MY REVENANT

RONAN MARLOW

Runaways Book One

ISBN 978-1-7643348-4-6 (ebook)

ISBN 978-1-7643348-0-8 (paperback)

To those who had to teach themselves how to love and be loved. I see you. You aren't alone.

REVENANT

/ˈrɛvɪnənt/

noun

a person who has returned, especially _supposedly_ from the dead.

CONTENTS

CONTENT WARNINGS

Please note the following list contains spoilers.

- Alcoholic side character
- Brief on page torture (of a SC by a SC)
- CNC (one scene where it is clearly established before that no means yes)
- Depiction of homelessness
- Depictions of mental illness and paranoia (including on page panic attacks)
- Drug and alcohol use
- Explicit sexual content between men
- Homophobia (including homophobic slurs, not by MCs)
- Mentions of abusive relationships, including physical abuse (of a side character)
- Mentions of car accident resulting in injury
- Mentions of child abuse
- Mentions of child neglect
- Mentions of death of a sibling (child)
- Mentions of parental death by suicide
- Mentions of sexual assault and grooming of a minor and resulting trauma
- Murder (by SCs and by one of the MCs)
- On page self-harm
- Stalking (by one of the MCs)
- Suicidal ideation (by both of the MCs)
- Transphobia (including deadnaming, not by MCs)
- Violence (by both of the MCs and between the MCs)

SC = Side Character

MC = Main Character

1

JONAH - PRESENT

HAUNTED OR HUNTED?

Ghosts are real. I know, because I'm being haunted by one.

It wasn't like the movies. There were no flickering lights, no cold patches of air, no odd smells or objects that moved on their own. I wished things were that simple, that easy to recognize. No, the ghost haunting me was far less obvious, and that somehow made him so much worse.

I saw him sometimes from the corner of my eye, only to turn and see someone else. I caught glimpses of him every-where—his leather jacket, his long curly dirty-blond hair, his old worn boots, that stupid fucking tattoo on his neck. I'd hear his voice, his laugh in a crowd, and I'd be so certain it was him that my heart would stutter and my stomach twist and bile would rise in my throat.

It was never actually him.

It was his ghost. Coincidences that dragged me back into the memories of all I'd left behind. They rose from the depths of me, made my bones vibrate and my skin itch with the need to escape. Escape from what? The ghost of him, my memories, myself. I didn't know anymore.

The truth was, I wasn't even *sure* my ghost was dead.

It had been almost a year since that day, and I sensed his presence now stronger than ever. I almost expected to see him around every corner, peering at me from dark alleys, staring at me across the bar. I could smell him in every cigarette. It kicked my senses into overdrive and made me jumpy. *Paranoia*, I told myself, my imagination playing tricks on me. *But what if it's not?*

The first time I was able to bring myself to look him up was a few months after I'd left. My stomach had twisted and my heart pounded as I'd guessed what the headlines would be: the confirmation of everything that had happened that day. Instead, I found... nothing. Not even a whisper of the name Dex Weller. No reports. No bodies. No murder investigation. I'd checked his social media accounts next, but they were all frozen in time. I still checked them regularly. It was the first thing I did when I woke up and the last thing I did before trying to sleep. My stomach always half dreaded, half hoped that something, anything, would change. Nothing ever did.

So here I was. I'd started running because I thought he was dead, and kept on running in case he wasn't. Until I knew which one he was for sure, I guess he was both. Schrödinger's boyfriend. Simultaneously dead and alive inside a box I wouldn't open and couldn't escape from, but fuck if I wasn't going to try.

That's how I ended up here in Hollow Creek, West Virginia. Another nothing town in the middle of nowhere. Another temporary stop on a journey with no destination, and fuck was I getting tired of it. This place was even shittier than the usual ones I stopped at. A crumbling old mining town with exactly one run-down motel, a diner that hadn't updated its menu or décor since the sixties, the sheriff's office at the back of the tiny grocery store, and The Rusty Nail, the bar I'd been working at for the past three weeks.

The first rule of running was to never get comfortable. The second was to always keep moving. Staying here this long? I was probably breaking both.

Not that anything about Hollow Creek was comfortable. The motel smelled like mildew, and the bed sagged heavily in the middle with a tired old mattress decades past its intended lifespan. The Rusty Nail wasn't much better: a dingy bar that reeked of old tobacco smoke and beer, with its sticky floors, flickering neon signs with dead letters, and a jukebox that only played sad country songs.

But they paid in cash, and they didn't ask questions. That was all I needed.

"Jack, my boy, another," said a rough voice from the other end of the bar. I smiled and nodded at Tiny, a regular. Why they called him Tiny, I had no idea. He was one of the biggest men I'd ever seen. I'm not even sure what his real name was. Then again, Jack wasn't my real name either, so who was I to judge?

"Coming up," I called back to him, getting a fresh pint glass and filling it before I slid it across the bar.

"Good man," he cheered, cheeks already rosy with intoxication, but this wasn't the type of bar that cut people off when they'd had too much.

I watched him stumble back to his booth, shaking my head softly before returning to wipe a damp rag over the bar counter again, half listening to the hum of conversation around me. It was the same faces every night, the same routines. I knew all their names; they thought they knew mine.

There was a sense of familiarity that I craved. I wanted to be known. I wanted to stop running and just breathe. Maybe make some friends who would actually give a damn if, or more accurately *when* I just stopped showing up one day.

The fact that I was thinking like this only proved why it was time to move on. It was probably also why my paranoia had kicked up a level. I'd been stagnant for too long, and the little voice inside my head that always whispered, "*Run, Jonah, run,*" was getting louder and harder to ignore.

Lost in the monotony of my temporary yet oddly comforting routine at The Rusty Nail, my mind drifted to planning what was next. I would probably head south again after this, find another bar job like this one and hope they didn't ask many questions. By now I had learned how to pick out the bars I knew wouldn't; they were the kind that didn't want questions asked about them either, and that worked just fine for me. I never stayed anywhere long enough to get caught up in any kind of shady business anyway.

"Didya hear?" came another voice from the bar that almost made me jolt, and I mentally scolded myself over letting my guard down. I knew better. If he noticed, he didn't say anything.

"Did I hear what, Hank?" I asked the man as I reached for a fresh pint glass, already knowing what he was after.

"Ya aren't the newest in town anymore," said Hank, amusement playing on his weathered features. Hank had been one of the people who seemed the most curious about me when I first arrived here, asked the most questions. Eventually, he'd learned I wasn't going to give him any interesting answers and had given up. Now, though, my interest was piqued, not that I wanted Hank to know that.

"Is that right?" I asked, keeping my tone carefully casual.

"Yep, 'nother young fella, 'bout your age. Said he's just passing through," Hank explained, and leaned forward over the bar like he was going to share some kind of secret he didn't want anyone else overhearing. I couldn't help but mirror him, my stomach twisting anxiously as I waited for his next words. "I don't like the way he's pokin' around, Jack. Don't like the look of him much either."

My mouth ran dry, and my palms grew clammy as I inhaled slowly and fought the urge to escape out the back door. "Yeah?" I tried to sound unaffected. "What's he look like, then?"

Hank leaned in closer, so I did as well, until I could smell the alcohol on his breath and had to fight the grimace from showing on my face. "He was dressed real nice. Too nice, I reckon, wearing a pink sweater, Jack, *pink*. I think he's... one of *those*."

I wanted to sag with relief and punch Hank in the mouth at the same time. Little did he know he was talking to one of "those" right now. But the risk of anyone here finding out wasn't worth it. Places like this didn't take kindly to differences, and I wasn't about to paint a target on my back. I had to fit in, be as unnoticeable as possible.

Pulling back and slamming his beer on the counter, I tried to keep my expression blank as I stared at the old farmer with his stupid cowboy hat and ancient flannel. I doubted I was doing a very good job of it, though; my best friend Becca had always told me I was complete shit at keeping my thoughts and feelings off my face.

"Don't reckon a sweater's a crime, Hank." My tone was flat, dismissive.

Hank was either too drunk to notice my thinly veiled bitterness, or he didn't care. "Still. Don't like him askin' so many questions. He was pokin' around, Jack, askin' who's who, where's good for food an' drinks, that kind of thing. Suspicious, if you ask me."

I reached for the rag so I'd have something to do with my hands and something else to focus on other than Hank and his suspicions over some very normal-sounding questions. The need to run vibrated under my skin. The description Hank gave of the guy was so far from what I had feared he would say, it was almost comical. I didn't know anyone who dressed "nice," at least not pink-sweater kind of nice. No, what I feared was leather jackets and dusty combat boots.

"Right, well, thanks for the warning," I muttered, reaching for an already clean glass that I started to polish just so I seemed busy.

Hank grunted. Now that he had his beer, he was significantly less interested in standing around gossiping, and he raised his glass in thanks before stumbling back to his usual booth.

⚬

At closing time, Marty, the owner of the Rusty Nail, showed up to lock up and put the cash in the safe in his small office out back. I'd told him I could do it so he didn't have to come in, but he either didn't trust me... *fair*, or he didn't want me seeing what else he kept in that safe... *also fair*.

It meant I got to leave as soon as the place resembled something close to clean. With a nod to Marty, who responded with a dismissive wave of his hand, I left him to it.

The walk back to the motel wasn't long, but it was starting to get real cold here at night, and it made my leg ache. At this hour, there were no cars in Hollow Creek. The drunken patrons of the Rusty Nail stumbled their way home, paths so well ingrained in their memories that they didn't even need the streetlights to guide them. I preferred walking under the streetlights, though, and took a slightly longer route just to avoid the poorly lit areas with too many shadows to be cautious of.

When I was within view of the motel, I stopped. Occasionally, someone would book one of the other rooms, but never for more than a night. The cars that would dwell in the small parking lot were usually just as shitty as my old '94 Ford Taurus, occasionally slightly nicer. There was never anything as nice as the sleek black Audi S7 currently parked next to me.

I scanned the area, the room windows facing the lot, but they were empty and all was dark and quiet.

Hank's story of the pink-sweatered stranger came to mind. Did that car belong to him? If so, why the fuck was he in a place like this?

With another quick scan of the windows, I walked quietly over to the new car, trying not to seem too suspicious in case anyone really was looking at me, but also wanting to get a peek inside to see if there was any indication of who it belonged to. Besides a few empty energy drink cans on the floor of the passenger's side, there wasn't anything noteworthy about it. I still didn't like it.

I'm being paranoid. It's probably nothing. I stepped back, giving my own piece-of-shit car a quick look over and checking it was still locked—not that there was anything worth stealing inside—before I headed up the concrete stairs to my room.

As I reached my door, I pulled the room key from my pocket but froze as my hand rested on the handle. The door was already unlocked. *I'm sure I locked it.*

Slowly, I put my keys back into my jacket pocket, fingers stiff from the cold yet tingly with panic as I grasped the handle of the switchblade there instead.

I had a moment to consider whether I should go in or head for the car, cutting my losses on whatever I left behind and the pay Marty owed me so I could get the fuck out of here.

I couldn't. I didn't have much, but everything I did have was in that room, and I wasn't too eager to start all over again with nothing.

Instead, I took a deep breath in and burst through the door before I could think twice about it.

I was greeted by darkness and silence.

Switchblade in hand, I punched the light switch, expecting to see someone, *something* maybe, that was here to get me.

There was nothing. No sound or movement, nothing that seemed out of place or different at all. Still, I did a sweep of the room and adjoining bathroom, expecting to find someone behind the door, in the closet, under the bed.

Nothing.

My heart was still thundering, my instincts refusing to believe that there wasn't any danger here. I checked the bedside drawer, picking up the old faded Bible and checking between the last page and the back cover. The money I had stashed there was still exactly where I'd left it. Untouched.

I checked everything again. Nothing had changed. Maybe I'd left the door unlocked when I went to work? I was *sure* I locked it, but now I was doubting myself, hoping I couldn't have been that stupid but also preferring it to the alternative of someone else coming in here.

Fuck, I didn't know what to think anymore. Maybe I really was losing it. Maybe no one was coming for me, and I was just running around in pointless fucking circles, stressing myself out over absolutely nothing.

It wasn't like there was another option, though. If I gave up running and it turned out I'd been right all along and Dex was still out there—hunting me down like I knew he would be if he was alive—I honestly had no idea what he would do to me. All I knew was that I was better off not finding out.

I dragged the small, creaky desk from the corner of the room to in front of the door. It wasn't sturdy enough to stop anyone who was determined to get in, but it would make a lot of noise and prevent them from sneaking in unnoticed while I slept.

Feeling a little better, I switched off the lights and made my way over to the bed. The mattress groaned as I sat down and unlaced my boots, kicking them off but keeping them close by. Scrubbing a hand over my face, I sighed and collapsed back onto the mattress.

Jonah - Present

PINK SWEATERS AND DYING DREAMS.

I always knew I'd spend my life running; I just never thought it would be like this.

Until three years ago, my life was centered around a very different type of running—the normal type, I guess. Days filled with counting miles and calories, nothing much to worry about but putting one foot in front of the other. I was good too. I started running in middle school, mostly just to burn off energy, and because it felt good. It also got me out of the house, away from Mom, her new husband Richard, who I could tell never wanted me there, and his son Liam, who also wanted nothing to do with me.

When I was running, none of that bothered me. It was just the wind in my face, feet pounding against the pavement, my heart soaring and my blood pumping. It was an escape. Freedom.

I never planned for it to go further than that. Becoming an actual athlete hadn't even crossed my mind until Mr. Stevens, the school gym teacher, started paying attention to me. He took an interest, gave me his time, and set me up with new targets and challenges, distances and times. It was fun, thrilling even. Mr. Stevens said I had potential. No one had ever said anything like that about me before.

He pushed me harder, probably harder than any gym teacher was supposed to push a ten-year-old, but I didn't mind. I enjoyed having someone's attention, and I enjoyed running, so it worked out. He would train me after school, and after a while he started training me in the mornings before school too. Mom didn't seem to mind, and Richard was probably pleased that I was around less. I was certainly happy to get away from him.

Then I started winning races. Small ones at first... school events, local competitions. Mr. Stevens took me to the races further from home, and Mom signed her approval with little thought to it, but when I started winning bigger races, she started to pay attention. Once I started winning medals, trophies, prize money—attracting attention from people with names that meant something—she *really* started to pay attention. So did Richard.

Suddenly he was all too happy to have me around, calling me "son" like we had that kind of relationship. I wish I'd rejected him more back then. But what can I say? I was desperate for attention and approval, and I was finally getting both. I soaked that shit up like a sponge.

Once I hit high school, I had a coach, like a real actual coach, not just Mr. Stevens with his whistle and a stopwatch, but someone who knew shit about actual potential. Someone who had credentials and got *paid* to focus her attention on me. Richard had decided I was worth the expense. When Coach Barnes started training me, I honestly thought she was trying to kill me. I missed Mr. Stevens, but under Coach Barnes that potential he'd seen actually became something more.

Barnes showed me a path that extended beyond where I was putting my next step. She sprawled out dreams and opportunities—talking about things like sponsorships, scholarships, qualifiers—and she would say that was just the beginning if I was willing to work for it.

Fuck did I work for it. Waking up every morning before the sun, running silent streets with the early-morning breeze whipping over my heated skin while the rest of the world slept. Afternoons were spent with Coach Barnes on the track, and she'd push me harder every day. I loved the way my heart would pump and my legs would burn and I could *feel* myself improving.

Those solo morning runs were always my favorite, though. When I was alone and I could run because I wanted to, because I loved it, without a finish line to race toward or a time to beat. Just me and the pavement.

My first big break came during regionals. The competition was fierce, with runners from all over the state. All of them were hungry for the win, but I was fucking starving for it. The starter pistol rang out, and everything faded away when my feet hit the track. I ran as if my life depended on it. I crossed the finish line first, obviously, but my time also broke a seven-year record.

My life was running full speed ahead after that, and I was just trying to keep up with it. In a blur, the years passed. Junior nationals, state championships, national qualifiers, international meets, endorsements... there were doors opening that I hadn't even known existed. Everyone wanted a piece of Jonah Hargreaves, and I fucking lived for it.

I let myself dream bigger, set my sights right for the top. I was on a track that I thought was taking me right to the Olympics. Really thought I'd get there. I thought I was fucking invincible.

But that's how it always goes. Rome wasn't built in a day, but it fucking burned in one.

All it took was a single instant for it all to come crashing down. Should have known better, really. I was reaching too high, standing too tall, and the universe decided to sit me the fuck back down.

I don't remember all that much about the accident. One minute I was running like I always did, and the next... headlights and screeching tires. Then my vision was blurring as fluorescent lights raced overhead, and I was being wheeled somewhere. People were in scrubs on either side of me. The smell of antiseptic and something metallic clogged my senses.

Crazy how much faster it was to lose it all. I got whiplash from how quickly my life changed... how quickly everyone around me changed. It wasn't my fucking fault, but when they looked at me—when Mom and Richard looked at me—it was like I was the death of *their* dreams. Like they were the ones who had to live with metal pins in their leg for the rest of their lives. Even Coach Barnes, my biggest supporter for so many years, didn't fight for me. There was no talk of recovery, of making a comeback. It was just *over,* and she was gone.

Of course I wasn't going to take it well. Of course I was going to be mean. For the second time in my life, I'd lost *everything.* Because I had. Both times. But this pain was entirely different from losing my sister.

I was hurting in ways the surgeries and physical therapy couldn't ever fix. Deeper than the agony constantly in my leg after the accident. I was wounded, and I lashed out like a bad dog at anyone who got too close. I didn't want their false sympathy, their judgment. I couldn't bear to see the pity in their eyes all over again, this time due to my own failures.

It was a blessing and a curse when Mom and Richard finally sent me away, back to my father in Port Skelton. Just like that, I was back in the hellhole I'd been born into before Mom upgraded with Richard and moved us to the city. It was rock bottom, but at least there I could lick my wounds in peace.

I thought I was fucking done, that I would never run again. Turns out, running was still my destiny. Only now, instead of chasing a dream, I was fleeing a nightmare.

These days, however, "running" mostly consisted of driving. Years after the accident, I still couldn't do much actual running. The pain that tightened my chest when I thought about those days hurt worse than the pain that would come and go in my leg. But on nights like this when it got real cold, the chill triggered a dull throb that made my limp a little more prominent if I wasn't focused on hiding it.

With more effort than it should have taken, I pushed back up off the too-soft mattress again, still too wound up to sleep, and limped over to the window. Dust coated the glass, making the view of the motel parking lot a little cloudy. But in the light of the flickering neon sign, I could still make out my Ford and the suspicious Audi beside it. Just the sight of it made my palms sweaty.

It's fine, I told myself. *A car like that is far too nice to be something* he *would drive.* I'd actually never seen him drive a car at all, just his precious BMW R51 motorcycle.

I cracked the window open slightly and lit a cigarette. Not sure why I bothered really, the room already stunk of old tobacco, and I could literally see the empty battery slot in the smoke detector. I stared outside for the time it took me to finish it and then another.

It was so quiet out there, nothing but the breeze rushing down the empty street and the faint buzzing of the too-bright vacancy sign.

Before I went back to bed, I double-checked that the door was sufficiently wedged shut by the desk, and my knife was still in its sheath hidden under my pillow. Satisfied, I crawled back under the too-thin blanket and stared at the stained ceiling. Like most days, I was too tired to bother changing out of my day clothes, and part of me still wanted to be ready to run out of here at a moment's notice.

Just a few more days, then Marty would pay me for the last week at the bar, and I could be on my way to the next place, the next bar, the next shitty hotel mattress. I should probably consider changing cars sometime soon too. I'd had this one for a while. Yeah, maybe I was being too paranoid, I didn't even know if anyone was actually chasing me, but there was this feeling in my gut that told me to keep running, that I shouldn't stick around to find out what would catch up to me.

There was another part of me I wanted to acknowledge even less, though. Buried deep under the logical thoughts and the paranoia was this sick, twisted curiosity, this little desire to stick around just to see if he would really show up, to see what he'd do if he caught me.

How both the self-destructive and self-preserving desires could exist within me at the same time, I had no idea. I wouldn't do that, though. It was stupid, and I still had a lot of running left in me, even if it wasn't the kind I'd ever anticipated. It wasn't time to stop yet.

⸺◆○◆⸺

I woke up to the sound of a car door closing. Whipping the blankets off, I made my way over to the window as fast as possible and parted the curtains just enough to peep through. The back door of the Audi was open, but from where I was, I couldn't see the person who'd opened it.

My pulse quickened a little in anticipation before a head of platinum-blond hair came into view. It was a face I didn't recognize, and I allowed myself to let out the breath I'd been holding in. This had to be Pink-Sweater.

Knowing Hank, I had kind of expected this "suspicious stranger" he'd mentioned to be just some regular guy who happened to be wearing a pink sweater. I doubted it would take more than that to flag someone as gay in a place like this.

I obviously tried to stay away from stereotyping, and never assumed anything about anyone. That being said, this guy was an absolute twink.

He closed the car door, a black bag slung over his shoulder, then locked it and started heading toward me. I lost sight of him for a moment as he started up the concrete stairs, but when he reached the top, I managed to get a better look.

He was, well... kind of gorgeous. He was short, but his long, *smooth,* slender legs took up more of his height than seemed fair. I could tell, because even though this was neither the weather nor the place for booty shorts, that clearly hadn't stopped him. I had to admit, they certainly did things for his thighs and ass. At least his arms were covered in a high-necked white sweater.

I stayed perfectly still as he passed by my window so he wouldn't notice me, but he didn't even glance in my direction. This close, I could get a good look at his face too, all full lips and high cheekbones. What really caught my attention, though, was the absolute shiner decorating his right eye. The black-and-blue bruise just made his eyes look even bluer.

He looked far too sweet and *normal* to be anything close to my type, but I could still appreciate what I saw. I watched him until he walked out of view, then heard a door close a couple of rooms down from me.

Seeing him myself had certainly made me feel less uneasy about the situation, and it figured that Hank thought the guy was "suspicious" because he wore pink, and not because of the black eye.

This fucking town.

3

Jonah - Past

MOODY SKIES AND PALE THIGHS.

The air was thick. It tasted of damp salt and smelled like the ocean.

At this time of year, very few people came down this path to the secluded beach, and I was counting on it being empty now. It had only been two weeks since I'd moved back in with Dad and I was fucking suffocating in that house. He didn't know what to do with me.

Why would he? He hadn't needed to be a father to me since I was seven. *Whatever*. It was what it was. I didn't need him to be my father. Well, no, that wasn't true. I *did* need him to be my father, as much as I needed my mom to be a mother. I needed someone to fucking help me. A father to guide me. A mother to soothe me. Some older, wiser person to just *help me*. Someone who had their shit together and who could just hold my hand and help me find my way again... because I was so fucking lost.

After Adaline, it was like they forgot they still had another child to parent. But if they hadn't changed in the fourteen years after her death, they just weren't going to. It made me so fucking angry.

There was this feeling in my chest most of the time, all tight and heavy. Like a weighted vest pulling me down. My throat tightened. I couldn't breathe, and I couldn't speak. Yet all I wanted to do was scream. My eyes were itchy, and my skin was too tight and too hot. I wanted to pull it all off. Maybe if I ripped myself apart, this feeling that was far too big for me could finally escape. I could finally be free of it.

Then again, I kind of liked holding onto it. Even as it burned me, as it shredded up my insides and turned me cruel, I clutched onto it. Because if I didn't have it, I'd be empty. And that was worse.

The path turned from solid dirt to soft sand, and the trees parted to reveal the small, sheltered area. This beach was quite shit for swimming or surfing—too much seaweed, and shattered shells to poke and cut at bare feet—but it was fine for walking on if you wore shoes. It was a good place to escape.

My Vans sank into the softer ground as I continued. The added resistance to my steps made a dull ache flare in my injured leg, but the pain fed my anger. That tight feeling in my chest and throat flared up, provoking me to drive myself forward faster, so the ache got worse. The two things fed into each other in an infuriating and vicious circle until the sand and crushed shells shrank into small patches between large rocks. I stepped onto them and continued on my way, rock to rock, until they flattened out.

There were tall cliffs on either side of the beach, and I walked along the bottom of one. When the tide came in, this place would go under, which meant I couldn't stay as long as I wanted to.

My shoes traced the edges of small pools of still water between rocks, some of which contained tiny fish or crabs that darted out of sight as my shadow cast over them.

I left them alone and continued on, following the curve of the cliff until I was far out of sight from the beach. If anyone came looking for me, they wouldn't be able to see me now. Not that anyone would.

Idly I wondered... if I slipped and fell into the ocean, got carried out to sea, how long it would take Dad to notice I was missing? How long would it take them to find where I'd gone? Maybe they'd never find me at all. Maybe they'd be relieved. *I think I'd be relieved*. My throat got tighter.

The wind picked up. It whipped my hair around my face and into my eyes, and I pushed it back in annoyance. It was past time for a haircut, but I'd rather shave it all off than let anyone touch me. I'd also feel too exposed without it.

I kept going. I knew this place from my childhood. Vague memories of Mom telling me and Adaline not to go too far away from where she was sunbathing. Not that she actually paid attention, immediately getting lost in one of her romance novels and trying to forget the fact that she, or us, or my father existed. We were disappointing to her. She'd always dreamed of a bigger life than what we could afford. She hated that she had to work and couldn't just stay home and be a well-kept trophy wife. Now Richard gave that to her. *I hope she loses it all*.

Despite knowing I shouldn't go too far, I couldn't actually bring myself to care as I continued onward. The hem of my jeans got damp, like my shoes, as I walked through some shallow water, and when the rocks inclined, I climbed.

The top of the cliff wasn't all that high. Tall enough that a fall would cause some nasty injuries but probably not kill me, unless I landed on my head or something. Would that be an instant death? Just the feeling of wind and then nothing? Or would it not kill me right away? Maybe I'd die slowly from my injuries, waiting for the tide to come in and drown me. Again, I wondered how long it would even take for someone to find me if that happened. Would they think it was an accident? Or would they think I'd done it on purpose?

Would it matter to them?

I kicked a small rock and stood too close to the edge as I watched it fall. Listened as it tumbled down and disappeared into the foamy ocean crashing below.

It was mostly flat up here. A few rocks covered in dirt stuck up above the others, one of which had a curved shape to it, making it almost look like a bench seat. I wondered if it had formed like that naturally or if someone had carved it out for that purpose. Then I decided I didn't care and plopped myself down on it, facing toward the raging ocean and the storm that brewed in dark heavy clouds over the horizon.

<•O•>

The shuffle of feet across dirt and rocks caught my attention over the sound of the waves crashing on the shore below. My jaw clenched in irritation that I was no longer alone. The best I could hope for was that whoever was approaching would see this particular area was already occupied and promptly move along.

No such luck.

The footsteps got louder. *Keep moving. Leave me the fuck alone.* I attempted to mentally project my thoughts onto the person. To make my aura and vibes as unwelcoming as possible.

They got closer.

Fucking seriously?

Closer and closer until the bastard literally plopped down right beside me on the rock, so fucking close they might as well have sat in my lap. Without looking at them, I shuffled over to give myself some more space until I was right on the edge of the rock seat.

"Do you fucking mind?" I said when a more appropriate distance had been established.

"Nope," replied a soft voice, popping the *p*. They sounded entirely too casual. Clearly, they hadn't picked up on the venom in my tone, and I needed to try a bit harder.

"Beach not fucking big enough for you?"

"I mean... it's not very big." That was true. This was a very small beach. However, it was large enough that sharing a rock was entirely avoidable. Before I could point that out, they continued. "Besides, this is like the best place to sit and watch the water. This rock is shaped—"

"Like a chair," I interrupted. "I know. But it's occupied right now, in case you hadn't noticed."

"No shit, Sherlock. But there's still enough room. Besides, you seem like someone who shouldn't be alone right now."

I tensed up even further. My chest and throat snapped tight, my ribs ached, and the urge to lash out bubbled within me, turning the core of me molten and explosive. "I don't know what the fuck you're talking about."

"Yeah you do."

"No I fucking don't." I snapped in indignation. "What do you know, anyway? You don't fucking know me."

"No, I don't know you, but I recognize it in you anyway. You're like me."

"What does that mean?"

"It means I'm someone who shouldn't be alone right now too."

The verbal vitriol bubbling up my esophagus came to an abrupt halt. I risked a slight glance toward them and caught a feminine profile with neon-orange, shoulder-length hair. Her eyes turned to look back at me, so I quickly snapped my attention back to the ocean in front of us.

I wasn't sure what to say in response to that. I wasn't here to fucking comfort anyone, especially not this random stranger. But knowing that *she* was hurting, that *she* didn't want to be alone, made me feel better. Because apparently I was an asshole like that. I didn't care about a stranger's feelings, I really didn't, but the tension inside me eased knowing she wasn't speaking from a place of judgment or pity.

"So this is because *you* need someone, then?" I said after a beat of silence.

"If I say yes, will you let me keep sitting here?"

"Yes." My voice sounded softer than I intended it to.

"Then yes."

We fell into silence again. I was hyperaware of her presence beside me. I noticed the soft gray of her hoodie from the corner of my vision, along with the pale skin of her legs between the hem of her skirt and the cuff of white knee-high socks that disappeared into black beat-up chucks.

At first, I couldn't focus on anything but her. She was too close, and I was too raw and vulnerable. The longer we sat there together in silence, though, the more I could tune her out. My attention turned back to the sea, and to the waves that crashed relentlessly against the rocks.

The ocean witnessed us as we witnessed it, silently observing each other as we fell into a fragile peace. My nose and ears hurt from the cold, and when the wind picked up, it sent whispers of chill down my neck and spine, under the cuffs of my sleeves at my wrists. It was cold, and it made me shiver, but it also felt real. Peaceful. I liked it.

There was movement beside me as she pulled her hood up over her head, and after a few minutes I did the same.

By the time she spoke again, I had almost zoned out, and the sound of her voice startled me. "We should probably head back soon. It's hard to navigate the forest path in the dark." She spoke so softly it was almost a whisper, like it was a secret, or maybe like she was just as worried about breaking whatever trance we were in as I was.

"Probably." I responded in the same tone.

We didn't move. We didn't speak again. The sun, already dulled behind thick storm clouds in a sky as moody as the ocean below it, darkened further, until it disappeared over the horizon and we were covered in a blanket of darkness.

It was colder now. Only when my leg ached fiercely did I dare to move at all. The rock we were sitting on was so hard and chilled that my ass had gone numb.

I was done here, but I didn't want to go back to Dad's. That didn't leave me with many options.

The rocky path I'd walked to get here had disappeared under dark waves at the base of the cliff. It meant the only way back was the path she must have taken through the dense woods behind us. I didn't know the woods *or* the path through them.

When I shuffled to my feet, she did the same, as if we had some sort of silent arrangement. She was a few inches taller than I was. I could tell now that we were standing, she must have been about six foot three.

I trailed a few steps behind her as she headed for a break in the dense trees. She was right; it was difficult to see where the fuck we were going in the dark. But she seemed like she knew the trail well enough, so I dared to keep a little closer as she led us through.

Eventually we broke through the trees and onto the quiet road barely lit by a lone streetlight before we came to a stop. Both of us stared at the poorly lit road rather than at each other. Each dared the other to speak first.

"Thanks for letting me sit with you."

I grunted in response, trying not to think about how long it had been since anyone had actually *wanted* to spend time with me, not to mention actually *thank* me for it. "Yeah, whatever," I mumbled as the weight of her gaze turned on me fully for the first time.

After a beat of silence, she startled me again, her voice booming like she couldn't help herself. Words tumbled out of her in an excited rush. "Holy shit! You're JJ, right?"

I stiffened. Shoulders rising. Fists clenching.

No one called me JJ anymore. Only people I'd left behind at high school back in the city had. And I hadn't started college here yet. I was supposed to, but I just hadn't turned up, and dear old Dad didn't seem to give a fuck about making me go. So no one here should have known me yet. I turned to glare at her stupid smiling face.

"OMG, it is you!" Before I could process it, she launched herself at me, wrapped her arms around me, and yanked me into a tight hug, with such a lack of hesitation it left me momentarily stupefied. "It's me, Bee. Fuck, I've missed you."

My hands twitched, but my arms remained hanging uselessly by my sides as I processed what the fuck was currently happening. Bee. I didn't know any girls named Bee. I had a friend named Bennet when I was younger, a scrawny little kid I thought was a boy who always insisted people call him Bee... not Bennet, or Ben, or Benny, only *Bee*. Mom always told me to stay away from Bee because she thought he was "weird," but he was probably my best and well, *only* friend back then.

The hug didn't loosen as my mind put it all together. "Bee?" I asked, my voice sounding soft and pathetic in a way I would have hated myself over in any other situation.

"Yeah." She pulled back just long enough to look at me, a brief moment of uncertainty in her features as she seemed to search for something in mine. Then she smiled again. "It's Becca now, but Bee still works just fine." She grinned, and hugged me tight again.

Okay. So it was Becca now. Fine. Processing that was easier than processing what was happening in my chest at being hugged so tightly.

She was so *warm*.

She hugged me as if she *missed* me.

"Welcome home," she said into my ear. My chest got even tighter. My eyes burned, and I realized I hadn't breathed for a while. Couldn't. It was too much. Being held was putting broken, jagged things inside me back together. I couldn't have that because I knew they would break apart again the moment she let me go.

Her warmth retreated as I shrugged her off, and I already wanted to claw at her to get it back. I hated myself for it. She frowned at me, but relented.

"Hey, do you remember the Cozy Cow?" she asked.

I cleared my throat as I tried to appear unaffected by what had just happened.

Cozy Cow was a small twenty-four seven diner on the main road. Her mom used to take us there after school sometimes. I nodded, still not trusting myself to speak.

"Let's go." She grinned, hooking her arm with one of mine and pulling me down the street toward the town center.

4

JONAH – PAST

SEXUALITY AND SHATTERED SILENCE.

I saw Becca every day after that.

We had a lot to catch up on. She told me about all that had changed in town, about the lives of all the kids we'd been in school with back then. Some of them I remembered, others not at all. To be honest, I really didn't give a fuck about any of them and had no desire to re-form any of those connections. But I liked hearing her talk.

When we were together, the ugly feeling that constantly twisted my insides eased.

It was nice to have someone who actually wanted me around. And I knew she *actually* wanted me around, because I'd tried to keep my distance from her after that day on the beach and she wouldn't allow it. She'd made us swap numbers at the Cozy Cow that evening, and she messaged me constantly. If I didn't respond fast enough, she'd be at my bedroom window to check what I was doing. That probably would have been weird if she didn't live two houses down from me.

Maybe she was weird, and intense, but after feeling so fucking alone for so long I wasn't complaining.

Becca told me about her life, her problems. She'd come out to her parents a year ago, and they hadn't taken it well. Her parents were divorced now. She lived in the house she grew up in with her mom and younger sister, and her dad had moved out to Meadow Park in the split. He'd told her he never wanted to see her again. Her mom didn't understand her either, and constantly used the wrong name and pronouns. It all made me so pissed off for her, and honestly, as angry as I was all the time, it was nice to hold some of that anger on someone else's behalf for a change. At least her sister seemed supportive. But if I ever happened to run into her mom or dad, I doubted I'd be able to hold my tongue.

I didn't talk a lot about myself, and she always seemed to know when to ask me questions and when to let things go. She knew about the accident, though, and had a vague idea of what it had taken from me. Instead of pity, she seemed angry on my behalf, and I much preferred that.

She was also angry that my mom had shipped me back here because I was too difficult to be around. Bee had used some very strong words to describe what kind of parent that made her—but had admitted she was grateful for it, because now we got to be together again.

As much as I missed the city at times, and as angry as I was at Mom for the same reason, I had to agree.

We didn't talk about Adaline.

It was nice having a friend again. I hadn't really had one since I'd left here, as it took a certain type of extrovert, like Becca, to drag me out of my introverted shell.

After a week of relentless pestering, she even got me to start going to college.

I fucking hated college. But we had a lot of the same classes, so I only went to those.

I didn't talk to anyone else. Unlike Becca, they seemed to acknowledge my foul aura and fuck-off vibes and had the normal reaction to those and kept clear.

It got me out of the house and away from Dad too, so that was something.

In the evenings we'd be at the rock seat on our beach, or at the Cozy Cow, where I mostly sat in silence and let her talk and ramble about whatever she wanted. Sometimes she'd hang out in my room with me, but I didn't like being there any more than I had to be.

The bed was small, the bedding the same as when I used it as a kid—with blue-striped sheets and a thin old quilt with bright primary colors and trains on it. Fucking ridiculous. But I didn't have money anymore, and I wasn't about to ask Dad for anything unless I had to.

I should probably look for some kind of job, but that would require me being at least somewhat pleasant to people, and that was too much to ask on the best of days.

Nothing about this house had changed since I'd left. Like it was frozen in time. It was small and old, but it wasn't run-down like the houses and trailers in Meadow Park. Just three bedrooms, a shared bathroom, and a kitchen with a joined living room.

It was all just how I remembered it, yet it somehow felt smaller, the colors dulled like they too had given up.

The pictures were missing from the walls. I couldn't remember what was in the photos, but there were faint discolored patches where they'd once been, like ghosts of them left behind.

Dad was a ghost most days too.

He woke up early, went to work at the factory, came home and ate takeout in front of the TV, and then drank until he fell asleep. At some point in the night, he'd wake up and stumble into his room to sleep some more, until his alarm blared at the ass-crack of dawn and he'd knock shit around getting ready and heading out.

There were usually leftovers in the fridge for me, or money on the table if there wasn't. Sometimes there was neither.

We hardly spoke to each other. What was there to say? Sorry Mom left you for another guy the first chance she got? Sorry some asshole hit me with his car, and all my dreams and hopes and desires had burned up in that moment, and now I'm stuck back in literal hell with you? We *certainly* weren't going to talk about Adaline. Yeah, it was better not to speak.

He was bitter that Mom had left him. He didn't have to talk about it for that to be obvious. I think he held some of that resentment toward me too, because she'd taken me with her. But I was seven. I didn't ask to go or stay. She'd made that choice for the both of us.

Dad hadn't called me in all those years I'd lived with her and Richard. Not once. He'd just let us go. Let *me* go. Either he didn't care enough about his kid or he hadn't wanted me anymore. I didn't care which one it was. He was a father in name only, and my being here now that Mom had decided I didn't fit her lifestyle anymore didn't change that.

We were strangers connected by blood. Nothing more.

"Earth to JJ," a voice said as a fry hit the side of my face. I scowled, and Bee laughed. She'd been rambling on about something again, and I'd zoned out rather than listen. I did that fairly often, but she only noticed sometimes. "What were you thinking about?"

"Nothing," I sighed, stealing her milkshake and taking a big sip. She always offered to buy me one, and food, and I always refused.

I didn't need her to pay for shit like I was some charity case. Didn't mean I wouldn't take some of hers, though. She hadn't drunk any of it yet, and had barely touched her fries. I was starting to think she just pretended to buy them for herself because she knew I would steal them off her. As long as neither of us verbally acknowledged it, I'd let that slide.

"Anyway... I was saying..." she continued, and I zoned out again immediately.

Her hair was always so perfectly straight and such a bright neon orange that it made my eyes hurt if we were in the sunlight. It wasn't so bad here in the back of the diner, though. The pleather seats were an equally offensive red, but everything else was monochrome or checkered in an aesthetic I couldn't imagine had ever actually looked nice.

Her eyes were an amber color, a couple of shades lighter than mine, and decorated in all sorts of bright colors each day. Today's eyeshadow was green. Lighter in the center and darker in the outer corners, paired with thick black eyeliner and lashes that seemed far too dramatic for spending the day at the diner with me. How long did she spend getting ready each day? It seemed exhausting to me. I barely even brushed my hair in the mornings.

Becca was always so animated when she spoke—long pointy nails sliced through the air with her hand gestures, and three sets of gold hoop earrings jingled together every time she moved her head. She was pretty, I guess.

I wasn't attracted to her, though. I wasn't attracted to anybody. Never had been.

Maybe I was asexual, but I still had urges, and I took care of them on my own. I just never liked the look of anyone enough to want them like *that*. Didn't like porn much either. I'd tried it, but it just felt so boring.

"*Jonah*." Bee's voice held that quality of exasperation that indicated that hadn't been the first time she'd said my name.

"Do asexual people jerk off?" I asked.

She blinked at me and simply stared for a long moment before sighing and going with it. "Asexuality is a spectrum. It would depend on the person. Some do and some don't. Doesn't mean they're not still ace. Why?"

I shrugged. I'd been on my own for so long I wasn't used to filtering out which thoughts were for speaking out loud and which weren't. Becca never judged me for anything I said, though.

"Do you think you're ace?"

I shrugged again.

"Well, you don't have to know. But if you are, and you want to talk about that, we can. Ace, gay, bi, demi, monogamous or polyamorous, any combination of any sexualities...shit, even"—she pulled a face—"*straight*." She said the word like it left a bitter taste in her mouth. "You're still my bestie, and you can talk to me about it."

I hummed my acknowledgment and stole more of her fries.

Bee was bisexual, or pansexual, or something. At least I assumed she was when she told me she'd hooked up with both men and women. I didn't question it, because I didn't care.

It was late afternoon now, the last of the sunlight falling in through the front window in golden rays that splashed over the gaudy decor, bathing the near-empty diner in a final wave of warmth.

There weren't many people here—too late for lunch and too early for dinner. It was quiet. That's why we picked this time to come. So when the doors opened, and a barrage of loud voices and laughter filled the diner, it *really* pissed me off.

Two figures stumbled in first; they were laughing like fucking morons. One of them had the other in a headlock while he laughed, and shouted, and tugged at his clothing in an attempt to break free. I hated them immediately.

And then *he* walked in.

And all I could think was that he was beautiful.

5

Jonah - Past

I STARED. HE STARED. WE STARED.

The obnoxious laughter faded to nothing. Cutlery clanked against porcelain. Spoons tapped against the sides of mugs. There was a low rumble of voices from the few patrons in the diner. It all faded into the distance as I witnessed him.

He trailed in after the idiots, and his aura poured out of him like the golden afternoon rays through the window. He was his own energy source, as bright and as brilliant as the sun.

I'd never seen anyone like him.

His hair was a dark blond—long, curly, soft—pulled back in a half-up, half-down style that exposed the shaved sides of his head. His skin was golden, sun-kissed and flawless except for a scar on the curve of his left eyebrow.

He was the sun, and his eyes were the sky. The lightest shade of blue I'd ever seen. It was like looking at an overcast sky through the clouds. No, that wasn't right. Clouds were soft. His eyes were like *ice*. Sharp. Dangerous. *Beautiful*.

It wasn't until he took a seat in the booth across from his annoying buddies that I could bring myself to break away from those eyes to take in the rest of him. He had a Roman nose, perfectly curved over the bridge, full lips, a sharp jawline, wide shoulders clad in a faded leather jacket... and the most appalling tattoo I had ever seen scratched across his neck.

I didn't know it was possible for a tattoo to piss me off, but this one did right away. A weird skull with round teeth and no bottom jaw was right in the center of his neck, over his Adam's apple, and what seemed to be angel wings extended out on either side of it, tracing the sharp edge of his jaw as they fanned out to the back of his neck.

It looked like someone with zero artistic ability had scrawled it on in Sharpie. I really hoped that's exactly what it was, because if it really was a tattoo and he had *that* permanently scarring his beautiful skin, I was going to murder something.

He had other tattoos too—something small on the left side of his face I couldn't make out from here and what looked like a spider web in his left ear. There were also letters inked onto his knuckles that I read as he tapped them against the table: HELL BENT. A rose decorated the back of one hand, a spider on the other. Thankfully, all the rest of his tattoos that were visible seemed better than the atrocity on his neck.

"Who is that?" I asked Becca, subtly tilting my head in his direction. The sound of her voice filtered back in, along with the rest of our environment. I took a deep breath, like maybe I hadn't done that in a while and not even noticed.

Becca being Becca, and lacking any sense of subtlety, turned her whole body in her seat to look in the direction I'd gestured toward. "Jesus, don't look," I whisper-yelled, as I grabbed her arm and forced her to face me again in a sudden and irrational panic.

"How am I supposed to know who you're talking about if I don't look?" she asked, rolling her eyes. "We're in a public place, JJ. I'm allowed to look around. You're the one being weird and attracting attention to us."

I looked around us and noticed that a couple of people at nearby tables were glancing in our direction. *Act natural.* Releasing her arm, I sat back in my seat, then snatched up her milkshake to take a sip. Strawberry milk hit the back of my throat so fast and suddenly that I choked on it.

"Smooth," Becca said, with brows slightly raised, before softly shaking her head at me. She turned again, and this time I didn't stop her.

I didn't look at the three of them on the chance they had noticed us, and I was by no means ready to make eye contact with Mr. Ice-Eyes over there.

"Those are Archer's little minions," she said as she straightened in her seat once more.

"What do you mean?"

Becca leaned forward a little, and I copied her. "Archer Kovats, you remember him?" she said with a slightly lower tone, and I frowned, combing through memories until the name slotted into place. I remembered Archer all right. One half of the terror twins.

"You mean that kid who bullied, like, *everyone* in elementary school?"

Archer was a couple of grades higher than us in elementary, but he was pretty notorious, and every kid had known to stay out of the way of the Kovats twins. Archer was the main problem; he called the shots. But Henrik was at least twice as frightening, he was just quieter.

Becca nodded. "Yeah, well, he's a bit more than a school bully these days."

She gave me a look as if I should know what she meant by that. I *didn't* know what she meant by that. Becca sighed, shuffling closer again. I copied her. "He like, runs a gang, or whatever."

"A gang?" I repeated, and it was my turn to give her a look. "In Port Skelton? You seriously think this town is big enough for a gang?"

"Yes, Mr. City Boy, Skelton is plenty big for a gang. Besides, they have bikes, and I heard they travel over to Deltran too."

I frowned at her, still not sure I believed her, though I guess I didn't have a reason not to. If anyone was going to start a gang, it would be Archer Kovats and his creepy twin.

My eyes drifted over to the group of guys again. The idiots were wrestling on one side of the booth while Ice-Eyes seemed kind of bored as he watched them, arms folded like he was too good for this place.

"So... who are they, then?" I gestured to their table once more. Thankfully, Becca was less obvious when she turned to look in their direction this time.

"Toby Attwood, Bryce Masters, and Dex Weller," she said, lowering her voice even further.

I recognized the first two names, and as my gaze drifted over to the table again, I could see the resemblance the two messing around had with the Toby Attwood and Bryce Masters of my childhood. Even if Bryce's hair was now bright blue.

They weren't really bullies like Archer had been, but they weren't exactly model students either. They came from Meadow Park, by far the roughest part of Port Skelton, and it had showed in their behavior back then. Apparently it still showed.

Process of elimination meant that Ice-Eyes' name was Dex Weller.

I ran it through the faded memories I had from back then, but couldn't match it up with anything I'd known before.

"Who's Dex?" I asked, in almost a whisper, hoping that Becca wouldn't catch on to the obvious interest I held for the leather-clad stranger.

She didn't seem to. She just thought quietly for a moment before speaking again. "That's right, he started school just after you left."

"He's not from here?"

"No, he is. He lives with his mom over in Meadow Park. I don't know for sure, but I heard his mom just didn't bother sending him to school, so by the time CPS got involved and made him go, he was like, super behind."

I frowned as I glanced over at him again, wondering how true that story was.

Could he really have a mother who just... couldn't be bothered sending him to school? My mother was neglectful, which was the whole reason she *liked* sending me to school—so I was out of her way. What about his father? And what would he do all day if he wasn't at school?

Rumors spread easily in Port Skelton, and the facts often had little to do with the stories people told. I hoped this one was fake.

Becca cleared her throat, snapping my attention back to her.

"Hmm?" I acted confused about why she would be staring at me like that.

"He's bad news, Jonah. You should stay away from him."

"Of course I will," I scoffed. "Why would I want to go anywhere near him? Or any of them?"

Becca narrowed her eyes. "I meant what I said before. You can like whoever you want—men, women, neither, both—doesn't matter, I'll still love you. *But...*" She paused and gave me a very serious expression. "You can't like *him*."

I rolled my eyes at her. "I said I'll stay away, fuck, would you drop it?"

She stared for a long moment, making a pensive sound before huffing and dismissing the topic altogether. I was grateful for that. I had more questions now than I did before, but I wanted time to run through them in private, to let myself examine this weird feeling in my chest that came with Ice-Eyes, Dex Weller.

As she rambled on about some girl in our class, I tried very hard not to let my eyes flick over to the table on the other side of the diner. The one in the fading sun's rays. The one that, quite coincidentally, currently sat two idiots and the most beautiful man I had ever seen in my life... who may or may not be part of a gang. I definitely tried.

I also failed.

Like a magnet, my eyes were repeatedly pulled back to him, and after the fourth time, all the oxygen left my body in a mad rush when those silvery blue ones locked onto mine in return. He was staring back at me.

I hated when people looked at me, but this felt... *different*.

Vaguely, I was aware I should do something. Look away maybe. Glare? I'd usually glare. What was I doing currently? I had no idea.

I stared.

He stared.

We stared.

Then he winked at me.

"I have to go," I snapped, slamming my hands down on the table as I stood to my feet and rushed to the exit, right past his table where I heard him snicker as I pushed the doors open and escaped into the breeze.

6

JONAH - PRESENT

VODKA LIME SECRETS.

I didn't see Pink-Sweater again over the next two days, but his car stayed in the lot, unmoving.

I wasn't sure what he was doing here, but as far as I was concerned, no news was good news. He would probably just move along like everyone else who came through here always did.

I only needed to be here for the weekend. Marty would pay me on Monday morning, and then I'd be out of here. I'd decided my next destination would be Darkwater Cove, but not for any other reason than that I'd seen the name on a map.

Another rule of running was to remain unpredictable, and I tried to be as random as possible in where I stopped.

I also lived out of a bag, so I didn't have to worry about packing anything and was always ready to leave at a moment's notice.

Of course, I wasn't going to tell anyone I was leaving. I'd just stop showing up the moment I got paid and block Marty's number. There wasn't anyone else here who had mine. There wasn't anyone *anywhere* who had mine.

The list of contacts on my blocked list was far longer than the number of contacts I'd had saved before all this started.

In fact, there were only two numbers I'd saved that weren't blocked—Bee and Devil.

I would never call either of them, but I couldn't bring myself to go without them.

Even though I'd changed my number, changed my phone, and they wouldn't be able to contact me, I still couldn't let them go.

Often I wondered about Bee. What did she think happened to me? Was she worried or maybe just angry? What had happened in Port Skelton after I left? Nothing was officially published or reported on, but surely there was... *something*.

On my weakest nights I would stare at her number, fighting everything in me not to call it and hear her voice. To tell her I was okay. To tell her when I wasn't. Would I ever get to speak to her again?

Had she reported me missing? I doubt Dad would have done it, but Becca seemed like the type to report me missing and then go searching for me herself when the police came up blank. She probably had a better chance of finding me. She would certainly be more dedicated to it.

Not as dedicated as *him*, though. Knuckles—inked and bruised—passed through my mind, making me shiver. HELL BENT. Yeah. He'd be hell-bent on getting me back... if he was still alive.

With work not starting until late afternoon, I made a trip to the laundromat. There was only one in town. It was small and aged, and the machine gave my clothes that musty old laundry smell, like fabric that had been left damp for far too long. Probably because the dryer seemed incapable of ever drying them fully, overheating and shutting off before it ever got the job done. Didn't matter much what I smelled like, though.

It was always empty. Not once had I seen anyone using it. So when I walked in, my bag slung over my shoulder, it took me by surprise to see that one machine was already going. And further still, when I noticed the figure sitting on one of the three chairs against the wall.

He was sitting on the middle seat—well, he was crouching—with his feet up on the chair, hugging his knees. His legs were exposed by tiny shorts once again, and he was wearing the pink sweater Hank had thought suspicious.

He was looking at me.

Bright blue eyes, one surrounded by an even bluer bruise.

I stalled, staring back at him in silence.

For a moment he looked me up and down, taking me in before his eyes met mine again. He made a little huff of a noise I wasn't sure how to interpret and looked away, eyes focusing back on his clothes in the machine.

Alright, then.

I unglued myself from the spot and headed to another machine to unload my clothes. With literally nothing to do in town or until my shift started, I'd intended to just sit here and wait for them to be done, but now I wasn't sure I wanted to. Then again, maybe this was an opportunity.

When the machine started up, I took a seat to the left of Pink-Sweater.

He didn't turn to look at me again, still hugging his knees and far more interested in watching his clothes spin than in me.

I was always awful at starting conversations, didn't know where to begin at the best of times, especially when I actually wanted to find out information from somebody without making it seem too obvious.

"New here?" I finally asked after a long silence.

"Yep," came his response. Only that.

Shit, what else could I say? He didn't seem as though he wanted to talk to me. I wondered how the fuck Becca had always got me to talk when I didn't want to. Had I also been this off-putting?

"Visiting family?" I tried.

"Nope."

Well, this wasn't happening. Whatever. If he didn't want to talk to me, that was probably a good thing anyway. Meant I had nothing to be suspicious about.

After twenty minutes of me scrolling on my phone and him watching the washing machine like it was a cinematic masterpiece, he finally broke the silence.

"Do you live here?" His voice was soft, and his eyes remained on the machine rather than turning to look at me.

"No," I answered simply. Then after a moment, "I'm just passing through." He nodded but said nothing more, so I continued. "Kind of shitty town to be honest."

He huffed in amusement. "Yeah. I'm not sure how it's possible for an entire town to smell like mold."

I couldn't help the genuine chuckle that earned. "Even the people."

He huffed again, this one almost sounding like a laugh. The leg closest to me dropped from the seat to the floor. "Shit, my clothes are gonna start smelling like yours, aren't they?"

So maybe it did matter what I smelled like because apparently I found that offensive. At least until he side-eyed me and his lips pulled into a brief smirk like he had to force himself to stop it.

I laughed.

How long had it been since I'd laughed?

"Hope there's nothing expensive in there." I gestured to his machine. "Because you'll never get the Hollow Creek stink off it."

"It's only Prada," he groaned.

Prada. Somehow I wasn't surprised by that. Not just because of the car he drove, but from the overall vibe of him. He seemed... expensive. Polished. Refined. He didn't fit here, and I was all the more curious to figure him out.

We fell back into silence, until his clothes were ready and he moved them to the dryer.

I tried not to be obvious as I took him in, but those legs seemed so long when his shorts were so small, and he definitely caught me looking at his ass. He said nothing about it, but I definitely noticed him smirking. When he sat back down, he seemed more relaxed.

"So, what is there even to do around here?" he asked.

"Drink, mostly."

"You do a lot of that?"

"I don't do any of that," I answered honestly. I told myself I didn't drink so I could stay alert, keep my mind sharp. It had nothing to do with *him*.

"So what is it *you* do around here, then?"

"Work."

"In the mines?"

"At the pub."

"Ah."

We fell into silence again, each of us no doubt trying to figure the other out. "I'm working tonight. You could stop by if you're bored."

"Maybe I will."

Was this normal? Was I making friends? It had been so long, I couldn't really tell.

⚫

Pink-Sweater did stop by the bar that night. I really needed to find out his name or something. It hadn't come up at the laundromat. Conversation had died off again until his clothes were ready and he'd left me there with a *"See you around."*

It was late, an hour until closing time, and I'd assumed that meant he wasn't coming. But then in he walked, booty shorts and pink probably Prada sweater.

Hank was here and gave him a glance over that wasn't at all subtle with his disdain. It made me wonder if I could get away with spitting in his next beer unnoticed.

The guy didn't seem to notice or care about the looks he was getting, though, as he made his way over and took a seat at the bar right in front of me.

"Hello again, Mr. Bar Man." He smiled at me, seeming far more friendly than he'd been this afternoon in the laundromat.

"Hello again," I grumbled back, trying not to seem pleased—to him or myself—that he was here.

"Know how to serve things other than beer here?"

"Not usually, but I'm sure I can figure it out."

"Vodka lime soda."

"Wow, so complicated." I rolled my eyes and started making his drink as he huffed in amusement.

I set his drink in front of him and went back to polishing glasses, serving a few beers here and there as I kept a subtle eye on him. He didn't seem like he actually wanted the drink, occasionally taking a sip, but mostly just running slender fingers up and down the sides of the glass, leaving trails in the condensation. When he started impaling the lime with his straw rather than drinking, I shuffled closer on my side of the bar.

He just seemed... lonely. Like someone who shouldn't be alone. Becca had recognized that in me back then. She said it was because she was the same. Maybe that's why I recognized it in him now.

"You look like you have a story," I tried.

"Can't possibly imagine what would make you say that." He rolled his eyes, that slight smirk pulling at his lips before he forced it away and frowned again. "It's not a nice one."

I nodded slowly. "Yeah, figured it probably wouldn't be."

His eyes remained fixed on the straw as he mashed the lime wedge into the bottom of his glass until it made the drink cloudy. "Why do you care?"

I shrugged one shoulder as I reached for a glass that didn't need polishing, but gave me something to look at other than him in case he found the attention too much. I knew all too well what that was like. "You just..." I smiled softly to myself. "You seem like someone who shouldn't be alone right now."

He seemed to consider that for a long moment, and although I could feel the weight of his gaze on me, assessing me, looking for... something, I kept my eyes on the glass as I wiped it clean of nonexistent smudges.

"It's... complicated."

I nodded. "Most things are."

"You really want to know?"

I shrugged one shoulder as I put the glass back down. "Well look, in a place like this I'm as close as it gets to a psychiatrist. It's pretty much part of my job description here. So why don't you tell me what's on your mind, and I'll prescribe you something to make it better." I held up a bottle of vodka in my left hand and tequila in the right, swishing the liquid around invitingly.

He huffed a laugh and rolled those pretty blue eyes again, wincing slightly at the discomfort he must have held in the bruised one.

"You're cute," he said with a sigh, like he was trying to pretend he was annoyed when he really wasn't. "Alright, Mr. Bar Man"

I held up a hand to stop him right there. "Ah, that's *Doctor* Bar Man, actually."

"Alright, *Doctor* Bar Man." He laughed again, shaking his head softly before eyeing me up, considering his next move.

A pink tongue darted out to lick a slow stripe over perfectly straight white teeth. Too perfect. Were they veneers? "I'll make you a deal, then. I'll tell you my story, and if you haven't heard one more complicated in the last..." He looked around, trying to determine just how complicated the people of Hollow

Creek could be. "Six months… then that 'medication' is on the house."

He didn't seem like the kind of guy who needed free drinks, but I was so desperate to know what brought him here, to understand him, that I was willing to go with it.

I snatched up two shot glasses and placed them on the bar between us as I poured the tequila. "Alright." I pushed one toward him. "A little incentive."

He smiled brighter this time as he took it. We clinked glasses, and both downed the harsh liquid in one go. One drink wouldn't hurt. I winced through the taste, but he seemed completely unaffected by it. "Go on, then."

"Well… my name… is Harper Lorens." He gave me another assessing look, like he seemed to think he'd already revealed something.

"Is this one of those 'do you have any idea who I am' moments?"

He huffed. "Well, I guess it doesn't matter. Basically… my family is in the spotlight a lot."

"Like celebrities?"

"Something like that."

"Alright. Proceed."

Harper's family sounded like a bunch of pricks. A different flavor of shitty than mine, but shitty all the same. They'd tried to put him in a box they created for him. They didn't like that he didn't fit. His dad didn't like that he was gay and tried to set him up with a woman, so he'd told him to fuck off and left to live with his boyfriend. It sounded like that was a big deal. With his family allegedly being in the spotlight as much as they were, it meant he had reporters following him everywhere.

He got quiet after that, and he hadn't explained why he was here alone.

"So... you know I'm going to ask. Who did you piss off to get that beauty?" I gestured to his bruised eye.

"You wouldn't believe me if I told you."

"Someone else I'm supposed to have heard of?"

"Maybe. Ever hear of Benny Forrester?"

"Oh, shit." Alright, so I actually had heard that name before. "As in MMA champion Benny Forrester? Wait, you got hit by an MMA fighter?"

"*Former* MMA fighter. His shoulder's all fucked from a fight last year. Now he just runs a gym."

"Okay. I'm starting to see what might have pissed him off, but proceed."

"Yeah, well, he's my boyfriend."

Oh. *Oh.* So he'd left his family for his boyfriend, and his boyfriend had given him that bruise. I was starting to get the unpleasant picture. What a piece of shit.

"So you're on the run."

"So I'm on the run."

"Me too." I wasn't sure what made me confess it, but I regretted it immediately.

"Yeah? What are you running from?" he asked, leaning in closer, attention obviously piqued.

My scalp prickled with unease, but I feigned nonchalance. "Mmn, I'm the doctor here, remember? I'll ask the questions."

Harper rolled his eyes. "Alright, then. Keep your secrets."

7

JONAH - PRESENT

LOYAL TO A GHOST.

Once the bar had closed, Harper waited for me to clean up. Marty hadn't given him more than a glance when he'd shown up to take care of the money, so I assumed it was fine for him to be here until I was done.

It was weird walking anywhere with company. I was extra jumpy in the short time it took to get back to the hotel, and I concentrated on concealing my limp from Harper as much as possible.

If he noticed it, he didn't mention it. He also, thankfully, hadn't asked many more questions about me either. Maybe it was obvious they made me uncomfortable.

Harper had been standoffish at first, but now he'd decided to open up to me, he wouldn't shut up. He told me about the city, about his friends, about Benny Forrester and how he *so* wasn't like what people would expect. I wasn't sure about that. A big man with violence issues as an MMA fighter kind of made perfect sense to me.

It was nice, though, just listening to him talk. Reminded me of when Becca would just talk at me. It filled the silence, and sometimes I really hated the fucking silence.

By the time we stopped out the front of my room, he was still talking. I reached into my pocket for my key card and turned to say goodnight only to find him stepping closer to me. Harper was so much shorter than me, but as he closed the distance between us, I shrank in on myself. Pale blue eyes flicked from mine to my lips, and I swallowed heavily.

What was this?

Harper was pretty—he was *really* fucking pretty—and the rest of his body was probably just as beautiful. But now that we were here and he was looking at me like that, my gut twisted in discomfort, telling me I should not be taking this any further.

The first real chance I had at getting laid in a year and my conscience decided it wanted to stay loyal to a ghost. "Well... I think... we should probably go to bed, right? In our own rooms?"

His confusion was clear as he took a step back. "What? I thought... Have we not been flirting all night?"

I gawked at him. Had we? Had I? Sure, I'd checked him out a couple of times, but had I been flirting? It was just so nice to actually talk to someone that I hadn't stopped to think about how that interest might have come across. "I uh... I can't."

Another long, assessing look. The feeling that he was seeing too much.

"You're with someone?"

"It's complicated."

"Most things are," he said quickly, echoing my words from the bar.

"Besides... I don't think this..." I gestured between us. "Would work."

"Why's that?"

"I think we might have the same... *preferences*."

"Preferences." Despite nodding, his expression told me he was waiting for me to elaborate on that.

I grunted my frustration. "I'm a bottom, okay?"

Lips parted, and there was a flash of those perfect teeth before he forced the amusement back down. "And you assume I only bottom as well?"

Oh. "Oh."

"It's rude to stereotype, Doctor Bar Man. Don't they teach you that in bar medical school?" His voice was playful.

"I uh... I shouldn't have assumed. I'm sorry."

"Pfft, don't be. You're not exactly wrong. I do like being the one with a cock up my ass. But what I do could hardly be classed as 'bottoming.'"

Well fuck if that thought didn't make my head spin, and if it wasn't for the guilt that churned my insides at just the thought of finding out everything that entailed...

Harper huffed. "Good night, Bar Man." He stepped forward and leaned up to place a soft kiss on my cheek. "It was really nice talking to you."

"It's... Jack, actually." For the first time in a long time, I wished I could give someone my real name.

He smiled sweetly at me in response. "Good night, Jack," he said before taking a step back and sauntering down the hall to his own door. I watched, somewhat stupefied, as he waved goodbye and disappeared into his room, closing the door behind him.

Well. That had been interesting.

Since the night I'd returned to find my door unlocked, I'd been extra vigilant in ensuring things were exactly as I'd left them. It hadn't happened again, and I was beginning to think I really had just forgotten to lock it somehow that day.

When I was satisfied nothing was out of place, I showered off the day and any lingering thoughts of Harper. I was interested in him, that was undeniable, but I was interested in him the same way I had been in Becca. As a friend.

It was annoying.

I was on the run, but I wasn't moving on. Part of me remained in the place that I'd fled, in hands that had once held me. Even if they were long cold now, *he* still held part of me. A part that would only ever belong to him.

When I collapsed into bed, I pulled out my phone to begin my nightly routine—looking up any news about Port Skelton, checking his social media. Everything was as it always was.

After that, I searched the name Harper Lorens.

I'm not sure what made me do it. I guess I just wanted proof that he was telling me the truth. I wanted to believe him about everything he'd told me.

Turns out I really should have heard of Harper Lorens. Literal fucking *billionaire* heir to Lorens Industries. Rich didn't even begin to cover it. Everything he'd told me was true. His pretty face was splashed over article after article, so many focused on his relationship with former MMA fighter Benny Forrester. There were photos of them together, articles that pried deep into their personal business. I couldn't think of anything worse. There was nothing covering Benny's true nature, though. No pictures of Harper's bruises... his *abuse*.

It was odd for me to feel protective of someone, to care about anyone but myself. Maybe it was because we were both on the run, something big and scary chasing after us in the name of love. Whether it was real or imagined, he was like me, and just knowing that made me feel less alone.

Alone was safe, though. I had to remind myself of that.

8

Dex – Past

BURNING. BLAZING. RAGING. SCORCHING.

I could feel the new guy's eyes on me whenever I was around him.

It wasn't in the way people normally looked at me—with a mixture of caution and disdain. No, his gaze was so much deeper. It made my skin prickle with an awareness I wasn't sure I liked.

He clearly didn't know enough about me to realize that having any kind of interest in me couldn't end well for him. So I was going to show him.

Apparently he was from here, moved away as a kid or something, but now he was back. Didn't know the details. Didn't care.

When my eyes first locked with those pretty honey ones in the diner, there'd been a tug toward him. It was magnetic. Something about him called to me, and that could only mean he was fucked up. Because only broken, deranged, and fucked-up things called to me. Like recognized like, or whatever the saying was.

I'd seen him around a fair bit since then, always hanging with that Becca chick.

They were opposites in both looks and personality. She was all neons and punk clothing, whereas he always looked as if he wanted to fade into the background—dark hoodies and jeans, dark brown hair that fell into his face when he tilted his head forward. It looked soft. I wanted to pull it.

Didn't think it was possible to fade into the background with a face like that, though. His eyes alone were the most intense thing I'd ever seen. The way he glared was so fucking pretty.

Then there were those high cheekbones and slender jaw, his perfectly pointed nose, his lips that looked so soft and pink. His skin was incredibly pale, and I wondered how easy it would be to make it flush pink in embarrassment, pleasure, or rage. I wanted to see if there was a difference between them all.

There was a fire inside him, wild and untamed. I wanted to watch it burn.

Toby told me his name was Jonah.

Jonah had my attention.

Time would tell if he'd be able to handle it.

"Dex?" A low voice snapped my attention, and I looked up to see Archer leaning against a pillar a short distance away.

"What?"

"I said, are you ready?"

"Of course I'm ready." I rolled my eyes. Wasn't like it was my first fight.

Occasionally, when the tide was low in the evenings, people would come down to the pier. There were barrels filled with firewood and fuck knows what else to burn.

Someone was blasting music from a speaker system.

Things were just getting started. People continued to arrive with coolers of drinks and food, and whatever the fuck else they thought they needed for an evening of watching men beat the absolute shit out of each other under the pier.

I didn't know who I was supposed to be fighting tonight. I didn't care either. Didn't care about the prize money, though it certainly was a bonus.

"Bryce is up first. You're following."

I grunted my acknowledgment. At least that meant I wasn't fighting Bryce. He was always such a crybaby when he lost, whining about his injuries like he hadn't signed himself up to be here. Last time we fought each other, he pissed me off so bad with his constant complaining afterwards that I beat him up again just for fun.

The area under the large wooden pier was illuminated only by the burning barrels half dug into the sand, and tiny specks of orange scattered among the crowd from the ends of cigarettes like cancerous fireflies.

The fights had already started. Bryce was beating some newbie from Deltran, so apparently that group had showed up tonight. Which explained why Archer was so tense and even more of an asshole than usual.

There was a territory war brewing between him and the Deltran guys. Well, *us,* I suppose. I hardly fucking cared. Archer would tell me who needed some new friends, and I'd introduce them to my fists because I'm just so friendly like that. That's all I needed to know. I didn't care who got hurt, and I didn't care why. That was Archer's business.

"What the fuck is he doing?" he seethed beside me.

"Uh, beating some rookie's ass?" I answered as I looked back over the fight, the sand spraying everywhere as Bryce wrestled the guy to the ground.

"It should have been over already. *You* would have finished it already."

"You know Bryce likes to make it into a show. Relax, he's winning, then we gotta deal with him gloating afterwards," I groaned. Somehow, the only thing more insufferable than Bryce losing was when he won.

"He's wasting time."

"So grumpy," I chuckled. "You'd think a guy who just had his dick sucked would be a little more relaxed."

He shot me a warning glare before he looked around us to see if anyone was listening. Of course I was going to poke at that. "What? I didn't say I was the one who'd sucked it." I spoke louder and laughed as I barely dodged the fist aimed for my jaw. "Now, now, you still need me to beat that Deltran guy's ass, right? No damaging the goods until after the fight."

"You're infuriating," Archer gritted out between clenched teeth as he tried to compose himself again.

Finally, the fight was called with Bryce as the winner. That meant it was me up next.

"You want me to shut up? You know exactly what to do with my mouth to make that happen." I leaned in to lick the shell of Archer's ear.

I ran off before he had the chance to respond in whatever sort of violent manner he decided that statement called for. I'd still get it from him later—I was counting on it—but I had someone's face to beat into the ground right now.

I recognized this particular motherfucker right away. Didn't remember his name because I rarely bothered to try, but I'd crossed paths with him before. He was big—bigger than me, just a little. More muscular too. Didn't matter.

Yanking my shirt over my head, I tossed it somewhere to the side, not caring if it landed on anyone in the crowd. The "ring" was made of spectators. A wall of bodies that formed a circle around the two fighters.

He looked pissed as he eyed me up, so I winked at him, and the sweet, sweet fury that flared in his eyes was more rewarding than throwing the first punch.

But I threw that too.

Adrenaline surged through my blood, more potent than any drug. And I was a fucking addict. The high I got while fighting was unparalleled. I came alive. I *lived* for this. The pain was inconsequential. *No*, it was everything. It was fuel. Every hit I took only made the fire inside me burn brighter.

I was burning, blazing, raging, scorching.

Euphoric.

Bloody-knuckled and split-lipped, we circled each other again. Predator circling predator. Seeking opportunity. Seeking weakness.

I was zoned in. I was *always* zoned in. Nothing that happened around me could ever take me out of a fight until it was over.

Or so I had thought.

Because then I saw *him*.

A honey-eyed inferno in the crowd.

My eyes refused to look away from him.

The light from the barrel fires reflected in the depths of Jonah's eyes, and his own fire burned bright and brilliant inside him to meet it in a fiery tornado.

He was scowling, and I'd never seen the emotion look so beautiful.

Then a fist connected with my jaw, and my brain shook within my skull as my head whipped backwards from the force of it.

And I went down.

9

JONAH - PAST

A BLOODIED ANGEL.

I wasn't sure how Becca convinced me to come to this. Crowds weren't my thing, neither were drunks or violence, but when she'd mentioned that Archer's group always came, I couldn't fight the weird pull at the thought of seeing *him* again.

I was no closer to understanding the strange feelings now than I was that first day in the diner. All I knew was that when he was around, I found it difficult to focus on anything else.

Becca noticed, of course, but I shut her down immediately when she tried to bring it up, so she'd taken to simply rolling her eyes at me instead when she noticed me staring.

It's not that I *liked* him. I didn't even know him. He just had the kind of presence that demanded attention. Without even trying. It pissed me off.

There were far too many people here, so it wasn't like I could even find him if I tried. Which I was definitely *not* doing. Not at all.

Becca pulled me by the arm through the crowd. She seemed to be looking for someone too, but I had no idea who that could be. If she found them, then I was leaving. I shouldn't have come here anyway.

We parted our way through all the excessive shouting, smoking, drinking, and the bodies grew denser the closer we got to what must have been the fighting ring. I hated it. Every time someone pushed against me, I wanted to give them their own fight if they were that fucking excited about it.

Someone to my left shoved me hard, and just as I was about to turn and shove them back—fuck the consequences—my eyes were drawn to the ring. Like a magnet. Like a homing beacon. An irrefutable pull I was helpless to defy.

It was him.

It was his fight.

Breath evaded my lungs as I took him in. He was shirtless. It was the first time I'd seen him without that old worn-out leather jacket, not to mention *shirtless*. I could see more of him than I ever had. All that tan skin, bathed in the glow of the barrel fires, which made the sweat running down his abs look like molten gold. *Fuck*. Of course he had abs.

He also had more tattoos, just as I'd expected, over his arms, his chest, his back. *Where else?* My eyes were particularly drawn to the scorpion on the right side of his lower abdomen. There was a tattoo of a knife on the left, the handle positioned just above his hip, and the blade followed the natural contour down and inward until it disappeared beneath the waistband of red boxers sitting slightly higher than his low-hanging jeans. That weird fluttering feeling I was getting familiar with in my gut transformed into an anvil.

He was a mess—bloody nose and knuckles, covered in sand, scrapes, and bruises—but he was smiling. Smiling like this was exactly where he wanted to be, and he wouldn't have had it any other way.

Dex Weller fought like he had nothing to lose, and suddenly I was wondering if that was true.

The guy he was fighting was bigger. He looked meaner. But there wasn't a doubt in my mind that Dex had this fight. There was a spark in his eyes, an unhinged madness that made up for any difference in size. He knew it too.

Then his eyes met mine and I couldn't remember how to breathe.

Look away, I willed him. *Focus and win this.*

Unfortunately, whatever this magnetic pull was between us, it didn't include telepathy. Because he didn't look away, so he didn't see the hit coming that had his head whipping back and his body falling heavily into the damp sand.

Fire. Burning. Blazing. Raging. Scorching.

It started in my chest and filled my veins like molten metal. My skin was hot, and my head was empty, and all I saw was red. Red. Red. *Red.*

His opponent didn't stop, was right there on top of him. Straddled him. Rained down pain over his beautiful face.

Get up. Get up. GET UP.

"GET UP!" I was screaming before I even realized, shouldering my way to the front of the ring. Further still until a hand yanked my hood to hold me back.

"Where are you going, idiot?" Becca hissed in my ear.

"GET UP!" I screamed at him again.

Punch after punch. But he wasn't done. I knew he wasn't. Unlike Dex, this fuckhead was wearing a shirt, and Dex dropped the guard he held over his face to grasp at the fabric. Instead of trying to haul the guy off, he did just about the last thing I would have expected. Using his new hold, he yanked the fuckhead down at the same time as he pushed himself up off the sand—just enough to lick a wet stripe over the guy's cheek.

The dumbfuck recoiled, as if that action had hurt him more than any punch to the gut. He tried to pull away, but Dex kept his hold until enough distance had passed between them that he could twist his body to slam the guy down into the sand beside him.

Dex's face was bloody, but he was *still* smiling. It wasn't a nice smile; it was unhinged. Deranged. Manic. Like he was high on the pain. I wasn't sure how anyone could find it in them *not* to be afraid of him when he looked like that. Like something certain. Something inevitable. A bloodied angel.

Limbs twisted. Fists landed. Sand sprayed up as the crowd cheered and hollered, and I understood for the first time in my life why people enjoyed watching violence.

I leaned closer. A magnet. An invisible rope. Pulling me to him. Each time Becca yanked me back by the hood, scolded something in my ear. I couldn't hear her. I couldn't hear anyone. Only the sound of every hit inflicted upon Dex as if it affected me personally.

On and on it went until my fists ached from clenching them so tight and the match was finally called.

Mason, the fuckhead, was called as the winner.

"That's bullshit!" I screamed, stepping forward again closer to the ref.

Becca yanked me backward, this time grabbing my arm and dragging me away. My eyes found Dex as he spat blood onto the sand, and someone I didn't quite recognize approached him looking furious. Who was that? What were they to him?

"Jonah!" Becca snapped, taking my jaw in her hands and physically forcing me to look at her. My face turned in her direction, but my eyes still attempted to stay on him. "Jonah!" she barked again, her voice dropping, and I finally looked at her. She looked bewildered. "What the actual fuck is wrong with you tonight? I swear you're one step away from getting into your own fight. Is that what you want?"

I tried to turn my head away.

"Is. That. What. You. Want?" She didn't release her hold on my face, and I grunted in frustration.

"No."

"Then what are you doing?"

"I don't know, okay?" I shrugged her off me.

"Maybe this was a bad idea. Let's just go."

I went to argue, but she silenced me with a glare. I rolled my eyes at her. So what if I got a little heated? Didn't mean anything. That's what this kind of sport did to people. That's why people liked it. Her expression dared me to talk back to her, and with another groan I tamped down whatever this pull was to go in the other direction as I followed her away.

Before we got far, some girl from one of our classes called out to Bee, taking her attention away from our exit. I didn't remember her name, but she seemed very excited to see Becca. She ran over with a beer in hand and practically hung off *my* best friend. Who the fuck was this bitch again?

I glared at them talking as if they were close. They weren't. Not like me and Becca were. All thoughts of the fight extinguished until, from the corner of my vision, I caught a big figure making his way through the crowd.

It was the fuckhead. He was scrubbing at his cheek as if he were trying to rid it of a disease.

"That stupid fucking cocksucker. I'll fucking kill him if he comes near me again. You hear me?" he said to another large man—probably equally a fuckhead—to his right. "I'll kill him."

RED.

That feeling—so big and ugly and uncontrollable inside me—twisted, like a beast attempting to break out of a cage. Clawing. Lunging. Thrashing. It was breaking free. I was powerless to hold it back as it burst out of me, swallowing me whole as it did.

Thump. Thump. Thump.

My heart thudded in my ears, louder with every step he took toward me. I couldn't think clearly. It was *stupid*. I knew it was stupid, and yet... I still did it.

My body moved on its own, leg swiping out, foot meeting foot, and the next moment he was crashing into the gravel with a grunt.

There was a beat of silence as I stared. He turned and stared back at me. His friend stared too. So did Becca and what's-her-name. All of us stared like idiots in stunned silence.

"Did you just fucking trip me?" he growled as he came out of his shock.

Unfortunately, I was slower to recover from mine.

He was up on his feet again with a fist full of clothing—my clothing. He yanked me toward him. I did the only thing I seemed capable of these days and glared. I wouldn't cower to this homophobic piece of shit. Instead of responding, I spat on him.

"Wipe that one off too, fuckhead."

I expected the punch that followed, but I still couldn't have braced myself for the white-hot pain of Mason's fist. Searing. My brain shook in my skull. I'd never been punched before.

"Jonah!" Becca shrieked behind me.

He shoved me backward. My leg flared with pain as my ass met the dirt. Through blurry vision, I glared.

"Stop fucking looking at me like that," he growled, lifting a boot, no doubt to stomp or kick or whatever else he deemed suitable. Still, I glared.

Rather than his boot coming down on me, Mason grunted as a body slammed into the side of him, taking him down like the sack of shit he was. Then Dex fucking Weller rained down pain twice as furious as anything he'd delivered during their fight.

It all spiraled pretty quickly from there. Mason's friend got involved, trying to pull Dex off, which got Bryce involved, which got someone else I didn't recognize involved, and then another person, and another, and pretty soon it was an all-out brawl.

The crowd dispersed, people running away from what quickly became more than they'd signed up for. Becca pulled at my arm, attempting to hurry me away, but I pulled back, away from her. My feet wanted to take me in a different direction, but she pulled again, and fuck was she strong when she wanted to be.

We scrambled away just as the sirens and red and blue lights came into view, running through the surrounding forest as fast as my limp would let me.

"Fucking *spill*," Becca demanded as she slapped a bag of frozen peas to the side of my face.

I winced and glared at her, but she remained unperturbed.

"What the fuck were you thinking tripping Mason fucking Bates?"

I shrugged, and she pressed the peas harder to my face as punishment.

"He said homophobic shit," I confessed after an argument that took place entirely through glaring at each other. I wouldn't specify who he was saying homophobic shit about, though. That was irrelevant.

Her expression softened a little at that. "Yeah, he's an asshole. But you can't just start a gang war because he said something fucked up, Jonah. You aren't violent like that. Are you?"

I looked away.

"Are you?" she repeated in a sterner voice.

"No. I don't know why I did it. Okay? I just... I had to do *something*."

Becca flopped back on the bed beside me with a sigh. I did the same. Side by side, we lay looking up at the ceiling, at the shitty glow-in-the-dark stars my mom had put up there after I'd begged her for them. They'd dulled over the years, or maybe they'd always been that shitty and I just hadn't noticed when I was so pleased she'd finally given in and got them for me to stop my nagging.

There were a few long minutes of silence before she broke it. "Well, that wasn't how I expected the night to go."

After a beat, I heard her snicker, and despite trying to hold in my own, I failed. The next moment we were both laughing so hard my stomach hurt.

"I swear it looked like Bryce was flying for a moment," she cackled, and I groaned as my lip split again. "No, but actually..." She turned on her side to face me, and I mirrored her. "What the fuck *was* that, Jonah? Dex literally came out of nowhere to save you after just getting his ass beat."

I scowled. "He didn't get his ass beat. That fight was clearly Dex's win."

"He only had a chance at the end because he *licked* the guy, JJ."

"So? That fuckhead didn't have to react like he was poison or something. Why? Because he's gay?" I paused for a moment, not able to meet Bee's eyes as I asked, "*Is* he gay?"

"Dex? Yeah. That's not a secret. I don't think he's ever tried to hide it from anyone."

Okay. So Dex Ice-Eyes Weller was gay. Cool. Cool, cool, cool. Didn't matter to me at all. I didn't care, and it wasn't like it affected me in any way whether he was or wasn't. So yeah. Not sure why I even asked, really.

"Jonah." Bee frowned. "I told you to stay away from him."

"I'm away!" I snapped back a little too quickly. "Haven't even said a word to him."

"But you want to." Not a question but a statement. I needed to defend myself. I opened my mouth to speak, but she beat me to it. "Oh, shut up!" The bag of peas in her hand smacked against my bruised cheek again.

10

JONAH - PAST

BABY, I'M THE DEVIL.

— ✶ —

I didn't feel like going to class the next day, so I didn't. Instead, I took a walk.

Rather than the beach path, I went in the other direction, through the thinner parts of the forest that blended with the large grassy field separating Port Skelton from Meadow Park.

I had no business going this way. There was nothing to see or do in Meadow Park. Nothing good anyway. But the beach felt like my spot with Becca, and I didn't want to go there without her. I didn't want to go there *with* her right now, though, either.

After Bee left last night, I'd found it difficult to sleep. The events at the pier played over and over in my mind. Dex shirtless. Dex spitting blood into the sand. Dex being hurt.

It was Archer who'd been the one to go up to him after the fight, I'd realized, after talking to Bee about everything that went down. What were they to each other? Was Archer the type to check over Dex's wounds? He didn't seem like it. Did he have someone for that? *Why does it matter?*

Then there was the brawl afterward, and the ugly feeling inside that had me tripping that fuckhead. *Why?* Because he was disgusted that Dex had licked him? Why did that bother me? I'd be disgusted too in his position... wouldn't I? Then

Dex came out of nowhere to defend me. Or was it just because he was pissed about losing the fight? Maybe it had nothing to do with me at all, and I was just overthinking it.

I had far too many questions and not enough answers, and they circled inside me like sharks going in for the kill, something awful yet inevitable swirling around and around.

Dex. Dex. *Dex.*

Everything revolved around him. All of it was his fault.

I needed to understand whatever these feelings were. I needed to make them *stop*.

The grass here was long, unkempt, typical of the area in and around Meadow Park. It was such a pretty name for such a shitty place.

Across the field were blocks of land containing run-down houses with yards full of junk. Their fences were a mix of metal or wood so aged they'd sunk into the dirt like skeletons in a boneyard—sagging outward like not even they could stand proud and tall in a place like this. It looked like a dump. Litter and trash tangled in some of the taller blades of dying grass, and weeds scattered throughout the field.

In the distance there was a dog barking, mean and ragged, answered by silence and something on the breeze, unpleasant and unwelcoming.

I shouldn't be here.

I kept walking, wading through the field, destination unknown until a new scent caught my attention, just as unpleasant but far more familiar.

Smoke rose from a grassy area about twenty feet to my left, so I altered my path to investigate. The long grass concealed its source until it was far too late to change my mind—because the body that lay in the grass was already looking in my direction when *he* came into view.

Ice eyes stared back at me.

Silence cut through my chest like a blade. A staring match that restricted my airflow like Darth fucking Vader was choking me with the Force as it caught me in its invisible and terrifying pull.

The voice in my head told me to turn around and back away, as if I were the prey in a predator's sights. But fear and something much worse kept me in place as Dex Weller stared back at me.

Pursed between wounded lips was the source of the smoke, a thin tendril that weaved and danced into the air from the end of his cigarette.

Despite the weight of his gaze, he seemed completely unbothered by my presence, lying in the grass with the hand resting behind his head obscured by thick curly locks a few shades darker than the dying meadow. The other was on his stomach over a dark green shirt and his faded leather jacket.

I forgot how to *be* when he looked at me.

There was always so much noise in my head, so many thoughts and feelings and *rage* that all tangled into a big ball of itchy *something* that I couldn't unravel no matter how hard I tried. But it wasn't there when he looked at me. It was silent. I didn't know what to do with that.

I'm not sure how long passed with us simply staring at each other before he finally broke the tension and spoke. "Are you waiting for an invitation or something?"

"What?"

He rolled his eyes. "Lie down or fuck off. You're blocking the view."

The view?

I turned and looked up at the sky. It was as bleak as the field below it, more white than blue with all the clouds. When I turned back to him again, his gaze had finally left me to cast upwards. He was cloud gazing?

I wasn't sure what to do with that. It felt like I should do *something* with that. Like this small piece of information meant something.

"Well?" He sounded annoyed this time.

Before I could even consider what the fuck I was doing, I was moving, my body obeying some unspoken command as I sank down into the grass beside him.

My heartbeat thundered in my ears as silence fell. I was looking up at the sky, but I wasn't aware of anything but him. He filled my senses. All I could hear was his breath, with each exhale sending a new plume of smoke twisting into the atmosphere. Any time he shifted, I had to fight the urge to look at him.

What the fuck was I doing here? Lying in the grass, looking up at the clouds. Why didn't I want to leave?

"Smoke?" He spoke again after what could have been seconds or minutes.

"What about it?" Something like panic fluttered in my stomach every time I heard the low rasp of his voice.

"You're kinda stupid, huh? I mean, do you want one? A cigarette, City Boy."

My brain short-circuited at the insult, and I sputtered and stuttered, torn between responding to the insult or the offer.

"Go to hell," I landed on.

"Where do you think we are?" I could *hear* the smirk in his voice.

It felt accurate, though. *Hell*, a.k.a. *Port Skelton*. "If this is hell, are you supposed to be a demon?" I responded before I thought better of it.

He chuckled, and my chest tightened.

"Nah, baby, I'm the devil."

"Don't call me that!" I snapped, mostly because I didn't like whatever feelings suddenly sprang into existence at hearing the word "baby" leave his battered lips. His very soft-looking battered lips. I hadn't even realized I'd turned to face him until he was staring back at me again.

"Whatever you say, City Boy."

It wasn't an insult, not really, but the way he said it made it feel like one. "Don't call me that either. My name's Jonah."

"I know." His lips tugged up in amusement. I don't know how he knew my name, but the fact that he already did made that feeling building up inside me even stronger. Made it feel more urgent, like again I was supposed to do something with it.

"I'm not stupid," I said after a moment, and even I could hear how sulky it sounded. I wanted to punch myself.

"Debatable."

"The fuck is that supposed to mean?"

"I mean you picked a fight with one of the Deltran fuck-heads last night and started a gang war. Sounds stupid to me."

"I didn't start a gang war. *You* getting involved started the damn gang war. If you hadn't gotten involved, he would have just beaten me up, and that would have been the fucking end of it."

He smiled again. "Yeah."

Yeah? I didn't know how to argue with *yeah*.

"Why did you do it?"

"Why did I get involved?"

I nodded. He shrugged. It pissed me off.

"*You're* the stupid one," I added, *stupidly*, knowing that provoking Dex Weller was not at all a smart thing to be doing, but instead of seeming insulted, he just smiled wider.

"We can both be stupid, then," he said simply and turned back to the sky. I did the same, expecting us to fall back into silence but he spoke again. "Why did *you* do it?"

"Do what?" I asked, even though I knew what he was talking about.

"Why did you pick a fight with that waxed sasquatch?"

It took more effort than I would ever admit not to smile at that. "He said homophobic shit."

He made a contemplative noise. "About me."

It wasn't a question, but I still answered it quietly. "About you."

From the corner of my eye, I saw him nod. "So you were defending me."

I felt like I had to defend myself against *that* accusation. "I would have done the same if he were talking about anyone!"

Would I, though? If someone had said something bad about Becca, I'd be the first in line to make them swallow their teeth, but if it was anyone else... would I have gotten involved, even knowing it was a fight I couldn't win? I was afraid of the answer.

"Sure thing, City Boy."

"I told you not to call me that." I glared at him, but he wouldn't look back at me to see it.

With his attention elsewhere, I took him in. There was a fresh cut on his eyebrow, and his nose had dried blood around the left nostril, like it had been bleeding again recently and had only just stopped. The dark shadows under his eyes told me it could have been broken. It definitely seemed kind of swollen. So did his split bottom lip. I glared at it like I could make the pain disappear if I intimidated it enough.

"Whatcha lookin' at?" Those full lips smiled again, the split opening in a way that must have stung, but I couldn't read any hurt in his eyes when mine met them again.

My mouth ran dry. "I want a smoke," I lied. I'd never touched a cigarette in my life.

"Mmm... is that why you keep looking at my lips?"

"Fuck you," I snapped. His eyebrow twitched up like I'd just suggested something he was considering. It was suddenly really hot. Wasn't it supposed to be going into winter? Why was it hot?

Instead of responding, he reached into his jacket pocket, I assumed for the cigarettes. I tracked his movements—the spider tattoo, the veins in his hands, his busted knuckles. Maybe he was just used to pain.

He handed me a pouch along with a small bag of white things and a slim cardboard package with tiny papers inside. I took them from him and sat up—using my back as a shield between us—and examined whatever the fuck he'd just handed me.

The pouch contained loose tobacco. The white things seemed to be filters, and I guessed I was supposed to roll myself a cigarette using the thin papers.

I pulled one free and added some tobacco into the crease in the middle, not knowing at all how much I was supposed to use, so I added a bit more, then tried to balance it all as I put the filter in the end. The paper wasn't sticky, so I guessed I had to lick it or something to make it stay shut? I thought I'd seen people do that before.

When I was done, it looked nothing at all like a cigarette, and most of the tobacco simply tumbled out of the loose tube-ish thing I'd created. So did the filter.

"You good?"

I flinched at the question, my cheeks heating in embarrassment. Why the fuck had I committed to this?

"Yes." I pulled another paper to salvage this abomination, tucked the filter back in, and rolled the whole thing up in a tighter tube.

"You generally only need one," said a voice right in my ear, causing me to drop the damned thing anyway. I recoiled as if struck, scampering back until I had some semblance of personal space again, my heart thundering as I glared at him.

He smiled, picking up the Frankenstein cigarette and examining it.

"Very... creative?" He didn't even try to hide his amusement.

"Shut up!"

"Temper, temper, all you had to do was ask." He smirked, reaching for the pouch again.

He made it look easy, rolled it like it was second nature, and when his tongue darted out to wet the paper, I noticed the glint of something in his mouth. *Fuck*, he had a tongue piercing. That... that was... something.

When he was done, it looked perfect. Dex brought it to his lips. Locked eyes with me as he lit it. Exhaled the plume of smoke in my direction before his hand extended toward me, the cigarette sitting pretty between tattooed fingers.

I took it from him, eyes refusing to leave his as it rested between my fingers.

"You gonna smoke that or you just want to hold it?" he asked after a long moment where we did nothing but stare at each other. I brought it to my lips quickly, taking a deep inhale that closely resembled a punch to the throat. Despite my best efforts, I couldn't help but choke and sputter at the vile taste.

The bastard cracked up laughing, reaching out to take it from me as I caught my breath and forced myself to stop from coughing further.

When I looked back at him, he was lying in the grass again, smoking *my* cigarette.

"Give me that," I snapped, voice slightly raspy from my coughing fit as I reached for it. He pulled it out of reach.

"Nuh-uh. I know you're not a smoker now, City Boy. These things are bad for ya."

Indignation burned within me at his condescending attitude. "You smoke them!"

"Yeah. But I'm bad for ya too."

I glared at him, not knowing what to make of that. Then I launched for the hand holding my smoke. No one was going to tell me what I could and couldn't do. He was fast, twisting his body away from me. We fumbled in the grass as I tried to grab for it again.

The next thing I knew, Dex's arm was around my waist as he tossed me onto the ground on the other side of him. I had a face full of meadow as I caught my bearings, and when I turned to glare at him he was so *close*.

Like a deer in the headlights, I froze as he shuffled even closer. *What the fuck is happening right now?* There were no words, no thoughts, just his face, his lips, so close... My lips parted against my will. For what, I wasn't sure, but it certainly wasn't for the mouthful of smoke he force-fed me with his lips a fraction of an inch away from mine.

I shoved him away as hard as I could manage and scrambled to my feet, ignored the pain that flared in my leg, and marched away as quickly as possible.

"Running away again?" he called after me.

I didn't even turn to look at him. I just stormed away from Dex fucking Ice-Eyes Weller. Away from hand-rolled cigarettes and cloud gazing in dying grass. Away from Meadow Park. Trying, while my gut told me I was heading in the wrong direction, to believe that he wasn't the entire reason I'd come this way in the first place.

11

Dex - Past

FROM GOLD TO GONE.

"Three times," I mumbled as Archer stopped yapping on about the things he'd heard through his connections about the Deltran Drakes. Stupid name, though ours wasn't much better. Archer had been so pissed when they'd dubbed us the Port Skelton Strays, but I kind of liked it.

"Three times what?"

"Three times Jonah's run away from me now," I said, rolling my eyes, because *obviously* that's who I was talking about. Who else would I give a fuck about? I wasn't entirely sure *why* I gave a fuck about him either, but that didn't matter.

"Dex. Forget about Jonah Hargreaves, for fuck's sake. This weird little interest in him has already caused me a fucking mess. We're lucky no one ended up dead last weekend. End it now."

"Ha! Good one, Archer." Bryce laughed from his sofa like the idiot he was. "You know you've just made him more interested in Jonah now, yeah?"

Maybe he wasn't such an idiot after all, because Archer telling me not to go after Jonah certainly *did* make me want to do it more.

"Who is Jonah?" spoke mister strong and silent from his brooding corner of the room. Henrik spent little time in Port

Skelton, unlike his twin, but with tensions as high as they'd been lately between the two groups—*perhaps largely due to myself*—Archer had asked him to spend some more time here.

His presence alone was definitely a deterrent. I'd been described as crazy before, but even *I* wouldn't mess with Henrik. Why would I? There was nothing to gain from messing with a guy who literally could not feel pain. All punching him would do was hurt your hand, and probably turn him on or something, I don't know. Henrik was a weird fucker.

"Jonah Hargreaves. He used to live here like forever ago but then his sister died or something and he moved away with his bitch of a mom, but now he's back and Dex is like crushing on him or something," Bryce so eloquently explained, but there was a new piece of information there he'd neglected to share with me previously.

I sprung on him, wrestling as he tried to wriggle away, all bony arms and legs as he screeched like a dying chicken. "What the fuck?" he squealed.

"His sister *died*? You weren't going to fucking share that with me earlier? You little fucking shit! I told you to tell me everything!"

"I forgot or something! I swear! Wasn't intentional, man! Lemme go, you're messing up my hair!"

Idiot. Never reveal your weaknesses. I grabbed a handful of artificial blue strands, not expecting them to be both crunchy *and* sticky. Disgusting. On point for Bryce, I supposed. I let him go, wiping my hand clean on his T-shirt before wondering if that was any cleaner.

"Tell me now. Everything this time," I demanded.

"I don't know everything." Understatement of the year. "She was a few years older than us in school. They both just stopped coming one day, and then the school announced that she'd died, and there was like a vergal or something."

"Vigil," Archer corrected as he flopped down on another sofa, eyes on his phone. This place had been thrown together for when we met up like this. A bunch of furniture that belonged at the dump had been pulled from curbsides and shoved into this crumbling shack of a home in Meadow Park. Not that any of us actually lived here.

"Died of what?" I pressed Bryce for more information.

"Dude, I don't know, okay? Ask Jonah."

Somehow I doubted that would do anything but get him to run away again. I'd find out, though. When I was determined to find something, there was little that could stop me until I got what I wanted.

"You were there." I snapped my attention to Archer.

"Don't know, don't care," he responded with a shrug.

"This Jonah," Henrik interrupted. "Why does he run away from you?"

"Who wouldn't?" Bryce added, and I punched him in the jaw. Pain flared in my bruised knuckles, but it hurt him more than me, so *worth it*.

"Maybe he just likes to run," I answered casually, though that question had been on my mind the entire week since our little moment in Meadow Park. I'd intended to provoke Jonah then, mostly because there'd been something building between us I didn't quite know what to do with. Jonah had caused a fight with Budget Hulk on my behalf over some homophobic comment, so I knew he didn't have that issue, but that also didn't mean *he* was gay. I could have sworn I'd made him blush, though, and given the opportunity, I was definitely going to do it again.

"And you can't catch him?" Henrik asked with a raised eyebrow. I smiled in response. That was an excellent point. If Jonah insisted on running away from me again, I would just have to chase him.

"He can't be too fast with that limp," Bryce added, and I hit him again. That one really hurt. I groaned as I shook it out.

I'd noticed the limp and was determined to uncover the story behind it. I wanted to know everything there was to know about Jonah.

Henrik left his corner perch, approached his twin on the decrepit sofa, and snatched the phone out of his hand. "What the fuck?" Archer snapped. "Use your own damn phone."

"No," was Henrik's curt reply as he typed something.

They were identical twins in their facial features and height alone. Where Archer was slim and toned, Henrik was fucking *built*. Widest shoulders I'd ever seen on someone who wasn't a professional bodybuilder. Archer kept himself clean-shaven, his light brown hair styled purposefully into something he definitely wanted people to think happened naturally—parted at the center, with soft waves that stopped over his cheekbones like he wanted to be some '90s heartthrob. Henrik, in contrast, had a full beard, and long hair that I'd never seen outside of its neat bun. There were scars all over Henrik's hands and arms that I didn't want to know the story behind. I mean I did, but I wouldn't ask. He also had all his fingers, unlike Archer, who was missing the smallest one on his left hand.

The way they spoke was different too. Even though they'd both grown up here, Henrik spoke like English was a second language to him—not that his English wasn't fluent and perfect, but his Hungarian accent was noticeable. I knew little about their family situation, only that Archer would shut down the topic any time I tried to pry.

"Amateurs," Henrik chuckled. "Jonah Joseph Hargreaves... *Local Deltran Teen Running Prodigy Breaks Regional Record... Track Star JJ Hargreaves Talks Dreams, Discipline, and the Drive to Win... From Pavement to Podium: How Jonah Hargreaves is Racing Toward Greatness...*" Henrik locked eyes with me for a moment before continuing. "*Olympic Hopeful Jonah Hargreaves Hospitalized After Hit-and-Run Accident.*" He dropped the phone back into Archer's hands, who picked it up to look at the screen with renewed interest.

There was something in my throat too big to swallow as I snatched Bryce's phone out of his hands to search his name and see for myself. There were so many articles, so many pictures of him—running, winning, *smiling*. I sank down onto the sofa as I opened up one of the more recent ones... *From Gold to Gone: Where is JJ Hargreaves now?*

I couldn't even bring myself to care as Bryce leaned into me to read off the broken phone screen.

No wonder he seemed so angry all the time. I hadn't even thought to google him, hadn't thought he was someone they'd write news articles about, but I could see it now. He still carried it with him... the pride. It was wounded and damaged, but it was still there.

Now he was here, in hell with the rest of us scum.

Jonah *Joseph* Hargreaves had just gotten a lot more interesting.

———◈———

"Remind me again why we are going to this?" Henrik's voice came through the intercom in my helmet as we pulled up to the extravagant house on the Port Skelton foreshore.

"I just need to see someone about something," Archer responded.

Henrik sighed. "Wow, very informative. You think the Drakes will be here?"

Archer shrugged. "Whether they are or not, it'll be good for people to see that you're back in town."

"What?" Bryce shrieked, the sound crackling through the comms as I killed the engine. I fought the urge to punch him, only because he was still on his bike and just out of reach. "Y'all, why did no one tell me it was a costume party?" he whined. "I would have dressed up. Now we look lame as fuck."

I did *not* want to see Bryce in a costume, so I wouldn't have told him about it even if I *had* known there was a theme night happening. It looked like a Halloween party even though Halloween was weeks ago.

I pulled my helmet off and secured it to my baby, then I retied my hair into a bun. I hated drunk people, and I hated parties. Everyone was far too loud and obnoxious and stupid. Bryce didn't need alcohol for that, but with it he was going to be even worse.

Still, I knew I'd seen Becca at these kinds of events, and where Becca went lately, so did Jonah.

"Let's go," I said after wiping a smudge off my rear fender. I led the way into the house, with its lights and music spilling out over the front lawn as if it were just as intoxicated as its inhabitants.

12

Jonah - Past

Okay, Rabbit.

✦

"How the fuck did I let you talk me into this?" I complained, uncaring of who was listening, as Becca dragged me through a crowd of way too many people.

"Oh, shut up, JJ! It's a fucking party. Have something to drink and try to have some fun, would you?" she shot back, pulling me between the bodies.

It was a big house, even bigger than Richard's, yet somehow there was hardly any space with all the people here. I recognized some of them from school, but I didn't talk to them there, and I had no plans to talk to them here.

Bee had tried—and failed—to get me to wear a costume tonight. It wasn't Halloween and we weren't children, so a costume party was stupid. Still, she did look cute.

She was a Playboy bunny or something? With a glossy white spandex-looking leotard she'd made me help her get into cut high over her hips, pink fishnet tights, and thigh-high white boots that brought her from six foot three up to six foot nine. Taller if you included the white-and-pink bunny ears on top of her head. So yeah, it was *unlikely* I'd lose track of her tonight when she stood above the crowd with her neon hair like a sexy lighthouse to navigate my way through this drunken storm.

While Bee *hadn't* convinced me to dress in costume, she *had* convinced me to wear something other than one of my hoodies. Instead, I wore one of her dark denim jackets over a knock-off designer black T-shirt and some ripped skinny jeans that I was surprised fit me. Her shoes were too big for me, much to her dismay, so I stuck with my checkered Vans. She'd also put some sort of product in my hair that smelled good, but I couldn't remember what it was supposed to have done.

I didn't care how I looked, but I'd let her style me since she was so excited about it.

"Want a drink?" Becca asked.

"Sure."

She cheered before letting go of my hand to get us some alcohol.

Being around my dad made me wary of ever touching the stuff, and before, my strict diet and schedule had never allowed for binge drinking, so I hadn't actually ever been drunk before. I wasn't planning on getting drunk now, but maybe one or two would help me relax.

Bee returned with two red cups and handed one to me.

"What's in it?" I called over the music as she dragged us into the main living room.

"Best not to ask. Just drink it," she responded, taking a big sip of hers.

As concerning as that was, *when in Rome...* I took a big gulp before I could think better of it and grimaced. It wasn't terrible, but it certainly wasn't good. I believed part of it was pineapple juice, the other part... some form of poison.

"It's best to drink it quickly," she called out, lifting her cup again. I followed suit.

I lost track of how many drinks I'd had so far. After I finished the first one, Becca had gotten me a second, and behold! Every cup I'd finished since was magically refilled. Whatever liquid was in the cup tasted better now than it had at the start. I'd even go so far as to say I liked it.

Bee was definitely drunk. She was singing and dancing to every song, even though it was very apparent she did *not* know the words, but she was having fun, and her fun was infectious. I'd never sing in front of people like that, but I enjoyed when she did it.

"I'm gonna go piss," she *whispered* into my ear, stumbling slightly.

"Go piss, girl!" I cheered. Why was I cheering again?

"Look after these." She pulled her bunny ears off and gently nestled the headband into my hair instead. "The band's too tight. It's hurting my brain."

As she stumbled away, I jiggled my head from side to side to watch the ears shake when I looked up at them. I could see what she meant. The headband definitely gave a little pressure, which I guessed was to stop it from falling off, or whatever. I didn't know, and I didn't care. Becca entrusted me with her ears. I was gonna take care of them.

One song turned into two, and I was suddenly worried about where she had gotten to. My cup was empty again, but I didn't want to brave whatever social situation was happening in the kitchen alone to get a refill. Becca did that for us.

When the next song ended, I wondered if I should try looking for her. I hadn't needed the bathroom yet, so I didn't know where it was, but if I had to go on that quest, then I would.

I walked into the hallway, noticing the way the walls seemed to be a little fuzzy and wobbly. *Weird.*

I decided the best approach to finding which one of these many doors was the bathroom was to open all of them. So I opened the first door, only to catch an eyeful of someone's ass as they were deep inside someone else's ass, and I very quickly slammed the door shut again.

"Whoops!" I said loudly to no one in particular.

That was *not* the bathroom.

I hadn't told Becca about my moment in Meadow Park with Dex, and I wouldn't, because it didn't mean anything. That didn't stop me replaying it in my head, over and over on a loop. That weird feeling in my stomach stirred to life every time I thought about how close we'd gotten before that asshole blew his ashtray breath into my mouth. It had caused some *confusing* bodily reactions, which I refused to examine past the basic fact that maybe my sex drive was finally waking up. That's all it was. It had nothing to do with *him*. Even if his face came to mind, against my will, when I was dealing with said bodily reactions.

It was the first time I'd thought about someone specific while jerking off. Normally, it was just sensations, a means to an end that I took care of as quickly as possible so I could get on with my day. It was perfunctory. So the first time after that day when I'd done it, the usual faceless fantasy had morphed into his arm around my waist as he shoved me into the ground, his hot, smoke-scented breath on the side of my face. I'd been so shocked I'd abandoned my mission in favor of a cold shower.

The second time it happened, though, I gave in to it.

Twenty years was apparently how long it had taken for my dick to figure out what it liked, and for some infuriating reason, it liked Dex fucking Weller. That didn't mean I did. I'd use him to get off, sure, but I still wanted nothing to do with him. Nothing at all. The fact that just picturing him gave me the best orgasms I'd ever experienced didn't mean I wanted to know what it was like to actually have those rough hands touching me. Those pale, intense eyes focused on me. Those lips that breathed smoky air from his mouth to my mouth...

When I eventually found the bathroom, it was blissfully empty, until I remembered the reason I was looking for it in the first place was to find Becca. Not so much bliss, then.

The combination of Dex surfacing in my thoughts and the scene I'd accidentally stumbled on in the bedroom made my dick stir in my pants. It wasn't like I wanted him to do *that* to *me*. The two things had *nothing* to do with each other. Still, it took longer than it should have to dismiss the idea of jerking off.

I used the toilet and then resumed my search for my sexy lighthouse best friend. Maybe she'd gone to get us more drinks.

She wasn't in the kitchen either, though. I refilled my cup. All by myself. *Go, Jonah!* Armed with my liquid fun, I kept looking. Maybe she was back in the living room, and I'd somehow missed her.

I turned the corner and ran into something hard and solid, almost bouncing right back off. "Shit," I cursed as I noticed the wet patch on the shirt of the guy I'd run into. "I'm so—"

My apology died on my tongue when my eyes drifted up, first to that ridiculous skull-and-wings neck tattoo, then higher until I was caught in the icy eyes of Dex Weller. He wasn't wearing a costume, of course he wasn't, just a gray shirt under his dusty black leather jacket, black jeans, and of course those scratched-up old black combat boots.

My mouth went dry. I couldn't find my words, and suddenly I was wondering if my hair looked okay. I panicked that it didn't when Dex's eyes left mine to stare at the top of my head for a few seconds before he huffed in amusement.

"Fancy seeing you here, City Boy." He grinned.

"Don't call me that," I scowled.

"Okay, *Rabbit*."

I stared at him in confusion. I'd expected something else… but Rabbit? His eyes flicked to the top of my head again. My fingers lifted to smooth out my hair and instead found the headband of Becca's bunny ears. The fucking bunny ears. I yanked them off.

"They're Becca's!"

"Sure they are."

"They are!" I'm not sure why, but it felt very important that he believed me.

"I know. Goes with the rest of her outfit," he chuckled.

"Wait, you've seen my Becca? Where?"

Dex turned his head to look into the hallway, and I looked at the wet patch on his shirt again. Deciding to at least try to brush it off, my fingers swiped at the fabric—well, more like rubbed. It wasn't coming off. I rubbed more vigorously, glaring at the spot. It wasn't easy without a free hand.

"Here, hold this." I lifted the headband and popped it onto his head instead. With my newly freed hand and my trusty denim sleeve, I rubbed his shirt in earnest.

Dex's hand reached out and swiped my drink from me in response.

"Hey, what the fuck? Give me that back!" I demanded, but instead of listening, he brought the cup up to his nose to sniff at the contents before grimacing.

"Fuck, how many of these have you had?"

"Some."

"Are you even twenty-one?"

"None of your beeswax, gimme drink!" I reached for it, but he kept it out of range by twisting his body away. I hadn't realized I was leaning on him until I stumbled, but before I could fall on my face, his arm was around my waist *yet again*, pulling me into him.

"Easy there, Rabbit. I'll give it back in a sec. Weren't you looking for Bee?"

Oh yeah. Bee!

"Where's Bee?"

"This way, come on."

I had little choice as he pulled me along with him down the hallway toward the back entrance. There were too many people out there. Too much noise.

"She's there." He pointed over the crowd, and sure enough, I caught sight of her neon-orange hair like a beacon. She was talking to some guy with a beard and a man bun, and I did *not* like him. Somehow the guy was only slightly shorter than her with her giant boots, and he was built like a brick wall. But it didn't matter; that was *my* Becca.

"Whoa there, little rabbit." Dex's hand caught the collar of my jacket as I tried to march over there and get my friend back.

"I'm not fucking little. I'm only like, an inch shorter than you." I pouted.

"It counts," he retorted childishly.

"Does not."

"Does too."

"Fuck you."

His brow twitched up suggestively, and heat flushed through me. Hell fucking no. I pushed away from him only to stumble, and he chuckled. "Come with me."

"But Becca—"

"She's with my friend. She's safe, I promise. Now let's go."

Dex - Past

SOMETHING MORE THAN WORDS.

Jonah was fucking trashed.

While I would normally enjoy watching a drunk idiot try to take on Henrik, I found myself feeling uncharacteristically fond of this particular drunk idiot.

He hadn't even noticed that I'd handed off his drink to the nearest stranger. After experiencing him rubbing my shirt like he was trying to start a fire, I wasn't about to leave him there alone.

This was *so* not like me. I didn't drink, and I made it a point not to associate with anyone who did. Yet here I was steering Jonah around the side of the property and away from the crowds and prying eyes so I could, with any luck, sober him up a little. I'd meant what I said to him. Becca would be safe with Henrik. In fact, she was probably the safest person in all of Port Skelton with that human weapon taking an interest in her.

"Sit down," I instructed, letting go of his arm and letting gravity aid in his obedience as he practically stumbled onto his ass on the manicured lawn.

He was pouting. He'd been doing that a lot tonight. It definitely wasn't doing what he thought it was doing. In contrast to his usual glare, this was *cute*. Not that the glare didn't have its own appeal.

I tugged the lopsided bunny ears off and tossed them beside him on the grass before I took a seat on the other side of him, crossing my legs so that my knee brushed his thigh, just to see what he'd do.

True to form, he glared down as if he could set it on fire with his vision alone.

I chuckled to myself as I pulled my pouch from my pocket to roll a smoke.

"Why do you smoke that?"

"Tobacco?"

"No, like... like *that*. Can't you buy them already made? Wouldn't that be easier?"

I shrugged one shoulder. "It's cheaper like this."

It wasn't exactly a lie. Rolling your own cigarettes *was* cheaper, although that wasn't the reason I did it. I did it 'cause my pops did it. He'd taught me how to roll them for him on the promise that if he did, I would never roll them for myself. I'd broken that promise years ago, but he'd broken the promise not to leave, so I'd say that was worse.

Besides, I liked to think he'd be proud of how good I'd gotten at it.

"Gimme one," Jonah said after I'd finished.

"Not a good idea, Rabbit."

"Fuck you. I do what I want. Gimme one."

He was pouting again. That must have been the third time anyone had dared to say "fuck you" to my face without fearing the consequences. It was also the third time I'd let it slide.

"Fine, don't say I didn't warn you." I lit the cigarette and passed it to him.

He stared at it as though, if he concentrated on it enough, he could force himself not to react like last time. Then, finally, he brought it to his lips and took a shorter drag on this attempt. It still didn't stop him from coughing.

I reached to take it back, but he pulled it away from me.

"It's mine," he snarled.

"Alright, alright." I raised my hands in placation. Some people just had to learn things the hard way. I rolled myself another while Jonah continued to struggle through his.

"Show me that."

I turned to see him holding out his hand for my lighter. I clutched it tighter, and he rolled his eyes. "I just want to look. I'm not gonna steal it."

If it had been anyone else, I would have promptly told them to fuck right off. Instead, for some unknown reason, I placed my father's lighter into Jonah's outstretched palm.

He angled his body toward the light to see it clearer, as his slender fingers traced over the flowers and leaves engraved on the front.

"It looks old." He flipped it over to examine the back as well.

"It is."

Older than either of us, for sure. It had seen better days, but wherever I went it came with me.

"Where did you get it?"

Here was the part where I normally lied. Except this time, I didn't want to. "It was my dad's."

Jonah looked at me for a long moment—maybe he was searching for something, or maybe he was just drunk and had lost his words—before handing it back. I tucked it back into my pocket. Safe and secure.

He groaned as he lay back in the grass, and I did the same. I would have liked there to be stars or something, but above us was the edge of the too-large house and a blank darkness beyond. Still, it was quiet enough out here that it was almost peaceful. Granted, there was a house full of drunk idiots beside us, but for the moment, it was just him and me again, like that day in the meadow. It was nice.

Nice was a dangerous thing for a guy like me to have. *Nice* and I didn't fit together, like two puzzle pieces that formed entirely different pictures. So I knew it was only a matter of time before something went wrong.

When the silence between us had extended long enough that I wondered if he'd fallen asleep or something, I turned, and found Jonah already staring back at me. We just looked at each other for a long moment. Something electric pulsed from his gaze to mine, sharing more than words. A quiet weight I'd never known. His eyes dropped to my lips.

Jonah moved closer, and my chest constricted in panic.

I was by no means a prude. I'd tongue fuck anyone decent-looking enough, and Jonah was so far beyond decent looking, but his eyes were still heavy and unfocused from intoxication. When I kissed him—and it was a matter of *when* and not *if*—I wanted him to be sober. I wanted him to choose it without the shield of alcohol to hide behind afterward. I wouldn't let him claim it was just a drunken mistake.

His lips were only an inch from mine when I turned my head away before they could touch, quickly occupying my mouth with my cigarette that had burned out without me realizing.

Then it was too quiet, and when I turned to look at him again, there was a fire in his eyes that I could almost feel burning me.

"Fuck you!" He raised his voice before shoving me.

That was four times now. Four too many. I shoved him back. "What's wrong, Rabbit? Pissed off I wouldn't give you a kiss?"

I'd known it was only a matter of time before something went wrong, and this time had been even shorter than I anticipated, because as Jonah's knuckles connected with my lips, my reflexes kicked in and I hit him back before I'd even thought about it.

He stared at me wide-eyed, his hand covering his struck cheek. I licked the blood from my lip. The split in the bottom one opened again, thanks to the kiss from his knuckles. Then he launched himself at me, and we were brawling in the grass.

Jonah had clearly never been in a real fight before, but he was fucking strong and he was pissed, and those things made him dangerous enough as I blocked his next hit.

"Fight!" someone yelled from further down the property, but I couldn't spare them a glance and give Jonah another opening.

Moments later there was a crowd of people growing around us, cheering and hollering obnoxiously, and if Jonah wasn't such a damn handful, I would have punched every single one of them too. As it was, I was mainly trying to block his hits and restrain him rather than actually fight him, but he was having none of it. Jonah wasn't above fighting dirty. When I had his wrists pinned, he'd try to kick me or bite me instead. It was like wrestling a rabid orangutan.

"Jonah!" came a familiar screech, then a flash of orange hair and white spandex as Becca threw herself into the fray. Then a freakishly large strong hand grabbed the collar of my jacket and yanked me up by the scruff of the neck like a misbehaving kitten.

"Enough," Henrik scolded, setting me on my feet.

Jonah was up again too, and he launched himself at me a second time, but Henrik was faster, and my rabbit coat-hangered himself on the immovable rod of Henrik's arm, sending himself back down onto his ass.

"Jonah, stop!" Becca begged.

"We're leaving," Henrik informed me, a firm hand on my chest shoving me in a challenge I was sorely tempted to take on. People really had to stop fucking shoving me today. I slapped his arm away, knowing the only reason it shifted at all was because he allowed it.

"Fine." I fixed my jacket back into place as I sneered at Jonah. "Better luck next time, Rabbit."

"Just go!" Becca snapped at me, using what must have been all her strength to hold Jonah back from coming at me again.

As we walked back to the bikes, I wondered how long it would be before I got another chance to kiss Jonah's lips rather than his fist.

14

Jonah – Present

You're Coming With Me.

—— ✦ ——

Despite my warnings to myself, I'd continued to hang out with Harper over the last two days. It wasn't like I'd gone out of my way to do it, but I'd been at work and he'd come in again, so it would have been rude to ignore him. Then the next day he'd knocked on my door and asked what I was doing because he was bored. We'd gone for a walk and hung out at the dilapidated park that honestly had so many safety hazards I wondered how any decent parents would ever let their children play there. We talked about nothing in particular. Mostly Harper talked and I listened, but it felt comfortable.

It was Monday, which meant Marty would pay me today and I'd be out of here.

I never told anyone when I was leaving town, but it felt wrong to just ghost Harper, especially with the little bit I'd shared about my past. Maybe he'd think something had happened to me. I knew it wasn't smart to care, but the decision sat in my gut like a burning coal.

Maybe just this once I could tell someone I was leaving. As long as I didn't tell him where I was going, that should be okay.

With that in mind, I pulled my jacket on, intending to head to the small grocery store. It had a surprisingly decent baked-goods section. I'd get us both some breakfast and tell him I was leaving while we ate.

I was so caught up in mentally rehearsing the conversation that I didn't notice the stranger until my foot hit the concrete at the bottom of the motel stairs.

He was *tall*, with short dark hair and a dark bomber jacket. His back was to me as his face pressed against the glass on the driver's window of Harper's car, hands cupped to reduce the glare as he peered inside.

"You need something?" I called out to him. My heart already thundered rapidly in my chest, but I wouldn't let it show.

The stranger didn't seem startled at being caught snooping. Instead, he stood to his full height, which was a lot, like six-five at least. He turned to face me—tanned skin, dark eyes, a square jaw with a short beard, and dazzling white teeth that he flashed me in a wide grin as he chewed on a piece of gum.

Recognition sparked in my mind, and with it a whirlwind of other emotions. Right here in the parking lot of this shitty Hollow Creek motel was MMA superstar Benny "The Bear" Forrester. Well... *former* superstar.

"Nope. You need somethin'?" he asked, that Boston accent deep and confident.

I had to figure out how to play this. I wasn't sure if Harper was in his room or not, and I absolutely was not letting this guy get so much as a glimpse of him. Taking on a professional MMA fighter, retired or not, was probably not the best course of action here. I guess that left talking. I fucking hated talking.

"You seem real interested in that car." I raised my voice slightly in a way I hoped was still casual but might carry through to Harper if he was inside and awake. It was the first time I was glad for the paper-thin walls of this dump.

"Why wouldn't I be? It's mine," he answered, still with that picture-perfect grin.

Fuck, Harper. That better not be the truth.

"I don't think I believe you."

"No? Well, call the cops, then. Though I'd really like to catch the guy who stole it myself."

Shit. Harper, did you honestly go on the run from a guy with his stolen car? I'd suspected the guy had more beauty than brains, but wow. "Sheriff's office is about four blocks that way if you want to report it stolen."

"Like I said, I'd rather catch the thief myself. Speakin' of, you wouldn't happen to know which room the driver's checked into, would ya? Since you're so sure this car ain't mine, ya must have seen him."

"Couple of days ago. Not since," I lied, turning to face the motel. "One of those two, I think." I gestured to two of the ground-floor rooms, well away from Harper's and mine.

"Hmm." He made a pensive noise as his eyes tracked over the two units I'd pointed out. "Thank you kindly."

That was it. He just stood there, waiting for me to speak again or move along, and my mind was fucking blank with panic. I didn't want to walk away and leave Harper alone, but going back up to my room would be too suspicious.

I nodded once, curtly, and continued walking. The weight of his gaze followed me until I was out of view from the lot. When I was sure he couldn't see me anymore, I pulled my phone from my pocket and continued on my way as fast as possible to the grocery store. I pulled up the social media accounts for Harper Lorens and quickly requested to friend him on all the ones I could find.

Of course, my account was a ghost account. I created new ones all the time, and my current accounts belonged to Rick Smith. Harper wasn't going to know who the fuck that was, but I hoped with as many friends as he had he was the type to just blindly accept requests.

I paced the bread aisle as I kept rapidly refreshing the page, waiting for him to accept.

He wasn't accepting.

I typed out a message quickly and sent it off, hoping to whatever gods or forces of nature landed us here that they'd cut us a fucking break and not let the message get lost in some void of spam messages.

Time passed with no response. No notifications. I cursed myself for not just getting his number when we had the chance, but the whole "form no connections" rule I had in place had prevented me from giving him my number when he'd asked. He'd been slightly offended and hadn't tried to hide it, but I'd just told him it was nothing personal, given him a free shot, and after ten minutes of silent treatment he got past it and talked again like nothing had happened.

Stupid, Jonah. Stupid, stupid, stupid, stupid.

The cashier was giving me weird looks now, so I paid for what I'd originally intended to buy and started on my way back to the motel.

When I got there, Benny was gone, and Harper's car was still parked in the lot.

I looked around, searching for any sign of the freakishly large man before I took the stairs two at a time and went straight for Harper's door, knocking furiously.

There was no response. I tried the handle. Locked.

I swear to god, Harper, if you've gotten yourself abducted by your ex—your professional fighter ex—I'm going to be so pissed at you.

I retreated into my room, keeping the window open as I stood by it, chain-smoking and listening for the slightest sounds or movements that would indicate *something*. My fingers traced over the engraved floral and leaf patterns on the old lighter. I usually found it calming, but there was little that would ease my anxiety at the moment with so much unknown.

If Benny had Harper, his car probably wouldn't still be here, right?

I couldn't remember if there'd been another car in the lot along with the MMA fighter because he'd taken up all of my attention. I just had to hope.

With nothing else to do but stew in my anxiety, I decided to head in to work as scheduled, hoping that maybe at least someone there, in this town full of gossips, had heard something of fucking value for once.

⚫◆○◆⚫

Two hours into my shift, and there was nothing. No news. No gossip. No Benny. No Harper. It was the one time I wished Hank was here, because at least that old bigot kept up with whatever the fuck was going on in this piece of shit town.

There were only the regulars here, but I was extra jumpy at every sudden noise and movement, constantly scanning the clouded windows for familiar shapes outside.

It took another hour before the door opened, and my breath left my lungs in a dizzying rush when a face I'd hoped I wouldn't see again so soon came into view.

Benny smiled at me again, that same perfectly punchable smile. It was a wonder the guy had any teeth left with how often people must want to punch him, and with his former career. Then again, they were too white to be natural, much like Harpers. Fucking rich people and their freakishly white teeth.

The giant approached the bar, and it was a miracle the glass in my hand didn't shatter with how tightly I was gripping it.

"Hello again," he said pleasantly, like we were old friends.

I nodded. "Drink?"

"Whiskey, thanks. Macallan twelve if ya got it."

"Yep." I made his drink, slamming it down perhaps a touch too aggressively in front of him, causing some of the contents to splash up over the side. He didn't seem fazed by it, and that somehow pissed me off more.

"Thank you kindly, Jack." He smiled, and my stomach churned. "It is Jack, right? Was talkin' to a nice fella named Hank just this afternoon. He mentioned ya."

Fucking Hank. Forget spitting in his drink, I was going to wring that old bastard's neck.

"No Jack here," I lied. "Must've been talking about the other bartender."

"That so? Well, any shot of him showin' up? I got a couple a questions about his new buddy Harper."

Yeah, I was definitely going to kill Hank. Fucking blabber-mouth bastard.

"It's a Monday, so no, don't need anyone else to get by when it's this quiet."

Benny made an amused noise as he nodded, those dark eyes boring into me like he could see the truth beneath my skin. Like if he stared at me long enough with that stupid fake smile on his lips, I'd start confessing.

I caught Tiny approaching at the other end of the bar, and made my way over before he said my name—well, *Jack*—and blew whatever cover I had left here.

Thankfully, I dodged that particular bullet, but Benny's eyes were on me as I stared at the pint glass in my hand, filling it with Tiny's beer. Before it was done, the door opened again and both my eyes and Benny's snapped to it at the same time.

The rapid beating of my pulse seemed to intensify and stop all at the same time as my heart sank and exploded simultane-ously, like a submarine kissing a sea mine.

In the doorway, hand still pressed against the glass, was fucking *Harper*.

Time seemed to freeze for a moment before a lot of things happened at once.

"Shit," Harper cursed, and he was off.

The door hadn't even closed behind him before Benny was up and wrenching it open again.

The glass in my hand dropped and shattered on the floor as I launched myself over the bar top to chase after both of them. Pain flared in my leg, but there was no way I was letting Harper face that piece of shit on his own. I pulled the door open and followed them into the dusk-lit street, running as fast as I could.

I should have been able to do it. I should have been able to catch up with them. Running was my thing. My skill. The one thing I was good at. *Had been good at.* I was broken now, broken and useless, and that had never been more apparent as the distance between myself and my new friend, my only friend, grew bigger.

A wretched sound pulled from the core of me as I lost all hope of catching them on foot. The pain that roared through my leg was nothing compared to the molten despair that unleashed through my chest. I couldn't let this happen.

Changing course, I sprinted to the motel as fast as my stupid fucking leg would allow me to. In the lot there was another car, a black Jeep that looked new. Praying it was worth the sacrifice of time and that this was actually Benny's car, I pulled my switchblade from my pocket and punctured the tires on the right side before dashing to my own car.

The motor sputtered before rumbling to life, and I pulled out of the lot as quickly as possible, heading in the direction I'd lost them.

It was darker now, and the headlights still made it difficult to make out movement beyond the road. If Harper had any chance of escape, it would have been through the woods. I hoped with everything left in me he'd done that. That he'd escaped.

As the clock ticked by, minutes into hours, the adrenaline faded enough that an overwhelming sense of helplessness threatened to consume me instead. I cried. I hadn't cried in so fucking long that once I started I found it impossible to make myself stop.

It wasn't my fault, I knew that, but I still felt so fucking useless. I didn't know what to do. Should I contact the police? After all this time avoiding the authorities, that suggestion burned away at my brain. Red flashing warning signs told me it would be stupid. The further from law enforcement I could stay, the better. Besides, I knew who the sheriff was, and that man wouldn't have stood a chance against Harper, let alone Benny.

It was pitch black when I finally caught movement on one of the dirt trails I'd been driving on through the woods. My car was not built for this terrain, but I hardly cared, especially not when that petite and familiar silhouette came into view. A choked sound escaped from deep inside me as I pulled the car to a stop and Harper turned wide, fearful eyes to me.

"Get in. Now!" I called as soon as the window opened enough for him to hear me, and the relief that washed over him made me want to burst into tears all over again. I found him. I had him. He was safe.

Harper got into the passenger side, and I took off before he'd even had the chance to buckle himself in. I hadn't seen Benny, but I wasn't taking the chance that he was nearby as I made my way back to the highway.

"Are you hurt?" I asked as wheels met asphalt instead of dirt.

Harper didn't respond. I glanced at him to find him curled up, facing away from me, his body shaking.

"Harper, I need you to answer me. Did he hurt you?"

There was a wet sniff, and he curled in on himself further, and I decided right then and there that I wasn't leaving him alone again.

"You're coming with me," I told him, the decision final.

15

Dex - Past

SO THERE'S THIS GUY.

Waves crashed endlessly. Water rolled over itself and thrashed against stone, carried by the current, by the wind. An eternal push and pull.

No matter what happened in Port Skelton, this place remained the same. It was unaffected by trivial human matters and pursuits. It felt real in a way that most things didn't, in the way that only the ocean could.

Being here always filled me with a sick sort of satisfaction. It made me feel small, made my problems feel small, like while I was here they weren't real and didn't matter. Like while I was here, none of it could hurt me. Ironic, I suppose, considering what had happened here twelve years ago.

"So there's this guy," I said with a sigh. I'm not sure why I was telling him, maybe because there was no one else to tell. Maybe because I thought he'd want to know. "I think I'm interested in him. Like, actually interested…" I brought my cigarette to my lips, taking a long drag and letting the wind steal the smoke as I exhaled, carrying it somewhere imperceivable, dispersing it into the atmosphere until it was nothing, along with the rest of my secrets. "It scares me."

My boots ground against the small stones and dirt beneath me, my eyes locked onto a small black ant on a mission, scouting the area, unbothered by my presence.

"I don't know if he's interested in me, but it feels like... something. Something I haven't felt before. I'm not sure what to do about it."

Another exhale, smoke whipped away before it had a chance to plume. The ant found a seed.

"What should I do, Dad?" I asked.

There was no response. There hadn't been a response for twelve years. I'd thought if there was ever going to be one, if there was going to be any trace of him at all, it would be here, where he'd died.

I clicked his lighter in my hand, watching as the flame died before it could even ignite. It didn't stand a chance at life against this wind. Twice more I tried; twice more it died. I turned my attention back to the ant, watching as it lifted the seed almost its own size over its head to carry back to wherever its nest was.

I understood why Dad had chosen this place. It was peaceful but not silent. Loud in ways that didn't trigger him. I didn't understand it at the time—why he had to leave so often, why he chose that day not to come back—but I did now. I understood it too well.

I didn't want to follow my dad's example, not because I didn't feel the call of the rocks at the bottom of this cliff, or of the waves that promised blissful silence and a watery embrace. A way to wash away my pain. No, that wasn't why I chose not to stay here forever like he had. It was because suicide felt like proving my mother right, and that was the last thing I ever wanted to do.

That being said, living wasn't great either. So I did it recklessly. I didn't care who I pissed off and picked fights with. I didn't watch my mouth. I didn't care about consequences. It was incredibly liberating not to give a single fuck about anything. And if doing whatever the fuck I wanted ended up getting me killed, well, that was fine too. As long as I was breathing, though, I was gonna make that everyone else's problem.

Standing up and taking one last long look at the ocean beneath the storm clouds that were rolling in, I crushed the ant and its treasure with my boot. Another miserable day in hell.

"Later, Dad."

⁂

"You're early," Roy grumbled from the reception desk as I walked through the door, his thick brows furrowed, that eternally displeased expression on his face.

"So?" I shot back as I attempted to continue past him, only for a large, callused hand to press against my chest and halt me in my tracks.

"So your shift don't start for another thirty minutes. Beat it, kid. I'm not paying you overtime."

"I'm not asking you for overtime."

"Damn right you ain't, cause you ain't working. Now get the fuck out of here till the shop opens."

"I'll do what I want, old man." I knocked his hand away with only half the force I would have used for anyone else.

"Not in my shop you won't, brat." Roy huffed. The thick curtain of his mustache hairs twitched with his breath.

"You gonna stop me?" I raised a brow in challenge. I didn't doubt he'd have the capability if he really wanted to. Roy was twice my age, but he was also twice as bulky. His dark shirt stretched to capacity over thick shoulders and sculpted biceps, the buttons clinging on for dear life down the center as his breaths expanded the muscle of his chest. He had a body built from hard work and heavy lifting.

"I will if I have to, boy." He didn't miss a beat, staring with the pale eyes of a predator, almost matching mine in color, though Roy's were more blue than gray, in stark contrast to his tan skin and dark hair.

I groaned. "But I'm bored, and I'm already here."

Roy huffed, a response I was familiar with. By now I knew the old mechanic well enough that I could translate entire sentences from his huffs. This one said, *"That's not my problem, and I won't be persuaded otherwise."*

"Ugh, fine, gimme some cash, then." I surrendered.

Roy didn't question me any further, simply retrieved his wallet from his back pocket and pulled out a twenty, holding it out to me between two thick, oil-stained fingers.

I snatched it up and tossed my helmet at him, which he caught with another huff as I turned and exited the shop again.

The Cozy Cow was only a five-minute walk from Roy and Declan's Auto Repairs, so I left my baby in the lot and made the trip on foot.

This early in the morning, there were rarely any dine-in customers, though office and retail workers would stop in for takeaway caffeine on their way into work. That was why the figure at the window caught my attention—well, that and the fact that Jonah Hargreaves always had a way of pulling my attention to him like a magnet.

Today's hoodie was a dark purple, pulled up over his head, which rested on the glass window. His eyes were closed, brow furrowed like he was annoyed that he couldn't sleep in the middle of the diner at seven forty-five in the morning.

It was impossible not to be aware of him, and as if he could feel it too, his eyes snapped open, immediately finding mine. The glare he sent me had twice the regular level of heat, and I knew without a doubt he remembered our last encounter very clearly despite the fact he'd been drunk. He looked ready to pick up where we'd left off, like any sudden movement and he'd jump the table and drive his bony fist into my jaw again. I almost wanted him to. My insides buzzed with the need to be pressed against him in whatever way I could get.

"Just the regular?" Amanda asked from the counter, breaking the building tension between us as I turned to look at her.

"Just mine and Roy's," I answered her.

"Bryce not working today?"

"He is, but he can get his own."

Amanda rolled her eyes, though her expression was amused as she put in the total, and I paid with the cash Roy had given me. "You're a menace." She smiled.

She was one of the few people in Port Skelton who didn't seem to find me intimidating or try to avoid me. It had been an accident, really, saving her. The piece of shit she'd called a partner had owed Archer money, and when I'd gone to collect he'd been in the middle of beating her, so I gave it back to him tenfold. He couldn't beat her with two broken arms, but I also broke a leg just cause I could. She'd finally left him after that, moved out of Meadow Park into a house share with some chicks she went to school with. I knew because for some reason she liked to tell me these things as she made my order.

While Amanda rambled on about her housemates, I turned back to my honey-eyed inferno, only to find his fire was no longer directed at me. Instead he was glaring at the barista as if she had somehow offended him. I didn't like that. I wanted his glare, his attention. All of it.

Picking up a plastic stirring spoon and a cube of sugar, I aimed, lining up my shot with my shitty catapult. Load. Aim. Fire.

The sugar cube soared through the air, hitting its mark—the side of Jonah's head—before crumbling over his clothes and the booth.

Attention successfully captured.

His fire intensified, igniting me where I stood. I smiled, and it just pissed him off further. When his eyes eventually left mine again, I watched him look over the contents of his table, undoubtedly looking for something he could throw back at me. I was worried he'd go for the ceramic mug steaming in front of him, if only because I didn't feel like causing Amanda the trouble of cleaning it up, but before he could decide, the door chimed and Becca breezed in.

"Dex," Amanda called behind me, and as Jonah's attention was stolen away from me once more, I turned to face her and the tray of three coffees she held out for me to take.

"I said Bryce could come get his own," I grumbled.

"You did," she agreed before waving her hand at me. "Now get out of here."

I rolled my eyes, and as I was about to turn for the exit, I felt the thump and crumbling of what was undoubtedly a sugar cube exploding as it hit the back of my jacket.

"Jonah!" Becca scolded as I turned, coffee tray in hand, and made my way over to their booth.

Jonah glared, and Becca's eyes were wide with shock and uncertainty at my approach. Plucking Bryce's coffee from the tray, conveniently marked with a B on the lid. I offered Becca my most dazzling smile and a wink as I put it down in front of her at the table.

Two birds, one coffee.

The shock garnered from both of them as I turned for the exit was incredibly satisfying, that was until another much heavier thump hit the back of my jacket, accompanied by hot, sweet-smelling liquid splashing up my neck and down the back of my jeans.

There was a heavy silence as every person in the diner stopped what they were doing. Even the buzz of the milk frother on the coffee machine halted as Amanda looked on in horror.

Well then. I wasn't about to let that slide, especially not with this many witnesses.

I walked back to the booth, keeping my expression neutral. Jonah's face flushed pink, either in anger or embarrassment at his own actions, like maybe he'd acted without thinking that one through.

"That was a mistake, Rabbit," I told him as I plucked my coffee from the tray and emptied it over his head.

Jonah gasped, like he hadn't quite expected I'd do exactly what he'd done.

The moment he recovered from his shock, he launched himself at me, knocking the remaining coffee out of the tray as we slammed against the table at my back. Roy's coffee, black and extra hot, burned in a way the other two hadn't, and all that seemed to do was ignite Jonah further as he clawed at me, hands going for my neck.

There were gasps and shouts of shock from the surrounding crowd, but I hardly cared. If my rabbit wanted to fight this out in the middle of the diner, I was happy to oblige.

We tumbled to the ground, trading hits and grabbing fists of each other's clothing as we fought to get the upper hand. Jonah snarled at me like a rabid dog, fueled by rage, but I was euphoric. Having his body thrashing against mine was so right, even if it hurt. Violence tasted a lot like passion, and I craved Jonah's passion.

With a grunt, I had him pinned to the ground beneath me, where I wanted him more than anything, his captured wrists pinned to the tiled floor on either side of his head. Before he could make a move to kick at me, I straddled him, weighed his lower body down with mine so any attempt to move only pushed him further into me.

Coffee dripped from my messed-up curls down onto his cheek as he glared up at me and attempted to thrash out of my hold, but I had him now, and I wasn't letting him go. Jonah grunted and tried to buck me off. I pushed down against him, and at the heavy pressure and friction I watched as his breath caught in his throat. Heat crept up his neck, his pupils expanding.

"Would you look at that. It seems my rabbit likes being held down," I said in a voice low enough for only him to hear, and whatever trance he'd briefly fallen into shattered.

"Get the fuck off me!" he shrieked.

Before I could respond, ice-cold water was being splashed over the both of us.

"Get out! Both of you! Out now!" Amanda shouted, brandishing a mop as a weapon.

Beside her, Becca stood with eyes wide, clutching a now-empty water jug.

With a grunt, I relented, releasing Jonah as we both got to our feet. I half expected him to launch at me again, but it seemed he couldn't even meet my gaze as he pulled his wet hood over his head and dashed out of the diner much like he had that very first day. Becca stared at me, both confused and shocked before she put the jug down, apologized to Amanda, and took off after him.

I sighed, watching them leave before reaching a hand out to Amanda for the mop.

◆◇◆

"The fuck happened to you, boy?" Roy asked from the desk where Bryce was now sitting. The bigger man rested a hand on his shoulder, which Roy quickly removed as my eyes locked onto it.

"Nothing happened," I grumbled as I made my way to the bathroom at the back to clean up. Fortunately, I kept a few changes of clothes here, in case of days I wasn't able to go home.

When I returned from cleaning up, Roy stared at me as he leaned against the wall, arms folded, brow furrowed. "Talk to me, son. What's going on?"

My eyes shifted to the door that led to the reception area.

"I sent Bryce to get more coffee, seein' as you decided to wear the first lot."

I rolled my eyes, ready to shrug Roy off again, but the way he stared at me told me he'd be having none of it. It was annoying, really, the way he genuinely seemed to care about me. No one else in my life would be bothered. It frustrated me. I didn't know what to do with it. For a moment we simply stared each other down, each waiting for the other to give in first, but the grumpy old bastard was infuriatingly patient.

I conceded with a groan. "So there's this guy."

JONAH - PAST

HYPOTHETICAL OPERATION.

I hate him. I hate him. *I hate him*. I fucking hate Dex fucking Weller.

I didn't wait for Becca as I stormed away from the Cozy Cow. The wind chilled my damp clothing. It hung heavy on my body, and my hair stuck to my face and neck in wet clumps that smelled like coffee and vanilla.

Granted, I had been the one to throw the first cup, but what else was I supposed to do when he'd bought a cup of coffee for *Becca?* He wasn't even interested in her. Was he? No, he couldn't be. The thought of him being interested in her made my blood boil and my vision turn red. I'd acted before I thought about it, hurling the coffee across the diner. What the fuck was that? That wasn't me. I didn't do shit like that, but when he was around, I couldn't think clearly. I became someone else, someone I didn't like. He did this to me. Somehow, it was his fault.

"Nah, baby, I'm the devil."

His words from the field that day circled around in my mind, and I couldn't think of a better way to describe him. Dex Weller was the devil, and he was set on corrupting me and dragging me down to hell with him. Well, I wouldn't allow it. Whatever this was, this invisible, immense thing that pulled me into his orbit like fucking gravity, it was over now. I wouldn't play his games. I wouldn't sink to his level. I never wanted to see Dex again.

"Jonah, would you wait up?" Becca called after me as she ran to catch up.

I didn't know how to explain myself to her. I'd called her non-stop until she woke up this morning, and demanded she come meet me at the diner because I didn't want to be alone. That old house and that old man made me feel like I was going crazy. The pain in my leg flared because it was colder today, and I wanted to tear it apart. Today was absolutely no good, and then *he* had to come in and make it all so much worse.

None of that was even the worst part. No. The worst part, the absolute *worst* part of it all was that Dex Weller had me pinned down on the dirty floor of a diner—both of us covered in scalding coffee, with me trapped by his stupid fucking strength—and *I got hard*. Just popped a fucking shame boner right then and there beneath him.

My dick and I really needed to have a chat about what the fuck it was doing. Waking up for Dex Weller in my weird little fantasies when I was in my bed alone was one thing, but in *public* during a fucking *fight* was entirely another.

"It seems my rabbit likes being held down."

His low gravelly voice circled around in my mind, and I couldn't help the frustrated shout that escaped me in response. *Whose fucking rabbit? Not yours, asshole. Never yours.*

"Jonah!" Becca grabbed my arm and turned me toward her. I shrugged her off, but she grabbed me again. "Nuh-uh, not this time. You are not getting out of explaining this. What the fuck is the matter with you?"

"I don't know, okay?" I yanked myself out of her grip. "I can't *think* when he's around. He pisses me off so much I can't control myself."

Becca gave me a long stare, and I couldn't meet her gaze, worried somehow she would see too much. She always saw too much. I didn't even know what I was hiding from her, but whatever these feelings were inside me, they were private, and shameful, and much too big. That's why I couldn't help but explode whenever Dex was in close proximity.

"Oh, sweetie." Becca sighed, and that pissed me off more. I pulled away from her and continued on my way. She followed me. "Let's go get you cleaned up, but then we're talking about this properly. Also, you are absolutely going back to the diner to apologize to Amanda. There's no way I'm letting you get us banned from that place."

"Now, I'm gonna hold your hand when I tell you this, but you're *into* Dex," Becca told me as we sat on my bed, like that wasn't the most ridiculous thing she had ever said in her entire fucking life.

"That's not funny." I scowled at her, snatching my hand back to continue drying my hair with my towel, pleased it no longer smelled of coffee after my shower. I'd told her, *mostly*, about whatever was going on with Dex and me. Of course, I left out the part where I'd almost kissed him at the party last weekend. Before he rejected me. It was a drunken mistake, one I wouldn't be making again, and it wasn't relevant to this, because although I might have thought about it often in the safety of my own mind, I definitely would never attempt it again.

"I'm not joking, JJ. You're into him. Like a *lot*."

"I *hate* him," I corrected her.

"You can be into people you hate."

I stared at her, processing that. I guess maybe you could, and maybe I was. "Whatever, it doesn't matter. It's never happening. I'd rather kill him than fuck him."

Becca smiled. "God, that'd be some hot sex, though, right? All mean and rough and intense. Yum."

She fanned herself with her hand. I dried my hair more vigorously, letting the towel curtain my face to hide the heat rising to my cheeks. Again my mind flashed to the way he'd pinned me to the ground, and again something hot twisted inside me. *No. Bad dick.*

"Maybe you just need to fuck it out of your system," she dared to add, and I let the towel drop so I could glare at her. She actually seemed serious.

"Yeah, I don't think that's it. Besides, aren't you the one who told me to stay away from him?"

"Well, yeah, and I stand by that, because look at the absolute dumpster fire you become when you're anywhere near him. But I'm not saying you should date the guy. Just have some absolutely filthy sex and then close that chapter for good."

I glared at her, mouth opening to retort, but no words would come. I settled for glaring some more instead.

"Holy shit, you totally want to!" she basically squealed, and more heat rose to my cheeks.

"I do not!"

"Do too."

"Do not."

"Do too."

"No!"

"Yes!"

I threw my damp towel at her, and she laughed as she caught it and flung it to the other side of my room.

"We are soooo getting you laid."

"Shut up! No, we are not! Plus, he fucking hates me too."

"You're kidding, right? That man basically dry-humped you in the diner today for everyone to see."

"That was a *fight*," I corrected her.

"He calls you *Rabbit*."

"Only because it pisses me off," I huffed. Becca laughed way too hard at that. "It's not funny."

"I mean, it's kind of funny. You. A rabbit?" she cackled. "I love you, JJ, but the only rabbit you could ever be is that one from Monty Python that eats people."

I tried glaring at her, I really did, but I couldn't help the smile that pulled on my lips or the laugh that followed, and soon we were both cackling like idiots on my bed over this entire ridiculous situation.

"Okay, so. Operation Fuck Dex is underway." She beamed and then squealed as I grabbed a pillow to suffocate her with, mostly to distract us both from where this conversation was headed, because I was not at all ready to deal with that. Even if my stomach fluttered with something dangerously similar to excitement at the prospect. "Come on, Jonah, don't be such a prude," Becca continued the moment I released her from the pillow prison. "It's not like you're a virgin." I turned away from her, the silence suddenly so loud between us. "Wait, are you?"

"Does it matter?" I snapped a little too aggressively.

"No. Not at all," she said, voice softer. "There's nothing wrong with that. Nothing wrong if you never want to have sex either, you know that, right?"

"I know," I responded quickly, but hearing that soothed me somewhat. It felt like the whole world was so interested in sex sometimes, that I was missing out on something fundamental by not wanting it. Like there was something wrong with me for not caring if I ever experienced it or not. Until now. Now Dex had woken something up inside me that I didn't know how to put back to sleep. "Hypothetically speaking, if I wanted to... you know. It should probably be, like, meaningful... right? The first time."

Becca was quiet for a moment. She turned to face me, but when I refused to look back, she seemed to understand that I needed to be shielded, at least from being watched, as we had this conversation. She turned her gaze back to the ceiling.

"That's entirely up to you, love. If you want it to be meaningful and special, then that's fine. But if you want my opinion on it, I think too much pressure and weight is put on losing your V-card. There's no reason the first time has to be any more meaningful than any time after that, and to be honest, the first time usually sucks anyway. There's no right time or right way to go about it, and anyone who tells you otherwise better mind their own fucking business."

A smile pulled at my lips. "What about you, then?"

"You are my business."

"I like being your business."

Her hand found mine on the bed, and she laced our fingers together. "I'm so glad I have you, JJ."

I squeezed her hand back, refusing to look at her, refusing to let her see how much those words meant to me. When I could trust myself to speak, I said, "I'm glad I have you too."

She turned to look at me again, but I still refused to look back until she snorted and whacked my arm playfully. "God, Jonah, you're so sensitive, damnnn." I turned and scowled at her, but I knew my face didn't actually look anywhere near as menacing as I wanted it to. "Okayyyy, so. Operation Fuck Dex?" She pumped her eyebrows at me. "Are we in? Or are we in?"

I stared up at the roof, feeling my cheeks heat and my belly flutter with that new sensation that happened whenever I thought about Dex. "Hypothetically, if we were in... what would that plan look like?"

◆○◆

It was all supposed to be hypothetical, just talking about it as a vague concept, a stupid, really fucking bad idea that Becca and I would talk shit about and laugh over before stomping it to the ground like it deserved. I hated Dex. I wasn't *actually* going to try to fuck him. It was just talk. Until it wasn't. Until the days passed and Dex filled my mind more and more, his words, his stupid pretty face popped up in my thoughts all the fucking time.

Then there were my ever-evolving fantasies. They'd taken a *highly* unpleasant and unwanted turn following the new knowledge of what it felt like to be held down by him.

Maybe Becca was right. Maybe I needed to fuck it out of my system. Then my mind would know what it actually felt like, and I could stop imagining it and move the fuck on.

I still wasn't convinced he'd be interested, but it wasn't like I was going to throw myself at him or actually proposition him or anything. I'd never put myself in a position again where Dex could reject me. But if he were the one to come on to me, well... maybe I wouldn't be opposed to it. Just once.

"This is so stupid," I groaned as I stared at myself in the mirror. Becca hovered behind me, her gaze scrutinizing as she looked over the outfit she'd put me in. I felt absolutely ridiculous. Becca was the most fashionable person I knew, but I had to wonder if she was joking with this.

The ripped black skinny jeans were acceptable, except maybe this pair had a few too many rips. Still, I could get behind them. What I could *not* get behind was the chunky platform boots with so many buckles that they jingled every time I took a step and the sleeveless black turtleneck *crop top* that exposed my midsection. I also couldn't get behind the smudged black eyeliner rimming my eyes. Well, I'd admit I liked it a *little* more than I'd expected to. I still felt ridiculous.

"It's *not* stupid. Don't insult my hard work like that. It's fucking hot. You're a goth baddie dream boy. Emo punk suits you. Dex is gonna come in his pants when he sees you, then he's gonna tear all your clothes off like a wild animal, and it's gonna be bye-bye virgin Jonah."

"You are so gross," I groaned, pulling away from her to go sit on her bed. This entire plan seemed so dumb now. We didn't even know if Dex was going to be at this party, and even if he was, I still wasn't sure that fucking him was a good idea. The fact remained that I fucking hated his guts, even if I also fantasized about him being up in mine. *Gross, Jonah.*

Becca hummed happily as she finished getting herself ready. She wore a patent leather mini skirt over fishnet tights that absolutely would *not* keep her warm. At least her boots covered most of her legs. They were heeled, as if she needed any extra height. She also wore a lacy deep-burgundy shirt over a black lace bra, a cropped black leather jacket, and more jewelry than most girls probably owned altogether.

"You look hot," I sighed.

"*We* look hot," she amended, and I rolled my eyes. "Are you ready to go?" she asked as she pulled out another leather jacket with studded shoulders from her wardrobe, this one for me.

"As ready as I'll ever be," I grumbled, taking it from her and shrugging into it.

Here goes nothing.

⚬

This party was in a house almost identical to the last one—with too many rooms, perfectly white walls, and beige furniture, like it came out of a magazine rather than being a place people actually lived in. I honestly didn't care for it. It was the kind of house my mom had always dreamed about, the kind she'd managed to get with Richard.

I spent most of my time trailing Becca and avoiding talking to anyone else, letting her do the speaking for us both. Unlike last time, however, I felt the weight of people's gazes far more intensely. I found myself trailing the hem of my crop top with my fingertips, pulling it down only for it to ride back up again immediately. It was too exposing, the neckline too constricting, like all the fabric was in the wrong place. It made my skin itchy, and all my clothes seemed wrong. I longed for my abandoned hoodie. This wasn't me. I didn't like it. It was just as well that Dex wasn't even here, because I didn't want him to see me like this. Who knew what infuriating fucking remarks he would make about it.

As Becca got caught in yet another conversation on our way to the kitchen for alcohol, I kept my gaze down and thought about what excuses I might give to get out of here. Maybe I could at the very least sneak away and raid someone's wardrobe for something that would cover me better. I didn't even know whose house we were in, or whose party this was.

I was about to reach for Becca, about to give her a look that I hoped would convey more than words could, when I felt it. Felt *him*. I knew it was him, even before I turned around, because only *his* gaze was that heavy, that heated, that magnetic. That pull between us was there, as it always was, growing stronger.

Before I could turn to find him, rough fingertips traced over my sides, just above the waistband of my jeans, on skin that was far too exposed and vulnerable. The scent of leather and smoke and something deeper and oaky had my breath catching in my throat as lips ghosted over the shell of my ear. "Have you had anything to drink?" Dex asked.

I couldn't remember how to breathe, let alone speak, but I still shook my head in response.

"Good. Keep it that way. I gotta see a guy about a thing, but then I'm coming to find you, Rabbit. Wait for me."

Then he was gone again. My pulse thundered beneath my skin, the ghost of where he'd touched still tingling, sending ripples of heat and want and excitement and fear over the entirety of me.

Maybe it was the outfit that had me feeling vulnerable, maybe it was this stupid half-baked plan Becca had talked me into, but the urge to punch him was second to the urge to see what would happen if I did what he said, just this once.

"I saw that." Becca gave me a Cheshire cat smile that was honestly a little creepy. She hooked her arm with mine, apparently done with her conversation and I hadn't even noticed. "Shall we get a drink to settle the nerves, love?"

Keep it that way. I swallowed and shook my head.

This definitely didn't feel so hypothetical anymore.

17

JONAH - PAST

BOOTS.

———————— ✦ ————————

This was a terribly bad, no-good idea.

I didn't know what the fuck Dex was here to do, but he'd disappeared a while ago now, and I was starting to think he'd just left me here. Maybe that was his new method of messing with me, just leaving me waiting. I didn't even know what I was waiting for. He hadn't specified that part. Just told me to wait as he went off to "*see a guy about a thing.*" What the fuck did that even mean?

I didn't have a drink to settle my nerves, as Becca had suggested, because he'd told me not to, and I'd listened. Why the fuck had I listened?

Well, I was done listening. Becca, as usual, was caught up in conversation with someone I really didn't want to talk to, so with a gentle squeeze to her shoulder, I left her side, wandering into the kitchen to see if I could figure out what the alcohol situation was here. Fortunately, it was empty for the moment, so I could poke around without anyone watching me.

After I'd successfully located a bottle of vodka and some lemonade in the fridge and filled my cup, I was already feeling more optimistic—at least until there was a "*tsk*" from behind me. I almost dropped my cup when I jumped, spinning to find Dex leaning against the doorway.

Pale eyes looked from me down to the cup in my hands, locking onto it for a long moment before he shook his head in disapproval and turned to leave. Panic clawed at my chest—sudden, confusing, and unwelcome. I slammed the cup down on the counter and followed him.

Dex had made his way across the room already, through the drunken crowd toward the door. I pushed through the bodies between us, catching the sleeve of his leather jacket just as he made it to the exit.

He tugged out of my hold. I frowned and grabbed him again. My chest constricted, my throat tight with guilt.

This time he spun, large hands grasping my shoulders as he flipped us, pushing me against the wall beside the door. I felt the shift of a frame at my back, but I hardly cared, too busy glaring at the man who held me there.

With the platform boots we were the same height, yet somehow I still felt smaller, boxed in between his arms. "Let me go," I warned him as heat rose over my chest and neck.

"You're the one who grabbed me, Rabbit." His expression seemed more amused now, and I preferred that to the disappointment I'd seen on him in the kitchen.

I opened my mouth to retort, but what could I say? He was right. When I'd thought he was leaving, I'd needed to chase after him.

His eyes dropped to my lips for a moment before he frowned again, his hands releasing me as he took a step back. "Pity."

"I didn't drink," I said quickly, barely stopping myself from reaching for him again before he could retreat any further.

A scarred eyebrow rose in question, lips pursing in disbelief. "I told you to wait for me."

"You're not the boss of me," I shot back, unable to help myself.

"You're right. And you made your choice."

This time when he shifted away, I didn't stop myself reaching out to grab the front of his jacket. "You took too long. I thought you'd left."

"Mmm." He made a contemplative noise and stepped in closer than he was before. "So it's my fault, is it? That my little rabbit got so impatient."

"I'm not yours."

He chuckled. "You want to be."

More heat flooded my face, flooded my whole body. I pushed him away. "Do not."

Dex rolled his eyes. "Then why are you sulking?"

"I'm not!" I realized only then that I was pouting and crossing my arms like a petulant child, and dropped them.

"Be honest with me and maybe I'll stay." His smile was slow as he stepped in.

I wanted to push him away. I wanted to pull him closer. Instead of doing either, I let my eyes drop to that stupid tattoo on his neck, letting him advance on me until he was only inches away. So close and yet still not touching me. If I just leaned forward slightly...

"Who are you all dressed up for, Rabbit?"

I couldn't think of a suitable response, not when his fingertips found the exposed skin of my waist, featherlight, his touch barely there and yet it was all I could focus on. "N-no one."

"Mhmm..." He nodded slowly. "You should be honest with me."

"I am."

"You're not." He sounded so certain. Like he knew me so well. Well, he didn't. He was quiet for a long moment, fingers tracing my skin as he waited for a confession I was determined not to give him. "Last chance," he warned, inching closer. "Who did you get dressed up for?"

I bit my lip to stop myself from answering, not trusting my tongue.

Then his leg pressed between mine, and my knees almost went weak.

"Pity your mouth isn't as honest as this." His voice was low and raspy as he angled his thigh up into the growing bulge in my pants. It was all I could do not to whimper pathetically. "But I'll accept it."

Laughter from someone nearby sent a stab of panic into my core. I'd *never* done anything like this before, and knowing I was now, here, with *him*, and there were people here to witness it, made me feel physically nauseous.

Dex turned toward the laughter, and whoever was making it immediately quieted down. I didn't look to see who it was. My eyes locked on his shirt, my cheeks still flamed with embarrassment. *I shouldn't be here. I shouldn't be doing this. I should just leave.*

"I need to go." I pushed at his chest.

"You're not running away this time, Rabbit." He stepped back, but only enough for me to feel like I could breathe again. "Come with me."

It sounded like a demand, but before I could argue with him, he turned and walked away from me. Oddly, I felt more vulnerable without his body there to shield me from prying eyes.

I took one long look at the front door, right beside me, before following Dex back through the crowd.

He made his way up the stairs, and my chest tightened as I followed him, uncertain of our destination and what would happen when we got there.

Ahead of me, he opened doors along the hallway until he found an empty room and stepped inside, waiting for me to follow. I did, then he shut the door behind us. The click of the lock felt as loud as a gunshot. Like something foreboding.

It was a bedroom. Beige and boring in decor, yet I'd never felt more intimidated by a room. I eyed the bed like it was a weapon set on my destruction, staying stuck in place right by the door. It wasn't too late to run. I was pretty sure I could unlock the door and make it out of here faster than he could stop me. Would he stop me? He hadn't dragged me here after all. I'd followed him on my own. Why had I done that? *Stupid, Jonah. Stupid, stupid, stupid—*

"Hey." My attention snapped from the bed to Dex. He was sitting on the edge, his legs spread wide, hands extended behind him casually, like he did this kind of thing all the time. *Maybe he does.* The thought sat in my gut like a stone. "You okay over there?"

I nodded. "Fine."

"Mhmm, so why don't you come over here, then?"

It was a good question, a perfectly acceptable question. Why else would I have followed him up here if it wasn't for... whatever this was? Fuck, I didn't even know what he was expecting to happen here. "No."

"No?"

"No."

"Okay?" he said, extending the word out as if he was waiting for me to elaborate on that. I didn't want to elaborate on that. He sighed before standing and coming over to me. My eyes found his boots—black, dusty, scuffed, with thick soles that probably gave him an extra inch of height. "Jonah."

Hearing my name was a shock. Not *Rabbit*, not *City Boy*, but *Jonah*. My eyes snapped up to find his, searching, looking for answers to a question we both knew but hadn't voiced. A question I wasn't sure I wanted him to find an answer to.

"I hate you," I blurted.

"Okay," was his response. As simple as that. He didn't seem offended, or surprised, or angry. Just *okay*.

"I do."

"I believe you."

"Well, good. As long as you know."

The corner of his lip pulled up in a smile. "Did you follow me up here just to tell me you hate me?"

"No."

"Then why did you follow me, Rabbit?"

I grunted.

"Answer me."

"No."

He stepped in closer, and I backed up to get away from him, until my back was against the wall. I could have gone for the door, but I didn't. I let myself get trapped by him. Again. Dex gripped my chin between his thumb and finger, tilting my head up to look at him. He was gentle, and I wished he wasn't. This soft touch left me with too much ability to think. I didn't want to think. I wanted whatever had happened in the diner, when he took control of the situation, of *me*. Why did he have to be gentle? Why did he have to look at me now like he cared?

"Talk to me," he demanded, but even that sounded soft.

"No."

His eye twitched, and I could tell he was trying to keep himself composed. I wished he wouldn't.

"Do you want me, Jonah?"

"No."

"Then why are we here?"

"Because!" I snapped, growing more frustrated. How was I supposed to vocalize my thoughts? They made no sense to me. They weren't normal. They were twisted and unknown, too big and too deep inside me. I didn't know how to get them out, but like a beast thrashing in a cage, they demanded release. Demanded him.

Dex sighed, keeping eye contact with me for a long time, trying to read me. *See it. See me. Don't make me tell you.* I willed it, pushing the thoughts through air heavy with tension. Heavy with *us*.

"You look pretty tonight," he said, releasing my chin and taking a step back. Resignation passed over his face, and with it more panic, twisted desire, and regret swirled inside me. He turned toward the door. I pushed him because I didn't know what else to do.

"God fucking damn it, Jonah!" he snapped. *Finally.* He shoved me back until I slammed against the wall. *Yes.* That was it. "What the fuck is your problem?"

"You're my problem!" I grabbed fistfuls of his jacket, holding him to me.

"So let me go!"

"No!"

"You're fucking infuriating. You don't want me but you don't want me to leave either? Which one is it? I can't read your fucking mind."

He was getting angry, and his rage called to mine in a way that felt familiar, dangerous, intoxicating. "Fuck. You."

Dex's hand grabbed a handful of my hair, and he used it to yank my head back harshly. Pain prickled over my scalp, and with it the sound of my thoughts quieted. *Yes.*

"Is this what you want, Rabbit? Want me to fight you?"

"No," I gasped as he tugged harder. *Yes.*

"I think when you say no, you mean yes."

"No." My heart thrashed rapidly in my chest, the pressure in my gut building. *Lower.*

"Pick a different word."

"What?"

"Pick a different word to mean no. A word you won't use for anything else."

Was this asshole really getting me to pick a *safeword* right now? Why did I want to? My mind raced, trying and failing to come up with something. He released the grip on my hair, letting me breathe, letting me think as my gaze cast down to his familiar black combat boots.

"Boots," I whispered.

For a moment he was silent, and I'd never felt so stupid. My skin heated with embarrassment, and just as I was about to tell him to forget it and fuck off, he nodded.

"Fine." I could hear the smirk in his voice, even though I refused to look at him. "Boots means no. Boots means stop. Okay?" he said, and I was silent long enough to realize he really wanted an answer to that. I jolted my head in a single quick nod.

"Nah, use your words, Rabbit. What means stop?"

God, I really was going to die of shame and embarrassment. I grunted as I tried to push him off me again, but he wouldn't budge. I waited for him to get impatient and just do what he wanted, but he seemed intent on waiting me out as well. With an exasperated sigh, I caved first. "Boots means stop," I grumbled.

"Good boy," he smirked.

"Fuck you."

"We'll get to that. For now, I'm going to suck your dick." I swallowed hard, and my next breath came out shaky. He looked so pleased with himself that I wanted to punch him. "Okay?"

I had the safeword. If I said it, everything would stop right now, and I realized with a bit of shock that I actually trusted him to stop if I said it. Boots means no. Boots means stop. We'd agreed to that. I could stop him right now with just that word. One little word... Why wasn't I saying it? *Boots means no*, I repeated in my head. No means... *yes*.

"No," I whispered.

He smirked, and dropped to his knees. My breath caught in my throat, and my pulse thundered in my ears as I looked down at him. I had no idea what my face was doing, but whatever it was, he seemed to like it. His pupils were blown wide in his icy eyes, darkened with lust as he devoured me with his gaze. Like a predator's eyes, locked on its next meal.

Fingertips brushed under the hem of my cropped shirt, and I sucked in a sharp breath that probably should have been embarrassing, but I couldn't really think clearly enough to be embarrassed when he was on his knees in front of me.

"Bite this," he said, voice slightly gravelly, and the sound of it sent sparks of *something* to *somewhere* he was dangerously close to. I wasn't thinking straight at all as I let him stuff the fabric into my mouth, and I gripped it with my teeth. I hadn't even noticed I'd done it until he grinned up at me wickedly and I could feel the way my face turned red. I still didn't drop it. The shirt hadn't even been in his way.

His hand took its time coming down from my mouth, over my chest... the skin twitched against the warmth of his fingers. How was he so warm? Over my ribs, my abs... They'd faded now that I wasn't running and working out as regularly, but they were still there, and I felt the appreciation in his touch as it traveled lower still to the waistband of my jeans. *Fuck.*

I could stop him. I could spit out the shirt and say that word, and it would all stop. Instead, I let him open the button and pull the zipper down torturously slowly.

"Is this what you wanted, Rabbit? Wanted me to order you around? To put you in your place?"

I shook my head, brow furrowed, gaze heated... angry. Still I didn't drop the shirt. Still I didn't say that word.

He used both hands to tug the skinny jeans down my thighs. There was a brief moment of genuine panic when I thought he was going to pull them all the way down and I realized quite quickly I wasn't ready for him to see *that* part of me, but thankfully he abandoned the fabric when it pooled around my knees and my scars remained covered.

"Look at you," he said, amused, his eyes finally breaking contact with mine to rake down my body, stopping at the hard bulge in the front of my black boxers. Fingertips traced the waistband, waiting long enough that I could protest if I wanted to before hooking beneath the elastic and tugging them down to sit with my jeans around my knees.

Unlike me, my cock had zero hesitation in expressing exactly what it wanted. Harder than I'd ever been, it jutted out, pointing to the person who had awoken true sexual desire in me for the first time. Reaching for him in a pulse of lust strong enough to drown me.

Dex also had no hesitation, his rough, warm hand circling around me. Just that one touch and my knees were about to buckle. A moan I unsuccessfully attempted to strangle ripped out from deep within my chest, and Dex's smile grew wider.

"That's it. Moan for me, baby."

Fuck.

One stroke. Two. My eyes would have rolled back into my head if I hadn't been so determined to watch what he was doing, drinking in his expression as if he were water and I was parched.

He kept his eyes locked on mine as he positioned himself, spreading his legs wider so his lips were level with my cock. Then they were on me, and I couldn't have held back the damn whimper if I'd tried. His mouth was so hot, wet, perfect. Lips closed over my tip, tongue tasting, exploring, like I was his new favorite flavor. He groaned as if this was just as pleasurable for him as it was for me, and that couldn't be possible.

None of my fantasies even came close to the real thing. The only touch I had ever known was my own, and I was left wildly unprepared for any of this. I was overwhelmed. I never wanted it to stop. I couldn't help myself as my hips bucked, forcing my cock deeper into the wet heat of his mouth, and though his eyes widened slightly in surprise, he quickly adjusted.

Dex kept his eyes on me, his tongue pressing firmly against my shaft, that piercing I'd spotted earlier tracing over heated flesh and veins, and it took all my willpower not to come on the spot. Fuck, I wanted to, but then it'd be over. I wasn't ready for this to be over.

He sucked up my length until just the tip remained between his pretty lips, then he took me in deep again, until his nose was almost touching the trimmed hair at the base of my shaft. Fuck, how was that possible? I'd never sucked a dick before, but unless I was in his throat, I hadn't expected him to be able to take the entire length.

The pressure, the heat, the suction. It was too much. Molten heat coiled in my core, building something explosive, something urgent, something I was powerless to fight against.

I lost control, my fingers finding their way into locks of curly blond hair that was just as soft as it looked. Grabbing handfuls of it, I *used* him. Used my grip to make him move faster, to take all of me as my hips stuttered, and I fucked his mouth with a desperation unlike anything I'd ever felt. Moans and whimpers muffled by the shirt still between my teeth poured out of me in increasing volume. But I didn't care. Couldn't find it in me to be embarrassed at all when I felt so fucking good.

And he let me. His hands rested on my hips, but not once did he fight against me or try to get me to stop. He simply opened his throat for me and let me use him, until that urgent pressure inside me built to be much too big and I couldn't fight it a moment longer.

With a strangled cry, I came. White-hot bliss pulled from my spine, and my body convulsed, my legs giving way as he kept me upright, greedily sucking down every pulse of pleasure like a hard-earned reward.

Only when I had nothing left to give him did he pull back, his lips a glistening mess. He licked over them, as if he didn't want to waste any of it. I shivered, my eyes wet, much like the shirt I finally let drop from between my teeth, damp with my spit as it fell back to my stomach.

"Fuck," I rasped, without the mental capacity to form any longer sentences.

"You taste good, Rabbit." His voice sounded deep and husky, like a man who had just had his throat well and truly fucked, I suppose. "Enjoy yourself?"

I grunted, because *obviously*.

Dex seemed all too pleased with himself as he rose to his feet again. It was all I could do not to sag against him. Instead, I leaned back against the wall behind me, still catching my breath.

"My turn," he said, and all the sweet relief twisted with sudden anxiety. Did he expect me to do the same thing to him? Did I want to? Would I be able to? He must have read the panic in my eyes because he chuckled and took my hand in his, lacing our fingers together and pulling it to the thick, hard bulge in the front of his jeans. "Just your hand, Rabbit."

Just my hand. I could do that... probably. I knew how to stroke my own dick. How different could it possibly be? Biting my lip, I nodded slowly.

"Take me out, then."

My pulse thundered in my ears, and my hands trembled slightly as I looked down at the front of his jeans. I could do this. I reached for him, working the button open, then the zip. I hesitated.

"Problem?" he asked, sounding far too amused. It sparked my need to prove myself to him. I tugged the denim and his boxers down together until they sat low enough on his hips for his cock to spring free. It was thicker than mine, hard as steel, and already leaking at the tip. Knowing he'd gotten that way just from sucking me off filled me with a sick satisfaction, at least until my eyes locked onto another very big difference between us.

"Holy shit," I gasped.

Holy fucking shit.

"Never seen a Prince Albert before?" he asked, a smile in his voice.

I wasn't about to tell him I hadn't even seen a cock that wasn't mine before outside of porn, but no, I had definitely not seen a pierced dick before. I didn't even know that was a *thing.* "Does it hurt?" I asked instead of answering.

"No," he answered, still sounding amused. "It's been healed a long time. It feels good."

The silver ring sat proudly, a contrast to the angry pink tip it circled through. My brain was still offline, unable to process this new information successfully. His fingers tangled in mine, and he pulled my hand up to my mouth. "Spit."

I hesitated for only a moment before spitting into my palm, surprised I could even manage it considering how dry my mouth felt.

Then he was guiding my hand to his length, wrapping my fingers around heated, velvet-soft skin. He groaned, and the sound knocked me out of my stupor. I tightened my hold around him, causing him to hum in approval again before I began to stroke him.

It was different from when I did it to myself. The angle was different. The feel and weight of him different. But I didn't hate it. Not at all. In fact, the more I stroked him, the more he made those deep masculine grunts and groans, and I decided I *very* much liked being the one who caused him to make those sounds.

"That's it," he moaned in encouragement. "That feels good, Rabbit, so good. Don't stop."

There was no way I was stopping, not when he sounded like *that* because of *me*.

I stroked him faster, held him tighter, all while I watched with intense fascination as the pierced head of his cock pumped through my fist. I felt him pulse within my grip, and the sensation almost had me letting out another groan of my own. His hips bucked, and he started thrusting into the cage of my fingers. Faster and faster.

"Yes, fuck, Rabbit. I'm close. Just like that," he moaned and praised, and my chest felt warm and proud. I doubled my efforts, and his words devolved into a string of curses and moans. "Gonna come, yes. *Fuck!*" he cursed, and his cock twitched in my hold as he came. Spurts of cum shot between us, landing on his shirt and mine, but I hardly fucking cared in this moment as I continued to stroke him through it.

I kept going until his fingers wrapped around my wrist, stopping my movements with a weak chuckle. "I think you got it all," he teased, and I quickly pulled my hand back.

Suddenly, I was completely unsure of what to do with myself. I'd just received my first blow job, just given my first hand job. I pulled away from him to pull up my pants and underwear, somehow not even noticing I'd been completely exposed for much longer than I had to be. Dex did the same, tucking himself away into his jeans again.

"This didn't mean anything," I told him. Told myself. "I still hate you."

He huffed and rolled his eyes. "Fine."

"It's also not going to happen again," I said confidently. Though as the words came out of me I already wanted to take them back. Because how was I supposed to experience *that* and then go without it again?

"Hmm, we'll see about that, Rabbit."

"Devil."

He smiled. A challenge rose between us that I hadn't spoken but he'd already accepted. As I turned and left the room, I tried very hard to convince myself that it wasn't a challenge I *wanted* to lose.

18

Dex - Past

WILDFIRE MEETS SEA.

— ✦ —

"You're in a good mood today," Roy grumbled from the desk as I waltzed into the shop.

"I'm always in a good mood." He gave me a long stare that spoke volumes, more than words ever could, because *yeah*, I was absolutely not *always* in a good mood. I wasn't even normally in a good mood. Good moods and I hardly knew each other. But now that I knew what Jonah tasted like, *sounded like* when I offered him pleasure, I could think of little else.

A week had passed since that party, since he'd hightailed it out of that bedroom like I was a fire and he was burning. I hadn't seen him around since.

He was in my dreams, though. In my fantasies. Jonah's pretty face, usually so sharp with rage, now melted into a desperate, whimpering mess of a man. Because of me. I did that to him. And I'd be doing it again the very next chance I got. Maybe even more next time. I wanted to know how much he would let me get away with. Because he had *let* me. I'd made sure he knew perfectly well that everything that happened that night was because he let me. I wouldn't force myself on him, or on anyone, not ever. I was an asshole, sure, but not like that. Never *ever* like that. Not like...

"Heard from Bryce?" Roy asked as I put my helmet on the shelf of my locker.

"Should I have?"

Roy grunted from the doorway, lingering for a moment longer as if debating saying more before he turned and stalked off to the front office. I rolled my eyes, but still pulled out my phone to shoot off a text to my least favorite buffoon.

> Hey dickface. You're working today in case you forgot.

I shoved the old Nokia back into my pocket and pulled on my oil-stained work shirt to get started for the day.

By closing time, Bryce still hadn't shown up. He hadn't responded to me either, which had left me with a grand total of *zero* new messages.

"I think Archer knows where he lives. I'll stop by and make sure he hasn't injured himself like a dickhead," I told Roy, who'd been even more silent and broody today than usual.

"No, that's alright. I'll handle it," Roy grumbled from the desk, squinting as he looked at the calendar for tomorrow.

"You need glasses, old man."

He huffed. It was all the response I'd expected as I zipped my leather jacket and picked up my helmet from the desk, as I turned for the door, Roy spoke up again. "How's that boy?"

I couldn't quite fight the way my lips tugged up at the corners. It was odd, having him know about Jonah—having him care—but I didn't find it as annoying as I'd thought I would. I'd told Roy more than I'd planned to. Part of it was a test. I wanted to see if the old mechanic was as closed-minded as most of the fuckers in Port Skelton. But as I should have expected, he hadn't even flinched when I told him I was into a guy. Roy was a man of few words, but he'd *listened*, and I'd needed that more than I realized.

"*Satisfied*. At least the last time I saw him," I answered, hoping to provoke a reaction from the man, but he remained as stoic as ever.

"And you?"

That was the question, wasn't it? I had been satisfied at the time. It brought me immense pleasure to watch Jonah unravel, to peel back his spiky layers so I could see him raw and unguarded in a way I suspected few others had. But the more time that passed since last seeing my rabbit, the more restless I'd grown.

I'd found myself looking for him each morning in the diner… waiting for him to show up again at the Meadow Park field. There hadn't been any more parties for me to hunt him down at yet, and I found myself increasingly opposed to that being the only time we saw each other.

"I will be," I answered eventually. "Once he's mine."

Roy nodded softly. "When I was courting my wife, I bought her flowers."

"And how is your wife, Roy?" I asked, defensive on instinct.

"Point taken," he huffed, and I almost felt bad for him. I knew Roy hadn't spoken to his ex-wife since the divorce. It was a shitty thing to have said, but even knowing that, it wasn't in my nature to apologize.

"I'll think about it," I said with a little less venom this time, and Roy simply nodded, turning his attention back to the computer. Somehow I didn't think flowers were the way to worm myself underneath Jonah's skin so deeply he could never be rid of me. In fact, I didn't think gifts seemed like the way to keep him fixated on me at all. So what would? What kept him coming back to me currently was violence, and that didn't feel right either. What would make my little rabbit stop running?

It was a joke initially, calling him Rabbit. It was because of the bunny ears. But now I couldn't think of a better nickname for the man.

Jonah was a rabbit. Not because he was weak or pathetic or helpless, like he probably thought I meant when I called him that, but because I could see it in his eyes—the desperation of something hunted, of something living on adrenaline and instinct, as if his constant state of being was a vulnerability he had to hide. He lived as if life was out to get him, like he was always looking for a threat, like a rabbit that knew that at any moment it might be cornered and eaten.

Jonah had the rage of a prey animal, all teeth and claws and a desperate instinct to lash out and fight for his life. He was scared and called it rage—perhaps it was both. Whatever it was, his eyes were full of it, and I couldn't help but think it suited him. Tough little rabbit, ready to fight the wolf. Too bad for him, the wolf doesn't care how much the rabbit fights back or tries to get away.

"Well, I'm going hunting." I pulled the helmet over my head and secured it in place.

Roy huffed from behind me, and I was gone.

My prized possession—my father's bike—roared over asphalt between buildings, then on dirt between trees. The wind screamed in competition. Tendrils of chill found the seams and gaps in my clothing and seeped beneath in an unwelcome caress.

Boots crunched over stone, over brush, over sand, and then I was standing at the peak, the ledge, the darkness deceptive enough that I could lose my footing if I didn't know this place like it was my own heart. Even more.

I don't know why I visited Dad so often; it never left me satisfied. I'd tried visiting his grave. His name was etched into the stone, cold and impersonal—Declan Ian Weller, beloved father and husband. Only half true. He wasn't there. It was a place for the dead. Not like here. Here felt like life—where I could see what he saw, hear what he heard. I could trick myself into thinking we were spending moments together across time.

When my father died, it left a void inside me. Roy soothed it, but he could never fill it, could never make me feel it less. I didn't *want* to feel it less. If I stopped missing my father, no one else would, and he didn't deserve that. If I let him go, he'd be forgotten. He'd die a second death. I was going to keep my father alive as long as possible.

"Bryce didn't show up to work today," I said, taking my usual seat in the dirt beside a tree that grew sideways, leaning over the edge like it too longed to soar. "He's a bit useless, but not showing up for work is new for him. He hasn't done that before. If I don't hear from him by tomorrow, I'll have to hunt the idiot down."

Pulling out my pocket knife, I resumed carving deep gashes into the stone beside me, the blade following the well-engraved lines so easily I didn't even need light to guide it. "Better not have gotten himself killed. Then I'll have to avenge him, and I just don't really have the time."

Bryce and I were by no means friends, but he was a Stray, and that meant he was under my protection like the rest of them. Even if I did beat him up more than anyone else, including the Drakes.

I continued to update Dad on my day, about Roy, and about the auto shop they used to own together. There was nothing new to update him on about Jonah, not yet, but I knew there would be soon. My rabbit. I wonder if he'd like it here?

When my fingers were stiff from the cold, I collected the butts from my smokes, shoving them into my pocket to dispose of later. I normally wouldn't give a fuck about the litter. But not here.

"I'll see you tomorrow, Dad." I stood up and dusted myself off. The ocean roared its unknowable answer in his place, and I started back for my bike, Delilah. I'd left her where I always did when I came here—where she'd been found when she was still his. She'd led us to him when he hadn't come home, and now she stood a silent sentinel, prepared to do the same for me if I ever followed. Only, there'd be no one else for her to watch over if I fell.

⸺◆⸺

Port Skelton Community College was made up of a cluster of tall brick buildings, each identical to the last in that none of them had an ounce of personality. While I wasn't a student here and had no desire to be, I often wondered how such a soulless place could ever inspire learning. It was no wonder Bryce struggled. Honestly, I wasn't sure why he was enrolled here at all. All he did was complain about the place, the teachers, the students. He and Toby probably spent more time fucking around than studying, but what the fuck did I care? Wasn't my tuition he was wasting.

He had responded to my text this morning.

Blue Haired Idiot

> sorry. ill sort it with roy.

That was it. No influx of emojis for my old phone to convert into blank squares. It didn't sit well with me. So when I'd asked Archer for his address and he'd told me he would probably be here instead, I'd decided to drop in and ensure nothing was wrong in a way that meant I had to get involved.

Leaving Delilah in the corner of the lot closest to the buildings, I started on my mission of locating that blue-haired moron. Most of the classroom doors had glass windows, which made my stalking incredibly convenient.

I found Toby first—glancing out the window and most definitely not paying attention to his lecture—and made a mental note to circle back to him if I couldn't find Bryce myself. Those two were practically joined at the incredibly annoying hip. Two halves of a whole idiot. It was a miracle Bryce hadn't gotten him a job at the shop too so they could sit in each other's laps—the two of them combined could do half the job of one regular person.

I continued on my mission, only it was brought to an abrupt halt when I scanned the next room. A flash of neon orange. Becca's hair, like a beacon that sent my heart into a crescendo, because where there was Becca there was—

My honey-eyed inferno. Already looking back at me. Brow furrowed in his regular scowl, except his cheeks held a sudden flush of color that didn't usually accompany his glare. I liked it. Wanted him to always react that way to seeing me. More.

I smirked at him. My gaze met the challenge in his. A raging fire, heated and set on destruction. Well, I was the ocean, raging in a whole different way. Fierce. Wild. Free. Untamable.

What happens when a wildfire meets the sea?

We stared at each other for seconds. Minutes. This pull between us as strong and certain as gravity, until his attention snapped to the front of the room and he glared at his professor with such heat it made me jealous.

I couldn't hear what was being said inside the room, but I watched as his lips moved and he shoved his things into his bag and stood, clearly ready to leave. Becca looked confused until her eyes found mine at the door, and she frowned. I gave her a wink and stepped aside, waiting for my rabbit.

The door slammed, louder than necessary, then Jonah grabbed my arm harshly and dragged me down the hallway without a word. I followed. Of course I followed. Through a door and up the stairs, and then we were on the roof.

The building wasn't tall, but from here I could see over the trees, to the ocean on the horizon. It was a decent view, but nothing compared to the fire in Jonah's eyes.

"You're stalking me." He pouted, but the venom in his tone sounded forced. In fact, I'd even say he seemed rather pleased to see me.

"No." I grinned. "I'm here for Bryce, actually."

There it was. The disappointment. Just as I'd hoped. A slight flicker of vulnerability immediately eaten up by his flames. "Well…" I could tell he was scrambling for something to say, something to make him feel less vulnerable, less embarrassed at his own assumption. At the disappointment he felt like a dirty secret. "Why the fuck did you stand there staring at me for so long, then? He clearly wasn't in there."

"How could I not, when you look at me like that?"

His mouth dropped open. Snapped shut. I liked leaving him speechless as much as I liked hearing his angry tirades.

"Well. Whatever, then. Fuck off and find him." He turned toward the door. I grabbed him by the arm, shoved him against the wall. Boxed him in, the way I knew he was hoping I would, and the fire in his eyes blazed and smoldered with new vigor. New purpose. His eyes dropped to my lips, and that fire burned with *want*.

"You don't get to run away now, Rabbit. Not after you basically kidnapped me and brought me somewhere we could be alone."

"I didn't—"

"You did." His hands grabbed fists of leather, pushing me away, but his grip on my jacket prevented us from separating. Such a contradiction. What he wanted and what he thought he should want at war with each other. "What do you want, Jonah?"

His eyes were still harsh as they searched mine, seeking a threat that wasn't there.

"I don't want anything," he said after a long moment.

Words spoken with distrust. I understood it well. But my rabbit would have to learn that if no one else, he could trust me. "Everyone wants something."

"Yeah? What do you want, then?" he said, defensive.

"You," I answered honestly.

He shoved me again, no doubt to distract me from the way his cheeks darkened and his eyes widened. I saw that want in him again. "Fuck off."

"Never," I said, and I *meant* it.

"I don't want you," he said, and he *didn't*.

"You're allowed to want me."

"I hate you."

"You're allowed to hate me too."

Something flickered in his eyes again. A vulnerability he was determined not to give me. But he would. Eventually.

I wasn't sure why I was so set on Jonah. I didn't understand this pull between us either. But unlike him, I wasn't going to question it. It was too big, too powerful, too inevitable for me to fight it. I didn't even want to try. Instead, I surrendered to it. I just had to figure out how to get Jonah to do the same.

19

Jonah – Past

I LOVE THE WAY YOU HATE ME.

———————— ✦ ————————

Dex Weller was a very, very dangerous man. Dangerous in ways I hadn't anticipated and was entirely unprepared to deal with. He had the power to hurt me in ways I was realizing extended beyond split lips and broken knuckles. Ways that would take far longer to heal if I didn't keep him out.

I meant it when I told him I hated him. What else could this possibly be? These feelings so bright and intense. Like a blazing fire. And yet I couldn't let them go. I let them burn me because existing without them felt so cold. I'd been so fucking cold for so long without him, and I hadn't even known it.

Willingly, I clung to the embers he ignited within me, but I blamed him for the way they burned. Of course I blamed him. Blaming him was simpler.

It had been a week since I'd seen Dex at the party. Since I *knew* what it felt like to have him touch me, so much more than the twisted fantasies I'd long given up fighting against. And although it was meant to be a one-time thing, a way to satisfy my fantasies so I could silence them once and for all, they had only grown more intense. I still wasn't ready to give in to *him* yet.

"You're the devil," I told him.

"Your devil," he replied without hesitation.

"What?"

"I'm *your* devil."

"What... what does that mean?"

He shrugged. This motherfucker.

"I don't understand you," I told him honestly.

"So ask me. Ask me anything, and I'll tell you."

Why did I believe him? Why did I trust him when I didn't want to? When all the logic and reason inside me told me I shouldn't.

Pale eyes locked onto mine—water on fire—like I was the only thing he could see. And it did feel like he *saw* me, like he actually looked at me and saw everything that was inside me. I didn't like it. I didn't want him to stop. Only Becca looked at me so closely, and even that was different. I didn't know what to do with this. With him.

"Why am I drawn to you?" I thought out loud, wondering if he had the answers that I didn't.

"Because something in you is the same as something in me. Feral dogs seek feral dogs."

It should have been an insult. He didn't know me. No one fucking did. But I felt like he wanted to, and that terrified me just as much as knowing that deep down I wanted to know him too.

"I hate you," I told him again, like I could convince him it was the truth, like I could convince myself.

"I love the way you hate me."

"I'm serious."

"So am I. Hate me more. Despise me, Rabbit. Loathe me. Detest me. Abhor me and let me feel it. Let me taste the hatred on your lips, let me drink it from your skin and feel the heat of it burning inside you. Burn me with it."

People didn't speak like that. Not to people like me. Like poetry. And yet he was. Offering up words as flowers. No—as *fuel*. Like oil to the flame.

My eyes fell to his lips, as if there was nowhere else they could have gone. Those lips had denied me once, and I'd promised myself I'd never seek them out again. I knew I should deny him now, but that felt like denying myself.

Incapable of answering him any other way, I used the hold I still had on his jacket and I pulled him into me. His hands slammed against the wall at my back from the force of it, and our lips crashed violently. An attack that he willingly fell into, that he forced back onto me. Another first, and I was beginning to realize he'd have them all.

His kiss was unlike anything I'd ever felt before. A pull like a physical thing. A magnet. A tree that sprouted roots in my rib cage, the kind that grew too big under the pavement, causing it to crack open and warp from the force of its growth. It took hold in the core of me and shattered everything in its path up my chest and throat, through my mouth, and it grew into him. Tethered me to him. Tied me to him like he was another part of me. A part I'd been forced to go without that had finally returned home.

He kissed me like he knew. Like he felt it too.

Lips gave way to tongues as we consumed each other. He tasted my fire, my hatred, just as he'd asked to, drank it down greedily like he'd said he would. In return, I tasted him, like smoke and danger. More. Like devotion.

I had only ever kissed him, yet I knew that no one else's lips could ever compare to this. No other kiss would ever be as tender. Tender like a bruise.

He crowded me in, hands leaving the wall on either side of me to tangle in my hair, to grab me by the hip and pull me into him. And I answered in kind, releasing his jacket only to slide my hands beneath the leather, to claw at his sides, his back. He wasn't denying me this time.

Dex Weller was the ocean, and I was drowning in him. It pissed me off when we needed to come up for air, and our lips parted only long enough to fill our lungs with something other than each other before I was diving beneath his surface again. Letting the tide drag me deeper. Further from the safety of the shore.

Lips found each other again. Our hands grabbed more frantically as whatever this was between us continued to escalate. I was burning up from the force of it. Dex's leg found its way between mine like it was supposed to be there, and he swallowed the sounds I made in response. I don't know why my body listened to him more than it did to me, but in this moment I couldn't bring myself to care, not when he rolled his hips against me again and I felt the evidence of how much he was affected by this too.

"Fuck," I panted the next time we broke for air. His chuckle was deep and breathy in response.

"Fuck," Dex echoed. "Let me have more, Rabbit. Let me have you again."

My cock throbbed as if it could answer for me, and maybe it could. I rocked against him, grinding my hips into the obvious hardness in Dex's jeans, and he groaned. He took it for what it was, his hands leaving my hair and hip to work open the button and zipper.

"What if someone comes up here?" I asked, a sudden stab of unwanted panic pulling me from beneath the surface of lust.

He looked at me for a moment before hands found my shoulders and he shoved me to the side, slamming me back again, this time against the door. "You'll just have to keep that door blocked, won't you?"

As if it were that simple.

Whatever further protests I had were lost as his fingers dipped beneath fabric to circle around me, stroking me so fast and firmly all I could do was gasp and moan and struggle to stay upright. "Fuck!" I cried, sounding pathetic.

"So hard for me, baby," he cooed, sounding incredibly pleased.

"D-don't call me—*ah*—baby."

"Hmm, fine. For now. Rabbit. But you will be my baby."

"Not yours." My hands clawed at his sides.

"Not *yet*."

His hands left me, and I let out a cry of protest until I saw where they'd gone and I knew what was about to follow. Dex freed himself, grasping his own cock in his hand before bringing our hips together, taking us both in his large warm palm and fingers and stroking.

Pleasure like an electric shock stabbed through me, and my head thunked back against the door with a loud *thud*.

"Careful, Rabbit," he warned, voice breathy with lust. "I'll punish anyone who hurts you. Yourself included."

"What about you?"

"I won't hurt you," he told me. "Never again."

Then he aimed and spat on our cocks, and the added slickness had me crying out again as he spread it over our lengths. His hand felt so different from my own. So much more intense. I thought maybe it was because he'd used his mouth last time that it had felt so fucking good, but now I knew it was just because it was *him*.

Lifting my head away from the door, I glanced down between us, at the obscene sight of his cock, thick and pierced, pressed against mine, tunneling through inked fingers. I couldn't look away. I wanted the image burned into my memory so I could revisit it in my dreams, in my fantasies, with the hope I could make myself feel even a fraction as good as he did.

"You gonna come for me, baby?"

There was that word again. Only now I had far more intense physical sensations that demanded my attention. Pressure built in my core, bigger and bigger, until I couldn't focus on anything else. I couldn't think about anything but the way he made me feel.

Words evaded me, so I attacked him instead—fiercely, violently—with my lips on his. This kiss was messy. Absolutely filthy. All open-mouthed and slick. His moans mingled with mine, sounding like *us*. It scared me how much I liked the sound of us.

"Come for me," he demanded, words spoken into my mouth and swallowed.

Like a spell. Like magic. My body obeyed, and I tensed, my cock exploding in white-hot bliss, pulsing pleasure between us that he collected and used to continue stroking until it was too much. Then he was coming with a deep and primal sound, the evidence of his own satisfaction joining mine.

Lips traced against lips in a not-quite kiss, not ready to be apart from each other as we shared heated air.

It wasn't until my heart rate slowed that I realized we had once again come all over each other's clothing. Unlike last time at the party, I couldn't just zip up my jacket the way he could to hide the evidence of what we'd just done. My dark purple hoodie was now streaked with both of us. Fuck.

I pushed him off me, tucking myself back into my pants quickly and retrieving my bag to look for something I could use to clean myself up.

Dex chuckled, clearly amused by the situation.

"It isn't funny. How the fuck am I supposed to go back to class like this?" I scowled. All I had in my bag that could even slightly be of use was a notebook, so I tore out a page and attempted to use the paper to wipe up. Unsurprisingly, it wasn't very effective.

"Here," Dex said, snickering as he shrugged his jacket off. "I'll trade you."

I halted my efforts, eyeing the offered jacket with suspicion. It had been unfairly spared from the event, unlike my hoodie and Dex's shirt. "But then you'll have the cum hoodie."

"And I'll wear it proudly," he told me, and it really seemed like he meant it.

"This is my favorite hoodie."

"This is my favorite jacket."

I tried to find another excuse, mostly because the thought of wearing his jacket made something in my chest feel tight in a way I didn't at all trust and couldn't allow.

"Come on. Off with it. It's fucking cold. We'll swap back later."

I gave him a glare, but I did what he wanted, pulling my hoodie off with its warmth and handing it over to him, taking his jacket instead. I shrugged my arms into the sleeves and was embraced by his lingering scent. Smoke and cedarwood.

Dex was slightly larger than me in build, but his jacket fit me well enough, and my oversized hoodie fit him like a regular one.

He truly didn't seem to mind at all that he was wearing our cum as he stepped in close to me again. My heart rate, which had finally slowed, hiked up as his hands found my waist over the jacket. On instinct my eyes sought his lips. No, it wasn't my waist he was going for, it was his pockets.

With a smirk that told me Dex knew exactly what I'd mistaken this as, he stepped back with his smoking supplies. I glared. "Roll me one," I demanded, hating that I sounded pouty.

"Anything for you, Rabbit."

This time when I took the first drag of his perfectly rolled cigarette, I managed not to cough. It felt like an accomplishment, and I glanced over at him to see if he'd noticed.

His own cigarette was lit, resting between lips puffy from the force of our make-out session. Dex wasn't looking at me, though, his eyes on his phone as he typed.

"You know what year it is, right? Why is your phone older than you?"

"It was my dad's," he said, his eyes remaining on the ancient piece of mobile history.

Was. Just like the lighter *was* his dad's. I wanted to know what had happened. Dex carried around pieces of the man in a way I could never imagine myself doing with my father. Did that mean they were close? Was his father a good one?

"What's your phone number?" he asked, snapping me from my thoughts.

"Why?"

"'Cause. Just give it to me."

"No."

"Now, Jonah."

I decided right then, even if I'd never admit it to him or anyone else, that I didn't like it when he called me by my real name. I liked the nicknames better, the ones only *he* called me. I knew I should have fought him more, and I blamed my lack of mental faculties on coming too hard as I gave him my number.

Dex sent off a text and I stared at him for a few moments before my phone pinged with a message from an unknown number. I opened it to see... a test sheet?

"Why did you send me a test paper?"

"I didn't. Bryce did." He grabbed my phone out of my hands. For some reason, I let him.

"You gave my number to Bryce?"

Dex didn't answer, just zoomed in on the image before he started typing.

He typed for a long time, and I just stood there waiting for him like an idiot, taking drag after drag of the cigarette until it was all burned out and my head spun from the rush of nicotine.

When he finally finished and handed my phone back over to me, the text thread was still open on the screen. He'd texted Bryce the answers on the test. Unable to help myself, I looked at the test paper myself and then at the answers he'd typed out.

"Number four is wrong," I told him, a slight curve to my lips in the knowledge that I knew something he didn't.

"I know," Dex answered simply, and that triumphant spark extinguished.

"Then why did you send it?"

"You think Bryce's professor is going to believe he got one hundred percent on a test?" Dex scoffed. "He'll get busted for cheating. He'll pass with that."

I looked again and yeah, a few more of the answers were wrong but like, believably wrong. He'd even included the equations so Bryce could copy it down exactly and it would seem like he'd worked it out himself.

That spark of pride that came with knowing things others didn't returned, only this time instead of knowing something Dex didn't know, I felt like I knew something about him that most others didn't. Not that I'd thought he was stupid, but that seemed to be the general impression people held of him, grouping him with idiots like Toby and Bryce.

While I continued to stare at my phone screen, a new notification popped up.

Unknown Number

You look so pretty when you come.

Heat rushed to my cheeks, and I glared up at the man snickering in front of me.

"I'm going to block you."

"No you won't," he said, sounding so confident about that.

I hated that he was right.

20

Dex - Past

THE FIRST BODY.

I'd buried a lot of bodies for someone who'd never killed any-one.

I wasn't *good*. Nothing about me ever had been. Those ru-mors? The things I got up to, the people I'd hurt… were more true than not. I'd done things for Archer, things for the Strays, things for my mother. Those things had secured my place in hell long before I reached adulthood. I'd accepted it. Long given up on trying to be anything else.

I was past the point of it bothering me, or at least, I had thought I was.

The closer I got to Jonah, the more I realized that if I wanted to keep him, I'd have to let him in. I'd have to let him see what his devil was capable of.

If I were a better man, I'd acknowledge that Jonah was too good for me, maybe keep away from him and let us live on our set paths. But I wasn't a better man. I didn't care what path he was supposed to be on. He was coming with me.

It was too soon, though. I'd barely got him within my teeth. He could still choose to run. He needed to be completely caught in my trap before I showed him what I really was. Helpless little rabbit at the mercy of the wolf.

It wasn't fair, I knew that, but I could see it in him. Pain like my pain.

He was hurting, like me. Maybe our pain wasn't the same, but both did what all pain does—it isolated. It was why Jonah lashed out, why he glared and snapped at anyone who got too close. He'd been alone in his pain for far too long, like me. Sure, he had Becca, but she didn't have what we had. She wasn't broken. She couldn't understand him like I could, and so he couldn't ever truly escape his loneliness with her. He could with me.

He'd deny it I'm sure, but I knew Jonah acted the way he did because he wanted people to notice that he wasn't okay. He wanted to drag his pain out into the open and force everyone to look at it. They didn't want to look at it. They never do. But I was looking. I *saw* him.

When he understood that I saw him, truly, as he was, and I wouldn't leave him no matter how ugly his pain might seem, then he'd stay. He'd be mine. Only then would I show him my own, because I knew he'd understand that too. He'd see me too.

Dropping my cigarette, I stomped it out right above where the bastard's head would be. The first body. Beneath the dirt, leaves, and roots. One day I'd bring Jonah here, where I'd never brought anyone else, because he wouldn't ever truly know me until he knew this place.

It was where I came when the nightmares happened. The ones *he'd* given me. Memories that played on a loop, reaching through time and dragging me back into a much smaller body. I came here to remind him, to remind myself, that he was gone—that he couldn't hurt me. I just wished I'd been able to kill him myself.

Tonight's nightmare hadn't been from him, though, not exactly. It was from her.

It was the night I'd had to bring him here. The scene was still so perfectly clear in my mind, like it had only just happened instead of all those years ago.

"DEXTER!" my mother had screamed, and just the sound of her voice was so loud, so hysterical, that it made me want to puke. I had to be quick, and I had to be cautious as I made my way to where her voice had come from. Downstairs. Kitchen. I couldn't keep her waiting.

Even though I never had any idea what to expect when it came to her, I never would have imagined what I found that deceptively sunny afternoon.

Her eyes were manic, her chest heaving and fingers trembling as she shakily lit a cigarette.

Before that moment, I hadn't known it was possible to smell blood so strongly, but it made sense when there was so much of it. I'd stared down at the body, my back pressing against the wall beside the entry, trying to stay as far from the situation as possible without leaving the room. His face was completely mangled, though it was hard to really see the damage underneath all the blood. Beside him on the ground was a pink stiletto shoe, its heel and sole covered in blood. So were her hands.

I'd fought to keep the bile down as I'd met her gaze again. The only question running through my mind was... *am I going to be next?* Was that why she'd called me into the room? My mother had finally snapped and was just going to go on an unhinged murder spree until the cops gunned her down?

"You need to fix this," she'd told me as she took another drag from her bloodied cigarette. Hair that had been bleached too many times was pulled back in a messy bun and splattered with red.

"Fix... this..." I'd echoed, wondering how the fuck I was supposed to do that. "He's... dead."

"No shit, Sherlock. Fucking king of observation, aren't you? Do something about it."

"Do... what... exactly?"

She'd looked at me like I was the crazy one, like I should know exactly what to do with a dead body. Like any of what had happened was fucking normal.

"Just... get rid of it."

"Get rid of it," I'd repeated dumbly, and she'd thrown a half-full box of cereal at me from the counter. Its contents spilled out onto the floor, soaking up the red that pooled around the man I'd hated but she was supposed to have loved.

"You deaf as well as stupid? Yes. Get rid of it."

"*It*," she had called him. Like he wasn't the man she'd allegedly been in love with, like he wasn't her entire world until she had jammed the heel of a shoe into his face over and over and reduced him to nothing but "it." A problem to be dealt with, apparently by me.

If she could be so cold with him, I wondered what she would have done if it were me lying on the floor.

I'd known then, despite his fate, that he'd been right. That the secret we shared, the one he'd forced upon me, could never be revealed to her.

I knew at that moment without a doubt, whatever compassion my mother may have at one time possessed, the drugs and alcohol had devoured it. It had died a slow but complete death until we'd ended up here. She was no longer my mother, but a monster wearing her haggard skin.

I'd listened to her. Of course I had. I'd rolled his body up in the living room rug while she chain-smoked by the window, watching on with disdain—for me or for him, I didn't know. I'd taken my mother's car and started driving, so sure I was going to get pulled over and arrested, for driving without a license at the very least, and if they'd found the body in the trunk...

Hours of driving with no other destination but *away*, I'd followed back roads and streets with no traffic until asphalt turned to gravel turned to dirt. Until my mother's shitty Corolla was bouncing along a rocky path, dodging trees and large stones, where I was certain no car had driven before and I prayed no car would go again. I drove and drove until the car got stuck and I couldn't go any further. Then I cried. Cried until the night passed into morning.

When I stopped crying, I started digging. Deeper and deeper. My hands were bleeding by the time day turned to night again and I finally felt brave enough to open the trunk.

When he was buried, the disturbed dirt covered over as best I could manage with dying leaves and forest brush, I'd set the car on fire. I'd used my father's lighter, the one I'd always kept with me even before I'd started smoking.

I'd stayed on my knees, covered in dirt and blood, and I watched it burn, convinced the smoke or the flames would draw attention, that someone would call and report the fire, that they'd come, and they'd find me and what I'd done. I'd thought maybe it would be better if they did, that I would have deserved it. I'd still thought I had a chance of being good back then, that maybe if I was punished enough I could be cleansed of all the bad things done to me, done by me, and I could go back to being good the way my dad would have wanted me to be.

I didn't have that hope anymore.

No one had come for me in the end. The flames had burned until there was nothing else for them to consume, leaving me with the husk of a car and a freshly dug grave.

I walked to the ocean after that. By the time I arrived, the blisters on my feet matched the ones on my palms from the shovel. They'd stung as I walked into the water, hoping the ocean would wash me clean far beyond the blood and dirt that coated me.

It hadn't. There were stains on my soul now that could never be cleansed. Stains I'd since added to. Each new one further cemented my place in hell. So no, I wasn't good, and I never could be. But I wasn't evil either.

Jonah called me Devil, and it was far from the worst thing I'd ever been called. I wished he were right, though. I wished I were the devil. I wished I were this vile, evil thing incapable of love. But I wasn't. I was human. And I craved love so much it made me sick.

Maybe, just maybe, he could be the one to love me.

I was so certain I'd never come back here after that day, but I did... the next time I needed to hide a body. After all, no one had found the first one.

Now I came here not only when I needed to remind myself he was gone, but when I needed to remind myself of who I was.

There were still hours left of the night. I'd have to go to work in the morning, but I knew sleep wouldn't happen for me after this. Pulling my phone from my pocket, I sent a text to the only person I thought I could stand talking to tonight. He wouldn't know what I was dealing with, not yet, maybe not ever, but I still hoped that maybe he could give me something anyway. Some small tether I could use to find my way back out of this darkness.

> You sleeping?

Five minutes passed. Ten. Until I assumed no reply was coming. Only as I was putting it back in my pocket did I feel it vibrate with a response.

Rabbit

> Yes.

A smile pulled at my lips.

> Liar.

A few more minutes passed before Jonah replied again.

Rabbit

> What do you want?

> You. Obviously.

Rabbit

Well I don't want you.

If you didn't want me, you wouldn't have replied.

There was more silence, and just as I feared I'd scared him off, another response came through.

Rabbit

You can't prove that.

I can actually. You can lie to me, Rabbit, but your dick can't.

Rabbit

Where are you?

I'll be at the field in an hour.

Rabbit

Isn't it cold?

I know a way to keep warm.

Rabbit

I'm not coming.

You will be ;)

Rabbit

Gross.

See you in an hour, Rabbit.

21

JONAH - PAST

THE TASTE OF CIGARETTES AND HOPE.

We were at the Meadow Park field again. We had been every other day for the past two weeks. Dex would text me to meet him here, I'd tell him no, and then I'd show up anyway.

The field was bathed in the warm light of the afternoon sun. It was a rare day compared to the weather we'd been getting lately, without a single cloud in the sky. It was still cold. The gentle breeze carried an unfriendly chill, but lying here in the grass, we were shielded from most of it.

I'd lost track of how long we'd been here, and I couldn't find it in me to care anymore.

I hadn't wanted to tell Becca about this, but when I was suddenly hanging out with her less and I wasn't at home, the beach, or the diner, she'd all but guessed what I'd been up to. To say she disapproved was an understatement, and I understood her concern. I did, and yet here I was again anyway, because he'd asked me to be.

That first night he'd texted me to meet him here, I'd fully intended to stay away. But then an hour had passed, and it was the time we were supposed to meet, and Dex was silent. He hadn't texted me again like I'd expected him to, hadn't followed up to see if I was still going to come.

It was the silence that had propelled me into pulling off the covers, getting dressed, and facing the ache in my leg as I made my way here. I couldn't shake the feeling that maybe something was wrong. By the time I got here, I'd half expected him to be gone, but there he was, lying in the grass, looking at the stars. In silence, I'd taken my place next to him, and we'd stargazed for an hour before he was on me.

That became our pattern. Dex would message me, and I would come, summoned like a loyal dog and hating myself for it. We'd lie in the grass. He'd watch the sky, and I would pretend I was as well until he decided that enough time had passed and he'd give his attention to me instead, his hands or mouth on my body in a way I was growing dangerously familiar with.

Whatever hopes I had of getting him out of my system were shattered a little more each time he broke me open beneath him. Each time I unraveled from his touch only left me wanting more.

It was a dangerous thing. His touch felt like a drug. Something powerful. Something deadly. Each time I'd swear it would be the last, and then I'd be back again at the very next opportunity. I guess that was the thing with drugs; no one planned to become an addict. "Just one more and then I'll stop" becomes a constant mantra, and suddenly there's a dependency that's increasingly difficult to overcome. I was at risk of becoming an addict for him. I still couldn't bring myself to stop.

I turned my head to look at Dex, still gazing at the cloudless sky.

His eyelashes were ridiculously long, and I wondered if they obscured his vision. Surely he could see them when he blinked. It wasn't normal, and it wasn't fair, how they framed his icy blue eyes and made them even more striking. His lips weren't fair either, full and pink and perfect. Fuck, he was beautiful.

"Something on my face?" Dex asked, those perfect lips pulling up into a smirk.

"No." My fingers reached for his as I stole the smoke from him, bringing it to my lips.

His eyes stayed on me, so I turned away, watching the smoke I exhaled dance in the breeze until it disappeared completely.

"What's your dad like?" he asked. The question startled me. We talked sometimes, but never about anything serious, and certainly not about our parents.

I took my time answering, wondering if he'd drop the subject if I was quiet for long enough. He continued to stare at me, the weight of his attention increasingly heavy, like an anvil slowly cracking open the shield I kept around me.

"He's..." I tried to think of a way to describe the man I shared a house with. When no good words came to me, I simply sighed and let out the truth that constantly bubbled under my surface like a poison. "He's a piece of shit, is what he is."

"Does he hurt you?"

"No, nothing like that. He's just... not there. Hasn't been for a long time."

"Since your sister?" came his next question, and I was startled for the second time. Unpleasant heat clawed up my chest and throat. I didn't talk about Adaline. Not ever. Not even to Becca.

"No, he wasn't much of a father before then either," I admitted. Whatever little fatherly instincts the man had possessed died along with his daughter.

"What about your mom?"

"She's worse."

"Does she hurt you?"

I turned to look at him, wondering where these questions were coming from and why he cared enough to ask them. That wasn't what this was. It wasn't what we did. My parents were none of his fucking business, and I was about to tell him as much, only when I met his pale eyes he looked so... open. His usual smirk was absent, his expression soft in a way I'd never seen on him before.

Lately, keeping my rage around him had taken conscious effort. Where it had usually been bubbling away in my core, it now simmered, cooled. Still there but tolerable. Just like when I was around Becca and her presence soothed me, like a balm on a wound. This felt similar, and yet different in a way I couldn't place, or perhaps didn't want to. Maybe acknowledging the way things were changing would make them real, and I wasn't sure I was ready for that.

"Why are you asking me this, Devil?"

"Because I want to know you."

"What if I don't want you to know me?"

"You do. You have from the start."

It pissed me off, how confident he always was, how sure. Especially in the things he assumed about me. But I couldn't even argue, because he was right. What I wanted—from him, from Becca, from my parents, from the world—was to be known. To be seen. To be understood.

"No, Dex. My mom doesn't hurt me. My mom doesn't care enough to hurt me, or maybe she isn't capable of caring at all," I started, and like a switch had been flipped, everything rushed to the surface. The floodgates had been opened, and I was powerless to close them again. That beast that always lurked inside me took its chance to claw its way up my throat and show its hideous form to whoever would look at it.

"Maybe she's just a human-shaped void where a mother should have been," I said as my throat grew tight and itchy and heat pooled behind my eyes. "Maybe whatever motherly love she had left in her died with Adaline. Maybe my dad was the same. Both of them died as parents when she died. And fuck, maybe that's to be expected after losing a child. Maybe their grief was too much for them. But I'm still here! I still needed them, and I was fucking hurting too! I lost her too! I lost my sister, my best friend, and I lost my parents right along with her. So no, they don't fucking hit me if that's what you're asking, but I fucking wish they would, because at least then they'd have to fucking acknowledge me."

"Hey." Dex spoke calmly, so infuriatingly calm, like he was trying to soothe a wounded animal, and that was exactly how I felt in front of him as my vision blurred. He closed in, moved over me, and his hand cupped the back of my neck like an anchor. But I didn't want to be anchored. I wanted to thrash and scream until this ugly feeling escaped enough for me to push it back down into the depths of me where it could continue to rot away inside me until the next outburst. "I've got you. You've been alone for so long, Rabbit, but you aren't anymore. I won't ever let you be again."

I didn't want to hear it, not those words, not from him. If I heard them, I might believe them, and I couldn't let myself believe them. It would leave me too vulnerable. Would give him too much power over me. Letting him have any part of me meant he could hurt me, or worse, he could *love* me. If he loved me, then I'd finally have something to lose instead of just something I yearned for.

"Don't fucking touch me!" I snapped at him, but I wanted him to touch me so fucking badly. I wanted him to hold me hard enough to bruise. To fucking hell with gentle caresses and soothing touches that faded away the moment they stopped as if they'd never been there at all. I wanted to be held with teeth and claws, touched only in a way that left marks behind. Scars. So that I could press and poke at the wounds and the pain could echo the touch for as long as I needed until it felt real.

"I've got you," he said again, and despite me pushing him away, he only pulled me closer.

I shoved him, because I wanted him to fight me for it. I wanted him to prove that he wanted to touch me because this was real and not because it was easy. Dex shifted, his body moving over mine, and I thrashed against him, trying to get away yet hoping I couldn't.

"I've got you." This time when he spoke, his voice was firmer. His hands, so big and warm and secure, grabbed my wrists, pinned them to the grass on either side of my head where I couldn't hurt him with them. Where I couldn't hurt myself. "I'm not going anywhere. You're mine, Jonah Hargreaves, and if you want to fight me, then you fight me. But it won't change anything. I know your parents made you feel like asking for attention was a bad thing, that it made you feel like too much, but it's not too much for me. You're not too much for me. I'll give you all my attention. I'll give you everything. All you have to do is ask, Rabbit."

"Let go of me!" I shouted, because the walls I'd put up were crumbling. Those walls kept everything that could hurt me out, but they also kept all the pain I'd been holding onto in as well, and I wasn't ready to let it go. I wasn't sure who I'd be without it. "I hate you!" I told him, like I'd told him countless times before, only this time when I said the words, they felt wrong; they tasted like a lie.

"Stop, Jonah." Dex's voice was firm but not cruel—in the way I both hoped and feared it would be when he finally realized how difficult I was. "It's time to stop running. I think you started running when you were a child, and you haven't let yourself stop. It's time to stop now. I know you're tired of it. It's okay to stop."

"I don't know how," I confessed, the words burning my throat like acid.

"I know. And that's okay. I don't know either. I've never wanted anyone like I want you. We can figure it out together."

"What if you change your mind?"

"I won't."

"How do you know that?"

"I just do."

I just do. Like it was that simple. I didn't understand how he could say those words, how he could be so sure and certain of them, but now more than ever I wanted to believe him. I was so fucking tired of doing this all on my own.

From the very first moment I'd seen Dex in the diner, something had been building between us. It was something I didn't understand, and every time we saw each other, touched each other, it grew. Bigger and bigger, like a balloon about to burst. That's where we were now. At the breaking point. I didn't know what would come after this; I only hoped it wouldn't break me right along with it.

"What do I do?" I asked him, and I didn't even try to mask the fear in my voice, the pain that came from not knowing.

"Well, that one's easy, Rabbit. Just let yourself be mine."

"*Easy*," he said. There was nothing easy about this. It was the hardest thing I'd ever had to do. But he wanted me, all of me, and I wanted to be wanted. More than that. If I was honest with myself, completely truly honest, I wanted to be wanted by *him*. Because I wanted him too. I had from the very first moment.

"Okay," I told him, letting my body still beneath him. Letting myself surrender.

"Okay?" he asked, his brow furrowing, like he expected it to be a trick, that I'd run away again the moment he released me.

"Okay." Such a simple word to change everything. "I'll be yours."

I watched as Dex's brows twitched again, and he swallowed heavily. Those eyes that matched the sky darkened like a storm, and then it rained. Droplets falling from him to me. Water on fire. His tears extinguishing me. His pain soothing me.

He wanted me so deeply that when I finally accepted him, his relief hurt more than my rejection ever could, and I understood that. I saw him now. I saw him, and I wondered how I'd been so blind to him before this point. He was just like me.

"Will you please kiss me?" I phrased it like a question, but it was a demand. Because I needed to feel him. I'd thought too much, and whatever this was now, we would figure it out together like he'd said... but later. Right now, I was tired. Right now, I wanted nothing else but to taste the lips of the man I belonged to. The man who belonged to me.

Dex fell into me. We'd kissed before, so many times, and each time it felt bigger than the last. This one was no different. He tasted like the cigarette I'd dropped somewhere in the grass around us when I'd tried to fight against this so futilely. More than that, he tasted like a comfort I'd never known. He tasted like hope.

22

Dex - Past

HIS FIRST, HIS ONLY.

HELL BENT. The letters inked across my knuckles. I was never the type to worry about my tattoos having meaning. If I liked the look of something, I'd get it put on my skin. Or with some of them, I'd just let Bull do whatever he wanted. When he'd told me to fuck off, I'd bought myself a tattoo gun and started doing my own ink, like the skull and wings on my neck. It didn't have any meaning apart from looking cool. However, the letters on my knuckles were accurate in describing the way I dealt with most things in life—stubbornly and recklessly determined.

I'd been hell-bent on getting Jonah to be mine.

Now that he'd agreed, I couldn't quite believe I'd done it.

I'd meant it when I told him I was fine with him hating me. Of course, I'd prefer it if he loved me, but if he couldn't, then hatred was the next best option. Love would give me his heart, but hate gave me his mind, and I would take whatever I could from him.

Lately, however, whenever Jonah told me he hated me, it felt different. It felt like maybe he meant something else instead.

While we'd evolved from sporadically meeting up at parties to meeting at the Meadow Park field on a semi-regular basis, I had yet to show Jonah where I lived. Showing him my mother's house felt like exposing a rotting wound, but it was a wound that had formed who I was. And with him accepting me, and finally being mine, it felt like it was time to expose that part of myself.

The house was deceptively ordinary from the outside. Two stories that had once been painted white, now faded and peeling like most in this area. The front deck was sagged, its rotten wood scenting the air, and it was concealed from the road by the piles of junk in the front yard that my mother kept around for purposes I could never understand.

Jonah was many things, but subtle wasn't one of them. I saw the judgment on his stunning features as I led him from the footpath to the front door, and I didn't fault him for it.

My mother hadn't been home for months. Maybe this time she wouldn't come back at all. She'd probably found some new piece of shit to feed her drugs and decided to live with him instead, like a parasite. Or maybe she'd died. Maybe I wouldn't ever know, but enough time had passed that I was confident bringing my rabbit to this place wouldn't put him in any danger.

The inside of the house was aged, damaged, from angry fists and the things she'd thrown at the walls over the years. But it was clean. All the evidence of the terrible things that had happened here were scrubbed away.

My honey-eyed inferno took it all in, his thoughts loud enough to hear even though his mouth was silent.

"So... where are your parents?" Jonah asked eventually as I led him up the stairs.

"My mom hasn't been home for a couple of months. She's probably living with a new boyfriend or something," I told him, heading past the closed door of her room, then the bathroom, to get to mine.

"Oh... and your dad?" Jonah's voice was uncertain, like he wasn't sure if he was allowed to ask, or maybe he just wasn't used to expressing an interest in other people.

"He's dead."

He didn't seem surprised by that, honey eyes casting down as he no doubt struggled with what to say in response.

It didn't hurt me to talk about my dad; I'd tell Jonah all about him eventually. I only wished they could have met each other. My dad wasn't like my mom. I'd told him about the crushes I had on boys in school, and he'd always smiled and told me I should invite them over sometime.

This had been a different house when he was here. He'd made it a home. Then he died, and whatever home was here died with him. The comfort he'd filled it with was replaced by my mother's drinking, her shouting, her constant stream of boyfriends.

My bedroom was childish. I'd upgraded the bedding to a solid navy blue, but the walls still had the old cartoonish dinosaur stickers I'd put up with my dad. I couldn't bring myself to remove them in case it also removed the memories. There were so many bad memories in this room of things that had happened since then. If the evidence of the good ones was removed, maybe the bad ones would consume me. Those exaggerated smiling dinosaurs were my anchor, what I'd focused on when I didn't want to focus on my body, on what was being done to me.

This was a house full of ghosts, but not all of them were evil. It's why I still lived here, even after everything.

Jonah took it all in as I sat on the end of my bed. Much like that first time at the party, he stayed in place by the door, like he was leaving himself with the best chance of escape while he pondered if he wanted to take it. Unlike then, however, this time he slowly crept further in on his own. Closer to me. Guarded, like this room could hurt him, but I'd never let that happen.

I remained where I was, letting him come to me at his own pace, until finally the bed dipped beside me and he looked at me, so unsure about what he was supposed to do now.

"Can I kiss you again?" I asked him, afraid if I moved too fast, I'd trigger my rabbit's survival instincts and he'd run again, like I could tell he was fighting not to do.

Jonah nodded, and I leaned into him, my nose brushing against his as I waited for him, despite the permission, to close the distance. He did.

This kiss was soft. Uncertain. Fragile.

I let him take his time. He was learning how to touch me softly, and I was learning how to be touched softly.

We were both damaged so differently by the people who were supposed to protect us. In my father's absence I'd only been touched with hands that had burned and voices that had made the walls tremble and the ground disappear beneath my feet. I'd learned to fear touch. Jonah feared it as well, but only because he *craved* it so much, had been starved of it, left in the dark and the cold. I was burned and he was frozen and neither of us knew how to love at the correct temperature because we'd never known it.

It would take time for us to learn how to touch each other in a way that didn't feel like violence.

Slowly, the kiss deepened. My hand found his arm, gently caressing from his wrist to his shoulder over the fabric as I slowly guided him back to lie beside me. I followed his lips, my body over his just enough to chase them, to keep them.

"I don't—" he started, pulling his lips away from me, his breath hitched up in a panic I could see in his eyes. "I haven't—"

"It's okay," I told him, understanding. "We won't do anything new. Just what you already know. You know what to say if you want me to stop at any point, don't you, Rabbit?"

He nodded, and the panic receded. When I was silent, watching him expectantly, he gave me the word I was waiting for. "Boots."

"Boots," I repeated in confirmation. "You say that, and everything stops."

Jonah nodded, and I claimed his lips again.

This kiss was soft. Certain. Strong.

It was a promise as much as a kiss. A promise that I'd take care of him. I would guard what he'd given me. He could trust me with it, with himself.

Slowly, I felt the stiffness in his body melt away. When he was relaxed, I licked over the seam of his lips and Jonah opened them for me. My tongue dipped inside to seek his, tasting him slower and deeper than I ever had before.

As I continued to kiss him, my fingertips brushed under the hem of his hoodie. This one was black. The purple one he'd given me in exchange for my jacket was in the top drawer of my dresser, and although I missed my leather jacket, I wasn't quite ready to trade it back to him. I liked having something of his, but maybe now that I'd let him into this place, I could convince him to come back. Maybe eventually he'd just stay, and I wouldn't need to treasure and hoard the small parts of him like a starving dog protecting its scraps.

When he remained soft and pliant, I let my hand explore further, over the heated, firm skin at his abdomen. I'd seen Jonah's pretty cock plenty of times now, but I had yet to see the rest of him. I was certain all of him was beautiful.

When I was done with him, there wouldn't be an inch of his skin I hadn't tasted and adored.

Jonah hummed his approval, and my hand continued its exploration, my tongue continued showing its devotion to his, until my fingertips brushed against his nipple and his lips flinched away from mine in a gasp. Jonah looked stunned, and I couldn't help but chuckle. "Never played with your nipples before, Rabbit?"

I flicked the hard bud, and again he gasped. His blush deepened, and I saw him debating whether he should lie to me or not before he landed on honesty. "No."

"Never had anyone suck them?"

Once more he warred with himself over opening up before surprising me. "I've... only been touched by you before."

The deep groan that rumbled up through my chest and poured out from my lips was entirely involuntary. I'd suspected Jonah wasn't very sexually experienced, but I'd thought maybe he just wasn't experienced with men. Knowing that no one had *ever* touched my rabbit before me stirred something in me I hadn't anticipated. Only I had touched him like this, *seen* him like this.

I'd never been a jealous person before Jonah, but the thought of anyone else getting to see him, touch him, taste him, had made my blood boil with something absolutely murderous. I'd never have to worry about that now, though, because I was his first. And I would be his only.

"Then let me give you another first," I told him, both hands sliding beneath the fabric now as I robbed him of the hoodie's warmth, intent on replacing it with my own.

I discarded it behind me, taking a long moment to feast upon the stunning sight of his upper body before my lips found his again, the kiss a brief thank you before my lips continued, to his jaw, his neck, over his collarbones and then down to his chest, until finally I kissed his nipple.

Jonah was already a gasping, squirming, blushing mess beneath me, hands twitching and unsure where to go. I answered the question he wasn't voicing. "You don't have to do anything, Rabbit, just lie there and feel."

He relaxed further. My tongue flicked over the sensitive bud on the left, and he gasped and shuddered. Then I closed my lips on him and sucked. His whimper was all the reward I'd ever need.

I played with him, sucking gently then firmer, rubbing the warm solid bar through my tongue over his flesh until his nipple was pink and plump and my lips left him only to give the other one the same treatment.

It turned out Jonah had extremely sensitive nipples, and I already knew this was something I'd be doing for him a lot.

His hips twitched up, his neglected cock seeking friction. I continued to mouth and suck at his chest as my fingers worked open the button of his jeans.

"D-don't take them off... my pants. Leave them—*mnn* on—please," he said through moans.

I wasn't sure why he wanted to hide his legs from me but not his cock, but I figured it had something to do with what happened to him. His accident. Whatever scars he possessed, physical or emotional, I trusted Jonah would show them to me when he was ready. When he did, I would show them every bit of affection I planned to show the rest of him, because there could never be any part of him I didn't want.

"I'll leave them on," I promised him as I pulled down the zipper, my hand dipping under skin-warmed fabric to find his cock like I was seeking home. It was already hard and leaking for me, and his spine arched up from the mattress as I stroked him.

My lips continued their descent, over pale skin flushed the perfect shade of pink, until I tasted his precum and Jonah cursed, his fingers tangling in my hair. We'd done this before, many times. He knew my mouth and how to use it. Jonah's confidence was a beautiful thing. I relaxed my throat for him, and his grip tightened as he pulled me down onto his length.

While I couldn't give Jonah my firsts of anything, I could use the experience and skills I'd collected solely for him from now on. He wasn't my first, but I could make him my last.

I knew I was good at this, had been told it many times, most recently by Archer. But not anymore. Now there was only Jonah. My rabbit. He was the only one I would ever give pleasure to again.

Jonah fucked my mouth, my throat, with a desperation that bordered on violence. We were lucky I didn't have a gag reflex with the force of his thrusts, but I would have managed regardless, because I already knew I'd never deny him anything.

With a beautiful cry, he came, his warmth coating my throat until I sucked up his pulsing cock to collect it in my mouth instead.

When he was finished, he collapsed back onto my bed in a panting mess, and I repositioned, hooking my leg over his as I straddled him and freed my own hard dick, spitting his cum into my palm and using it to slick myself up. Jonah watched me closely, brows rising in surprise, which quickly morphed into aroused approval.

It didn't take long. Having him use me for his pleasure was almost as good as feeling it myself, and when I came, my cum splashed over him in ropes, marking him as mine in a way I wished was far more permanent.

23

JONAH - PAST

MILKSHAKES AND MAXXXINE'S.

———— ✦ ————

I tried not to squirm under the absolute contempt in Amanda's eyes as Becca and I walked into the Cozy Cow. We hadn't been back here since the coffee incident.

Bee nudged me with her arm, prompting me to step closer to the annoyed barista.

"Sorry about what happened last time I was here," I grumbled, and Amanda crossed her arms over her chest, looking at me skeptically.

"What are you sorry for exactly?" she questioned, as if it weren't obvious. I guess she needed to see me more uncomfortable or something, and I fought the urge to roll my eyes or snap at her because I didn't actually want to get banned from this place if I hadn't been already.

"For spilling coffee—"

"*Throwing.*"

"Throwing... coffee."

"And?"

"And... for fighting."

"And?"

Fuck, what else was there? "Um... for not cleaning it up?"

"And?"

"And *what?*"

"And it won't happen again?"

Oh. "It won't happen again," I assured her.

"Not even if Dex comes in here at the same time?"

"Well, he started—"

"Jonah!" Becca scolded, and I stopped myself.

"It won't happen again. We've, uh... sorted it out. Between us. Worked it out," I told Amanda, not liking the heat I felt rising inside me from just talking about the man who took up all of my attention lately.

While I still didn't know what had come over me that day when we were last here, why I'd acted without thinking, I knew that I—*we*—wouldn't be doing that again. Whatever had changed between us didn't make me immune to being pissed off by him, but my feelings toward him had shifted away from that all-consuming rage. What they'd evolved into I didn't yet understand, but I was done fighting it.

I tried not to fidget as Amanda gave me a long, assessing once-over. Her eyes lingered on the leather jacket I was currently wearing. His jacket. I saw her fighting a smile before her eyes met mine again. "Fine. But if you cause any more problems, I'm banning you. Understand?"

I nodded stiffly, and Becca hooked her arm in mine as she stepped forward and ordered for us: a coffee, a milkshake—which I knew she got only for me—and fries to share. Even when she was pissed she still had to take care of me. It was cute, but I wouldn't tell her that.

I knew why she was pissed at me. I'd been avoiding her since that day in the field when I'd agreed to belong to Dex and he'd taken me back to his house. For four days, I'd blown her off to hang out with him instead. I hadn't even gone to school, spending my time around the beach or Meadow Park even when Dex was at work at the mechanics. But it was more than just that. I knew I couldn't have seen her without telling her everything, and I knew she wouldn't approve when I did. I knew she wouldn't understand it.

My eyes were fixed on the table between us as we sat at our regular booth, seeking anything else to look at that wasn't Becca's disapproving stare. I wasn't used to that, not from her, and although I knew her negativity came from a place of genuine concern, it was difficult not to get defensive right away.

"He's bad for you, JJ," she told me, apparently already knowing without me even needing to tell her. The defensiveness I was trying to tamp down inside me sprung up again with new force, only it wasn't for me.

"You don't even fucking know him," I told her, my eyes snapping to hers.

"And you do?" she asked, arms folded.

"I know him better than you do."

"I know he's in a fucking gang, that he fights people for fun. He's violent, Jonah. *Enjoys* being violent. We saw it with our own eyes. Have you even heard what people say about him? Liking his dick is one thing, but you're what, dating the guy now?"

Dex and I hadn't had that conversation. He'd asked me to be his, and I'd agreed. I'd surrendered myself to him. Did that mean we were dating, though?

"So what?" I snapped because I didn't know what else to say. She was right. He was in a gang. He was violent. But he was so much more than that.

"So he's fucking crazy!"

"Okay? And? Maybe I'm crazy too!"

"You're not, Jonah. You're not like him."

Why was that so insulting? I hated him, or at least I'd believed I had until a few days ago. But things had shifted. Maybe things that were always supposed to. "Maybe there's nothing wrong with being like him."

"It won't end well. Not for you."

"You don't know that."

"I do. But whatever. Don't listen to me. I'll still be here for you when it all goes to shit, but I'm gonna say 'I told you so,' and then we'll figure out how to hide his body together."

The tension broke, a laugh I couldn't quite suppress pulled to the surface. "You're going to kill him if he hurts me?"

"Damn right I am. *When* he hurts you. You really going to make a murderer out of me, JJ?"

"He told me he wouldn't. Never again."

Becca didn't seem convinced, and I couldn't blame her, not when I didn't even understand why I believed him.

"Well, I hope for his sake he doesn't." She sighed before letting her arms untangle, and she reached for a fry, the tension between us fading further. "Also, stop fucking avoiding me. Just because you have a boyfriend now doesn't mean you're allowed to forget about me, your bestest friend and one *true* love. Okay?"

"Okay," I said, releasing whatever tightness remained in my chest and throat. I reached for the milkshake, taking a long sip—

"The sex is good, then?" Bee asked, and I almost coughed it all back up. With a smile, she handed me a napkin.

I coughed and wiped my mouth, feeling my cheeks flame with a new sort of embarrassment. "I haven't—*we* haven't... done... *that*."

"Anal?"

My skin prickled from the sudden heat as I nodded.

"But you want to?"

It was all I'd been able to fantasize about lately, but it still felt too big, too intimidating. Dex hadn't tried to pressure me into it like I almost wished he would, rather he seemed perfectly content in continuing to just do what we'd already been doing. I was starting to think he'd be satisfied even if that was all we ever did.

I nodded again. I knew I should talk about it with him instead, but Becca felt like the safer option, maybe because she was separate from it. I couldn't say or do anything to fuck it up with her. "I don't... know how."

"You've watched porn, though, right?"

"Yeah, but doing it is different. What if I get it wrong?"

Bee's smile was warm as she placed her hand over mine. "Oh, my sweet innocent bestie. That man should feel incredibly grateful for any part of you he gets. Besides, I think he knows exactly what to do and would be more than happy to show you." She winked.

I hated the thought that Dex knew what to do because he'd already done it with other people. What if they were better at it than me? What if I disappointed him?

I didn't even know what "role" he'd want me to take. In my fantasies, it was always him over me, inside me. But is that what he'd want too? I groaned, pushing my milkshake to the side and smacking my head down on the table, hiding myself there.

Talking about sex with Becca didn't bother me exactly; it was a little uncomfortable but only because it was new. It was helpful, though, and if there was anyone I could trust not to judge me, it was her. She was the most sex-positive and judgment-free person I'd ever known. Maybe she could help me with something else too. Something I'd been thinking about for a while but couldn't bring myself to do alone. I sat up slowly.

"Would you... come with me to... Maxxxine's?"

━━━◦○◦━━━

The outside of Maxxxine's Treasure Trove was all black and incredibly intimidating. I'd walked past it once last week, but I couldn't bring myself to go inside. It wasn't like I had the money to buy anything anyway, but I was so curious about what was within those walls.

Becca's arm hooked through mine as she pulled me fearlessly toward the entrance. She'd been delighted when I'd asked her to come to the sex store with me; however, I was already having my regrets.

Despite my hesitation, Becca soldiered on, dragging me right along with her until she pushed open the doors and my eyes were assaulted with the bright fluorescent lighting from inside. Why the fuck did they make it so bright in here?

My heart thundered in my chest as we walked in. It was still pretty early in the day, so thankfully there weren't many other people here. The shop assistant didn't even look up from the counter she was leaning on, her eyes glued to her phone instead of her new customers.

"Alrighty, what are we looking for? Dildo? Butt plugs? Maybe something sexy to wear?" Becca questioned, and I wished she'd keep her voice down.

"I don't know," I whispered back harshly.

"Well, let's start here and see what catches your interest," she answered just as loudly, as she pulled me into the first aisle.

My stomach twisted with nerves as I took it all in. The wall was covered in so many brightly colored plastic dildos, all so well lit up there might as well have been a spotlight on them. Some of them were normal shaped and sized, others definitely not. I didn't know so much variety existed, and seeing it all made this somehow more intimidating rather than less.

Becca let go of my arm to touch things, and I immediately felt exposed without her. Remaining close, I followed her lead, reaching for one of the less intimidating toys. Apart from being pink and sparkly, it seemed relatively normal—a safe option. It wasn't as thick as him, though. I put it back.

I looked at a few more before a "*psst*" caught my attention, and I turned to see Becca holding up a very alien-looking... thing. She wiggled her eyebrows at me before pressing a button, and the thing buzzed to life, the middle of it contracting and extending in a thrusting motion while the bumps on the top of it rotated.

"Absolutely not."

"You're no fun." Becca pouted, turning the thing off and putting it back on the shelf.

"This isn't fun. This is... research."

She scoffed. "Research you're gonna put up your butt."

It took a lot of self-restraint not to throw one of the heftier dildos at her. "I am not. I don't even have money, okay? I just wanted to look. And now I have. We should just go."

"Nuh-uh, JJ. You're getting something. I have money."

"Normal friends don't buy each other sex toys."

"Since when have we ever been normal?"

That was a fair statement. But I was stubborn, and she knew that about me.

"Listen, I just have a real urge to buy one, ya know? And I already have so many, it wouldn't even get used. It would just go in the drawer and be wasted, so you'd really be doing me a favor if you took it."

"Mhmm." I folded my arms, scowling at her, but she didn't seem at all bothered by it.

"What about this one then, Mr. Boring?" She grabbed a purple, thankfully *human*-shaped dick from the wall. It was bigger than the first one I'd picked up—thicker, like him. I must have revealed more than I'd thought on my face because Becca smiled at her perceived victory, putting the display back to reach for one still in its packaging. "This one, then. Okay, next. Lube. And condoms. Who knows where that man has been."

When we were done, Becca had a basket with a whole variety of things, some she'd let me pick and others she told me weren't any of my business. We turned to make our way to the counter when I came face to face with someone I very much did not want to see here.

Green eyes widened in surprise as Bryce recognized me.

"Oh, hey!" He smiled as though we were friends, clearly not planning to just look away so we could both pretend this hadn't happened and move on with our lives. "What's up?"

What's up? What the fuck did he think was up? Like there was any other reason we would be here aside from the obvious. Becca knowing about my sex life was one thing, but Bryce was entirely another.

"Is that Dex's jacket?" he asked, like he was proud of himself for recognizing it.

"No," I lied.

"Nah, it is. Same stain on the sleeve. Does he know you have it?"

How else would I have gotten it?

"He knows," Becca answered for me, amusement in her voice.

"Oh. Cool, cool. So you guys are like together, then? Or just fucking? Wait, are you two also fucking?"

"No, Bryce. We aren't fucking!" I snapped, and Becca pulled me closer to her, no doubt sensing I was about to cause a scene and get us banned from here.

"We're just friends." She smiled, and it was far more than Bryce deserved. "Happy shopping."

Bryce seemed like he wanted to say more, but Becca was already steering us swiftly away, toward the exit. We stopped so the cashier could bag up the items, and Becca paid while I lingered nearby, trying not to draw any more attention to myself and thinking with an uncomfortable twist in my gut... what if Bryce tells Dex he saw us here?

24

WHERE I GO, THE GHOSTS FOLLOW.

———⋆———

No one ever suspected me of being gay until I started traveling with Harper.

Even though there was no change in the way I dressed or carried myself, arriving together had them assuming I was gay by association or something. While they were right, and I had no shame in it, it made it harder to blend in without drawing too much attention to us in these small towns clearly filled with equally small-minded people.

There were people who tried to be "supportive," like the motel receptionist where we were currently staying, who had happily informed me with a wink they had rooms with one bed available when I'd just asked for a room with two.

Of course, I'd rather have my own room entirely, but with leaving Hollow Creek in such a rush after the run-in with Benny, we hadn't been able to go back for our things or the pay Marty owed me. Everything I had was abandoned in that hotel room except the clothes I'd been wearing and whatever I had stashed in my car.

Harper was a lot more distraught about it, telling me about all the expensive clothes he wouldn't be able to replace, but there was no way I was letting us risk his safety by going back for them.

It meant starting all over again.

Harper, thankfully, had an obscene amount of cash in his wallet, and we'd used it to buy ourselves just enough of a wardrobe to get by—none of it designer, much to his dismay. It was also why we were sharing rooms, so we could make it last as long as possible.

We didn't stay anywhere for more than a night before we were on the road again.

I'd traded my Taurus for an even shittier and incredibly hideous red Pontiac Aztek. I fucking hated the thing, but it was functional enough for us to keep moving.

This motel was a little nicer than the usual ones we stopped at. It had been refurbished at some point in the last decade, and I was hopeful I'd hear less of Harper's complaining because of it.

He still hadn't opened up to me about what really happened that day back in Hollow Creek, in the time between him running out of the bar and when I'd finally found him. He'd been quiet for the rest of that day and the next before he returned to his usual self, but whenever I attempted to broach the subject, he'd quickly shut it down or start talking about something else.

I could understand that. At the very least, he didn't seem to be seriously injured beyond a few scratches and scrapes on his otherwise perfect skin.

I still hadn't opened up to him about my past either, and he no longer pushed me to. We just bonded over the secrets we refused to share but still recognized in each other. Different but the same.

"Can we stay here for a bit longer?" Harper asked, throwing his bag on one of the two single beds and collapsing down after it. "I'm fucking tired, Jack. My back wasn't made for sitting in that shitty car so much. At least the Audi had heated seats."

"The Audi you stole from your ex?" I asked, because yes, I'd confirmed that Harper had in fact gone on the run from Benny in his fucking stolen car.

Harper rolled his eyes at me. "Yeah, 'cause my custom-painted Bugatti Mistral would have been so inconspicuous."

As if those had been the only two options for him to choose from. I'd grown protective of the guy, but fuck did I want to smack some sense into him sometimes. Without his money, I seriously doubted Harper would have made it very far in life. He had almost no survival skills, so there was no way in hell I was going to let him go off on his own. Without me, it'd be all too easy for Benny to catch up to him again.

I dumped my bag on the bed and made my way over to the window, parting the curtains to check what was visible outside. Even this late at night, it was a busier road than Hollow Creek had at any time. The parking lot was half filled, the Aztek in clear view, and neon signs lit up old buildings across the road: a liquor store, a convenience store, and "Garden of Eden," which I assumed was some kind of sex shop from the signage and posters in the windows. No security cameras that I could see.

It had been over a week now, and I'd chosen our destinations randomly, sometimes not even picking where we were stopping until we ended up somewhere decent enough. This place was slightly bigger and busier than where I usually chose to stay, but enough time and distance had passed that Benny couldn't have been on our tail anymore.

"We can stay for a couple of days, but then we have to keep moving."

"Ugh, fiiiiine," Harper groaned.

It had been a long time since I'd had to think about anyone other than myself. Before Harper, I'd been getting tired. Slowing down. But now that I had his safety to look after as well, I had a new purpose. I was still tired, but now it wasn't just me. I wasn't alone.

"It's time to stop running... It's time to stop now. I know you're tired of it. It's okay to stop." Unwelcome whispers of a ghost. False security even more now than it had been back then. It wasn't time to stop. Not ever. Still, his words circled my mind like a physical thing. He was an ache I'd never be free of.

"It won't end well. Not for you." Becca had been so right, only she wouldn't get to tell me *"I told you so."* I wouldn't get her involved in any of this. Running protected both of us. *"We'll figure out how to hide his body together,"* she had said. If only she'd known then what the future held, I'm sure she would never have said it.

"What are you thinking about so hard over there?" Harper asked, and I finally pulled away from the window, drawing the curtains shut.

"If you knew this was where you'd end up, would you still have gotten involved with him?" I asked. It was the question I'd been asking myself since that day. The one I still couldn't answer.

"Benny?" he asked, and I nodded. Harper thought about that, pale eyes staring up at the ceiling like it held the answers for him. "Yeah," he said eventually, turning to look back at me again. "I would. No matter what happened, I don't think I could have made any other choices."

"You really wouldn't have stayed away from him?" I asked as I came to sit down on my bed, beside his, uncertain how he could be so sure of it all. Then again, he hadn't done the things that I had done.

Harper shook his head softly. "I wouldn't give it up—the good times. He loved me more than anyone ever had. Without him, I never would have been able to experience that, you know?"

I knew. "And you still love him?"

This time he didn't take as long to think about his answer. "I do."

His answers didn't satisfy me, though. Maybe nothing ever would.

"What about you?" he asked after I'd been silent for a while. "Do you still love whoever you're running from?"

"It doesn't matter." I stood to my feet again. "Love isn't always enough. Sometimes it's the entire problem."

"What makes you say that?"

"You wouldn't understand."

"Maybe, but we won't know unless I try. Maybe I'll surprise you."

I doubted that, but what else did I have to lose? I eyed the door, where I'd intended to go outside to smoke, before I sat back down on the bed, pulling the lighter from my pocket and rubbing my thumb over the engravings. This lighter had meant so much to him, but he'd given it to me anyway.

Dex had given me so much for someone who had so little.

"Love is supposed to be good. It's supposed to make you better," I told him, and it felt like ripping a scab off a wound that could never heal. "My love made him worse."

25

Dex - Past
DEVIL OR COYOTE?

I'd expected to find Archer at the Strays' house, but when I arrived it was Henrik who was waiting for me. Archer had been around less and less lately. I didn't even know where he lived. The bastard was almost as private and guarded as his twin. Whenever we met up for Strays-related business and *other* business, it was here.

I'm pretty sure Archer didn't want anyone to know he was gay. In contrast, I didn't give a fuck who knew about my sexuality. I might never have known, or cared, about who he was into if he hadn't suggested our *arrangement*.

There were never any emotions involved between us. I respected the man, but I didn't have an ounce of romantic feelings for him, just as he didn't for me. It was just physical between us, and it was very limited, because he preferred not to bottom and I refused to even try. Mostly it was blow jobs and hand jobs, just a way to let off some steam. He hadn't particularly cared when I told him it was over. Just said *"fine"* and then tasked me with retrieving the money someone owed him but swore they couldn't pay.

Surprise, surprise, when I'd paid them a visit, that money had magically appeared.

"Get it?" Henrik asked, straight to business as I expected.

"Most of it," I answered, pulling out the envelope of cash and tossing it over to him.

He pocketed it. I wasn't concerned. Archer ran this thing, but Henrik was his twin and far closer to the man than I ever cared to be. I trusted he'd give it to his brother.

"How's your hunting going?" Henrik asked me, a smile pulling at the corners of his lips. I knew little about the man, who he was into beyond the occasional times I'd seen him flirting with Becca. Didn't really care. Becca seemed smart enough not to get seriously involved with him.

"Very successful," I told him. "I've caught myself a rabbit."

"Congratulations." Henrik smiled, and it seemed genuine, but he was always a tough one to read. "Will your rabbit be joining us?"

"No," I answered quickly. I wanted Jonah to be close to me at all times, but not here. It wasn't safe. I wouldn't let him be tainted by this part of my life.

"Pity, he's a pretty one. Wouldn't mind seeing his face around some more." So it seemed Henrik liked men too. That was fine, except that was *my* man he was talking about.

"I don't share, Hound," I told him, a warning in my eyes as I stepped forward, and he raised his hands in placation.

"Calm down, Devil. I'm not going to take him from you. I'm just saying he's pretty. He seems feisty. Maybe he would do well here."

"No," I told him again. It didn't escape me that he'd called me Devil. We all had names here, ways we referred to each other through messages and when we weren't sure who was listening. Archer had given them to us: Wolf, Hound, Fox, Jackal,

Raven, Bull, Cupid, Snake, Reaper, Ghost, Halo, Knives... the list went on. I was Coyote.

"Where did you hear that name?"

He shrugged one shoulder. "A birdy told me."

"Birdy..." I made a pensive sound. "Or a Bee?"

Henrik smiled. "So... you don't trust him, or you don't trust the others?"

I trusted no one. Not ever. "He's not one of us."

"Hmm. Maybe. Maybe you would feel differently if you were the one running things. You could use them to keep him safe. To keep him yours."

I didn't know what to make of that. The direction this conversation was heading in felt dangerous, completely uncharted and forbidden territory. "But I'm *not* the one running things."

"No. Not now. But what do you think is stronger, a wolf... or the devil?"

"You're implying I what? Take over the Strays? Usurp Archer?"

Henrik shrugged one shoulder, as if this entire conversation wasn't a betrayal of his twin brother. "Just something to think about. When you're tired of being a little coyote in the shadow of the wolf, you call me."

"And Archer?"

"You let me worry about him."

I'd never felt any particular need for power. Sure, maybe I'd do things a little differently to Archer, but he'd brought me in, he'd seen a kid who was lost and without a purpose and given him one. It was the only purpose I'd had until now, until Jonah. I knew I should dismiss Henrik. How could I trust someone who'd betray his own twin? A couple of months ago I would have dismissed him outright and probably brought this whole thing to Archer's attention. Now, though?

I didn't need help keeping Jonah safe, or keeping him mine, but the thought scratched its way into my mind like a parasite. Too fast and too deep to squish like the insignificant bug it should have been.

"I have to go," I said to Henrik instead of responding. He nodded simply and watched me leave in silence, but his words followed me, like a toxin in my system. A poison in my blood I couldn't purge.

***

"Don't talk with your mouth full, pig," I told Toby as he attempted to speak around a mouthful of fries. He scowled at me, continuing to chew before swallowing and starting again.

"I said the Drakes should be at the pier tomorrow night. Archer wants us all there," Toby repeated, more comprehensible this time.

I huffed. "I'll be there." I was always there, unlike Toby who thought he could pick and choose what Strays business he'd participate in. I had nowhere else to be, not until recently, and for the first time I found the thought of going to the fight night at the pier annoying. It was time I could spend with Jonah instead.

Bryce was quiet beside his moronic best friend. He'd been quiet a lot lately, and while he hadn't missed any more shifts at the shop, something about him still seemed off. Snatching the basket of fries from in front of Toby, who scowled at me, I slid it in front of Bryce, who seemed to be off in his own world and not paying any attention to us.

He looked down at it in surprise, his face doing something complicated for a moment before he slid it back to Toby. "I'm not hungry."

I moved it back in front of him. "I didn't ask."

Bryce scowled at me, and that was new too. They said ignorance was bliss, and Bryce was the most ignorant person I knew, so he should have the most bliss. He had sunshine beaming out of his annoying ass at any point in time. He didn't scowl. Except he was. It didn't suit him.

"I'm really fine, Dex. I don't want to eat."

"I said I'm not asking, dickface. Just do it."

"No."

"Eat, or I'll make you."

"Jesus, why are you so pissed off all the fucking time?" he snapped. Beside him, Toby's eyes widened in surprise. "Give me a fucking break. Shouldn't you be happy now you've made Jonah yours? You got what you wanted, is that still not enough?"

The outburst was certainly unexpected, but I hadn't told Bryce that Jonah was mine. Hadn't told any of the Strays but Henrik, and he didn't seem the type to gossip. "What do you know about that?"

Bryce shrugged. "He was wearing your jacket at Maxxxine's."

There was a bit to unpack there. First, Jonah was actually *wearing* my jacket. I hadn't seen it since the day we'd traded clothing. It made me wonder how often he wore it when he thought I wouldn't know about it. Second, Jonah had been at a sex shop. What could my rabbit possibly want from there? I found the idea offensive, that he'd need anything apart from me to satisfy him.

My issues with Bryce were immediately shoved to the back of my mind as I retrieved my phone from my pocket, my fingers clicking over the buttons rapidly, my messages barely coherent in my haste.

> my place. now. bring wat u bought @ maxxxines.

I grabbed my keys and helmet as I got up from the booth. "Gotta run."

Jonah's response came as I reached my bike.

Rabbit

> Fucking Bryce.

> if ur not there in 30 ill find u. bring everything. ill no if u dont.

Truthfully, I'd have no idea if he brought everything or not, but he didn't need to know that. I thought for a moment before adding another message, then I yanked on my helmet and sped off to where Jonah would join me very soon. If he didn't, I'd hunt him down and drag him home myself.

> u better still b wearing my jacket.

26

JONAH - PAST

FROM WALLS TO RUBBLE.

Fucking Bryce.

I knew he wouldn't have been able to keep his obnoxious mouth shut about this, but I still couldn't have prepared myself for getting Dex's messages. He wanted me to bring the fucking bag of sex toys with me to his place. For what? Was he just curious, or did he plan to do something else with them? My head thumped face down onto my pillows, barely muffling my scream.

He also knew I'd been wearing his jacket thanks to Bryce, the fucking snitch. I'm not sure what had possessed me to wear it, but it was going down on the long record of stupid fucking things I'd done and would beat myself up for.

Would Dex really know if I didn't bring everything? I tried to remember if Bryce had gotten a good look into the basket, but I couldn't be sure. I had no doubts Dex was telling the truth about coming to find me if I didn't do what he wanted, and my dad would be home soon. As much as I didn't give a fuck what the man thought of me, I wasn't particularly fond of the idea of Dex being here in my room doing god knows what to me while he was home.

With a long, exaggerated groan, I rolled off my bed, snatch-ing the unmarked black plastic bag from the floor and shoving it in a backpack instead. Fucking *fuck*. I hadn't even gone through it on my own yet. Becca had only just left for the day. I'd just showered, and I was building up the nerves just to open the damned bag.

I got dressed, then after another moment of indecision I pulled his stupid leather jacket back on. Why did I always just do what he told me?

There was no time to think about it. I'd already be struggling to make it to Meadow Park in the thirty minutes he'd given me to do so.

Fuck!

By the time I made it to his house, Dex was already waiting for me out front, leaning on his bike as though he really had been preparing to come and find me.

Saying nothing, he turned and marched inside, and I followed him, my heart rate escalating as he took the stairs two at a time in front of me up to his room. The moment I walked in, he snapped his fingers at me, holding out his hand for the bag. I took a step back, my hands defensively circling around behind me to guard it.

"Give it to me, Rabbit," he demanded.

"Why?"

"So I know how much trouble you're going to be in."

Indignation flared in my core. "I'm allowed to buy sex toys if I want to."

"No you're not," he said, matter-of-factly. "You're mine, Jonah. You agreed to that. No one else is allowed to touch you, not even you, and especially not some fucking toys. Now give them to me."

Toxic. Obsessive. Unreasonable. Unfair. All true. And yeah, they absolutely should have been red flags. I knew they were. But the jealousy in his voice, words, and actions? No one had ever wanted me so much that my own fucking touch made them jealous, and it ignited something twisted inside me.

I handed him the backpack. Dex yanked it open, grabbing the plastic bag from Maxxxine's and emptying it over his bed. Everything was still in its packaging. Untouched. The purple dildo, condoms, lube, a glow in the dark butt plug Becca must have snuck into the basket, along with... an anal douching kit.

I wanted to fucking die.

I thought I might with how rapidly my heart was beating in my chest. On the off chance that I didn't die from embarrassment, or whatever Dex planned to do to me, then I was absolutely going to kill Becca instead.

Dex *tsked*, his eyes finally leaving the items on the bed to look at me again. "If you wanted something up your butt, all you had to do was ask, Rabbit."

"I just—" I stalled, really not knowing what I could say to make this situation any better for myself. "I just wanted to practice. And you didn't seem like you wanted to anyway!"

"What gave you that idea?"

"You haven't tried anything!"

"I was waiting for you to tell me you were ready."

"How was I supposed to know that?"

"You'd know by talking to me."

"You don't talk to me about it either!"

"I'm telling you now. If you want to do something, tell me. Whatever it is, we'll do it together. You're not dealing with anything on your own anymore, Rabbit, not even this."

My stomach twisted, definitely in anger, but also in something else that always came when I was around Dex. Whenever I was with him, I felt like the walls I'd built up around me were one slight push away from crumbling. He made me feel vulnerable, and like maybe it would be *okay* if I were. It terrified me.

"You say it like it should be easy. It's not easy."

"It's not easy," he repeated, walking over to me, and I barely resisted the urge to shove at him when his warm hand cupped the side of my face, his other hand found my hip, and he pulled me closer to him. "I know it's not. I'm sorry."

"Don't do that," I told him, my throat feeling tight. "Don't be gentle with me."

"Why?" Even his voice was gentle.

"I don't know what to do with it." But it was more than that. "I don't deserve it."

"This isn't something you have to earn, Rabbit. I'm giving it to you. It's yours."

"What if I get used to it?"

"You should. It's not going anywhere. *I'm* not going anywhere. It's safe to let me in."

The walls crumbled to rubble at my feet.

My hands found his hips, and I pulled him closer, so his body could replace the shield he'd torn away from me. I couldn't protect myself anymore, so now he'd have to be the one to do it. My lips found sanctuary in the warmth of his neck, in the strong arms that wrapped around me. Safe, like a cage was safe.

"I want you," I told him, the words too small to encapsulate the magnitude of everything I was feeling in this moment.

"You have me," he answered, his lips kissing the side of my head so softly it burned.

"More."

"My rabbit, you can have everything."

He shifted ever so slightly, and I clung to him, terrified that I'd crumble along with my walls if he parted from me for even a second. He understood. His hands moved down over my clothes to my thighs. Then he was lifting me. I wrapped my legs and arms around him tightly so he could carry me over to his bed.

Even when he laid me down, I refused to let him go.

"I have you," he told me. "I'm not going anywhere."

I believed him, letting just enough space pass between us so he could take off his jacket, then mine. His shirt, then mine. His pants, then mine. Repeating until we were both stripped bare for each other for the first time in a way that was deeper than lost clothing. I'd tensed when my scars were exposed to him, terrified he'd see the ugly marks and be as repulsed by them as I was, but he barely even glanced at them. No, when he looked at me, he saw all of me, everything I was, and that was deeper and uglier than any surgery scars. Still, he looked at me like I was something he craved, something he loved.

Dex Weller was the devil, and he touched me like I was sacred, like it was some form of worship, so what the fuck did that make me?

His hands explored me, all the parts I'd kept hidden. Gently. Reverently. His body over mine, skin against skin. He mouthed at my jaw, my neck. He tasted me. Breathed me deep into his lungs.

His cock was hard against mine, sparks of pleasure and heat rippling over my body as they pressed against each other, but it didn't feel urgent like it usually did when he touched me, or at least it felt urgent in a different way.

Dex rested his forearms on the bed on either side of me, supporting just enough of his weight that I didn't feel crushed by him. I wanted to be.

I felt trapped by him, like he was a cage I couldn't escape from, with walls so thick and high I couldn't see past them and so little space I was always pressed against him. And it felt so safe. I couldn't get away, but nothing else could get in either. He'd keep the bad things out, he'd keep the world away, and finally, *finally*, I could relax and let my guard down. Only in the prison of his love did I feel safe enough to be gentle. I could exist here without baring my teeth and snapping at anyone who came close.

"More," I whispered to him. "I want you to fuck me. Please."

He groaned against my skin, pulling back to seek my lips, claiming them like he would claim the rest of me. Then he was pulling back again, and I fought myself not to chase him, knowing he was coming back to me. Trusting him to.

Dex grabbed the condoms and the lube from where they were scattered further down on the bed, his arm swiping everything else onto the floor for good measure before he was over me again. "I'll take care of you," he told me.

"I know," I answered, and I did know.

I parted my legs for him, seeking his lips again when my stomach twisted with nerves. And he gave them to me, kissing me so deeply I couldn't think as his slick fingers pressed at my crease, finding my hole, circling it. I tensed on instinct.

"Shhh... it's okay, Rabbit. Open for me. I won't hurt you."

I nodded, forgetting how to breathe as I claimed his lips again, harder, desperately, in need of a distraction that he granted me by taking my bottom lip in his teeth and tugging on it. I groaned. His finger slipped inside me.

"That's it." Words spoken against my lips as he sank deeper. "Let me in."

It felt strange, neither pleasant nor unpleasant, until his lips found my neck again. His teeth traced my skin and then sank in. I cried out, turning my head to give him better access. He bit me again.

"You like that, don't you? I'm going to mark you up, Rabbit."

"Do it, then," I gasped out, and he did, teeth sinking into my flesh in a way that hurt and soothed simultaneously.

As he sucked a bruise into my skin, his finger pressed deeper, searching, stretching, until he withdrew it to press in two. He bit a second mark on my neck, harder than the first, successfully distracting me again.

Then he touched something inside me, like a bolt of lightning pleasure to my core. "Fuck!" I cried out. Dex did it again, over and over, and I broke apart under him. Moaning and writhing. Melting under his teeth, around his fingers.

"That's it, baby. Feels so good, doesn't it?"

I nodded frantically, because I wasn't capable of speaking, especially not when he added another finger and I felt so fucking full. "More. Want you. Please," I begged. Because I was feeling too much, and I didn't want to come undone until I had him inside me properly.

He listened, slipping his fingers free, and even though he needed to in order to give me what I wanted, I still whimpered at the loss of them.

I was impatient as Dex opened the box of condoms, pulling one free and rolling it down his hard length, so much thicker than his fingers, and I already knew it would feel even better. Already dreaded how empty I'd feel without it afterwards.

"Relax for me, baby," he said after he'd applied more lube, lining himself up until I could feel the pressure of him where his fingers had just been.

"Bite me again," I demanded, needing the distraction, needing the pain, the feeling of possession from him. He gave it to me, biting me hard enough that it stung as he pressed inside. Pressure that burned as he sank deeper.

Then he was inside me fully. His tongue licked an apology over my skin before his lips found mine again. "Alright?" he asked, pressing his forehead against mine.

"Yes," I whispered, still adjusting to him as the burn faded.

"You feel so good." His voice was strained. "So fucking perfect for me, Rabbit."

I made a pathetic sound in response, but I didn't even care as my hands smoothed over the skin of his back, where I'd clawed him without even realizing it.

Dex kissed along my neck and jaw softly, letting me get used to him until the burn was nothing compared to the urgency that hadn't faded with our joining.

"More," I said. He found my lips again, kissing me as I felt him shift, his hips rolling as he pulled out of me and pushed back in. I whimpered, "More."

He did it again, and again, until the roll of his hips turned into thrusts, and with each one I cried out and clung to him harder. That pleasure was back, his cock pressing against that sweet spot inside me every time his hips met mine.

I couldn't think, couldn't exist beyond this. Just his body and mine and the sounds we made together. Louder, harder, faster. Until I broke, convulsing beneath him in pleasure as I came harder than I ever had before, without even touching my dick.

Dex was grunting as his thrusts picked up speed, using my oversensitive body to take his own pleasure. Sweat coated his skin. Then he groaned loudly, his hips stilling deep inside me as he came. "Fuck," he panted.

"Fuck," I whispered back in response.

His lips found mine, a kiss that was gentle and affectionate, and after what we'd just done... the softness of it made my eyes prickle with heat and my vision blur as I opened them. And suddenly I was crying.

"I'm sorry," I sniffed, trying to get myself to stop, but the tears wouldn't listen.

"What for?" Dex asked me gently. A hand cupped my cheek.

"'Cause I'm being pathetic." I cleared my throat, but the tears still didn't stop running down the sides of my face—to my ears and into my hairline—as I looked up at him.

"Why?"

"I don't know. I just am."

"No, I mean, why do you *think* you're being pathetic?"

"'Cause we just had sex and now I'm fucking crying."

"Who told you crying was pathetic?"

"I'm sure most people don't cry after sex."

"So fucking what? You're not most people, and neither am I. When you feel things, you feel them deeply. You feel them with all of you. I like that about you. Don't hide it from me."

I nodded, because I didn't know what else to say. He kissed my forehead, and I cried harder. I cried without trying to stop myself until the feelings emptied themselves out of me. Dex held me the whole time, kept me in his arms, peppering soft kisses over my face so much that when I finally stopped and he kissed my lips again, he tasted like my tears.

I was shivering now, from the cold, from the fragile state I'd found myself in. Dex pulled out of me, and as I feared, I suddenly felt so empty without him. "I'm going to get something to clean us up," he told me, and I grabbed him in a panic.

"No, don't leave me."

"Okay, baby." He reached for his discarded shirt instead and used that to clean us up as best he could, then tossed it with the tied condom to the floor and shifted us until he could peel back the covers of his bed, pulling me into him as he covered us with them.

He was so warm. I wrapped my arms around him and nestled in closer. I felt so tired and so secure, and I knew if I didn't move from here, I'd fall asleep like this.

I couldn't bring myself to care.

27

Dex - Past

RABBIT IN THE SHEETS, FIRE IN THE STREETS.

The nightmares didn't come for me. With Jonah's body against mine, I slept deeper and more peacefully than I could ever remember doing before.

When my eyes opened to the early-morning sun leaking in between half-closed curtains, I knew it was later than the usual time I'd wake up. I didn't even set alarms anymore, because I never slept in, yet here with Jonah I didn't even have to try.

I just had to hope he wouldn't run from me again when he woke up to realize he'd spent the night. Yesterday's progress extended far deeper than sexual. He'd let me into his soul as well as his body, and I so desperately wanted to carve out a home for myself there in the depths of him. I wanted to live in his soul, let it soothe what was lost of mine.

It didn't matter that I'd be late for work—if I wasn't already. I didn't dare move in case he took this away from me again. I wanted to soak up as much of him as I could so it'd sustain me for the time we had to be apart.

By the time Jonah stirred beside me, I'd been lying there for hours, just holding him, watching him sleep, committing him to memory. I was no artist, but I could paint a picture of him with my eyes closed from how deeply I'd etched the image of him into my psyche.

Peaceful features twisted, regaining their sharp edges. His brow furrowed the way I'd expected it would, and his eyes opened slowly, as though waking up was an extremely difficult task and he had to fight himself to do it, both winning and losing simultaneously.

"Morning, Rabbit." I spoke softly, bracing myself for the moment he'd pull away. Jonah's eyes finally focused, taking me in, and he surprised me as he softened again, letting his eyes close once more as he grumbled unhappily and wriggled closer to me under the covers. His arm, which had been lying lax over me, tightened once more with consciousness. His nose was cold as it burrowed into the curve of my neck, but I didn't mind. I'd give him my warmth. I'd give him everything. "How are you feeling?" I received another incoherent murmur in response.

So, my rabbit wasn't a morning person, then. I pulled him in closer, wrapping my body around him, my legs tangling with his until we were a knot of limbs, and Jonah sighed with what sounded an awful lot like relief.

He mumbled something else.

"What was that?" I asked, unable and unwilling to mask my amusement.

"Time is it?" he repeated, only slightly more comprehensible.

"Mmm, does it matter?"

"Don't you have work?"

"I'm already late."

He pulled back from me, that pretty frown twisting his features.

I couldn't fight the way my lips tugged in a smile.

"What are you so happy about?"

"Nothing... I just... I've never had anyone in my bed in the daylight before."

Jonah seemed to consider that for a moment, finding it agreeable before he snuggled closer. "You won't have anyone in your bed at all anymore," he grumbled, and my chest warmed at the possessiveness in his words.

"Except you."

"Except me."

"Because you're mine," I couldn't help but add, and Jonah groaned into my neck. "Because you're mine?" I prompted him again, giving him a squeeze.

"I already said I was."

"I wanna hear you say it again."

"You already know."

"I do, but I need to make sure *you* know. Who do you belong to, Rabbit?"

Silence.

I roughly grabbed a handful of his ass cheek. "Answer me."

Jonah gasped out a sound suspiciously like a moan, but he still didn't speak. I squeezed again, and this time it definitely sounded like a moan. He rocked his hips against me, seeking friction for his cock—which was always significantly more honest about what it wanted than my rabbit seemed able to be.

"Answer me, and..." I kissed the side of his head that wasn't hidden away in my neck. "I'll make you come."

Jonah groaned, and I gave him some time to think it through. "You," he whispered after a minute.

"What about me?" I couldn't resist provoking him further.

"Urghhh. I belong to *you*, Devil."

"Good boy."

"Fuck you."

"Mmm, you first, Rabbit."

Jonah shivered, his hips impatiently rocking against me again.

"Okay, okay, you'll get what you want." I pulled away from him, and he seemed unhappy about that until I grabbed his hips and rolled him onto his back. The blankets slipped down my back, exposing us to the cold morning air, but it didn't matter, because I was about to make my rabbit feel a different kind of heat.

As Jonah came undone from my lips, my tongue, my throat—writhing in my sheets and making the most beautiful sounds—I knew I wanted to start every day this way.

I came over his flushed, sweat-damp skin when I finished myself off, looking down at the beautiful mess of him beneath me, covered in my cum, my marks. I wasn't ever going to let him be without my marks on him again.

"Time to shower," I told him, spanking his thigh lightly. His brow twitched as he decided whether he liked that or was offended by it before deciding on both. I made a mental note for next time. "Come on. Up. Or I'll carry you."

His lip curled in annoyance, but he knew I fully intended to follow through and finally got moving, shuffling out of bed and coming with me to the shower.

When the water was warm, I pulled him under the stream after me, closing us in with the curtain. Jonah was quiet until I lathered up the soap and brought it to his chest.

"I can do it myself," he snapped.

"I know," I answered and continued washing him anyway. He gave me a glare that could set fire to kindling, but he let me continue. My soapy fingers traced the curve of his ass. "Are you sore?"

"I'm fine," he growled, but he was still letting me wash him, clearly not hating it as much as he wanted me to think he was. That was fine. Jonah wasn't used to anyone taking care of him, so to finally have it felt like a weakness. But he'd get used to this, and eventually he'd feel safe enough to ask me for it.

"You can be fine *and* sore."

"I'm fine," he repeated, softer this time.

"Okay, baby." I waited for him to tell me not to call him baby, but he didn't, just turned away from me so I couldn't see his face. I reached for the shampoo, adding some to my hand, and as he tensed again, I cut him off before he said what I knew he was about to. "I know you can do it yourself. But I want to do it."

"Okay," he said quietly, and I let my fingers run through his dark locks.

I took my time washing his hair, and the tension in his shoulders melted away the longer I did it. When I was done, I tilted his head softly to the side, my lips tracing over the marks I'd sucked into his neck last night.

"I'm fighting at the pier tonight." Words spoken softly between kisses. "Will you come over afterwards?"

"I'll come to the fight."

"I'd rather you stay away from—"

"I said I'm coming!"

I sighed. "Then just promise me you won't put yourself in any danger, especially not because of me."

"What if that fuckhead says something again?"

I loved seeing him angry on my behalf. "Then you tell me and I'll fuck him up myself. Okay?"

"Mnn."

"Promise you won't get involved?"

Jonah groaned. "Fine."

"Thank you."

I washed myself, not nearly as carefully as I'd washed him, and turned the water off, stepping out to get us towels.

When we were back in my room and dressed, I made sure Jonah put my jacket on again. I liked seeing him in it.

"I'm going to fuck you while you wear this next time," I told him, and his cheeks immediately flushed pink, his brow furrowed, and he tried to make himself look angry about it.

"When's next time?" He sounded so pouty it took all my self-control not to strip right now and throw him back on my bed.

"Tonight?"

Jonah nodded.

"I gotta go to work. I'll see you there, then?"

He nodded again.

"You can stay here as long as you want to," I told him, circling my arms around him again, and his eyes widened in shock as he looked up at me.

"You'd let me just stay here without you?"

"I doubt you're gonna rob me, Rabbit, and if you wanted to, I wouldn't care." I'd give him everything I had right now if he wanted it. "The spare key is in the dead plant by the door. Now, I really gotta go. Roy's gonna be pissed off as it is," I said, silencing any further protests with my lips on his in a kiss that was meant to be quick but ended up lingering, leaving me wanting more when we parted. I groaned. "Okay." One more kiss. "I'm going." Another. And one more and then he was shoving me.

"Get outta here, Devil."

"Yeah, yeah. See you soon, Rabbit."

⸺◆⸺

After work, I made my way to the pier. Roy had been very *Roy* about my arriving so late. Just an "Oh good, you're alive," and then carrying on with his tasks, leaving me to mine and asking no further questions, the long, scrutinizing look he gave me enough to satisfy him that nothing was wrong.

Being a weekday, Bryce was thankfully at school, so I didn't have to deal with him. Jonah probably should have been there too, but if he didn't want to go, I wouldn't tell him to. I'd leave that in Becca's very capable hands.

As I pulled up and parked my bike with the others, I knew I'd have to deal with a fuller crew tonight. Given what happened last time, Archer had clearly called in all the fighters this time. It wasn't that I didn't like the others... I just didn't like *most* of the others. The ones I did anything more than just tolerate—Bull, Cupid, Halo, Snake—wouldn't be here. Their value lay outside the fighting ring.

"Coyote," said Raven, giving me a lingering once-over I didn't much care for. As usual.

"Raven."

"Still gay?"

"Last I checked."

"Maybe we should check again," she said, licking over black-painted lips.

"Pass."

"Hmm. Your loss."

"I'm sure."

"Pity."

"I'm sure you have many other men and women who'd appreciate your talents." I cast a glance at Reaper, already shooting daggers at me like I was the one flirting with the woman who'd sleep with anyone but him. I didn't blame her. Reaper was a creepy fucker. I didn't even know his real name; he just insisted everyone call him Reaper. He was a mean fighter, though.

As Archer and Henrik pulled up, I thought again about the conversation I'd had with the bulkier twin yesterday. It was something I shouldn't have been thinking about at all, but the thoughts rose of their own accord—what would happen if I tried to take over the Strays? If Henrik did what he'd implied and somehow got Archer out of the picture, I still had no guarantee the rest of the Strays would follow me instead. Particularly Reaper.

As night swallowed the sky, and the sand was lit only by the stars and fires that slowly warped the barrels that sustained them, my eyes were more focused on the crowd than the fights. I needed to find *him*. Not knowing where he was made my skin itch uncomfortably, like a junkie in need of a hit and Jonah was my drug. Without him, I was unmoored. Agitated. Distracted.

There.

I breathed a sigh of relief as my eyes caught him from a distance, walking onto the sand with Becca. He was still wearing my jacket. I never wanted to see him without it again. In fact, maybe I'd replace all his clothes with mine. He already smelled of my soap and shampoo after our shower. I liked the way Jonah usually smelled, but having him smell like me satisfied a primal part of me he'd woken up.

His eyes found mine right away.

My honey-eyed inferno.

Becca had her arms folded across her chest as she caught sight of me, and clearly I'd earned her disapproval. I wondered if it was the markings I'd left all over Jonah's neck, or maybe it was just me as a whole she disapproved of. Didn't matter to me either way. She might have been Jonah's best friend, but he was *mine*.

"Who's that?" Raven asked, holding her pack of cigarettes out to me. I glanced at her just long enough to take one before looking back at Jonah, who was watching us with a glare.

"My rabbit." I leaned down so she could light it for me. Raven took her sweet time, a knowing smirk on her lips as she stepped in far closer than necessary, hands shielding the flame from the wind as a much hotter flame burned in Jonah's eyes.

"Rabbit, hmm? I'd go for something a little more territorial and murderous."

Jonah kept walking, his limp faint, and I knew that was because he was doing his best to cover it. Becca reached for his arm to stop him, but he yanked out of her hold, continuing on his way. Coming to me.

The rest of the Strays and I were hanging out under the pier until it was time for our fights, smoking and drinking—well,

I wasn't drinking. Overall, we were causing a general ruckus that most people kept clear of. Not my rabbit. He had a point to prove, and I was going to let him do just that.

The moment I was within reach of him, he had both hands gripping the collar of my jacket, and he smashed his lips against mine. I smiled against them even as they bruised me with the force of his public claiming.

When he considered his point successfully made, he released me, shooting a glare at Raven. She smiled back widely. Raven had never been easy to intimidate—came with being the only woman in the Strays. She could hold her own against the rest of us, so she certainly wasn't about to cower down to Jonah. If anything, he'd just given her something fun to poke at.

"You should piss on him next," she said with a sneer. "You know, just to really mark your territory."

Jonah's scowl deepened, and I saw that flame roar inside him—a lit fuse, and he was ready to explode. I grabbed his jaw in my hand before he could feed her more ammo, turning him toward me to steal his lips again in a far deeper kiss. My tongue sought his, found it, claimed it, used it until he went weak in my arms. A bomb successfully defused.

28

JONAH - PAST

COYOTE VS JACKAL.

There weren't many people I liked. Until recently there was only one—Becca. And though I never expected it, there were now two. I tolerated everyone else at best. That being said, I fucking hated this bitch.

All night she'd been standing way too close to Dex, offering him cigarettes, lighting them for him, touching his arm, leaning on him. I wasn't stupid. I knew she was doing it specifically to piss me off. Every time I felt like I was about to explode and fucking tell her to keep her hands to herself, Dex would be on me—his hands, his lips—and I struggled to hold onto the rage.

It wasn't like he was letting her touch him or seemed to enjoy her company. He'd shrug her off, roll his eyes when she spoke, but he still seemed fucking amused about the whole situation, and that pissed me off too.

I guess she was part of his gang or something, so yeah, maybe he couldn't just tell her to fuck off. Still, the more she reached for him, the more I wanted to cut her fucking hands off. Maybe she thought because she was part of his group that she had more power than me, but I didn't fucking care.

I could hardly spare a moment to take in whoever else was in the area. Archer was—I'd seen him with Henrik—and Bryce had shown up not too long ago too.

I didn't look at any of the others long enough to work out if I knew them or not. But I could feel them looking at me, monitoring me. I was a stranger, an outsider. I wasn't welcome here with them, that much was obvious, even if no one had the balls to come out and say it. But Dex wanted me here, and that was all that mattered. And apparently that was enough for them not to get involved. I wasn't sure if they just trusted his judgment or if maybe they were afraid of him. I didn't care either way.

Most people were cautious of Dex, if not downright terrified. I wasn't one of them. I knew him better than any of them could. They called him Coyote. It didn't suit him. Maybe to them he was a wild dog, but to me he was the devil. My devil. My beautiful twisted angel of light. Because that's all the devil really was—an angel. *Fallen,* but still an angel. I'd seen the softer side to him, the side that was good, and I wondered if the devil was only ever the devil because he was unloved. Maybe if I loved him, he could be good. Maybe no one had ever given him the chance to be good before.

"JJ." Becca's voice sounded from behind me, and I turned to find her looking wary. She clearly didn't want to be here, but I should have expected my best friend wouldn't let me face the wolves on my own.

"Bee." Dex's head nodded in greeting. Beside him, the black-haired bitch gave her a long, assessing once-over, and my hackles rose, ready to fight her for a whole new reason until her lips pulled into a grin.

"Well, hey there, gorgeous," she said, her voice smooth as silk rather than the sharp edge she'd used with me. "Bee, was it? I'm Raven."

I watched as Becca looked Raven up and down, the slight tug on her lips indicating she approved of what she saw. Perfect. Becca could get this bitch away from me and my man.

"Raven was just saying she liked your boots," I told Becca.

"I was? Oh yeah. I was. Super cute," Raven agreed quickly, and I hated that I was basically being her wingman now, but it served my purposes.

"Well, Raven has excellent taste," Becca responded, that faint smile on her lips pulled wider. Fuck, I really hoped I wouldn't regret this.

"You know what else I have excellent taste in? Beer. Want one?"

Becca's eyes flicked to me, giving me a once-over to make sure I was okay before she nodded, following Raven over to where her half-drunk six pack was dug into the sand.

"Sneaky rabbit." Dex's low whisper traced the curve of my ear with his lips as his arms circled me from behind.

"Don't know what you're referring to," I told him.

"Mmhmm."

⚬

Watching Dex fight was like watching a natural disaster. An earthquake. A hurricane. Something devastating and powerful. Unstoppable.

It was like everything that had built up under that scarily calm facade he always maintained was suddenly unleashed. His violence felt like passion in such a way that I almost felt jealous

I wasn't the one receiving such beautifully strong emotions from him.

He fought as if it were his purpose.

And he fucking loved it.

Like last time, his opponent was bigger than him, but the man was struggling to keep up, and though they both traded blows—fresh blood spraying the sand to be washed away by the rising tide—Dex was maintaining the upper hand.

Every new scrape and split to his skin fueled me with fire, an inferno of vengeance I longed to unleash on the fucker he was up against.

I was both relieved and annoyed it wasn't Mason fucking Bates again. He was here, though, watching the fights as well. He'd fought someone the Strays referred to as Reaper, and he'd lost. It wasn't enough, not if he could still stand there, glaring at Dex like they had unfinished business.

I'd promised Dex I wouldn't get involved, but I don't know how I could be expected to keep that promise if the fuckhead really did anything beyond glare in disapproval at him.

Becca was beside me, cheering Dex on. The alcohol Raven had fed her loosened her up enough to enjoy herself. She still monitored me, though, and yanked me back if I tried to step into the fighting ring. Which happened only when Dex received a particularly hard blow. I moved without even thinking about it, just like the first time I'd watched him fight. When it came to Dex, I could hardly think logically, and that was only stronger now we belonged to each other.

Dex and whatever his fucking name was tumbled into the sand, Dex on top, raining down punch after punch until the fight was called and he basically had to be dragged off the guy.

I hated him. Hated that Dex had been all over him, even in violence.

It wasn't a surprise when Dex was called the winner, and then not even Becca could hold me back as I practically attacked him, throwing myself at his sweating, bloody, shirtless body with enough force I almost took us both to the sand again. His arms wrapped around me, and he kissed the side of my head.

We pulled away from each other, only just enough to walk, heading to where the others were waiting so the next fight could be called. Toby—Jackal, as the Strays called him—was up next. The crowd parted to allow Dex to leave.

Becca stepped backward as we passed, into Toby, who was right behind her.

"Fucking watch it, *Bennet*!" he snapped as he shoved her, sending her into me.

There was a moment of silence, Becca's eyes wide as we processed what had just happened, her expression morphing from shock to hurt. I saw red.

I turned to glare at Toby, but before I could even move in his direction, his face was on the receiving end of a punch so powerful his neck was whipping backward and he was dropping back into the sand. Dex was on him. Fists with knuckles already busted landed hit after hit so quickly all Toby could do was grunt like a wounded animal and try in vain to shield himself from the attack.

People scurried back, trying to get out of the way of the unexpected brawl, no doubt fearing a repeat of the complete battleground this beach had devolved into the last time. But this fight wasn't between opposing gangs, and no one quite

seemed to know what to do with it. Stray-on-Stray violence...
even their own members seemed hesitant to throw themselves
into the fray. Bryce stood next to Becca, right next to where
Toby had been standing only a moment ago, his features pale.

"Coyote!" A voice shouted above the commotion, a figure
shouldering their way to the front of the new ring forming
around us. Archer made it through, grabbing Dex and attempting to haul him off Toby's prone form, but my devil
was set on destruction, pulling out of every hold and attempt
at restraint to deliver more pain. "Hound!" Archer shouted,
calling for backup.

I turned to see who Hound was, my eyes landing on the far
more intimidating half of the terror twins. He didn't even need
to push his way through the crowd; they just moved for him as
if they were afraid to touch him.

Henrik took in the situation. His eyes scanned from Archer
pulling at Dex, to Dex beating on Toby, to Becca clinging to
me like a life raft in a storm, then to Bryce pale as a ghost, and
Raven glaring down at Toby, her hand finding Bee's back in
a soothing gesture. He reached his own conclusion, standing
tall, arms folded over his chest.

"Hound!" Archer yelled at him again. Henrik still didn't
move. His silence made it clear whose side he was taking in this
fight.

It was Reaper who ended up pushing his way through to
help Archer pull Dex off the now sobbing Toby. It took both
of them to pull him back, and even then it was a struggle.
Reaper helped Toby to his feet as Archer made himself a physical barrier between them to stop Dex from going at him again.

"Enough!" Archer warned Dex, but he was having none of it, adrenaline still pumping through his system as he stood up to the man in front of him, stepping closer until his chest barged Archer and the man had to brace himself so he wasn't pushed backward. "Stand down, Coyote."

"Or what?" Dex snarled.

A vein bulged in Archer's neck. "Or I'll make you."

"Will you? Think you could? Try it, Wolf. See what happens."

"That's quite enough of that, I think." Henrik finally spoke up, placing a hand on Dex's shoulder that he attempted to shrug away, only Henrik didn't budge. "Wolf will deal with Jackal. Won't you, Wolf?"

Even in the dim light, it was clear Archer's face was turning red. I knew rage well enough to know it wasn't all Archer was feeling. Two of his own gang had fought with each other, and Dex had challenged him in front of the crowd—all completely fucking silent so they could hear every word.

"Stand. Down," Archer said again, and Dex stayed right where he was, jaw and fists clenched, aching for more violence.

It wasn't possible to stop a hurricane with physical force, or by command, but I knew if he wasn't stopped there'd be more destruction to himself as well as everyone else around him. I didn't care about anyone else, but he'd taken enough damage for one night.

"Devil," I called out to him, and my voice reached him more than the hands grabbing at him. His eyes found mine, the storm within them explosive, wild, raging. It needed to be acknowledged. Witnessed. Seen. *I see you.*

I reached my hand out to him, watching the conflict in his features. He wanted the violence and the pain, but he wanted me as well, and he didn't want to mix the two. He had to choose one. He chose me.

His hand found mine as he stepped away from Archer, and I laced my fingers between his, pulling him to my side.

Archer took a deep breath, giving him a final stare down before shooting me a glare full of hatred—like any of this was my fault. Then he was pushing his way back through the crowd to stalk off.

The edge of Henrik's lips pulled up in a grin as he looked at Dex, then me... then faded as he stepped forward, a large hand cupping the back of Toby's neck as he pulled the man along with him back through the crowd that parted for him as if he were on fire and they didn't want to get burned.

Reaper lingered, staring at Dex. I saw something in his eyes that called to the beast caged inside me, made it thrash at my ribcage with the urge to get between them. Protect him. Then he huffed and turned, following Henrik.

"I... I'm sorry, Becca. He didn't mean it, I'm sure. Sorry." Bryce bobbed his head in apology before he was slinking his way back through the crowd to seek his bloodied best friend.

When it was obvious there was no more fighting to spectate, the crowd dissipated. I held Becca with one hand and Dex with the other.

"You shouldn't have done that," Bee said, clearing her throat, her eyes on Dex. "But thanks."

He nodded in response, and I could see the storm in him fading, leaving him hollow in its absence.

"We should go," I said to Becca and to Dex.

"Need a ride home?" asked Raven, who was apparently still here.

"You've been drinking, Raven." Dex's voice sounded so fucking tired.

"Barely," she argued, but he still shot her a glare that made her roll her eyes. "Ugh, fine. Come on, pretty lady, let's get you an Uber."

Becca nodded, stepping in to give me a tight hug. "I'll text you when I get home. You too?"

"I will," I answered, and she nodded.

Raven and Becca walked off together toward the main road.

I turned to Dex. "Let's go home."

29

Dex - Past

HANDS ON THE HEADBOARD.

———— ✪ ————

"You wear it," Jonah said, crossing his arms. As if I'd given him a choice.

I wasn't in the mood for an argument, not with him, so instead of replying I just stepped forward and shoved the helmet over his head.

"But you nee—"

"If you don't wear it, then we're walking back to my house, and I'd rather not leave my father's bike here, Jonah." I cut him off. Maybe it was my harsher than usual tone, or that I'd called him Jonah instead of Rabbit, but either way he crossed his arms over his chest and fell silent. I didn't need to see his face to know he was probably pouting under there, but as long as he didn't take the helmet off I didn't care.

I swung my leg over Delilah, settling into the seat as far forward as I could in order to make room for Jonah behind me. My bike wasn't equipped for a passenger—single saddle seat with no passenger foot pegs. She was designed for solo riding, and that had never been an issue for me before.

Jonah looked between me and the bike, hesitating.

"Come on, Rabbit. She won't bite you."

With a muffled huff, he stepped forward, a hand on my shoulder as he swung his leg over and slotted in behind me,

"Delilah isn't used to taking two, so stay as close to me as you can." I grabbed his hands, lightly resting on my waist, and pulled them tight around my middle. Then grabbed the underside of his knees and hiked his legs up. "Hug me with them, tight as you can. I don't want your legs dangling like spaghetti when we hit the road."

Whatever he grumbled in response was swallowed up by my helmet.

Delilah's engine rumbled to life. Jonah clung tighter to me as we started moving, and soon the wind was stinging my face, knotting my hair, but with his warmth at my back and my heart in tune with the bike beneath me, there wasn't anywhere I'd rather be.

When I modified my bike to carry Jonah, and I already knew I would, then I'd take us on a longer ride. As it was, I made my way straight to Meadow Park, taking us home.

Jonah's legs were a little shaky when we stopped. I smiled to myself as I dismounted and took the helmet from him. His cheeks were pink, his hair ruffled, and he fidgeted with the sleeves of my jacket.

I took his hand and pulled him along with me into the house, up the stairs, desperate to get him into bed, not even in a sexual sense. I just needed his body on mine somewhere we could just breathe and exist with nothing but each other.

Jonah let me pull him along until we passed the bathroom door just before my bedroom, and he came to a stop, yanking his hand out of mine.

"What?" I sighed, for once feeling far too tired for this game of cat and mouse, of the push and pull.

"Shower first."

I sighed again. "Fine."

Jonah stared at me expectantly until I stomped into the bathroom ahead of him. I stripped quickly, letting my clothes fall to the floor with little care or finesse. Jonah watched in silence.

"You going to get undressed too, or do only I need to shower?" I asked him, my voice dry. I couldn't be too displeased with his request; echoes of blood, sweat, and sand still clung to my skin.

Normally after fight night, when the storm of adrenaline and thrill of violence faded from my system, I'd crash hard. It was one of the few times I could sleep with little trouble, so I rarely bothered showering until the morning after. If that habit grossed my Rabbit out, though, I guess I'd have to change it.

Jonah started to strip, his cheeks flushed and signature scowl firmly in place. I turned away from him to start the water. When it was warm enough, I stepped under the spray, followed closely by a very quiet Jonah. I reached for the soap, pausing when Jonah's hand shot out to block me.

"I want to do it," he told me.

"This again? I know you can do it yourself, Jonah, but it's okay to let me—"

"No." Jonah cut me off. "I mean... I want to do it... for you."

"You want to wash me?"

His cheeks darkened as he nodded.

I felt my lips tug into a smile. More than the hot water cascading over our bodies, I was warmed by the understanding that Jonah had wanted me to shower with him, not because he thought I was dirty, but because he wanted to take care of me.

"Okay, Rabbit."

He couldn't meet my eyes as he reached for the soap, lathering it up in his hands before he brought it to my chest, washing away so much more than the sweat and dirt. He was gentle, particularly over areas that were scraped up or split open from the night's events. He didn't need to be gentle. Jonah wasn't capable of hurting me. Any sensations delivered by Jonah's hands were welcomed and wanted. Even pain would feel like a reward from those slender fingers.

When he'd washed my front, his hands urged me to turn around, and as much as I wanted to tease him, I resisted. My rabbit could be skittish at best. I didn't want to scare him off when he was initiating affection.

He gave my back the same level of care. His touch was soft, affectionate, intimate, but not sexual. He'd avoided washing my dick too closely, even though it was already desperate to show him just how appreciative it was.

When he was done with the soap, he reached for the shampoo, lathering it up in my hair and combing his fingers through to detangle the many knots from riding without a helmet.

I'd never had this before. I'd never given it to anyone either, except for Jonah, but I'd never given him anything with the hope of getting it back. I understood now why he was so cautious of care. Touch was foreign to him, and this type of touch was foreign to me too. It would take time for our minds to process it, to understand what it was, what it meant, what to do with it.

Jonah urged my head to tilt back under the water, washing away the foam. I was thankful for the heated stream that ran over my face, even as it stung at the cuts, because I wasn't sure that everything trickling down my cheeks was water anymore.

His hands left me, and I remained where I was, secretly hoping they would find me again, and opening my eyes only when they didn't. I attempted to turn around. Jonah stopped me.

"Don't look for a second." He shoved my shoulder to turn me back around.

"Why can't I look?"

"Because. You just can't."

"What are you doing, Rabbit?"

"I'm... washing."

"Washing what?"

"None of your business," he snapped, and the defensiveness told me enough.

"You should let me do it."

"No!"

"I'll use my tongue." The sharp inhale behind me brought another smile to my lips. I dared to push him a little further. "Let me taste you, baby."

"I'm..." He took a steadying breath. "You mean... my dick?"

"Were you washing your dick?" I asked, already knowing the answer.

"No."

"Then that's not what I meant."

Jonah was silent, no doubt considering what I was offering, deciding whether he could let himself be that vulnerable with me.

"Just turn around, Rabbit. Put your hands on the wall."

More silence in response.

"Given I'm not allowed to look, you'll have to tell me when you've done that."

Jonah snapped, "I've done it!"

"And I can turn around now?"

A longer pause before he responded. "Yes."

I tried to keep my amusement to myself as I turned around, finding him exactly how I'd told him to be—his pale back exposed to me, lithe and toned, and his skin flushed pink from more than the temperature of the water. I trailed a fingertip between his shoulder blades before tracing down the curve of his spine, watching as the muscles reacted to me, rippling and shifting in anticipation.

Then I was on my knees. My hands cupped his firm cheeks, massaged them in appreciation. Jonah shivered under my touch, but he didn't tell me to stop or shift away, so I continued. Rough hands on smooth skin—kneading, squeezing, soothing. I spread his cheeks, revealing his hole, taking the chance to appreciate this part of him that had accepted me last night for the first time. Now it belonged to me and only me. All mine. Just like the rest of him.

I wasted no more time, diving in tongue first, and Jonah made a startled sound that morphed into a moan. He was stiff, trying to decide if he liked the new sensation or not, but the more my tongue lapped and stroked at his sensitive opening, the more he melted against the cool tiles of the shower wall, until his back was arching and he was tilting his ass toward me, offering himself to me, and seeking more of the sensations I was eager to give to him.

His legs quivered, and his breath was heavy, soft sounds leaving his perfect lips as I licked and probed, and when my tongue pressed lightly inside him, he cried out. I pressed in further, until my tongue was fucking him in shallow thrusts and Jonah was a whimpering mess. Using one hand to keep his cheeks spread for me, I let the other smooth between his thighs, fingertips tracing along the skin below where I was licking, then forward to cup his balls.

"Fuck," he whimpered. "Devil, mnn *fuck*."

"Like me eating you out, baby?" I asked between licks, his pretty hole twitching in need every time I abandoned it. "Like it when I taste what's mine?"

"Fuck, Dex."

Jonah's hips thrust forward, and I pulled back enough to see that one of his hands had left the wall and he was stroking himself off.

"That's mine too," I growled, grabbing his wrist and pulling his hand away. "You're not allowed to touch it."

"Please," he whined. "I need more, Dex, please."

I smiled. "Of course, baby. All you had to do was ask."

My hand replaced his, wrapping around his cock as he moaned again. Then I was picking up right where I'd left off, my tongue pressing as deep into him as I could manage.

With the dual sensations, it didn't take long before Jonah was coming, his voice high-pitched and needy, his cum shooting onto the shower floor as he twitched and clenched around my tongue. I didn't release him until he was shivering from overstimulation, his hips trying to pull away from me.

I placed a kiss on his cheek, then another, and then Jonah yelped as my teeth sunk into the firm curve of his ass, delivering a mark I couldn't resist leaving on that perfect skin. I sucked on the abused flesh, a beautiful bruise blooming to the surface. If only it were permanent.

I pulled myself up to my feet again and reached around him to turn off the water.

Jonah was still panting softly when I stepped out to get us towels, and when I returned to hand one to him, he was pouting. "What's that face for?" I asked him.

"I was supposed to be the one taking care of you."

"You did."

"Yeah, but then you..."

"I enjoyed it as much as you did, Rabbit."

His eyes glanced down at my dick, hard as steel and leaking for him, demanding attention that I was content not to give it.

"I could... try... to use my mouth on you... this time."

I stepped forward, placing a kiss on his forehead, which he responded to with another superficial scowl. "I appreciate the offer, baby, but I'd rather have this," I said, reaching around to grab a handful of the cheek now proudly wearing my mark.

It was the truth, but not the whole truth. I'd tell Jonah soon about why I was the way I was, and why there were things I was happy to give him but just couldn't enjoy receiving myself. But I didn't want the way he looked at me to change, so selfishly, I kept my secrets a while longer.

"Should I... put the jacket back on?" he asked, and my grin pulled wider.

"Definitely."

Jonah was still scowling, but he somehow also looked pleased as he toweled himself off quickly and reached for my jacket among our pile of discarded clothing. I'd clean them up later.

I laced my fingers through his and pulled him to my bed-room. This time, blissfully, there were no more objections.

Jonah fell onto the bed beside me, our skin still slightly damp, and naked except for my jacket on him. I claimed his lips. He kissed me back eagerly, tongue dancing with mine. He was bolder now than he used to be, more confident in what he was doing, and I loved it. I wanted him to always be confident in touching me. There was nothing he could do that I wouldn't like.

While we kissed, my hands trailed over him, finding all the hard edges and softer curves I adored. Perfect. All of him. When his hips rocked against mine, his cock was hard for me again. I pulled back from him to locate where we'd last abandoned the lube. It took a minute of aggressively pulling back blankets before I found it, then I was on him again, slick fingers seeking their new favorite place.

Jonah was softer for me this time, thanks to my efforts in the shower and him already knowing what to expect. One finger slipped in easily, Jonah pushing back to meet it with a whine, so I gave him another. When he'd adapted to two, I gave him three, and his tight, welcoming heat pulsed around the digits as he moaned into the skin of my neck.

I knew I'd found that spot he liked so much when he yelped out, fingers clawing into the skin at my waist. I targeted it. Jonah writhed in my arms, his hips wanting to both push against me harder and also pull away, chasing and evading the pleasure overwhelming his beautifully sensitive body.

"More," he gasped into my neck. "Need more, need you."

"Want my cock, little rabbit?"

Jonah nodded.

"Tell me, then. Tell me exactly what you want."

Jonah moaned, his grip on my skin tightening in his frustration. My hand stilled, leaving him full but without friction. His hips rocked, trying to chase it again, trying to spur me into movement without asking. My hold tightened to keep him still and unsatisfied.

With a long, exaggerated groan, he thunked his head roughly against my collarbone. "Just fuck me already, you dick."

"Now, now, that's not how you ask for something, is it?"

There was a displeased huff, and I thought he'd give in, but then his teeth were biting down roughly on the curve of my shoulder and I jolted with a groan. Sneaky rabbit.

My fingers slipped out of him and he whined softly, shifting onto his back, legs spread wide and ready for me, his face pink with his blush but a cocky smile on his lips like he thought he was about to get exactly what he wanted.

"You wanna play dirty, baby?" I smiled down at him, and his own smile turned downward into a pout. "Forget telling me what you want, now you're gonna have to scream it." I grabbed both of his hands, pulling them above his head until they pressed against the headboard of my bed. "If your hands leave this spot, I'm not fucking you tonight."

Before Jonah could reply, I was moving down his body again, my hands spreading his legs wider, and I swallowed his cock until my nose pressed against the neat curls at his base. He cried out, hips bucking up into my mouth, but his hands stayed exactly where I'd put them.

I moaned at the feeling of him in my mouth, my throat, the taste of him on my tongue. I sucked up to his tip, and plunged my fingers back inside him again, completely intending to overwhelm my little rabbit. My tongue piercing teased over his slit, then I took him to the back of my throat again, while my fingers pumped into him fast and hard.

"Fuck, *fuck!* Gonna... mnn..."

I stopped. My fingers left his opening, my mouth sucked off of his dick. Jonah sobbed, his hips stuttering, unsure if they wanted to chase the heat of my mouth or seek the lost fingers. His cock and hole both twitched in need. He made another sound, desperate and needy, as his orgasm retreated, the peak of his pleasure ripped away from him before he could obtain it. "Fuck you," he panted.

"Not with that attitude," I smirked, nipping at his inner thigh.

"Nng. You're the worst!" he told me with a heated glare, but his hands were still on the headboard because he still wanted me to fuck him.

"Mhmm," I hummed in agreement, nipping at his skin again.

When his body relaxed again and the need to come wasn't so urgent, I returned to my tasks without warning, my fingers and mouth resuming their attack. Again, I played with his body until he was right on the edge, muscles quivering with tension, and *again* I denied him, pulling away seconds before he found relief.

He was panting, sweating, his eyes glassy with tears of pleasure and frustration.

"*Devil*," he panted like an insult.

"Rabbit."

I did it again, and this time when I stopped before he could climax, he was trembling all over, making the sounds of something wounded. "Fucking fuck!" he cried out. "Please." Sweet surrender. "Please, p-please, *please* make me come. Please d-don't tease me anymore."

"Good boy." I took him to the back of my throat and slipped four fingers into his hole, the extra stretch making him cry out again. This time when I felt him tense with the need to release I didn't stop him, letting him coat my mouth and throat with his cum, swallowing down my reward greedily.

Pulling off, I took a moment to appreciate the blissed-out expression on his face. Wet strands of his hair clung to his sweaty face, but he didn't move them, because his hands were still where I'd put them.

I shuffled off the bed to locate the box of condoms, which had tumbled to the floor during our activities, then I was on my knees between Jonah's still-parted thighs.

He was a vision. Skin flushed and damp from sex. Naked apart from my jacket. His chest still heaved as he caught his breath. His relaxed cock still wet with my spit. His hole stretched and glistening with lube. Beautiful.

I'd let him recover before we continued, his hands still on the headboard telling me he wanted to, except when I put the condoms on the bed beside him he frowned at them.

"Do we need to use those?" he asked me.

"I always do," I told him, and his expression soured into a glare before I continued. "But we don't have to."

"Really? You've never fucked anyone without one?"

How did I answer that without revealing too much? "Whenever I've chosen to fuck someone before, I've worn one."

"So I'll be your first at something, then." He smiled, and like a knife twisting in my chest, I wished he could have been.

"I'll get tested, and when we're all clear, we can go without them," I told him instead of acknowledging his words. Guilt that I kept chained in the depths of me seeped to the surface.

Jonah pouted, brow furrowing. Rather than let him dwell on my words, I opted for distracting him. "Want to feel my cum filling you up, baby? Want me to mark your insides with it?"

It worked. Jonah inhaled sharply, his spent cock twitching against his thigh, and I decided to see just how many orgasms he was capable of in one night. "Turn around, Rabbit. Present that pretty ass to me and show me what's mine."

Jonah bit his lip, but he did as I asked, turning on shaky thighs. It was a little awkward as he was determined to keep his hands in place. He didn't need to; he'd get what he wanted either way, but I didn't tell him that.

I reached for the condoms, already eager for the day soon when I could take him without one, to feel him and only him. It wasn't like I even slept around that much. I didn't have concerns that I had anything I could give him, but I wouldn't risk him. I'd promised my rabbit I would never hurt him again, and I intended to keep that promise.

His hole was still stretched, still shiny with lube, but I added more over the condom. His cock hung heavy between pale thighs, half hard, and I used the excess lube on my hand to stroke him, feeling him plump up for me again until he was a mewling mess—hands still on the headboard, face buried in my pillow, and ass raised and presented to me.

I didn't wait any longer, lining myself up and pressing completely into his heat in one thrust. His body welcomed me, tight and warm and perfect. I didn't give him any time to adjust, my hips pulling out to slam back in like an attack, with a passion so much sweeter than violence.

My thumbs spread his cheeks, smoothing over that pretty mark I'd left behind in the shower, so I could watch where we were joined as my cock pistoned in and out of him. "Fuck you're beautiful. Your ass is swallowing my cock so perfectly, baby."

Jonah seemed incapable of stringing words together to respond, his voice muffled and hoarse as he practically screamed into the pillow with every thrust. Harder and faster, until his hands made the headboard slam against the wall every time I drove into him.

Thwack, thwack, thwack.

An increasing tempo as I gave him everything I had left. Harder. Faster. Until the room was filled with the sounds of the bed against the wall, Jonah's cries, my grunts, and the slick, sharp sound of our skin slapping together.

Jonah convulsed around me, his body giving out as he came a third time, and my hands gripping his hips hard enough to bruise stopped him from collapsing into the puddle of his cum until I groaned, releasing deep inside him.

I fell onto him, but he didn't seem to mind, turning his head to the side to find me, and I pressed a firm kiss to his sweaty temple.

"You're heavy," he panted.

"Want me to get off you?"

"No." After a moment, he added, "Jacket off."

I smiled. "Okay, baby." I pushed myself up, my hips pulling back until his hand shot out to stop me from withdrawing any further.

"Stay. Just the jacket."

"Okay." I placed another kiss to his hair before helping him wriggle out of the leather jacket—a slightly awkward task when he didn't want me pulling out of him, but we made it work—and I cast the jacket to the floor as I returned to him, my body over his, and he sighed in contentment.

Once our breathing returned to normal, I could feel the exhaustion pull at me, threatening to take me under into sleep. With a groan, I pulled back. Jonah grumbled unhappily as I slipped out of him, but he didn't stop me this time.

I left the room for as brief a time as possible, returning with a cup of water and a warm cloth. Jonah's eyes were closed, and I gently nudged him awake. "Sit up for a second."

He wasn't happy about it, but he listened, shuffling up enough for me to pull the blanket stained with his cum off the bed. I cleaned him up, then handed him the water to drink as I stripped the bedding, replacing it with new linen from my wardrobe.

"Why are your cups plastic?" Jonah asked as he put the cup back on the nightstand.

Because they hurt less when my mother throws them at my head, I thought. But to Jonah, I shrugged.

30

Dex - Past

KILL LIST.

— ✦ —

Jonah spent the night again, waking up in my arms, his body shuffling closer to soak up more of my heat. I huffed softly in amusement, and he tensed, realizing I was awake.

"Ugh. You're totally a morning person, aren't you?" he groaned into my skin.

"Mhmm. But I'm also a Jonah person. Means I get to just lie here and watch you sleep and listen to your cute little grumbles."

He pulled away from me. "I do not grumble in my sleep!"

"You do. You snore too, just a little."

"No I don't!" he argued, apparently very offended by the simple fact.

"No? Record yourself sleeping, do you? Or sharing a bed with anyone else who can verify?"

Jonah huffed, stealing the blanket and rolling away from me, probably because he couldn't think of an argument.

"I don't mind, Rabbit," I told him as I followed him, wrapping my arm around his waist and pulling him in close so he couldn't escape from me further. "It's cute."

"I'm *not* cute."

"Baby, you're *very* cute."

He tried to wriggle out of my hold, but I just tightened it around him. His struggle rocked his ass back into my hips, and he stilled when he felt what was waiting for him there.

"You're especially cute when you're crying from the pleasure I'm giving you." Jonah's breath shuddered, and he rocked his hips back into me again, all attempts at retreat apparently abandoned in favor of feeling my cock against him.

"Prove it," he breathed out, rocking against me again, and I would do just that.

◆

"You're late again," Roy said from the desk as I strolled in.

"Sorry," I told him, and I meant it.

I tried to get here on time, but Jonah had been staying with me every night for the past week and a half now. We hadn't talked about it, he'd just text me to ask what I was doing, I'd tell him I was home, and shortly after he'd be there, falling into my bed with me. I'd fuck him until he cried, and then sometimes I'd fuck him again. Then we would sleep, and when we both woke up, we'd fuck again.

I'd gotten tested, and I expected the results back either today or tomorrow. Just the thought of being able to take my rabbit raw, with truly nothing between us, to mark him with my cum, it made my dick firm up in my jeans.

Roy huffed. "Honestly, son, I'm glad."

"You're glad I'm late to work? Kind of a shitty work ethic, boss."

He rolled his eyes. "I'm not glad you're late, smart ass. But you're late 'cause you got somewhere else you'd rather be 'sides here with me. It's good for ya."

"Don't go getting sentimental on me now, Daddy Roy. It'll ruin your grumpy reputation."

I was deflecting. I didn't know what to do with the warmth his words filled my chest with. Didn't know how to express whatever these feelings were.

Roy seemed to understand. "Parts you ordered came in," he told me, thankfully changing the subject.

"Fuck yes." I smiled, taking my gear to the locker so I could get started on the day and hopefully still be able to finish up early enough to work on my personal project.

Two years ago, a customer had brought in a 2004 Jeep Cherokee with a blown transmission. She didn't have the funds to repair it, so Roy had taken pity on her and offered to buy it from her instead. Since then, the car had sat out the back of the garage completely neglected and almost forgotten about. When I offered to buy it off Roy, he'd given it to me.

Sourcing a brand new transmission would cost more than the thing was worth, but I'd managed to find a replacement at a scrapyard and had it delivered to the shop. The old girl wasn't too pretty, but she'd be functional when I was done with her, and that's all she needed to be. I hoped Jonah would like her.

He walked everywhere despite the pain his leg obviously gave him, but he didn't complain about it or seek an alternative. Maybe that would feel like admitting he had a weakness. I wasn't sure if he even knew how to drive, and I hadn't told him about the car yet, but if he didn't know, I could teach him.

I got home a little later than usual, having spent some time on the Cherokee. When I walked in, I heard noises from the kitchen and followed them to see my rabbit attempting to cook... something. Something that had definitely already passed the stage of "cooked" and was well on the way to becoming charcoal.

"What you doing there, Rabbit?" I asked him from the doorway.

Of all the rooms in this house, I hated the kitchen most. It was better now than it used to be, and it certainly helped that Mom hadn't been home in so long, but I still spent as little time here as possible. Even though the floor and walls had been scrubbed clean so many times, until my hands ached and the tile was shining, sometimes I could still see the blood.

"Cooking," he grumbled, glaring at the frying pan. "Or... trying to. Why are you late?"

"Work project," I told him, not exactly a lie.

"Well, if you'd gotten home on time, maybe it wouldn't have burned."

"Ah, so it's my fault. I see." I smiled, leaving my post in the doorway to approach him. My finger hooked the back of his jeans as I yanked him into me, trapping him within my arms. "In that case, I'll order in for us, to make it up to you."

Jonah sighed softly as he leaned into me, and I inhaled his scent deep into my lungs. He used my soap, my shampoo, but it smelled so different on him. Better.

"It's only fair." He shivered when my lips found the curve of his neck.

Just as I was about to tell Jonah that maybe I'd just have rabbit for dinner instead, my phone rang in my back pocket. I sighed, still keeping him close to me as I retrieved it. Only when I saw the name on the screen did I pull back and step away.

"Hey, little Cupid, how's my favorite Stray?" I asked, only because I loved the way Jonah glared at me. I loved seeing him jealous, possessive. Adorable. I wanted him to always be like that—needy and demanding, entirely unreasonable.

"Coyote," said a voice on the other end of the call, far too deep and Hungarian to be Cupid.

My smile faded. "Bull. Where's Cupid?"

"Injured."

"Yeah, the man of few words and many grunts routine is fine under normal circumstances, but I'm going to need more from you than that."

"Drakes attacked him pretty badly. You can handle it?"

"I can. Have you called Wolf?"

"Unavailable." That was becoming a pattern with Archer.

"Name?"

"Petrov brothers, and Bates."

"Of course it was fucking Bates." My fists clenched in rage; that particular motherfucker was becoming an increasingly large pain in my ass. Cupid wasn't even a fighter, he just peddled drugs, and not even well. To have three of them rough him up... something wasn't right. Then again, looking the way Cupid did was probably enough of an offense to trigger tiny-brained Mason Bates. "Alright, I'm on it. He's alright, though?"

"He'll live."

"Thanks for the reassurance, Doc. I'll keep you updated."

I ended the call, turning to see Jonah scowling at me. "Sorry, Rabbit. Why don't you order something? I'll eat while I'm out."

"Where are you going?"

"I've got some business to take care of."

"With that homophobic piece of shit?"

I gave him a strained smile. "Unfortunately."

"Fine. Go fuck him up." Jonah crossed his arms over his chest. "Just don't fucking lick him this time."

I laughed. "I promise."

"And... Cupid?" He said the name as if it tasted bitter on his tongue.

"Just a friend. I promise."

"Have you ever—"

"Just a friend, Rabbit." I cut him off, because I *had*. Just once. But Cupid was rarely sober when I saw him lately, and I wasn't getting involved with that. "Will you wait for me here?"

Jonah nodded, that familiar pout on his lips.

"I'll be as quick as I can, Rabbit."

"'Kay, just be careful."

"I will, baby," I assured him, stealing his lips in a kiss that promised far more than I could deliver right now. I pulled back before I could get too caught up in him, stepping away to unlock my phone and text Bryce, Raven, and begrudgingly, Reaper.

I normally would have messaged Toby, but we still hadn't spoken since the last fight night, and I wasn't sure I wouldn't try to deck him again on sight. Supposedly Archer was dealing with him, but I doubted that. Archer wasn't transphobic, to my knowledge, but he was still in the closet with his sexuality and not exactly an outspoken ally. He kept his voice to Strays business only, and even that was enough to keep him highly strung and on edge at all times as it was. Stick a lump of coal up Archer's ass and in a week you'd have a diamond.

It didn't take long for us to locate Bates and the Petrov brothers. The Drakes had a few regular hangouts in Deltran, Molly's being one of them. It was a prohibition-style speakeasy, with low lighting and lots of dark corners for whatever shifty business the Drakes dealt with here. It was unofficially their territory. While it wasn't gang owned, the Drakes held a regular presence here—enough that when I walked in with Bryce, Raven, and Reaper, the atmosphere grew cold and voices quieted down.

The fuckhead trio were still together, but there were two others with them too. We were outnumbered by one, but I still liked our odds. Bryce was our weakest link. Reaper could hold his own even against me, and Raven was both our fastest rider and fighter, definitely enough to make up for what she lacked in strength.

Mason fucking Bates smiled, like he was happy to see us.

"That didn't take long, did it? Should have known the bitch would go crying to the other homos right away." He spoke loud enough for us and everyone else in the bar to hear.

I smiled at him—a deceptively calm surface. Like the ocean with its raging, unknowable depths, sharks swam beneath my skin, and there was blood in the water. "Why don't we step outside, Budget Hulk? This is a lovely establishment, and I'd hate to ruin it with all the blood."

"Your blood, asswipe."

"Witty. Guess that's expected when you have steroids instead of brain cells."

"At least I'm not a cocksucker."

"Hmm... you think about my sex life a little too much. Kind of suspicious, don't you think?" I turned to Raven.

Dark-painted lips pulled into a smirk. "Definitely suspicious," she agreed.

Mason stood up with enough force that the table in front of him rattled and his drink tipped over, beer spilling over the edge and onto the floor. Fucking idiot. I turned and left the bar, my crew following me. Reaper seemed pissed, Bryce offended, and Raven amused.

The Drakes stepped outside a moment later, and Mason didn't even take one moment to think before his fists were swinging. He came straight for me, as I'd hoped. I was here for vengeance for one of our own, but it was deeper than that. This fight felt personal. This wasn't like fight nights; there was no referee to call the match before things got too serious, no crowd cheering. It wasn't sport. It was violence, plain and simple, and it would end only when one of us couldn't get back up again, whatever form that took.

For a big guy, the meathead was quick.

I didn't have a chance to check in with my people, which meant I'd just have to deal with this sasquatch first.

First punch, and I dodged. Second punch, and he didn't. My fist connected with his ribs. But he was a big guy, and one hit was hardly going to knock him back. His elbow collided with my jaw, and I tasted blood, but I wasn't easily knocked back either, and I was on him again, knuckles bruising skin.

We traded blows, blood spilled on both sides. The metallic taste in my mouth was like a drug. Fuel. I hit him again, and my fist came away with our blood combined, red gushing from his lips down his chin. I had this. Mason fucking Bates was going down.

A sharp cry to my left and I spared Raven the briefest of glances, not wanting to give Mason any advantage by being distracted—but it was enough to notice with our uneven numbers, *two* of them had gone for her. Should have figured the fucking Drakes would gang up on who they saw to be our weakest link. One of them shoved her into the bricks.

The flurry of other fights and bodies slamming into each other faded when a fist slammed into the side of my head hard enough for my vision to blur and my ears to ring with the force of it.

As I stumbled backward, losing and finding my feet again, Mason took the chance to deliver another. I raised my arm fast enough to cushion the blow, but it still sent me staggering back further.

Raven made a wounded sound, and despite Mason boxing me in, I was determined to get to her. He swung, I dropped, his fist catching the air above me as I took the lower ground, landing a hit to his gut, then my boot kicked at his knee. He shouted and stumbled, giving me the out I needed to get to Raven.

I cocked my arm back to take a swing at one brute attacking her, but before it landed, a fist was in my hair dragging me back. I spat. Red landed on the cheek of the guy pinning her to the wall, who turned to look at me, giving Raven an opening as she kneed him in the balls.

Mason's grip left my hair, only for his arm to circle my neck. I clawed at him, but the bastard wouldn't budge. I attempted to elbow him, to take out his feet with mine. No luck. His arm tightened, the headlock stealing away my oxygen until heat flushed over my face, my lungs burned, my vision blurred.

As I faded, I took in the carnage surrounding us. Raven on someone's back, inflicting a headlock of her own. Bryce on the ground, straddled, but still fighting. And Reaper, the last thing I saw before I faded was Reaper, a knife in his hand as it plunged into the gut of one of the Petrov brothers.

When I opened my eyes again, it was to Raven shaking my shoulder frantically. "Come on, Dexy, we gotta bounce, dude."

I sucked in a breath that felt like inhaling fire, my hands finding the pavement as I pushed myself up. The Drakes were no longer here, but I couldn't have been out for more than a few minutes at most.

I quickly accounted for my own: Raven, her nose probably broken, but otherwise she seemed fine; Bryce, who stood just behind her, with an eye already swelling shut; and Reaper, leaning against the brick, blood on his hands and his clothes.

"Status?" I croaked.

Reaper looked up at me with cold, dead eyes and a blank expression on his pale features. "Scurried off into their cave. One unconscious."

"You stabbed him."

"Had to."

"You didn't have to. Fuck, Reaper. If you've killed him, it's an all-out war."

He shrugged one shoulder. "He was breathing when they ran off."

"That isn't good enough."

"Who the *fuck* put you in charge anyway?"

I stumbled toward him, my fingers grasping handfuls of his dark clothing. "You think because Archer isn't here you can just do whatever the fuck you want?"

His jaw ticked. "You think because Archer isn't here you're automatically the one in charge? You aren't. I don't have to listen to a fucking thing you say."

Using the grip on his clothing I shoved him until his back pressed against the wall. One of his hands wrapped around my wrist, and as the heat in my eyes clashed with the ice in his, I had a pretty good idea of where his other hand was.

"Going to stab me too?" My voice was low but firm.

He didn't answer, but the way his jaw ticked told me I was right. He was either bluffing to get me to back down, or the sick fuck had actually thought about using that knife in his hand against me.

"Try it," I threatened.

"For fuck's sake, that's enough." Raven appeared beside us, a hand on each of our chests as she shoved us apart. "Why are boys so fucking stupid? You dumbasses are on the same side here."

Despite the feisty woman between us, neither of us was willing to break eye contact first. Not until Raven clasped my tender jaw in her hand and forced my face in her direction. "Enough."

I could see it in her eyes, beneath the exhaustion. The fear. I nodded and she sighed in relief.

When I looked back at Reaper that coldness had been replaced by something far more intense. He said nothing as he glared at me, then Raven, then turned and shouldered passed Bryce as he walked off and left us.

"You sure you're not interested in him?" I scoffed when he was out of ear shot.

"Not even if he had the last dick on earth. Now let's fucking go."

"Yeah, yeah."

Once we made it to the bikes, I reached into my pocket for my keys, only to come up empty. My heart sank to my gut, lower. They were gone. *Everything* was gone. My keys, wallet, phone, and... my father's lighter.

"Who took my shit?" I asked through clenched teeth.

"Bates, probably. He was the only one with you. We were a little preoccupied with the others," Raven answered.

My head was already pounding as I tried to make sense of that. I don't know what he thought he'd gain from taking shit that had no value to him, but Mason fucking Bates was officially on my kill list.

There were sirens in the distance, growing louder, closer. "We have to fucking go, we can get your shit back later, Dex."

Bryce and Raven lingered anxiously for the time it took to hot-wire Delilah. I gave her a silent apology for the treatment, and then we were off, heading away from the noise and the lights and back to Port Skelton.

By the time I pulled up at the house, I was fucking exhausted. I needed to find Mason. I needed my shit back. I had spare keys for my house and bike inside, and I could replace everything in my wallet. I'd even be okay if I couldn't get Dad's phone back. But there was no replacement for that lighter.

JONAH - PAST

YOU COULD NEVER HURT ME.

It was late when I finally heard the familiar sound of Dex's motorcycle roaring down the street and into the driveway. I felt stupid just waiting around for him to get back. I wasn't sure if I should head back to Dad's or stay here. If I stayed here, was I supposed to wait up or go to bed? What would he expect me to be doing?

The longer the night dragged on without him returning, the more my anxiety over what I should be doing faded to anxiety over what he was doing. The phone call had revealed three names: Cupid, Bull, and fucking Bates. Bates was the more pressing concern. I didn't know what Dex dealing with him meant—how much danger he'd be putting himself in.

Bull didn't seem like much of a threat, but Cupid—*"my favorite Stray"*—I didn't like him, not one bit. I knew Dex well enough to know it couldn't have been Bryce, or Archer, certainly not Toby. Henrik was Hound, and Raven was... well, Raven. So who was Cupid? How many more of them were there? *Doesn't matter,* I tried to tell myself. I really did. But my mind kept circling back. I wasn't stupid. I knew Dex had slept with other people before me. Probably a lot of other people.

Every time I thought about it, I was filled with this big ugly feeling that scratched at my insides and made me feel reckless.

Like there was anything I could do to change his past. I knew it shouldn't have mattered, really I did, but I hated that other people had seen him how I'd seen him. Felt his touch like I'd felt his touch.

It wasn't rational for me to be mad about him fucking people before he even met me, but I wasn't rational and he knew that. So this was on him.

So there was that, and there was the increasing worry that something had happened to him and that's why he hadn't come home to me.

Hearing his bike alleviated the latter, and I was ready to be unreasonable about the former when he walked in. Only, when I caught sight of him, it all vanished. All thoughts of being intentionally difficult so he could prove yet again why he wanted only me faded. Because he was hurt.

"What the fuck happened?" I asked, on him before the front door was even fully closed. His eyebrow was split, so was his lip, his cheek was puffy and bruised, and there was bruising on his neck.

"I'm fine, Rabbit," he sighed, but as my hands cupped his face, he melted into the touch. Like my hands alone could soothe away all the hurt.

I held him there, my thumb lightly tracing over his cheek. "You have a first aid kit?"

"I'm fine, reall—"

"Do you have a first aid kit?" I snapped again.

"Bathroom."

"Okay." I nodded, reaching for his hand, threading my fingers between his and pulling him upstairs to the bathroom.

"Under the sink," he sighed, after I'd forced him to sit down on the closed toilet seat and looked at him expectantly.

I opened the cabinet, located it, and pulled it out, placing it on the bathroom counter to go through its contents. I'd had enough scrapes and cuts when I'd tripped on the running track over the years, which I'd tended to myself in the school's medical bay. It wasn't the same, but I was sure I could make it work.

"Clothes off," I told him, my tone leaving no room for argument. "I need to see where you're hurt."

Dex was quiet. Too quiet. He did what I asked, shedding his clothing piece by piece, revealing more bruises and evidence of what he'd been through. I watched his face when he winced slightly, indicating more soreness beneath the surface.

I started up the shower for him, and he stepped into it, washing off the surface grime and dried blood as I pulled what I wanted out of the first aid kit. Some things were empty, others mostly used up, and I wondered if he often came home like this and patched himself up. I hated the thought of anyone else being here to do it for him, but I found the thought of him doing it alone much worse. My throat tightened, somehow already knowing he had. He wouldn't have to anymore. I was here now. I could do it for him.

Dex stepped out, and I handed him a towel. He was still silent as he dried off and sat back down.

I started by applying antiseptic to his split and bruised knuckles, which must have stung the open wounds, but he didn't react. Then the antibiotic ointment. Then I wrapped them in gauze bandages. Next I took care of his lip, with the antiseptic and ointment. His eyebrow was still bleeding slightly, so after the ointment I pulled the split skin together with a closure strip. There wasn't much I could do for the bruising. "Got an ice pack or any ice?"

He shook his head softly.

I cupped the cheek that wasn't swollen gently in my hand. He turned into it, placing a kiss on my palm.

It occurred to me now just how different we were when it came to certain things like pain. When I was in pain, I was mean. I snapped at anyone who got close to me. I got loud and demanded attention because the ones who were supposed to take care of me weren't there. When Dex was in pain, he was quiet. He made himself smaller, and I had to wonder what that meant about the people who were supposed to have taken care of him.

I ran my thumb over the healed scar on his eyebrow, just next to the new split.

"What's this from?" I asked softly, wanting to know all of his scars, so that I could know all of him.

"I used to have an eyebrow piercing," he answered, just as quietly.

"And?"

"And now I don't."

I sighed, understanding that he didn't want to offer any more information about it right now, and I wouldn't push him for it. Instead, I reached for the hairbrush on the counter, gently pulling the long wet strands of his hair back out of his face before I started to brush them.

His eyes closed, head tilting back as I pulled gently through the locks. I'd never brushed anyone's hair before but my own, but it was nice. I found it soothing, and I hoped he did too.

Except when I looked at his face again, his eyes weren't closed anymore. He was staring at me. Pale eyes. Ice that melted. Pools of emotion that welled until he couldn't hold it all in anymore and he sobbed as they flowed over. Tears cascaded down his cheeks.

His hands found my waist, and he pulled me in, burying his face in my shirt, letting it soak up his sadness. I hugged him as best I could from my standing position.

"I lost it." Words muffled by fabric, but still they sounded so broken. Distraught.

"What did you lose, baby?"

He cried harder. I held him, waiting patiently for him to let it out. When he was done, there was a damp patch on the front of my shirt, but I didn't care.

"I lost my father's lighter." His voice was low and rough.

"Lost it where?"

"Bates."

My fists clenched. "We'll get it back," I promised him, and it *was* a promise. I didn't know how, but I knew that I'd get it back for him if it was the last thing I did.

He nodded, pulling me closer again.

"Let's go to bed."

He sniffed and nodded, getting to his feet and following me to the bedroom.

"Can I use your phone?"

"Where's yours?" I asked, but I handed it to him anyway.

"He took that too."

Well, I'd be getting that back as well. Dex opened my browser, typing something in as I got undressed. At Dad's I'd just toss my clothes onto the floor, not caring about them until they needed to be washed so I could wear them again, but here I noticed Dex would often clean up after me in the morning before heading to work, so I put my clothes in the hamper instead.

The air in the bedroom was cold, and I wanted to steal as much of his warmth as he'd allow, and whatever else he wanted to give me tonight.

A smile pulled at his lips, and he handed the phone back to me. I glanced at the screen.

> **Port Skelton Medical Clinic Patient Portal. Patient: Dexter Ian Weller.**
>
> *Your recent STI panel returned with no abnormalities. No follow-up is required at this time. If you have ongoing symptoms or concerns, please contact your provider.*

I felt my cheeks heat.

"Get the lube for me," he requested.

"You're hurt."

"Just... please."

I switched the screen off, placing my phone down on the nightstand and picking up the bottle of lube as I walked over to Dex and placed it in his hand. He put it on the bed next to him, shuffled back, and patted his thigh.

"Dex. You're hurt."

"I'm *fine*."

I eyed him doubtfully, even if my cock was immediately on board with this idea. Dex just looked at me expectantly, patting his thigh again, firmer this time as if I hadn't understood what he wanted when he last did it.

Carefully, I climbed onto the bed, straddling him, watching his face closely to make sure he wasn't in any pain and trying to keep most of my weight on the bed on either side of him. Dex was having none of it, his hands finding my ass and yanking me firmly into him until our hard dicks pressed together and I sucked in a sharp breath at the feel of him.

"Kiss me," he demanded.

"But your lip—"

"Kiss. Me."

I did, cautious of the split, but he pressed his lips against mine firmly, clearly not having the same concern. His tongue licked over my lips, pressing inside, coaxing mine out, and I was helpless to deny him. I melted into him, the taste of him overriding all my thoughts until his hands left my hips and I heard the cap of the lube bottle opening. I'd finally get to feel him and only him, with nothing else between us.

I relaxed, knowing what was coming next, and his fingers found my hole, probing at the soft muscle. Two slipped inside, and I groaned at the feel of them.

"Rabbit." Dex's voice was stern, threatening, but there was a curve to his lips that made me feel warm inside, because that was how his lips should always be. Smiling. I pulled back so I could see it properly. "What did you do?"

So, I may have had a shower while I was waiting for him, and in said shower I may have decided to clean up ahead of him getting back, and may have gotten carried away with that. In my defense, I didn't think he'd be able to tell. But as he pressed a third finger inside, it was clear my body was accepting him faster than when he usually prepped me.

"Have you been playing with what's mine?"

"I was just, mnn, getting ready for you."

"Naughty little rabbit. I should punish you for that."

"Punish... how?" My fingers dug into his shoulders unconsciously, and I realized only when I saw the soft wince that flickered over his features. "Stop," I said, trying to pull away from him, but he just held me tighter.

"I need you, Rabbit. Need to feel you. It doesn't matter if it hurts me."

I sighed. "Lie down, then, at least."

"But I need to punish you."

"Punish me tomorrow."

"But I can still have you?"

"Yes. But only if you lie down."

He sighed, as if I was being unreasonable. I could be, I knew that, but I thought this time it was entirely called for. Dex released me, shuffling back on the bed until his head was on the pillows. Most of his injuries were on the same side. I could have tried riding him, but I wasn't sure my leg wouldn't fuck it up, and potentially having to change positions after I'd just demanded that already felt entirely too embarrassing.

Instead, I crawled onto the bed and lay beside him, and right away he curled into me, his body a blanket of warmth on my back, his lips trailing kisses along my neck. "Is this okay?" I asked him.

"Yes," he whispered against my skin.

"You're sure it doesn't hurt?"

"I'm sure, Rabbit."

"Okay, but if it hurts, tell me and we—*ah*!" His fingers plunged back into my body suddenly, and my sentence devolved into a moan. "Fuck."

"Lube."

I stalled for a moment before realizing that was a request and reaching for the bottle, handing it to him. His fingers pulled out of me to take it.

I expected them to push back in again, but his slippery hand found my cock instead, stroking me slowly. So slowly it was more frustrating than pleasurable. "Please, Dex."

"Call me baby again."

I groaned, debating whether I should give in, before his grip on my cock tightened and stilled to show he wasn't fucking around.

"Such a dick."

"Mmn, close. I think you meant to say, 'Please can I have your dick, baby?'"

I bit my bottom lip, not wanting to give in, but as his hips rocked forward and I felt the slippery sensation of his cock along my crease, the stubbornness inside me receded to make room for desperation.

"Please can I have your dick?" I grumbled. And when he made no movement at all, I added in a much quieter voice, "Baby."

He chuckled softly, warm breath over my ear, before stroking my length a couple of times. Then his hands withdrew. "Of course you can, baby."

He sounded entirely too smug about it, but I couldn't bring myself to care when I felt the slick tip of his cock against my opening and the metal of his piercing. I relaxed for him, the pressure increasing as I bore down and he slipped inside.

Dex kissed gently along the back of my shoulders, and I tilted my head for him, enjoying the softer touches and the increasing fullness as he gradually eased deeper.

Once he was fully inside me, his hips pressed firmly against my ass, his hand found my cock again. This time he stroked me holding nothing back.

"Gonna come... too fast... if you do that."

"So come. I know you have more than one in you anyway."

His hips withdrew and thrust back inside, the glide of his length and the feeling of the piercing so much better without the usual barrier between us.

I had no doubt he could make me come again, but I still tried to hold out as long as possible. It was a losing battle right from the start when his thrusts increased in speed along with his hand on my dick, working in tandem. Then the bastard bit my neck, hard, and I was helpless to stop the cry that escaped me, my cock exploding in his hand as my body convulsed around him.

Total bliss overwhelmed my senses as the waves of pleasure pulsed through me, his thrusts slowing but never stopping. Dex kissed the mark he'd left on my neck softly, his hand leaving my oversensitive cock to run his fingers through the mess I'd made on my stomach.

Fingers slicked with lube and cum smoothed over my chest, tweaking my nipples and making me jolt against him again. His tongue traced the shell of my ear. "That's it, baby. Made such a mess for me. But you're gonna make more, aren't you?"

His hand traveled higher, over my collarbones, my neck... and then two wet fingers were tracing over my lips. Gently. Experimentally. Waiting to see if I'd part them for him. I did.

I was possessed by the devil, and I'd do anything he wanted me to—including, apparently, tasting my own fucking cum on his fingers. I didn't want to like it, would never even have thought to try it, but as his fingers slid over my tongue and the saltiness of my pleasure filled my senses, I groaned, my cock already twitching again.

"Perfect, baby. So good for me." His low voice rumbled in my ear, so close it felt like a physical thing. The vibrations of it tingled over my skin and down my spine, and made me clench around him. He groaned, causing the same reaction in me again. "Fuck, you're so perfect."

All I could respond with was a whimper around his fingers, my tongue slipping between them.

"Gonna fuck you hard now," he warned me, and I nodded, his fingers slipping out of my mouth so his hand could circle my neck instead—not hard enough to cut off my air, just enough to feel the pressure of him there, for him to keep me perfectly in place as he pulled his hips back and slammed in again fast and hard.

I pushed back against him, trying to keep up with his thrusts, but with the feeling of his piercing rubbing my over-sensitive prostate making me jolt and squirm, his hand had to leave my throat to grip my hip and keep me where he wanted me. All I could do was lie there and take it as he chased his own pleasure.

"Fuck. Ready to feel me fill you up, baby? Ready for my cum inside you?"

"Yes," I cried out. "Pl—*fuck*—please."

My cock was iron-hard again, and as his thrusts picked up speed—no longer a steady rhythm but a race toward the finish line—I stroked myself quickly, crying out pathetic noises into his pillow.

Dex groaned next to my ear, slick warmth erupting deep inside me, and I moaned as I came for the second time, adding to the puddle over the front of myself and the blankets.

We were both panting, covered in sweat and sex. His arm wrapped around my center, pulling me in closer, so there weren't any gaps between us, and we lay like that until the chill of the night air on our drying skin had me shivering. Dex tried to pull back, but my hand shot to his hip to stop him. "Can we stay like this?"

"You want to sleep like this?"

I nodded, and even in the dark of the room, I knew he could see it.

"You're sure?" he asked, and I nodded again. "You want me like this? Inside? While we sleep? You're absolutely sure?"

"Yes, I'm sure!" I said, trying not to snap. I liked having him close to me, especially when we were sleeping, and there was no getting closer than we were right now. Dex's hand left me as he grabbed for the blanket, pulling it over us. I knew we needed to shower, but I didn't care. I was tired, and so was he.

"Are you hurt?" I asked once we settled in, his arm wrapping around me again.

"No, baby." He placed a kiss to my temple. "You could never hurt me."

32

JONAH - PAST

BOOTS.

✦

I woke up with Dex still inside me. He was wrapped around me as if he was shielding my body from some unknown thing. His cock was hard, and so was mine. I considered whether it would be acceptable for me to rock myself back into him and fuck myself on his dick until he woke up and fucked me again properly.

Before I could reach a decision, a small noise left him as his body tensed behind me.

"Are you awake?" I whispered.

He didn't respond.

"Dex?"

I wondered whether he was dreaming, and if so, was it a sex dream? Was it about me?

He made another sound—quiet, choked, *pained.*

"Dex?" I asked again, a little louder this time. I winced as I peeled his arm off me and rolled to face him, his cock slipping out of me. It was still dark, and I could hardly see his features.

He mumbled something in response I couldn't quite make out.

"Devil?" My hand smoothed over the skin of his shoulder, finding it heated and damp with sweat. Any remaining tiredness evaporated in an instant, concern taking its place. I rocked him gently.

"No," he choked out.

"Dex, what's wrong? Talk to me, please."

"No! Stop it!"

"It's a dream," I told him, shaking him harder. "It's just a bad dream, baby, wake up."

He sobbed, his body trying to twist away from me, but I didn't let him, determined to wake him up from his nightmare. Then he gasped sharply, his breathing coming in short and sharp and far too fast.

"Are you awake?" I asked again, my hands still rubbing his arms in an attempt to soothe him.

He sobbed and flinched again in response.

"I'm here. I have you."

"—oots."

"What?"

"Boots."

Boots means no. I pulled back, taking my hands off him even though all my instincts screamed at me to hold him together while he was breaking apart. Heat prickled behind my eyes. I didn't understand was happening, why he'd used our safeword for something as simple as my hands on his shoulders. But he didn't want me to touch him right now, so I wouldn't, despite how badly I wanted to. *What did I do wrong?*

"L-lamp," he choked out, and I scrambled to the nightstand to switch it on for him.

Warm light flooded the room, and I took him in. He wasn't looking at me, his head tilted back to look at the bedroom wall.

"Baby, please look at me."

He didn't. His face was wet, tears streaming steadily from the corners of his eyes as he kept them focused on the wall.

What was happening? What did I do? *How do I help?*

Without thinking, my hand rested over his, but he pulled it back as if I'd burned him.

"I'm sorry!" Emotions swirled around inside me in a panicked and confused storm. I wanted to touch him again, to comfort him, but that seemed to be the problem. "Tell me what to do. Please. Tell me what you need. I'm sorry!"

He let out a broken sob, and I shuffled closer without touching him. When he still wouldn't look at me, I followed his gaze, finding the childish dinosaur stickers on his bedroom wall. Their exaggerated smiling faces blurred as I looked at them, becoming a smear of color. A truth I didn't want to know became clearer as they distorted.

It wasn't a nightmare at all. It was a memory. Here, in this bed, someone had hurt him.

I stayed where I was, trying to think of something I could do that wouldn't make things worse for him, but I felt completely useless.

When his breathing finally evened out again, he turned to look at me, and I'd never seen so much pain in his eyes. I sobbed.

"Come here," he whispered, his hand finding mine.

I shook my head. "I don't want to make it worse. I'm sorry."

"I'm okay now, baby. I need you to hold me."

I fell into him, wrapping my arms around him, and he held me just as tight.

"I'm sorry," I said again into his shoulder.

"I know, Rabbit. It's not your fault."

Maybe he was right, but I still felt like I'd made it worse for him. I needed to apologize for not being able to fix it, and I didn't want him to comfort me. He was the one who was hurting. I needed to just be here for him now, without him feeling like he needed to take care of me as well as himself.

We lay in silence, holding each other until his breathing was slow and deep and calm once more. Until I might have thought he was asleep if I weren't paying quite such close attention.

"Who was it?" I asked eventually. Dex was silent for too long for him not to know what I meant, for it not to be a confirmation of my fears. "Give me a name." My voice sounded way more affected than I wanted it to. "Or... names?"

"Just one."

"Where are they?" Something dark and ugly bubbled inside me, something I didn't know how to deal with. But I couldn't shove it back down. I wasn't sure what I'd do with the information I was asking for, but I already knew I had to do something. I'd hurt whoever had hurt him. I was sure of it.

The pillow we were sharing shifted as he turned to look at me, and I pulled back to look at him better. I expected to see... something, some emotion he was choking back. Instead, I just saw a crushing amount of nothing. Whatever panic and fear he'd felt earlier was now absent, like just thinking about who this person was had scooped the emotions out of him. No, that wasn't it. They were still there, shielded behind a wall to keep him safe from them.

He searched my eyes for something, and I didn't know what it was, but he must have found it because after a long moment he spoke again. "I'll take you to him."

That wasn't the response I was expecting.

"When?"

"Now," he said, surprising me again, but I didn't have time to question it, because Dex was already pulling away from me and rolling out of bed. I scrambled to follow him.

I didn't know what was going on, but as he pulled the drawers of his dresser open, yanking out the first items of clothing he found, I rushed to get dressed as well.

Once we were clothed, I was running to catch up to him as he charged down the stairs and out the front door without a backward glance. Wherever he wanted to take me was his only mission, and it was urgent enough to him that he didn't even spare the time to lock the door.

When he reached his bike, he took the helmet and thrust it wordlessly in my direction.

"You wear it," I said, not taking it.

"Just put it on," he sighed.

"No, you put it on."

This time, instead of speaking, he stepped in closer and shoved it into my chest with enough force that I grunted. I pushed it back at him. "You wear it, Dex."

I was expecting him to fight me more on it, but he just snatched the helmet and flung it to the side where it crashed into a pile of junk. Neither of us was wearing it then.

"Wh—"

"If you won't take it, then we'll both risk dying from grievous yet preventable head wounds."

"If you're dying, then I'm dying. You don't get to leave me," I told him, my words teasing softly, trying to coax out his regular self. Because he was being too serious, and I didn't know where he was taking me, and I didn't want to ask because I wasn't sure I'd like the answer.

The ghost of a smile pulled at his lips, his eyes softening just slightly as he swung his leg over the bike. "You saying I'm your 'ride or die,' Rabbit?"

There it was. My lips pulled into a slight smile as I stepped forward, resting my hand on his shoulder as I pulled my leg over the back of the bike and settled into him.

Delilah's engine roared to life, and a few minutes later we were tearing down the highway.

⊰◦⊱

By the time we arrived at what was apparently our destination, we were a long way out of Port Skelton. I couldn't ask Dex questions while we were riding; the wind was far too loud to compete with. My face stung from the cold of it, my hair no doubt a tangled mess just like his.

He stared at the forest as if he were mentally preparing himself to enter it. Like it was a danger to him. Given that we were allegedly here so he could take me to the person who'd hurt him, I was starting to feel the same.

"Why are we here, baby?" I asked cautiously.

The wind rustled through the trees in the early-morning light. This place felt foreign. Undisturbed. Unwelcoming. Foreboding. Like something big and heavy waited here to be discovered, and yet something inside me was reaching out to meet it. Some unspoken knowledge seeped into me that I should have been afraid of, but I wasn't, because I was with him. Whatever secrets and terrible things undoubtedly waited for us, I didn't fear him. I didn't fear what I'd learn beyond the veil of the trees. Not if he was the one to lead me there.

"This way." He spoke softly, like he didn't want to disturb this place any more than we already had. Then he was following a path I couldn't see, and I was right there behind him.

My leg ached from the uneven terrain, but I kept up with him, leaves and twigs crunching underfoot as he led me through the dense foliage.

The forest opened up again into a clearing, shielded by a wall of trees. There was a slight ditch in the center where maybe a river had once carved out a path through it, but all that remained in it now was dirt and leaves and the burned-out shell of a car.

Dex stared at it for a moment before continuing onward.

"Here," he said, staring at the ground.

I followed his gaze, but all I saw was dirt and the remnants of cigarettes. Some that looked recent.

"What's here?" I asked him, but I already knew.

"The body."

33

DEX - PAST

IT'S NOT YOUR FAULT.

———— ✦ ————

I'd always intended to bring Jonah here eventually. I wanted him to know my scars. I just didn't expect that he'd see the wound first.

When we were done here, if he still wanted me, I'd make sure he knew everything. All my secrets. I hadn't told him about my past, had been very careful not to reveal it to him, not to burden him with it. But it was too late now. He knew. And if he was going to see the festering wound I carried with me always, then he should know the weapon that caused it.

I didn't want this to be the way he found out about it. I thought maybe we'd be able to avoid it happening like this. Because when Jonah was with me, the nightmares weren't. Until last night. Hours after experiencing his touch—wanted, craved, perfect, safe—and my mind had twisted. The demons I'd thought were missing when I was with him were only sleeping, and they'd woken. They'd tainted us, forming vivid pictures of another time, another touch—unwanted, despised, repulsive, unsafe.

The nightmares were *his* way of reaching me, even from here, beyond the veil of death. His touch corrupting the best thing I'd ever had. My rabbit.

"Who's body is here?" Jonah asked me.

I'd brought him out here, to this dreadful place, and he hadn't questioned it. I'd isolated him here in the middle of the forest and told him about the first body, and still he didn't have any fear of me. All I could read in his eyes was a genuine desire to know me. To understand me. I just hoped he wouldn't regret that when he did.

Jonah had dropped his walls for me, and it was time for me to do the same, to let him see all of me.

"His name was Pierce." The name alone felt like a curse. "He was my mother's boyfriend."

Jonah's hands clenched into fists at his sides, that fire that had once been directed at me igniting, blazing hotter and fiercer. It wasn't directed at me anymore, but at the ghost of the man who had hurt me. Now his fire burned on my behalf, and I loved it more than ever.

"And..." I knew the question that was coming before it even left his lips. "You killed him?"

I searched his eyes, looking for the fear that should have come with a question like that. It still wasn't there, as though whether I was a murderer wouldn't change anything between us; he just needed to know.

"No," I answered honestly. "But I wish I had. I wish with everything inside me I'd had the chance to make him pay for what he did to me."

Jonah's eyes burned, fire into lava, molten, liquid rage filling his eyes and seeping out, trickling down his cheek as he nodded once. "So who killed him?"

I felt a smile pull at my lips—a disguise, a mask—because that was the rest of the wound. "My mother."

"For what he did to you?"

I laughed. Mirthless. Bitter.

"No. You know, all these years and I never asked her why. Figured she might put me in the ground right beside him. She would if she ever knew what we'd done."

More tears. His brow furrowed as if he were fighting rage with rage. Fire with fire. I'd always found his rage so beautiful, but it was so much *more* when it burned on my behalf. It was ethereal. It was sanctifying. It was holy. No one had ever cried for me before.

"Then *she* should be in the ground with him."

Vindication. A weight on my chest I'd carried for years easing, cracking, crumbling. I could breathe deeper.

"Maybe," I admitted. It wasn't the first time I'd thought it.

His eyes turned away from me, and I felt more vulnerable without them than when he peered right into the center of me. He glared at the ground, as if his anger could seep beneath the dirt and find the soul in hell that had hurt me. "When?"

"When did I bring him here?"

"That too."

"Ah, when did he hurt me?"

"Yes."

"I was thirteen the first time." Jonah's jaw clenched. I'd thought it would be difficult to tell him, to let it out after all these years. It wasn't. Rather than letting it out, I was letting him in. And letting him in was the easiest thing I'd ever done. "Sixteen the last time. That's when I brought him here."

He nodded again. Processing. "And..." He hesitated a moment. "He touched you... the way I touch you?"

"No. Not like you do. Never like you. Your touch is wanted, Rabbit, always. His wasn't." Even though Pierce told me it must have been, because I'd reacted to it. Against my will, I'd reacted to the foul hands that touched me, even as they burned. My body listened to him instead of me. I hated him for that too.

Jonah stepped closer to me, his hand unclenching to rise to my cheek. His touch was warm even though his hand was cold. "It wasn't your fault."

"I know, Rabbit," I told him.

"No, I don't think you do," he said firmly. So certain. Like there really was no doubt in his mind. "It *wasn't* your fault."

"I know that." Something inside me squirmed uncomfortably under his gaze.

"It wasn't your fault, Dex." His tone was so rigid. Immovable. Steady.

"I know," I whispered. The thing inside me bubbled and oozed under the fire in his eyes. Black ichor. The guilt that seeped from the wound.

"It wasn't your fault."

"I—"

"It wasn't."

I sucked in a breath. I'd told myself those words so many times, over and over like a mantra. It wasn't my fault. It wasn't my fault. *It wasn't my fault.* It felt like a lie.

His palm guided me to him until his forehead pressed against mine, his eyes blurry this close, but still on me fiercely. His gaze still burned the thing inside me that had made a home in my soul like a parasite in the wound.

"It wasn't your fault." He spoke directly to it. Intimidated it. It shifted inside me, hearing him in a way it had never heard me. "It wasn't. You didn't do anything wrong. You didn't deserve it. *It wasn't your fault.*"

I choked. A strangled, awful sound rose from my depths as it broke me. Tears flowed freely, cleansing me the way I'd hoped the ocean would cleanse me the night I brought the body here. "You don't know that."

"I do."

"H-how can you know that? You don't know that I—when he—I didn't like it. I didn't want it, but he touched me, and I—I couldn't stop myself from reacting to him."

"It. Wasn't. Your. Fault." Every word spoken with intensity. With purpose. "I'll tell you that as much as you need me to. Every hour of every day for the rest of our lives. It wasn't your fault."

I sobbed again, the parasite inside me burning away.

"It wasn't your fault. It was his fault. All of it. And when I get to hell, I'll make him pay for what he did to you."

I smiled even as I sobbed again. "You're not going to go to hell, Rabbit."

"Of course I am," he said, his voice softer now. Tender. He'd scraped the ichor off the wound, and now his words soothed over it, tended and cared for it. "I'm in love with the Devil. There's no place I'd rather be."

I fell to my knees, and Jonah fell right along with me, his arms around me, holding me as I cried as much as I'd cried the day I'd brought the body here. More. I cried harder because for the first time since I'd lost my father, there was someone here to listen. To care. To soothe.

Jonah held me through it all, until there was nothing left for me to give and I felt hollow and empty inside. Because the ugly thing that had always eaten away at me had *finally* left. It might come back, and that might be soon, but I didn't have to face it alone anymore. I had Jonah, and if I didn't believe myself, he would tell me. I'd always believe him.

"Will you tell me what not to do? So I won't hurt you?" he asked once I'd calmed down, pulling back to search my eyes.

I smiled at him and nodded softly. "You won't h—"

"I don't want to risk it, Dex. I don't want anything I do to make you uncomfortable."

"It might be different, because it's you," I told him, because if there was anything Jonah wanted to do, I wanted to do it with him. "It's just... he would... when I was sleeping... that's when..."

"Okay." He leaned in, his lips pressing against mine softly. "I won't touch you while you're sleeping. I promise."

"But if you want to, then—"

"No." He silenced me with another kiss. "I don't want anything that isn't good for you too. If it's not good for both of us, then I don't want it at all. I'm more than happy with what we already have, and if that's all we ever do, it's more than enough for me. Do you believe me?"

I nodded, because I did.

"So you just tell me anything that makes you uncomfortable and we won't do that. Okay?"

"Okay. Later, though?"

"Of course." He kissed me softly again. "Whenever you're ready."

I hated that there were things that had been ruined for me. Things I'd never get to experience the way they were supposed to be experienced the first time, and every time after that. I couldn't have him touch me in a sexual way while I was sleeping. I couldn't have him give me a blow job. I couldn't bottom for him. Those things were tainted, taken from me, and it felt like now I was taking them away from him in a different way. Denying him the experience of even trying them.

More than anything, I didn't want Jonah to feel like he had to be cautious around me, or for him to treat me like I was weak, fragile, broken. I loved it when he got needy, when he was demanding and selfish. Especially when it came to sex. It had taken him time to relax around me and be confident like that. I didn't want to lose it again.

I kissed him again, gently at first, then deeper. He matched me, softly, cautiously, until my tongue pressed into his mouth and his was eager to meet it. Until he kissed me back the way he always did.

When our lips parted, I rested my head against his again, the tip of his nose cold as it brushed against mine.

"So…" I smiled softly. "You're in love with the Devil?"

Jonah huffed, rolling his eyes. "Apparently."

"Would you still be in love if I had killed him?"

He looked at me for a long moment, processing, before he spoke again. "I would."

I believed him.

"I love you too, Rabbit."

I kissed him again, deeper. I wanted him, craved him, *needed* him in ways so much more than sexual. He kissed me like he understood. Like I wasn't tainted.

"I need to feel you."

He nodded softly. "Take me home."

"Are you sure?" Jonah asked me, his skin flushed pink and bare beneath me.

"Don't do that," I pleaded with him, stealing his lips again. "Don't treat me any differently."

"I'm not." He spoke between kisses. "I just—" I silenced him with another kiss, not wanting to hear it, because if he felt like he needed to check in with me when I said I wanted to do something, then he *was* treating me differently. "I—" another kiss. Jonah shoved my shoulder, forcing me to release his lips. "Will you fucking let me speak?" he snapped.

I sighed, an ache in my chest. "What?"

"I was just trying to say, you got fucking injured last night. If this position hurts, we can just lie down like we did last time."

I laughed softly, relief easing the tension that had built in my chest.

Once we'd arrived home, we'd wordlessly taken a shower together. I washed him, and he'd done the same to me, cleaning away the remnants of that forest from our skin. Now I was more desperate to feel him than ever. To have a connection with him that brought us as close as physically possible. I didn't think I could take it if he rejected me right now.

But he wasn't. He was accepting me as I was. Even knowing what lived beneath my skin, he still wanted me—still loved me.

"I'm okay, I promise."

He nodded. I reached for the lube and kissed his lips as I uncapped it. Refused to leave them except when we needed to breathe as I opened him up with my fingers. Then I was pushing inside him, where I needed to be. Where I belonged. And he accepted me like he always did. Until my hips pressed against his ass and I was home.

It wasn't possible to be closer to him than I was right now, but still I wanted to be. I didn't even want skin between us. I wanted to become this beautiful grotesque combination of the both of us, where there was no place he ended and I began. I wanted to fuse our bodies, our souls, until there was no way we could ever be separated. But I suppose this would have to do.

I fucked him in short strokes, barely able to bring myself to pull back before I was plunging deeper again, as far into him as I could reach. His hands were on my back, nails biting into my skin as he angled his hips for me.

When he came, he did so with my name on his lips, and I followed him, pouring myself inside him as tears of bliss streamed down his face. Again he was crying for me. Tears that I treasured, that I tasted as I licked them from his skin.

Then I collapsed onto him, and he held me. It felt so good to be held by him. To know the person holding me knew exactly what was in his arms and he was still choosing to hold me anyway.

"I love you, Rabbit," I whispered into his neck.

"I love you too, Devil."

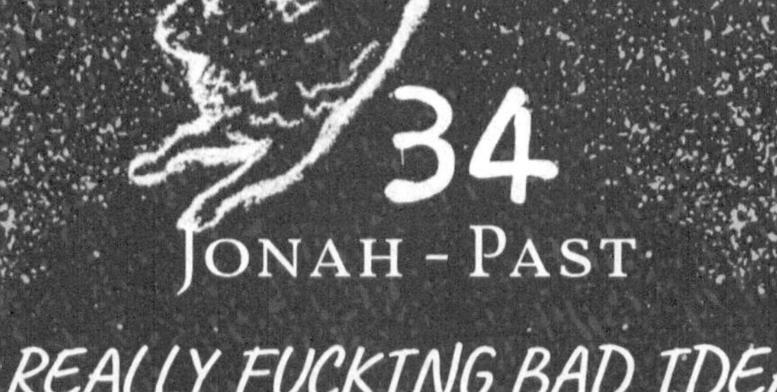

REALLY FUCKING BAD IDEA.

———✦———

Since Dex had taken me to the forest a couple of days ago and revealed to me that part of himself, I was absolutely sure of two things. The first being that I would never let anyone hurt him again. The second was that I was getting him that lighter back even if it killed me.

Of course, if I'd told him what I was planning, he wouldn't have allowed it. Dex had taken a couple of days off work, and we'd spent the time around the house, cloud gazing while lying in the field, on the rock seat at the beach. We'd even gone to the Cozy Cow. Amanda had seemed way too amused at seeing us together, so different from the last time we'd both been there.

Mostly, though, we'd chosen to be alone, to block out the world and be together. Just existing in our own bubble for a while. It meant we'd had a lot of sex too. Dex had opened up to me more about the things he couldn't do, and I got the sense he was waiting for me to be disappointed. I wasn't. It didn't matter what he couldn't do. What mattered was that nothing we *did* hurt him. He still fucked me like he was trying to make up for it.

It meant I had to wait until today to do what I was planning, though, and I just hoped like fuck things worked out. Because if they didn't, then I was about to cause some major fucking problems I may or may not live to see the consequences of.

"JJ, it's too fucking early. I know I told you not to avoid me for your hot new boyfriend, but *please* avoid me before nine a.m. at the earliest," Becca said with a yawn, her hands resting on the aged ledge of her bedroom window.

I rolled my eyes. "There's just no pleasing you," I teased.

"Come in, then," she sighed, reaching for my hand and basically dragging me up through the window until I stumbled to my feet inside her room. "If you're gonna wake me up early, the least you can do is come cuddle me. Didn't even bring coffee."

Bee shook her head at me before flopping back onto her bed, pulling the plush covers back up over her shoulders until she was just a pile of neon hair in a sea of black bedding.

I shifted from foot to foot, because this was not what I was here for, and I didn't know how long what I needed to do would take. With a sigh, I kicked off my shoes, trudging over to join my best friend.

The bed was warm and so soft as I slipped in beside her. Becca's hand reached back to grab mine and yank it around her. Affection came so easily to her; even on that first day we'd been reunited she had hugged me. Whenever we met up or parted, she would hug me in greeting or goodbye, and then there were just the random hugs that happened for no reason but because she wanted to. I wondered at first whether this was normal—if this was what other friends did, what other families did—or maybe it was just her. Either way, I was used to her now, and it wasn't the first time she'd made me hug her like this. The feeling of it was entirely different from anything I felt when I was touching Dex, but it was just as warm.

"I need to ask you something." I spoke up after a couple of minutes, not wanting her to fall back to sleep again.

She groaned, "Ask me later."

"It's important. I need to know now. I can't stay very long."

She was silent for a few minutes before turning around to look at me. "What's up, bub?"

"So, I've seen you like, around Henrik a couple of times."

Her brow furrowed, clearly not expecting this to be the direction I took the conversation.

"Okay?" she said slowly, prompting me to proceed.

"Do you like... have his contact details or anything?"

"Why?"

"I just need to talk to him about something."

"About what?"

"Just something with Dex. Please, Bee."

She watched me for a long moment, her eyes seeking answers I was determined not to give her, because then she wouldn't help me.

"You haven't got yourself mixed up in Strays' business, have you?"

"No, it's just something personal about Dex."

"You aren't in any trouble?"

"No." *Not yet.*

Bee sighed. "Okay fine, hand me my phone from the nightstand."

I turned to grab it and give it to her. She unlocked it and passed it to me a few moments later, open to a contact screen with the name "Really Fucking BAD Idea."

I smiled. "He is."

"I know."

"So's Raven."

"Mmm, but she liked my boots."

I rolled my eyes, pulling my phone from my pocket and copying the number across before handing hers back to her. "I need to go."

"What's so urgent you can't even stay for ten minutes of cuddles?" She pouted.

"Will it only be ten minutes, though?"

"Promise. I miss my JJ time. Let me soak you up a little like the needy sponge I am."

I sighed, giving in, because she was right. I hadn't been hanging out with her as much, and I did feel bad about that.

Becca was asleep within five minutes, but I stayed the full ten anyway, just in case she woke up while I was leaving and got moody with me.

I left the same way I'd entered, out the bedroom window, pulling it slowly closed behind me.

When I was what I deemed a reasonable distance away, I made the call.

He wasn't expecting me, and I didn't know what kind of life he had. Maybe he had a job or something, but I had to try.

"Igen?" came the deep voice on the other end of the line after only the second ring.

I stalled. "Um... what?"

"Who is this?"

"Uh... It's um, it's Jonah. Hargreaves."

There was a pause. "The rabbit," he said, and his voice sounded amused. "To what do I owe the pleasure?"

"I was hoping you might, um, help me. With something. Without telling Dex? Uh, I mean, Coyote?"

Henrik laughed. "Alright."

"Alright?"

"Yes. I'm interested. What are we doing?"

That was... much easier than I'd expected it to be. It took a minute for me to get past all the planned convincing I'd been prepared to offer him to find the reason I'd called. "I want to find someone. Bates."

Henrik made a pensive noise. "And what will you do when you find him?"

"I need to get something back. Something he stole."

"And if he doesn't want to give it back. What will you do?"

"I'll get it back," I said, knowing it wasn't exactly a plan, but I didn't have one of those yet. "Can you take me to him or not?"

"I can."

I waited for him to elaborate, but he didn't. "When?" I prompted.

"One hour. I'll pick you up. Where are you?"

"I'm um... I'll be at the diner," I told him, because I didn't want him to know where I lived. I might have been asking him for help, but that didn't mean I trusted the guy. As Becca's contact name had aptly referred to him: Really Fucking BAD Idea.

"Okay. Anything else?"

"Um..." I honestly hadn't thought I'd even get this far. "No?"

The line cut out as he hung up on me. I had nothing else to say to him, but it still pissed me off.

I turned and made the short trip back to my dad's house, knowing he'd already be at work. There was something I had to get first.

———◆◇◆———

It was exactly one hour after the call that I heard the roar of a bike pulling into the Cozy Cow parking lot. I was leaning against the bricks outside, smoking from a pack of cigarettes I'd bought with money I found on Dad's kitchen table. They didn't taste as good as the ones Dex rolled.

I knew little about bikes, but Henrik's suited him. He was a big, intimidating man, and his bike was no different. It was all black and *much* bigger than the bike Dex rode. Still, I hadn't expected he'd come here on *that*. Not when he was supposed to take me to Bates.

He left the engine running as he pulled his helmet off, spotting me and staring. Assuming he was waiting for me to come over to him, I stomped out the cigarette before doing just that. "You don't have a car?"

"I do."

"Why didn't you bring it?"

"Bike's faster."

I was already regretting this entire idea. "But there's... two of us?"

"Wow, nothing gets past you, does it?" he said, sounding overly impressed. I scowled, not appreciating the sarcasm. He seemed amused by it, and that just pissed me off more. "Show me your weapon."

That snapped me out of the indignant tirade building in my throat. "My what?"

"Weapon, Einstein. You want me to take you to Bates, no? You're not planning on just talking to him, I assume. So show me what you have."

Heat crept up my neck. The weight in my pocket felt like it was burning a hole through the leather as I looked around us to make sure no one was nearby. When I was satisfied, I pulled out my father's pistol. The thing was old, and to my knowledge had never been used, but it was loaded, and I just hoped I didn't have to find out whether it worked or not.

Henrik glanced at it, his lips twitching as he tried not to smile. "Are we going to shoot him?"

"What? No, I mean, I don't know. Maybe. If he doesn't give back what he took."

Henrik nodded slowly. "Okay, Rabbit."

"Don't call me that."

He put his hand up to quiet me. "Just making sure we're on the same page. You want to find him, talk to him, threaten him maybe with that toy, get back what he took, and then just walk away? Is that the plan? You think any of the Drakes will just hand something over because you have a very small gun, and then let you leave with no consequences?"

Embarrassment and rage bubbled in my core.

"You've never even shot a gun before," he continued.

"How would you know that?"

"The way you hold it. They'll know too."

My eyes cast down to the ground, my breathing faster as my chest ached. "I need to get it back for him. No matter what."

Henrik was silent for a moment before holding his hand out. "Give me the gun."

I did. He shrugged his backpack off and unzipped it. There was a second helmet attached to the side that he took off and handed to me. Then he disarmed the gun and tucked it away, digging around before retrieving a switchblade and handing that to me too.

"You think I have a better chance with this than the gun?" I asked as I took it.

The knife looked old. Well used. It felt heavier than the mix of metal and pale wood it was composed of, as if it was possessed by something unseen. I flicked it open, eyeing the cloudy silver of the blade with its razor-sharp edges. Where it had come from and what I would do with it, I didn't know, but I clenched it tighter, accepting the feel of it, the warmth of my palm seeping into its coldness.

"I don't think you need a weapon. But just in case."

"Why don't I need a weapon?"

"Because I'm coming with you. Now get on."

He was an arrogant bastard, but I didn't question him further. Henrik knew what we should expect better than I did, as much as I hated to admit that even to myself. I wasn't sure how involved he was planning to be in the confrontation with Bates, but I felt better with him on my side.

I pulled the helmet over my head, and Henrik gave me the bag to put on my back as I got on behind him. His bike was much better equipped for carrying two people, but I still tried not to get too close to him.

"You'll have to hold on tight. We'll go faster than you're used to on that old relic of his. Don't want to tell Coyote his rabbit is now roadkill. I don't think he'd like me anymore."

I shuffled a little closer. My hands rested on his waist, but then the bastard took off at a stomach-twisting speed. The moment we were out of the parking lot, the front wheel was lifting off the asphalt, and I screamed as I clutched onto him with my arms and legs so I didn't get thrown off.

I could almost hear my heartbeat above the roar of the bike's engine as it thumped rapidly with adrenaline. I could also hear the bastard's laughter, and I might have fucking hit him if I wasn't so concerned about him doing that to me again and ending up as a smear on the road.

Thankfully, for the rest of the long trip—that would have taken *much* longer if he wasn't speeding like a madman—he kept both wheels on the road.

We pulled up at an old warehouse on the outskirts of Deltran.

It took me a moment to find my balance on shaking legs as I got off, immediately scrambling away from Henrik. I'd spent far too long clinging to his body on the ride, and when we were done here, I didn't want to be in so much as the same room as him ever again. I yanked the helmet off to heave in blissfully cool air.

"Alright? Looking a little green there."

"I'm fine," I snapped, trying to convince myself of that as well, because the twisting of my stomach was only half due to the ride. We were here. And now I had to face whatever came next.

Henrik took the helmet and backpack from me, securing them to his bike.

"How do you know he's here?"

"I just know things," he told me, fixing up his stupid man bun. "Come now, Bunny. You can do the talking, but when things turn violent, you stay behind me. Don't get in my way."

When and not *if* things turn violent. My mouth dried up.

I took a deep breath, steeling myself for what lay ahead, and reminding myself of why I was here. For Dex. For his father's lighter. For the pain this fucker had inflicted on him multiple times now. Never again. Getting his lighter back wasn't enough. I had to make sure that when I left here, Mason fucking Bates would never be a problem for my devil ever again. I couldn't do anything about Pierce, or about Dex's piece of shit mom. But *this* I could protect him from.

Henrik stood behind me, waiting patiently for me to lead the way.

The warehouse, with its boarded-up windows, chipped paint, bright graffitied walls, and dark abandoned interior, stood like an enemy fortress. Still, I pushed forward, hiding my limp to the best of my ability, in case anyone was watching from somewhere unseen.

When we stepped inside, it was too quiet, motes of dust illuminated by the limited light that streamed through gaps in the window boards and broken glass. I pushed onward, all my senses on high alert.

With nothing here but the silent darkness, a wave of coldness rushed over me. Henrik had brought me out here alone. I'd told no one where I'd gone, and they certainly wouldn't expect me to be with him. What if he brought me here to get rid of me? To get me away from Dex and the Strays?

"Keep going, Bunny," he whispered in my ear, far closer than I expected him to be. My pulse thundered, my hand dipping into my pocket for the switchblade. "That way." I followed his gaze, his profile only just visible enough. There was a closed door on the other side of the room.

Keeping the knife in my hand, I walked over to it, feeling Henrik's presence directly behind me even though I couldn't hear him. That was incredibly unnerving considering how quiet it was here and how large he was. Dex had felt like a predator before I got to know him, but this man was something else entirely. I just hoped I hadn't made a really big fucking mistake in asking him for help as I twisted the handle and the door creaked open.

HOUND AND RABBIT.

The light that streamed in on the other side of the door was unexpected and almost startling. It took a moment for my eyes to adjust again, and when they did, I saw what used to be an office of some kind with an old desk in the center. The walls were covered in graffiti, broken furniture and books were thrown about, but my attention snapped to the three men waiting for us—Bates in the middle, leaning against the desk, and two others I didn't recognize.

Bates looked unimpressed, and unsurprised, to see us here. His eyes landed on me only for a moment before they flicked to Henrik.

"Who is this?" he asked.

"Mmm... Ghost," Henrik answered, and the two men I didn't know stood up straighter, their eyes wide with the surprise I would have expected when they first saw us come in. Bates looked at me again, closer this time, my hand clenched tighter around the switchblade in my pocket.

"No. I remember you. You're that fucker who tripped me." He looked back at Henrik, brow furrowed in anger. "What the fuck is this?"

Henrik laughed. "You tripped him?"

"I'm here to get back what you took," I said, heat building in my chest. Anger that always seemed to show whenever this fuckface was around, only hotter this time, because now I was here to do something about it. Provided Henrik hadn't brought me into a trap for his own amusement, which I still hadn't ruled out.

"What did I take?" Mason stood to his full height, and I fucking hated that he was taller than me.

"You know what you took from him. I want it back. All of it."

A smile pulled at Mason's lips as he looked up at Henrik—*up,* because even if the bastard was a giant, Henrik was bigger.

"You heard the man. He wants back what you took," Henrik answered, and I could hear the smile in his words.

"You told me to come here for this shit? To what? Hand over some fucking junk for some fucking cunt?"

I pulled the knife from my pocket, flicking it open. "Don't fucking call him that."

"What? Cunt? He is. Fucking cock-sucking bitch."

The fire built, burning, blazing, too big to contain.

Mason's eyes flicked to the knife and stayed there. "We had a deal, Kovats."

"Mmm yes. But I made a better one." Henrik's hand landed on my shoulder as he pushed me forward. "Go on, little rabbit, show them your teeth. I'm right behind you."

I stood taller. "Where the fuck is it?"

"Up your fucking ass." Mason gestured toward us with his head and the two others stepped forward, fists raised and ready to fight.

The only person I'd ever fought was the man I was in love with, and even when I fought him, my fire burned for him in ways other than violence. I'd longed for him even before I understood it. This was different. Adrenaline pumped through my system, steadying my hand, because this was it. The moment to prove myself or go down with nothing to show for it.

One of them, the smaller one, came for me, and the other went for Henrik. I raised my fists, one clenched around the knife. I swung at him the moment he was within reach, but he blocked the hit and followed it with his own to my gut, knocking the air out of me.

Pain to fuel the fire. I swung the other arm and nicked him with the knife. A superficial cut that made him angrier rather than slowing him down. He hit me again, and I raised my arm too slowly to block the force of the impact as he knocked my arm into my face and the inside of my cheek sliced open on my teeth. More pain. More fuel. More *red*.

He stepped forward to come for me again, but a muscled arm shot out, catching him around the neck and swiping him with inhuman force down to the concrete floor. He gasped, the move stealing his ability to draw in a full breath. Henrik stood in front of me, blocking my view. I turned to see the man he'd been fighting, only to find his body crumpled on the floor as well.

Henrik didn't even hesitate when he stepped forward and his boot slammed into the side of the guy's head. Just like that, he was out. In seconds.

Mason pulled a knife, taking a fighting stance as he eyed up the demon in human skin between us. Then he rushed forward, blade first, aiming for Henrik's gut. I jumped back as bodies collided, out of reach as limbs moved and struggled against each other. Mason grunted. Henrik smiled.

Red dripped onto the concrete. Fresh blood. Henrik's.

His hand was holding the knife by the blade, fingers wrapped tightly around silver even as it cut into him. Using the hold on it, he wrenched the weapon from Mason's hand and flung it across the room. It clattered against a wall, leaving a bloody splatter on impact.

"What the fuck are you?" Mason asked through gritted teeth.

Henrik replied, but his words weren't in English, just a simple short phrase, then he was punching, blow after blow to Mason's stomach, his face, until the man was stumbling backward, losing ground rapidly. He fell into the desk behind him and Henrik kept hitting. Fists a mix of both their blood. Wet smacks echoed through the cold, dilapidated room until Mason stopped moving.

Henrik wasn't even sweating, not even an increase in his breathing. With the same amused smile on his lips, he stepped back from Mason's bloodied form on the desk. I watched him until I saw the slight rise and fall of his chest. He was still breathing. Still alive. I was... disappointed by that.

"Knife." Henrik spoke to me, and after a dazed moment, I handed it to him. He went back over to Mason and gestured for me to follow. I did. I didn't know if my heart was beating too rapidly for me to feel it or if it had stopped entirely.

"There's a tradition in my family," he said, and I wasn't sure if he was speaking to me or the barely conscious man on the desk. "When someone is a thief, they take something that doesn't belong to them, so in return, we take something that does."

Henrik reached for Mason's bloody hand, laying it flat on the desk surface, and with no hesitation he ran the blade over Mason's pinky finger. A wet crunch and then Mason was conscious again, conscious and screaming, clutching his hand to his chest as his blood wept over his shirt. His finger was still on the desk next to the knife until Henrik flicked it to the ground and kicked it away.

"Now I think maybe you will answer the question." Henrik looked at me expectantly, but my mouth was dry, my words evaporated as I watched red continue to seep into Mason's clothing. "Remember what you came here for, Rabbit." My eyes broke away from all the red and found Henrik. He smiled and nodded toward Mason. "Why are we here?"

For Dex. This was all for Dex.

"Where's the lighter?" I asked, my voice sounding far calmer than I expected it to be.

Mason only screamed.

"Where is the lighter?" Henrik repeated, speaking loudly into Mason's ear as he gripped him by the hair. "Or I'll take another finger."

"Bag!" Mason sobbed. "In my bag!"

I looked around, spotting three bags against the wall. I walked over to them, unzipping the closest one and spilling its contents over the ground. There were a shocking number of weapons, but no lighter. I emptied the second one, and among all the other things that scattered over the floor, silver glinted like a beacon. The lighter. I looked through the other things, finding Dex's phone, his keys, his wallet, quickly stashing them all into the safety of my pocket.

I'd done it. I got them back.

I couldn't fight the smile as I looked at Henrik, who smiled back at me. "That's it, smile. Show them your bloodied teeth. Maybe you aren't a rabbit after all, hmm?"

There was a man holding his mutilated hand as he sobbed, and I was smiling. The realization sobered me, and the smile fell away as I walked back over to Henrik, to Mason. "What do we do now?"

Henrik held the knife out to me. "That's up to you."

I took it, staring down at the now bloodied blade. *What do I do now?*

I'd gotten what I came here for. It was done. Over. Except it wasn't. Because Mason knew who I was, and I knew he'd want revenge on me after this... on Dex.

He glared at us, still clutching his hand to his chest protectively. "You'll fucking pay for this," he said, as if reading my thoughts. "You and your piece of shit fucking boyfriend. I'll fucking make you pay. I'll slit his fucking throat while you watch, you piece of shit fucking fa—"

I didn't plan to do it, but he was threatening Dex, and I was holding the knife, and without conscious thought I moved, and it was so easy. The blade sank into flesh, a bit of resistance at first but then it just plunged in with barely any effort at all.

Mason stared down at the knife in his stomach, his un-injured hand slowly reaching for it. I let it go, taking a step backward.

Henrik rolled his eyes, slapping Mason's hand away as he gripped the knife and yanked it free, plunged it in again, over and over until Mason slumped forward, his body falling gracelessly to the floor.

Then he walked over to the body of the man on the floor closest to him, repeating the action. More red. Red. Red. Red.

Then to the next.

"Y-you promised me vengeance," the final man said, glaring up at Henrik through an eye almost swollen shut. "For my brother. You promised me Reaper."

Henrik gave his face an affectionate pat. "Don't worry, Mikhail, I'll send him to you in hell, hmm? You get your vengeance there." He plunged the knife into Mikhail's gut, watching with what could only be described as fascination as the light left the man's eyes and he slumped to the ground.

Bile rose in my throat. I hunched over, heaving, but before I could get out the acid that burned up my throat, a bloodied hand was clamped over my mouth. I struggled against Henrik's hold but he wouldn't budge, the vomit trapped in my mouth until I swallowed it back down.

"Can't leave any traces of you at a crime scene, Bunny."

I yanked away from him, frantically wiping at the blood that was now smeared over my face. "Your blood is fucking everywhere!" I told him, and he smiled.

"Allegedly."

"What does that mean?"

"It means don't worry about me."

"You... you just killed three people..."

"Allegedly."

"I just fucking saw you do it!"

Henrik fucking laughed. "What did you think? We could just walk out, and they wouldn't come for us afterward? Now they can't. You got what you wanted, and now..." He gestured to the bodies. "Now they can't take anything else. No? It's a good thing."

A good thing. I looked at Mason's body, face down on the concrete. Endless red seeped out of him.

"Do... do we need to... hide the bodies?" I asked, my mind trying and failing to just fucking *think*.

"No," Henrik said simply. "I'll handle it."

"What if people find them?"

"I said I'll handle it."

It was too much. Too much to process. Because of a decision I had made, three people were now dead.

But it wasn't my fault, was it? Not really. I might have stabbed Mason, but *I* wasn't the one to kill him. And he had been threatening Dex. If he hadn't been stopped, he would have hurt him again or worse. There was no other way. Henrik killed him. He had to. This... this was a good thing.

36

Dex - Past

TREASURE AND INK.

I was late home from work again. Roy hadn't mentioned the time I'd taken off, but I felt his eyes on me more than usual throughout the day. It was his way of checking in. The grumpy bastard cared and didn't know how to show that, but I appreciated it all the same. I was honestly okay. Better than I had been in a long time.

Letting Jonah see that part of me no one ever had before had just entwined our lives deeper. He was under my skin, deeper than my bones, in parts of me no light could reach but his. I hated being apart from him, even for work. I wanted him with me always. Wanted to know what he was doing, what he was feeling.

After my shift, I'd done more work on Jonah's car. It was almost ready for him. I'd also ordered what I needed to modify Delilah to carry a passenger more comfortably. Those parts would arrive soon too, and between the bike and the car, there was no reason we'd have to go anywhere separately again, and Jonah wouldn't have to stress his leg as much as he did.

I'd sent him a text on my lunch break, asking what he was up to, but he hadn't responded. Knowing him, he might have been giving me the silent treatment for needing to leave him to go to work.

The house was dark when I arrived home, and the thought that he wasn't here waiting for me felt even darker. I made my way inside, deciding to check that he wasn't sleeping in my bed or something before I went out to hunt him down and bring him home.

The shower was running upstairs, and I breathed a sigh of relief, taking the stairs two at a time to get to the bathroom. I was surprised to find it dark as well.

"Rabbit?" I called out cautiously.

"Yeah?" Jonah answered softly.

"Why are you showering in the dark, baby?"

"I just... didn't want to see it."

I wondered if he meant his scars. I knew he hated when I paid any attention to them at all, but some days were worse for him than others. "Can I turn the light on?"

"You won't like it."

Alarm bells tolled in the back of my mind as I hit the light switch, the old bulb flickering in the ceiling before staying on, yellow-white light illuminating the tile and the clothes strewn over the floor covered in blood. My heart stopped as I approached the shower, yanking the curtain back to find Jonah sitting on the floor, hugging his knees. His cheek was bruised, but the water running off him was clear.

"Are you hurt?" I asked the most important question first.

He shook his head in response.

"Whose blood is that, baby?" I asked, speaking softly because he still wasn't looking at me, and he needed me to be gentle with him despite the panic clawing up my ribcage.

Jonah turned slowly, brown eyes dulled of their usual flame until they locked with mine and life sparked once more in their empty depths. He smiled. "I got it back for you."

My breathing came a little faster, the panic scratching, gnawing, clawing. "What did you get back?"

"All of it. It's in the pocket."

I turned slowly from him to my bloodied leather jacket on the bathroom floor. Reaching for it without leaving Jonah's side, I pulled it over to us, my heart thumping rapidly as my fingers dipped into the pocket.

Heat prickled behind my eyes, blurring my vision even before I pulled the familiar-shaped items free from the leather. My keys, phone, wallet... and my father's lighter.

"You got it back for me," I whispered, words pulled from my weeping soul, from the wound that losing this piece of my father had left. I'd lost it, and my rabbit had brought it back to me.

I placed the items down, uncaring about my clothing getting wet as I stepped into the shower and sank to my knees in front of him. My arms held him as if I could pull him into me, into my core, so he could feel the way he soothed me without words. He held me back the same way.

Long minutes later, I reluctantly pulled back from him, smoothing his wet hair back from his face as I examined the bruise on his cheek. He didn't have any other injuries that I could see. "You need to tell me what you did, Rabbit," I told him, because if it was what I thought, then there was another body that I needed to stash away somewhere no one would ever find it.

"I stabbed him," Jonah answered, eyes searching mine like he was lost at sea, drifting without an anchor, without a way back to solid ground.

"Okay," I said simply, reaching for him, my soul seeking his in the darkness, trying to guide him back to me. I'd be the strength he needed. The lighthouse. The anchor. I'd be whatever he needed me to be. "Okay. Is he dead?"

Jonah nodded. "They all are."

"Okay. How many of them, baby?"

"Three."

I stroked his bruised cheek gently. Three bodies. More than I'd dealt with at one time before, but it didn't matter. I'd make it work. I'd do whatever I had to in order to protect him from this. "Where are they?"

"In the warehouse. Henrik said he'd take care of them."

I let out a long breath. "Henrik was with you?" Relief mixed with other emotions, and I tamped down the anger that rose with knowing that psychopath had taken my rabbit into danger. There'd be a time for it later, but right now, Jonah needed me calm.

"He killed them. I didn't kill anyone."

"It's okay if you did. You were just protecting yourself—protecting me—weren't you?"

He nodded, more life filling his eyes. "He can't hurt you again."

"Yeah. I'm safe. You're safe too. I'll make sure of it. Okay?"

Another nod, and then Jonah was wrapping his arms around me again. His lips found my neck, trailing kisses there. His hands made their way under the wet fabric clinging to my body. "I want to feel you."

I helped Jonah get my wet clothes off, tossing them to the bathroom floor to deal with later. Each layer, until we were both naked, hands gripping skin. Jonah was frantic in the way he touched me, grabbed at me, refusing to let any space pass between us.

I turned the water off. "Bedroom," I said when he finally released my lips long enough for me to speak. He frowned, trying to capture them again, but I pulled back just out of reach. "Bedroom," I repeated, a little firmer this time.

Jonah pouted, but he stepped out of the shower, over the bloodied clothes on the ground, dragging me along with him, not even stopping to dry off. Then he was spreading himself out on my bed and pulling me down with him.

I pulled away, enough to take in the perfect image of him in the moonlight. "Where were you hurt?"

"Nowhere."

"Bullshit."

Jonah groaned. "I was hit twice before Henrik stepped in. That's it. Nothing serious."

After I'd murdered Henrik, I'd thank him for presumably taking on three men and attempting to protect Jonah from serious harm. "How did you get there?"

"Does it matter?"

"Damn right it fucking matters. You tell me everything, Rabbit."

If Jonah really was okay, and it seemed like he'd returned to me from wherever he'd been in the shower, then I fully intended to punish him for putting himself in danger on my behalf. Even if I was eternally grateful for what he'd done for me.

"I called him. He picked me up. We went to the warehouse. I got back your stuff, and Henrik killed three people. Will you fuck me now?"

I knew that was a way too oversimplified version of the story, but it was enough for now. I might not know all the shady business Henrik got himself involved with, but I knew those certainly weren't the first bodies he'd dropped and they wouldn't be the last. He'd sort them out, and I'd be sure to get all the details from him the moment I stepped away from Jonah next. But for now, there was something far more urgent demanding my attention.

"I love you, Jonah, more than I can put into words. What you did for me is more valuable than any gift. That lighter is irreplaceable. But so are you. And I treasure you far more than anything I own, including the lighter. Do you understand? You put yourself in danger, and I could have lost you as well."

"But you didn't."

"No. But I could have. And it would have destroyed me. I need you to promise me you won't ever do anything like that again. Don't put yourself in danger, especially not for me."

Jonah crossed his arms over his chest, clearly annoyed that I was dragging this out and not just giving him what he wanted, but this was far too important to put off. Because the world I was involved with was cruel. It was dangerous, and it was cold, and I couldn't have him stepping into it. I had to protect him from it, but that wouldn't be possible if he ran headfirst into danger any moment my back was turned.

"Promise me," I demanded.

"No."

"Why?"

"Because it'd be a lie, and I don't want to lie to you. I'll never stop protecting you, and you'll never stop protecting me, and that's just our life now, Devil, so get used to it."

"I don't need you to protect me," I told him.

"No. But I'm going to do it anyway," he replied, as stubborn as always.

"Jonah."

"Dex."

"Fuck, you're so frustrating sometimes. I just want to keep you safe."

"Yeah, well, same."

My eyes, fierce like the ocean, locked with his, a blazing inferno. Two immovable extremes, clashing while longing to coexist. I groaned, sensing that anything else I said to him now would just take us in circles. If I couldn't get him to agree not to put himself in danger because of me, then I'd just have to get better at protecting him, as well as myself. So there'd be no need.

"Will you fuck me now?" Jonah asked impatiently.

"No," I answered, and he pouted. "I'm going to punish you first for being reckless."

I watched his expression shift between intrigue and indignation before settling on the former. "Punish me how?" he asked, trying very hard not to smile, but I could still see it in his eyes.

"Turn around."

Jonah eyed me with cautious curiosity, no doubt internally debating himself over whether he wanted to listen or continue to be a brat, before he did as I asked and rolled onto his stomach. I switched on the lamp, using the light to give his back a careful check for any injuries I might have missed while we were in the bathroom, but he was as perfect as ever.

"Hurry up," he demanded when long moments passed with me just standing there taking him in, admiring the toned muscle in his back, the firm curve of his ass. Mine. Forever. Always. I let my hand come down on the perfect milky surface, the slap making him jump.

"If you keep mouthing off, I'll gag you," I warned, and he groaned, rutting against the bedding to get some friction on his hard cock.

"You like that idea, Rabbit?"

"No."

"Liar."

I would gag him. Maybe later I'd make him come in his underwear and then I'd shove them into his mouth and make him taste himself. My cock twitched, approving of the idea. Later.

My hand smoothed over the red mark from where I'd spanked him. It wasn't enough. I pulled his hips up, guiding him to his knees, and Jonah quickly moved to get into position, feet hanging off the bed, angled apart so there was room for me behind him, his ass at the perfect height for me to fuck him.

I spanked him again, harder, and Jonah let out another startled moan. He pushed back toward me, seeking more. I alternated sides, a crisp *thwack* every time my palm connected with firm skin, until his ass was red, and still he twitched and shifted toward me for more.

"I want to mark you," I told him, a twisted thought resurfacing, one I'd had every time I'd marked him before, and every time they had faded.

"So mark me."

"I mean, I want to *mark* you. Something that won't fade. Something permanent."

Jonah was quiet for a moment before looking over his shoulder at me. "You mean like... a scar?"

A smile pulled at my lips. "No, Rabbit, like a tattoo."

"A tattoo... where?"

"Right here," I said, smoothing my thumb over the pink skin of his ass cheek. "Put my name on what's mine."

"You want to put your name on my ass?"

"*Mine*. Belongs to me and only me."

Jonah groaned, his head falling forward for a moment before he angled his hips toward me again. "Alright."

"I'm serious, Rabbit."

"So am I. Do it."

"I'll do it right now, Jonah. I'm not playing around."

"So do it. Mark me, Devil."

I wasn't sure if he was actually on board with this idea, or if he still didn't believe I'd do it. With one more firm spank for good measure, I stepped away from him.

After I'd bought my tattooing supplies, Bull had reluctantly shown me the basics, but I was a shit artist and after a few attempts at doing my own ink, I'd left the rest of them to him. It wouldn't take much skill to just write my name, though. As long as it was legible, I'd be satisfied.

I got what I needed from the bottom drawer of my dresser, bringing it over and chucking it on the bed next to Jonah, waiting for him to see it and protest, but he simply looked at it and remained in position. So perfectly presented for me.

Next, I took the lube from the nightstand, slicking up my fingers with it.

"Mnn... I thought you were going to mark me?" Jonah's voice was low and needy as my fingers circled his rim, teasing him before I pressed one slowly inside.

"I am."

"After you fuck me?"

"While I fuck you."

He moaned again, pressing back against my hand.

Jonah's body welcomed me as I opened him up, just enough to take me, until he was soft and pliant and moaning into my bedding. I slicked up my cock, wiping the excess lube off on the sheet, then I was pressing inside him.

I gave him a few fast, hard thrusts before stilling, buried deep inside.

"Stay still, or you'll make a mess," I told him, and Jonah whimpered. I reached for the supplies next to him, filling the small plastic pot with ink and balancing it precariously in the dip of his spine. "If you make it spill, I won't let you come."

"Fuck you. Hurry up and do it so you can fuck me properly."

"I think I'll take longer now just for that."

Jonah whined, his hips shifting slightly, the pot of ink shaking without toppling over. "I'm serious, Rabbit. Stay still."

Moving as little as possible inside him, I tore open the sterile packaging of the needles, clicking them into place on the tattoo pen. It buzzed to life, the low rattle of the machine echoing in the form of a shiver down Jonah's spine.

"Ready?"

"Yes."

I pulled the skin taut over Jonah's ass, waiting to make sure he was still before dipping the needles in the ink then bringing them down on his flushed skin. Jonah yelped, jolting as the needles punctured him. I pulled the pen away, *tsking* as black ink spilled over his spine from the pot.

"It's not my fault," he said defensively. "I didn't know what to expect! That doesn't count!"

I switched the machine off, picking up the inkpot that had rolled onto the bed and placing it back on his spine to refill.

"It doesn't count," Jonah said again when I didn't answer.

"We'll see. If it happens again, it definitely counts, but if you stay still, maybe I can overlook it."

"Okay," he said with a heavy exhale, bracing himself as I switched the pen on again.

This time when I brought it down on his skin, he twitched and clenched around my cock, but he didn't spill the ink.

D

Jonah whimpered and tightened around me, testing my resolve as I lifted the pen from his skin.

E

He was shivering, his ass tightening up so much around me that I couldn't help but groan. I picked up the inkpot, taking a moment to give him a couple of thrusts, causing him to moan in relief, before I placed it back down. "Almost done, baby. You're doing good."

I was briefly tempted to drag this out, to put DEVIL on him instead of DEX, but I needed it to be my name there so there'd be no doubt who he belonged to. Not that I ever planned to let anyone else see it.

✗

The name wasn't my finest handwriting, but it was readable. Big letters over his left ass cheek.

I switched the pen off, wiping away the excess ink as Jonah continued to whimper and shiver, still trying so hard not to spill the pot. Perhaps it was cruel to leave that bit to last, but the way he twitched and clenched around my cock was addictive.

The moment I lifted it safely off him, he was pushing back against me, rocking back and forth, trying to fuck himself on my dick.

"So impatient," I groaned, dropping the supplies on the bed, not caring about the mess as I gripped his hips and used the hold to fuck him properly. Jonah moaned, loud and needy, as I pounded into him, my hold on him firm enough to bruise. If he wanted me that badly, then I wouldn't hold anything back.

"Fuck, you feel so good, baby. This ass that's all mine—*mnn*—now you have the ink to prove it. Forever."

Jonah was beyond words, his response coming as moans, the sound of them joining the slick rapid slapping of skin against skin. Faster, faster, faster. He screamed as he came, his cum mixing with the ink on the covers of my bed.

It only took a few more thrusts before I was coming too, marking him on the inside with my cum while I stroked a thumb over the other more permanent mark on his skin.

I pulled out, spreading him open to watch as it seeped out of his twitching hole. The sight of it next to my name was the single hottest thing I'd ever seen, and I wanted this moment branded into my mind as clearly as possible.

"Fuck, you're so perfect."

Jonah panted. "Kiss me. Then clean me up."

"Of course, baby," I chuckled, rolling him over to steal his lips hungrily.

"And you're sleeping inside me," he mumbled against my lips.

"Of course, baby."

37

Dex - Past

TROUBLE.

⭐

"We have to run," Jonah told me, hands holding mine and panic in his beautiful brown eyes. Still burning like fire, but a fire uncontrolled. A fire burning too rapidly. Unpredictable. Threatening to consume him and everything in his path.

I placed a soft kiss on his forehead. Over the past two days he'd been volatile, switching between panicking about what he and Henrik had done and clinging to me like a life raft in a storm. Like he needed me more than air. He needed me just to *be*. Just when I thought he'd stabilized, Deltran Police Force had found the bodies.

I'd tried and failed to contact Henrik. He wouldn't answer his phone, not to me, not to Jonah when I stole his phone, and not to any of the Strays I'd called. No one had seen him, and the bastard better have been dead or dying to disappear after all the shit he had caused.

While I wanted to hunt him down and get some fucking answers, Jonah was increasingly becoming a flight risk, and I didn't want to leave him alone for even a moment.

"I won't let anything happen to you, Rabbit," I promised him. "I can't leave here, not while the Strays need me, but if it comes down to it, and there's no other way, then we'll go. Okay, baby? I won't let anyone hurt you or take you away from me." Words spoken with a calmness I didn't feel. But I wouldn't let him see it. I was his anchor, and an anchor needed to be strong, firm, immovable.

"What if you get hurt again?" he asked, hands holding mine tighter.

"I won't."

"You don't know that!"

"I'm just going to go to work, baby. It'll just be me and Roy. There's no danger there."

It was a lie.

I intended to go to work. Roy had been accommodating of me taking even more time off, but he needed more of an explanation, and I needed to get Jonah's car finished. Maybe if he had his own way of getting around, he'd be able to relax a little more, knowing he wouldn't be trapped in place without me to take him everywhere. I just hoped he'd never use it to run without me.

After the shop, though, I was going to find Henrik.

"Why don't you call Bee? She can come hang out here, or I can take you to her place on the way to work."

"No," he answered quickly. "I don't want her to know."

"You don't have to tell her anything you don't want to."

"I can't lie to her. She's too perceptive. Pisses me off."

I kissed his forehead again, if only to cover the smile that threatened to pull at my lips. "Okay, I won't be long. And I'll have my phone on me, so if you need anything at all, you just call me, Rabbit. Whatever I'm doing, I'll drop it to answer you."

Jonah huffed, burying himself in my arms as he locked his own in a cage around me, pulling me close and tight. I held him back the same way.

"Everything will be okay, baby." I'd make sure it was.

Jonah shook his head, arms tightening around me. "No."

"No?"

"No, don't leave me."

I sighed, rubbing his back soothingly. "I need to go to work."

"Then I'm coming too."

If I denied him, I expected there'd be little chance of me prying myself out of his koala grip, and if I was honest, I didn't particularly want to. I'd just have to hope Roy would be okay with Jonah being my shadow for the day, and look for a moment I could get away to find that big bastard.

<hr>

Roy raised an eyebrow when we walked into the shop. His eyes flicked from Jonah to me, a question on his face I was going to force him to ask before I answered with as little detail as possible.

"All good?" he spoke after a moment.

"Will be." Because it wasn't yet, but we'd find our way through.

Roy nodded his head once, looking back at my rabbit again. "Jonah, I assume?"

Jonah's fingers caught the back of my jacket as he stepped in closer, that harsh mask he always wore around people he didn't know firmly in place. He nodded.

Roy grunted. "Well. I ain't paying you if you ain't workin'."

I huffed in amusement, and Jonah stiffened, obviously trying to figure out how to respond to that.

"You can start by getting the coffee order," said the grumpy mechanic, already putting Jonah to work. No doubt sending him off so we could speak privately.

He pulled cash from his wallet and held it out to Jonah, who was still trying to figure out the situation he was in and how to respond. Roy made that decision for him. "Black, no sugar. Whatever this one wants." He gestured his head toward me. "And you." Jonah looked at me, mild panic beneath the scowl as Roy stepped forward and slapped the cash into his hand. "Go on, then." Roy ushered him out, and I smiled and gave him a reassuring nod as he was whisked toward the entrance.

The door chimed, and I heard Jonah grumble something under his breath, but he started walking toward the diner.

"Well then." Roy turned his attention back to me. "You takin' time off and then bringin' him here. Now, I don't have a problem with that, provided he doesn't get in the way, but I need to ask you, son. You boys in trouble?"

Briefly, I wondered what might happen if I told Roy everything. Would he still have the same level of care for me? Would he still want me working here for him? Would he still call me "son?" I couldn't risk it. Couldn't lose him.

"I'm sorting it out." I settled for. Not a lie.

Roy nodded and waited for me to continue. When I didn't, he sighed, crossing his thick arms over his chest. "Boy, you want him to stick around here, you're gonna have to give me more than that."

"You really gonna kick him out, Roy? He doesn't want to be alone right now."

Roy stared at me, and I stared right back, both of us waiting for the other to give in. He huffed, and I won.

"Just... what do you need from me, kid?" he asked. I wasn't sure what I needed, but I had the urge to confide in him, like a scared child seeking the guidance of a parent, someone older and wiser who could make promises like "it's going to be okay," and it'd be believable because there was no reason to doubt them. But that wasn't my life, and Roy wasn't my father. That was something I didn't have anymore. I had to do this on my own.

"I need to go somewhere for a bit. Can you keep Jonah busy? Tell him I had to do something for work? I don't want him to worry."

"Should he worry?" I knew what he was really asking was, "Should *I* worry?"

"No, everything's going to be just fine." Words spoken with hope rather than confidence.

Roy stared at me with an intensity that threatened to shatter the walls I kept between us. "I don't talk much, 'bout your pa."

The mention of my father was so unexpected that I couldn't help the sharp inhale it provoked. "You don't talk much about anything." I tried for teasing, but it fell flat.

"*We* didn't talk much 'bout what really mattered. And I could see—" Roy cleared his throat. "I could see he struggled, and I'd ask him if he was good, and you know what he'd say to me, son? He'd say, 'Everything's going to be just fine.' Now, I ain't no fool, and I knew he wasn't feeling all that good, but like a fool I let him go with that. Because that's the type of men we were. But—" He cleared his throat again, his jaw clenching, his eyes piercing right through me, and I felt heat behind my own as he continued. "But maybe if I hadn't, he wouldn't have—" His eyes glassed over. "He wouldn't have done what he did."

My throat tightened, and as a tear escaped the pale eyes of a man I was used to always seeing so stoic, it felt like my own were being unwillingly drawn from my depths like water from the bottom of a deep well. Because I'd been selfish enough to believe I was the only one who'd missed him, who remembered him, who'd cried for him.

"But I can't fix that now. He's gone, and I can't bring him back. He asked me somethin', though. Made me promise him somethin'. You know what that was?"

I shook my head as my vision blurred.

"He made me promise if somethin' ever happened to him, that I'd look out for his boy. Now I've tried, kid, and maybe I coulda tried harder, and I'm sorry for that. But I failed him once and I'll be damned if I do it again. So, I'm gonna ask you one more time. You boys in trouble?"

The bucket pulled to the surface of the well and spilled its contents in rivulets down my cheeks. "Yeah," I whispered. "We might be."

Roy nodded firmly. "Alright, then. Now what do you need from me?"

"Time." I cleared my throat. "I need to find someone, and Jonah can't come after me."

"Okay. I can handle that. What else?"

"I don't know."

"You gonna be safe?"

"I don't know," I repeated, and the honesty of it threatened to pull more tears from the well.

"Whatever this situation is you're in, you ain't alone. And I'm not losing you too. So if I can help, you tell me."

"What if you don't like what I tell you?"

"Mm, I suspect I probably won't. But I'll help you all the same."

I wasn't about to tell him that my rabbit was directly involved in the murder of three people, whether they deserved it or not, but maybe I could tell him something. Maybe it was safe—he was safe—like my father had been safe. "I have to go before Jonah gets back or he won't let me leave alone, but later?"

Roy nodded, clearing his throat and wiping away any remaining dampness on his cheeks. "Right. Best get on with it, then. You need me—"

"I'll call," I finished for him. "I know."

⚬

I didn't have high hopes that Henrik would be at the Strays' house. With the bastard being as mysterious as he was, I really didn't know where to find him if he didn't want to be found. But I had to try.

When I walked through the front door, I heard a commotion from the next room over. It was Archer, tearing apart the cushions of the sagging sofa like they owed him money.

"All good?" I asked from the doorway.

He startled, scrambling to his feet to face me. "Oh. It's you. What do you want?" he asked, returning to his destruction of the furniture.

"I'm looking for Henrik."

"Haven't seen him," Archer responded distractedly.

"Do you know where he might be, then?"

He didn't respond, instead flipping the sofa over onto its back with a crash.

"Archer?" I snapped.

"What?" he shouted, turning to glare at me. "I don't fucking know where he is, okay? I haven't seen him, and I'm fucking busy."

"Busy?" I scoffed. "Is this why you've been so hard for everyone to contact lately? Because you're fucking up sofas?"

"The point, dickhead, isn't to fuck up the sofa."

"Then what is the fucking point?"

"I'm looking for something."

"For what?"

"Just something!" he snapped, but I wasn't tolerating it.

Archer had been a shitty leader lately, but that hadn't always been the case. When he'd first brought this group of misfits together, he'd been an anchor, the solid foundations that held up everything we'd built. He'd found broken people and given them a home, a purpose. But he'd been absent far too often lately, and the ripples of whatever was happening with him were echoing throughout the Strays.

It wasn't just my conversation with Henrik, there was doubt creeping in when it came to Archer's leadership. Some of the Strays had lost their faith in him. He was unreliable, unreachable, unfocused, and therefore they sought me out instead.

"If you tell me, I can help you," I said through gritted teeth.

Archer glared for a moment, giving me a long, assessing look before sighing as he relented. "My knife."

All this over a knife? "What's it look like?"

He chewed his lip as he looked skyward and inhaled deeply, as if seeking patience and composure. "Switchblade," he said after exhaling. "Pale wood handle."

"Alright," I said, stepping forward to look. Maybe once he had the damned thing he'd calm the fuck down so I could ask him about Henrik.

We searched the living room, the kitchen, and despite telling me it had to be there because he didn't go anywhere else in the house, we searched the other rooms too. Still no knife, and the longer that passed without it, the more I could see him unravel.

"What's so important about it anyway? Can't you just get another one?"

"No!"

"Why?"

"Because."

"Because fucking why, Arch? I'm trying to help you here. Can you stop being so fucking unreasonable?"

Apart from the most recent fight night at the pier, I rarely had reason to be confrontational with Archer. He clearly didn't like it, but at least this time the words sank in instead of bouncing off.

"My father gave it to me," he said after a moment, and the words were soft, like an exposed wound. "It's the only thing he's ever given me. And it's lost."

I knew very little about Archer's father, except that the man was still alive. I wondered what kind of father would only ever have given his kid a knife, but if I could assume Archer and Henrik were products of their environment, I'm not sure I wanted to know.

"Where else might it be?"

"Nowhere." Archer ran his fingers through his hair, leaving it sticking up in every direction instead of the purposefully styled waves he was always meticulous about. "I've searched everywhere else. It's gone."

The panic and rage burned away, revealing something vulnerable and raw he never let anyone see, and given the conversation I'd had so recently with his brother, I wasn't sure I deserved to see it either.

It lasted only a moment before he pulled those walls up again. "Doesn't matter. Just a knife, right?" he said clearing his throat. "Bigger things to worry about."

"Arch..."

"No. It's fine." He exhaled, slow and measured. "It's fine," he repeated, and I knew it wasn't me he was trying to convince but himself. "Listen... I know I haven't been around as much lately. I'm slipping up, I am, and I know that. But I'm trying. Just... just give me a little more time. I'm sorting everything out. Then it can all go back to normal." That part was harder for both of us to believe.

"Is it the Drakes?"

He scoffed. "You could say that."

"What does that mean?"

"It means they know things they shouldn't know, and I'm trying to find out why."

"You think one of us is working with them?"

"Do you have the money?" he asked, changing the subject.

"What money?"

"The money I asked you to get from Phillips."

"I gave it to Henrik. He said he'd give it to you."

Archer's face did something complicated before the mask slid back into place. "Fine."

"I need to find him."

"Yeah. You and me both."

38

Jonah - Past

NOT SAFE.

✦

Dex was gone.

I returned from the diner, and he was just gone. Roy said he was picking up some parts for the shop, but that was a lie. He was lying to me. Dex had lied to me. His bike wasn't here. I might not know shit about cars, but I know you can't pick up parts on a fucking motorcycle.

"Where is he really?" I asked, intending to sound as stern as possible, but my voice didn't listen. Emotion, raw and vulnerable and disgusting, laced my words.

"Told you."

"I don't believe you."

He grunted in response, arms crossed over his chest as he watched me from the desk.

"Who is he with?"

Silence.

"What did he say he was going to do?"

Roy's eyes flicked from mine to the coffee in my hand and back.

"Did he at least say when he'd be back?"

"Jesus, kid." Roy grabbed a handful of tissues from the desk and marched over to me, prying the cup from my vise-like grip. Only then did I register the wetness on my trembling fingers.

I let him take the cup. My breath was coming in short and fast. I tried to steady it. When he attempted to take my hand, I yanked it back, snatching the tissues from him instead to wipe up the spilled coffee. My skin was pink underneath from the hot liquid, but I hardly felt it. All I felt was the heat inside me, scalding, boiling, burning me from the inside out. I didn't know how to let it out without Dex.

I paced, watching the empty lot outside the shop window. Waiting. Listening. Roy went back to the desk, but I still felt the weight of his eyes on me. I hated it. It made my skin feel too tight, too itchy. If he were as concerned as he was pretending to be, he would just tell me where Dex was.

Rather than writhe under his relentless supervision, I pushed the door open and stepped into the cool air, taking my panic with me out into the lot, and yeah, maybe I'd scare off the customers, but who the fuck cared? Dex was gone.

I pulled my phone from my pocket and called him until the line rang out, and then I called him again. Stupid fucking bastard lied to me about that too.

Heat bubbled over inside me, rising up my throat. It made my jaw tighten and my vision blur. I ran my fingers through my hair, tugged at it, tugged harder. The pain across my scalp forced some of the heat to recede. I couldn't breathe. Couldn't fucking breathe.

My back thumped against the brick of the shop's outer wall, the leather probably getting scraped up as I slid down the rough surface until my ass hit the cold ground. I still yanked at handfuls of hair over my scalp.

What could I do? What if he was hurt? What if he was in trouble?

I couldn't go to him. I didn't know where he was. Even if I did, how would I get there? My vision blurred further, and even though I tugged at my hair until the strands came free, it wasn't enough anymore.

"Hey," a voice spoke to me softly, like he was trying not to spook a feral animal. Roy had followed me outside. I didn't want him near me. Didn't want him to look at me. I wanted only one person, and he wasn't here. He wasn't here.

Every breath burned as I inhaled, unable to hold it in for a moment before I was chasing the next one, and the next. Too much. Not enough. Dex.

A warm hand rested on my shoulder, and I pulled away as if struck by it. "No," I choked out around a sob. Was I crying?

"Shit," Roy grumbled, hovering over me without touching me again, clearly uncertain what to do, and I didn't have answers for him.

"Dex," I choked out again.

"He'll be here, kid. Any minute now he'll be here, and he'll be okay." Roy's words were supposed to soothe, but they didn't. He didn't know. He was a liar. He'd already lied, and he was doing it again.

Dex.

I wanted to scream, but I couldn't get enough air into my lungs. Was I suffocating? Was I going to die because I couldn't remember how to fucking breathe? The sound of my own ragged breathing drowned out everything else.

Knowing Roy was there, watching me, made it worse. But I couldn't tell him to fuck off like I desperately wanted to. I couldn't tell him anything. My words were caught in my chest, tangled like a ball of string I couldn't find the end to. Building, building, building. Heavy. Itchy. Hot. Too much. Dex.

I needed Dex. Needed him more than air. Needed him more than I'd ever needed another person. Even Adaline. I hadn't felt like this for a long time, not since I was a child. Not since I had her to help me. She always knew how to help me. She was the only one who tried. Until Dex. But she was gone now. And so was he.

I blamed them both. I only felt like this because they let me *feel*. They made me think it was safe. Without them I'd learned to feel only rage, because I knew how to deal with that, how to use it. My rage felt like a weapon, like a protection. I wasn't protected now. My rage was out of reach, and I wasn't safe.

Not safe. Not safe. *Not safe.*

The only reason I didn't throw up was that my mouth and throat had dried up, air passing in and out too rapidly to be useful. Until my head spun. Until my vision was blurring and my limbs were stiff and trembling. Twitching like a dying spider as it curled in on itself. Vulnerable. Weak. Pathetic.

Not safe.

Then I was being touched again, cradled by warmth, the scent of smoke and leather and safety as familiar arms wrapped around me. "Shhhh... I'm here. I've got you, Rabbit."

Dex.

I sobbed. Heat flowed freely down my face as I let him surround me.

"I've got you," he said calmly, always so calm. I breathed deeper, my body only accepting air when it tasted like him. The burning fire receding to embers in my core, his presence water over the flames. Drowning me. Saving me. "I'm right here."

He was here. He was here with me, and he was safe.

My limbs unlocked, melted into him, falling and trusting him to catch me. He did. His hands smoothed over my hair, his touch soothing the hurt I'd inflicted.

I must have been a mess, but I didn't care, and he didn't seem to either as he held me tighter, letting me bury my damp face in the warmth of his neck. He was here. He'd come back.

I clung to him like I'd die without him, and honestly maybe I would. It had felt like I was going to. But he was with me now, his pulse warm and beating beneath my lips. I let it soothe me, like sunlight above the surface of deep water, guiding me up, guiding me back. Only when my pulse matched his could I bring myself to pull away again.

"You left me," I told him, whatever fire remained seeping into the words.

"I did. I'm so sorry, baby. I shouldn't have done that."

There was more I wanted to say, wanted to know. But now my head was heavy and spinning, and I felt so tired.

"Can you stand?" he asked, and I nodded softly, still giving him my scowl because I was too tired to give him anything else.

Dex pulled me to my feet, and I wiped the back of my hand across my face, trying to erase the evidence of the disgusting feelings that remained on my skin.

Roy wasn't here anymore. He must have left when Dex had come back. He probably thought I was completely fucking ridiculous, and maybe he was right. I hated when anyone looked at me at all, and I'd let him see far too much.

"Come on." Dex's fingers laced between mine as he pulled me inside.

Thankfully, Roy was nowhere in sight as Dex made his way through the office and into the garage, and I let him pull me along with him until we reached an old Jeep in the back corner.

Dex opened the driver's door and gestured inside.

I rolled my eyes, and the action only reminded me of how heavy they felt as I got in and he closed the door, walking round to the other side to get in beside me.

"Do you like it?" he asked me, looking hopeful.

"What?"

"The car."

I shrugged one shoulder. "It's fine. Why? Whose car is this?"

"It's yours."

I thought I was done crying, but as his words sunk in I felt that icky heat pooling behind them again. "You... you got me a car?"

He nodded. "It was supposed to be a surprise when it was finished. I still have to do a few more things, but then it's all yours. You'll have a way for us to get around, and you won't ever be stuck in place."

It was all too much, all of it too big to fit inside me, but I didn't know where else to put it. So instead of speaking, I rested my hands on the wheel, sniffing as I nodded firmly, once, letting the tears fall again, feeling safe enough not to stop them when it was just the two of us.

"Come here, baby," he said, his voice soothing and warm like nothing else I'd ever known. I wanted to be angry at him, wanted to hold on to my rage over the fact that he'd left me, that he'd lied. I couldn't. Even now, when I was so broken because of him, I still wanted him.

My hands left the wheel and I went to him, climbing over the center console, my limbs and shoes knocking things awkwardly as I scrambled over it and into his lap. Warm. Safe. His arms circled me, cradling me to him as if I were smaller than I was. Lips pressed a soft kiss onto my hair, and then I was crying again.

We didn't speak. I wasn't sure if I'd even be able to. But this was enough. I *let* myself fall apart this time because I knew he was there to hold me together.

By the time I was done, what felt like hours later, I felt empty and exhausted. My eyes were too heavy to keep open, but still he held me close to him, waiting for me to be ready to just *be* again.

"Roy thinks I'm a freak," I told him, my voice quiet and hoarse.

"He doesn't think you're a freak, baby," Dex replied, his voice just as quiet. "He's probably just worried. But you're not a freak."

I turned into him further, unsure if I believed his words. But it didn't matter, not really. Not what Roy thought of me, or anyone else. The only person who mattered was here with me now, and he saw me. He knew me. He loved me. It's all I needed.

"Will you be okay if I go back to work soon?"

Despite just thinking that I didn't care what Roy thought, I decided I still didn't want to see him again so soon. "Can I stay here?"

"Of course. This is yours now, baby. You can stay here as long as you want."

"And you won't leave again?"

"I won't, I promise. I'll stay in the garage where you can see me, and if you need me, I'll come back and be here with you again."

"You lied already."

Dex inhaled deeply, trying to find the right words to say because he knew I was right. He couldn't deny it, and if he even tried, I wouldn't be able to handle it.

"I did," he answered eventually. "I did, and I'm so sorry. I thought I was protecting you by keeping you out of it. But that was a mistake, and I know that now. And I'm so very sorry, Rabbit."

I didn't want his apology to soothe me, but he always had a way of influencing my emotions more than I wanted him to. Like parts of me obeyed him as if they belonged to him instead of myself. Like he possessed me.

"Fine," I grumbled. "But if it happens again... I won't forgive you."

"It won't happen again," Dex told me, and against my better judgment, I trusted him.

* * *

The rest of the day passed uneventfully. When Dex was sure I was okay, he got back to work, bringing me a fresh coffee that apparently Roy had gone to get. I sipped as I hid out in the car—*my* car, that he was fixing just for me.

When it was time for lunch, he asked me if I wanted to go to the diner with him or just have him go pick something up for me. While I did trust that he wouldn't take off without me again, I still didn't want him going anywhere I couldn't be with him, so I had to leave the safety of the vehicle I'd locked myself away in.

I avoided Roy as much as possible, and he didn't seem to mind that. When the shop closed for the day and Roy left, I felt brave enough to leave the car again, only to hover around Dex as he continued the repairs on it. I didn't know shit about engines, but Dex still explained to me what he was doing, still tried to keep me involved even though I'd much rather watch him work than do it myself.

By the time he was done, it was late, and I was so tired. Dex brought the Jeep out from its corner, and after I assured him I was perfectly capable of driving it—Richard having paid for my driving lessons when he still thought he'd eventually get something out of me—I drove home, following Dex on his bike.

We stumbled through the door, up the stairs, and into each other's arms as we fell into bed. I was hard and so was he, but it wasn't about being sexual. It was the connection, the intimacy. I needed to feel him on me—in me—so that we could be as close as possible. So that my mind and my body were filled with nothing but him. Only with him could I stop myself from spiraling when all I wanted to do was run and hide from the world.

39

JONAH - PAST

CHOICES.

When I woke up, the room was still dark. Shadows enveloped our surroundings, the furniture only discernible by its faint outlines from the moonlight streaming in through the uncovered window. It meant we had more time together before the world woke up and he had to leave this bed, only when I shuffled back to find Dex, he wasn't there.

The sheets were still warm on his side, but he wasn't there. Shards of ice sliced through my chest, and suddenly I was wide awake, ripping off the blankets, determined to find him.

The rest of the house was dark. He wasn't in the bathroom, and I stumbled down the stairs without bothering to even put clothes on first. The front door was slightly open, and as I approached, the sound of his voice on the other side already had the ice embedded between my ribs melting. He was still here. He hadn't left.

I took a deep steadying breath before approaching, wondering who he was talking to.

"Whoa there, calm down, little Snake Prince."

Little Snake Prince? I stalled in place. A new kind of cold spread through my core. Who the fuck was he talking to? My gut twisted with adrenaline. I stepped a little closer to the door, trying to hear better. Through the gap I could see him; his back was to me as he faced out over the blackness of the front yard. He was alone with his phone to his ear.

"Okay, stop. Don't say anything else. I said stop... Okay. Breathe in deep and just listen for a second. Do not tell me any more details right now. Do not tell *anyone* any details right now. Don't call anyone else. Just tell me where you are and explain when I get there. Got it?"

What the actual fuck was going on?

"Okay. I'll be there in an hour. Stay put and stay quiet... Okay... I'll see you soon."

He hung up the phone, and I darted backward, away from the door and back into his room. By the time he came back in, I was pacing, and it felt like there were bugs under my skin making me all kinds of itchy.

"Hey, you're awake. So—" he began, but I immediately cut him off.

"Who the fuck is Snake Prince?" He stared at me instead of answering, so I continued. "Seriously, Dex? Little Snake Prince?"

"He's just a friend," he explained slowly, softly. I hated it. "Just one of the Strays, Rabbit."

"Who is he? What's his real name? And what the fuck is he doing calling you at three a.m.?"

"Like I said, he's a Stray."

"Why. Was. He. Calling. You?" I said, clapping my hands between each word impatiently. Dex might have been trying to stay calm, but I wasn't, and I wouldn't be until I had fucking answers.

"He needs my help with something."

"With what?"

"Stray stuff. Does it matter?"

"I don't fucking know, Dex. What do you think? He's calling you of all people in the middle of the night when he's upset, and you're just going to leave me and take off to go help him? Why can't he call someone else?"

Dex sighed, taking a deep breath in as if seeking composure. I hated that. Hated that he was masking himself from me. "He doesn't trust anyone else with this. He just... broke something. Something important. He needs me to come help him fix it."

"Why you?" I pressed again.

"Because, Jonah! Just because!" The mask of calmness cracked. "Because things are happening. Things I'm involved with that I don't want to put on you. Archer isn't reliable anymore, so people are looking to me instead." He spoke as he crossed the room to his dresser, pulling the top drawer out so harshly that the handle broke off. Dex grunted and tossed the handle across the room, causing it to collide with the far wall. He pulled out the first dark shirt he found and pulled it over his head.

"You're seriously leaving? You're just going to go and leave me?"

"I have to, Rabbit. Something bad happened, and I need to fix it. I'm the only one who can fix it. I'm sorry."

Panic clawed up my chest. "No. You can't go. You can't leave me. What if I need you too?"

Dex sighed. "Then call me and I'll come back. But you're okay. Just stay here in bed and I'll be back soon."

"That's it? You're not even going to explain where you're going?"

"I have explained."

"You haven't told me shit. Not who you were talking to, not where you're going, and certainly not fucking why."

Dex grunted instead of responding. He grabbed his jacket from the top of the clothes pile we'd left before stumbling into bed hours ago, and slipped it on.

"I'm coming with you," I told him, crossing my arms over my chest.

"No. You aren't."

"Yes, I am. Unless you can tell me what's actually going on. Why are you keeping secrets from me?"

He sighed and crossed the room toward me. Large warm hands cupped my arms just below my shoulders, gentle for a moment before I shrugged him off and took a step back. I glared at him expectantly, waiting for him to explain.

"I'm not keeping any of *my* secrets from you, Rabbit. Ask me anything about me, and I'll tell you. But this isn't my secret, and I don't even know the details yet, okay?" His voice was soft when he spoke to me, and I hated that more. I wished it wasn't. I'd rather he yell at me if he wasn't going to tell me what I wanted to know. At least then it would feel like a fight and not me one-sidedly losing my shit. "I'll be back in a few hours. So wh—"

"Don't go."

He sighed and stepped closer to me, reaching for me again. "I have to."

Like before, I shrugged him off, his arms dropping as my fists clenched in rage. I didn't understand why he wouldn't just tell me what the fuck was going on. Why couldn't I come too? And most importantly, who the fuck was little Snake Prince?

"If you leave now, don't bother coming back."

Dex's jaw clenched. "I live here, Jonah. If you don't want to see me, you're the one who has to leave."

There was rage in my veins instead of blood. I didn't fucking want him to go anywhere if it wasn't with me. I didn't want him to know people I didn't know. I didn't want anyone to need him. Because I needed all of him. He was mine. Every part. Mine. "Don't go."

"Get some sleep, Rabbit. I'll be back before you wake up."

Dex reached for me again, but this time instead of shrugging him off, I shoved at him.

Before I gained any distance between us, his own larger hands were wrapped around my wrists and he used the hold to yank me forward, causing me to stumble and fall right into his firm chest. His shirt smelled of cheap detergent, and *him*, and I hated how much just the scent of him calmed me down. His arms were wrapped around my shoulders before I could pull away, and he held me close as he dropped a firm kiss to the top of my head. "I won't be long," he repeated. "I'd like it if you were still here when I got back."

"I won't be." I pulled away, turning my back to him as he sighed and collected his keys, wallet, and lighter. He left without saying anything else. I listened to the sound of him walking down the stairs, the shuffle of him putting his boots on, and then the door closing. His bike started up and sped off.

My eyes burned. Rage pulsed through me, looking for a destination. Looking for destruction. He'd seen what had happened to me yesterday when he left me alone. He'd seen that, and he still left now. Granted, he hadn't lied to me this time first, but he hadn't exactly told me the truth about what he was doing either.

Part of me wanted to go after him, to take the car he'd given me and follow him to see what it was he was really doing, who the fuck little Snake Prince was. It wasn't just him. He'd had another phone call before—*"little Cupid, my favorite stray."* Who the fuck were these people? Why did they need him? Why did he *let* them need him? Were they really just friends, or had he fucked them before too? Did they know him like I knew him?

I screamed, grabbing the lamp from beside me and hurling it across the room. It crashed, and for a brief moment I felt better, the sound echoing something inside me as it shattered, but then it was gone and I felt worse.

Why did he need other people? Why couldn't it just be me? What happened if shit hit the fan? If the police somehow found out it was me and Henrik at that crime scene? Would he really run away with me? Or would he stay and protect his precious Strays? Maybe they meant more to him than I did. If it came down to it, and he had to choose between them and me, would he really choose me?

Fuck him. I'd been serious. He didn't believe me, obviously, but I was. I wasn't going to be here just waiting around for him to get back.

40

Jonah - Past

FRESH WOUNDS OVER OLD SCARS.

✦

I waited around for him to get back.

Of course I did. Where else would I have gone? I considered waking up Becca, but I didn't want to explain what had happened, and there was nothing I wanted less than to go back to Dad's. That left me with going to the diner, maybe, or the beach.

I'd thought about it. I'd even got dressed at one point and made it as far as the car before stalling, because what if he was in danger? What if he came home again like the last time he'd been called away from me, bloody and beaten. Who would take care of him if I wasn't here?

He'd lied to me. Shocker. Even if I *had* gone to sleep, he wouldn't have been back before I woke up. It was just after ten in the morning, and he still wasn't back. I paced back and forth in front of the door as if waiting here would bring him home faster.

I cycled between panicked, enraged, and this other feeling from deeper inside me I didn't know how to name. It was both, and it was more. Bigger. Heavier. It sat uncomfortably in my gut, clawing up the inside of my rib cage and threatening to spill free until I swallowed it back down. Because it felt like darkness. Like destruction.

It was rising again, creeping up my chest, up my throat like it could possess me to lash out—to break things—so Dex could see with his own eyes the storm that was inside me. Logically, I knew it was wrong, that breaking things wouldn't change what had happened and would only make things worse for the both of us when he returned. But still it was there, impossible to ignore.

"Fuck!" I shouted, and not for the first time since he'd left. I was thankful that the houses on either side of this one seemed empty or abandoned.

Leaving my post at the entrance, I stormed into the living room and slammed the door so hard that the wall rattled and a picture fell to the ground. The glass shattered, and the wooden frame splintered.

Fucking fuck!

Why not, then? If just existing was going to cause destruction, why not fucking lean into it? My arm swiped out, knocking tacky trinkets from an accent table across the room as they shattered and broke as well. I flipped over the table itself for good measure, then stood there seething, fists clenching and unclenching in the heavy silence that followed.

Panic clawed up my throat, and I tamped it down, but it was getting harder, and I knew I was getting bad again. Pride had stopped me from calling Dex when he'd already made his choice, but I needed him. I needed him even if I was pissed at him right now. It had been long enough.

I'd left my phone in the bedroom, because having it on me had only made the temptation to call him stronger, and I hadn't been ready to give in to it yet. I was now. I pulled the door handle with as much force as I'd slammed it earlier, only this time it didn't budge.

I tried it again, and the handle twisted, but the door didn't open. I pulled harder, but it was like it was locked from the other side.

Clawing, slashing, scratching panic.

With both hands I jostled the handle, pulled the door with everything I had, but it was jammed. My vision blurred, and the panic blazed. Engulfed me. I couldn't fight it. I couldn't breathe.

I took a step back, raising my leg to kick at the door. My foot made contact, and I screamed as searing pain enveloped the limb like fire.

FUCK. FUCK FUCK FUCK FUCK FUCK FUCK.

"FUCK!" I screamed, clinging to the rage because without it there was only panic, and I was just scared and trapped in a room alone.

I put my weight on my leg, and it gave out immediately, sending me to my knees. I screamed again. Then I was grabbing whatever was within arm's reach just to throw it, set on taking the destruction inside me and pushing it outward. I crawled to the dropped picture, my hands ripping apart the pieces of the still-intact frame just so I'd have more to break, more to throw. I threw the back of the frame, hearing it smash against something else made of glass across the room. Then I went for the shards.

One piece of jagged glass thrown, and on the next I felt the sting of cold edges as it sliced into me. I hissed, watching as red beaded slowly from the break in the skin, bubbling, oozing to the surface.

For a moment, everything was quiet.

Then the sting faded, and noise was back—the thoughts, the panic, the rage, the thing inside me climbing back up. I clutched at the shard again until the pain pushed the demons away, my blood a sacrifice that appeased them.

Not enough.

Pain in my fingers. Pain in my leg.

More red. More quiet.

I didn't think. Couldn't.

I just wanted it to be quiet.

It was finally quiet.

Then I was done, and the panic was gone, and in the quiet it left behind, seeping out of the wounds with the red and the pain, was shame.

I curled in on myself, hugging my knees, my sleeve soaking in the red I'd caused on my leg, fresh wounds over old scars, but I didn't care. Dex would come home, and he'd find me like this, and he would finally see that I was too much.

You're too much.

Why can't you be different?

Why can't you be better?

Why can't you make yourself smaller?

This is why they don't love you.

This is why no one ever will.

*You're crazy. Insane. Unreasonable. Stubborn. Frustrating. Too much. Too much. **Too much**.*

I sobbed into my arm, panic replaced by hopelessness. My anger had been loud so I hadn't had to listen to the doubts that whispered in the silence. The fears. But it was silent now.

Why couldn't I just be like Dex? He was in pain too, he was hurting too, but he could control it. *Why can't I control it?*

I'm not good enough.

Dex would return and see that he'd been right to leave me. And the next time he left... he wouldn't come back.

By the time I heard his bike coming down the road and into the driveway, I didn't want to move. I didn't have any rage left for him. All I could do was sit here and wait for him to find me. Wait for him to decide that this was it, this was too much for him.

The door opened and closed so softly that if I hadn't been sitting in the next room over, I wouldn't have heard it. Maybe he was worried about what he'd be walking into and was trying to be cautious. I heard the creak of the stairs as he climbed them, but I didn't make a sound. Let him think I'd left.

After a minute, I heard the creaks again as he descended. Closer. Until all that remained between us was a jammed door. Only when *he* turned the handle, of course it opened for him.

Dex inhaled sharply, no doubt taking in the chaos I'd caused. I'd thought maybe I'd get some satisfaction from him seeing the destruction, but all I felt was more shame.

After a moment, he pushed the door open the rest of the way, and then disappeared out the way he came. I figured he'd go for the front door, but he took the stairs again. Was he waiting for me to leave now that it was open?

I didn't have to wonder for long before his heavy footfalls bounded closer, like maybe he was taking the stairs two at a time. Then he was back, kneeling in front of me, concern and hurt in his tired eyes as he gently pried my arms away from where they hugged my knees, getting a better look at what I'd done to myself.

Leaning forward, he placed a kiss on the top of my head, achingly soft and lingering. Then without speaking, he opened the first aid kit and got to work.

41

DEX - PAST

NO MORE HIDING.

The door to the living room was one of many things on my list to fix. The handle twisted on both sides, but the latch only engaged if you turned it from the outside. I'd made a mistake by forgetting to mention that to Jonah. But the biggest mistake I'd made had been leaving him. Again.

It shouldn't have mattered that the Strays needed me. I'd been trying to contact Snake for the past two days, and when he called, I figured he was just calling me back. How wrong I was. Another body. He'd been so panicked. I wasn't used to hearing a man usually so cold, arrogant, and sure of himself crying like a baby, barely able to get a breath in. Still, Jonah should have been my priority.

I'd done what I'd needed to and stepped up while Archer slacked off, but I couldn't keep it up, not with Jonah needing me as much as he did. If it were between the Strays and Jonah, I'd choose Jonah every time. But I hadn't shown him that.

A conversation needed to be had with Archer. He'd asked me to give him time, but I couldn't. He needed to get his shit together or start delegating to others, because I was done. It didn't matter what conversations had been had with Henrik. It didn't matter that there were others who'd put their trust in me. The only person who mattered was sitting in front of me, and even then, he wasn't truly there.

Jonah's eyes were dull and vacant, like the day I'd found him in the shower; violence had carved out the fire from the core of him, only this time it was violence against himself. I'd rather bury a thousand bodies for him than patch up a single wound on his perfect skin. I wished I could take them from him, because each laceration hurt me twice as much as if they'd been carved directly into my flesh.

There were two that were particularly savage, marking an X over the existing scars on his outer calf. He'd carved them right through the denim of his jeans, the fabric as torn as his skin. They seemed to be the only ones still actively bleeding. I tore away the rest of the ruined material as gently as possible to reveal the full extent of the damage, then applied gauze firmly to the wounds, adding another layer when it soaked through too fast, waiting patiently until the bleeding eventually slowed and then stopped.

"This is going to sting," I warned, my voice just above a whisper after I'd pulled the bloodied gauze away and reached for the antiseptic. Jonah nodded softly but didn't speak, still numb to me and to himself until the damp pad made contact with wounded flesh and he hissed, gritting his teeth and groaning. He didn't stop me, so I continued cleaning and disinfecting his leg and then his fingers.

I placed more closure strips than was probably necessary to the worst of the damage, holding his split skin together, and I hoped reducing the chances of further scarring. Then I wrapped his leg and fingers in more gauze until his pain was hidden beneath deceptive white.

There was blood on the floor, soaking into the carpet. I didn't care. Tomorrow I'd figure out what to do about that; today I'd been away from Jonah long enough. We still needed to talk about what happened, but he was tired, and so was I. What I needed now was to hold him, to have him, to keep him. I believed he needed the same.

Without forcing either of us to speak more than necessary, I gently eased my hands under his legs, around his waist, waiting for him to protest and then lifting him when he didn't.

I carried him to the bedroom, setting him down softly on the bed before undressing him, cautious of his injuries. He let me, and when he was left in only his underwear, I did the same.

Just before taking my place on the bed beside him, my phone rang again, and I didn't miss the way Jonah tensed at the noise. I reached for it, seeing Bryce's name on the screen before switching it off. Whatever he needed, someone else could deal with it.

Where I needed to be now was here, with him. I found my place beside him and pulled him into me, his skin against my skin. Then I tugged the blankets over us both, sealing us in with each other like the covers could shield us from the rest of the world.

I kissed the back of his shoulders, inhaling the scent of him deep into my lungs. The scent of my home.

He was quiet and still, and I listened to the sound of his breathing, my hand smoothing over his chest to feel the pace of his heart for long minutes before whispering, "I'm sorry."

For a moment there was silence, and I wondered if he was already asleep. Then quietly, he spoke. "I'm sorry too."

I kissed his skin again and moved in closer, so that as much of me was touching as much of him as possible. And like that, like we should always have been, we both fell asleep surrounded by each other's warmth.

***

I wasn't sure what time it was when I woke up, but Jonah was already awake, his fingers tracing idle patterns over the skin of my arm around him.

"I'm glad you didn't leave," I whispered. He stiffened when he realized I was no longer sleeping. I followed the words with another kiss on his shoulder.

"I was kind of trapped," he scoffed, wanting the words to sound harsher than they did. Because he was guarding himself against me again, and it pained me deeply knowing I'd made him feel like he had to.

"I'm sorry I forgot to tell you about the door. I'll fix it. I never wanted to make you feel trapped, Rabbit."

Jonah was quiet again, so I continued. "You were going to, but you changed your mind. Thank you for changing your mind." Now that I'd started, the words were pouring out of me. "I'm sorry I left. I'm sorry I made you feel like you had to leave too, even for a second. I always want you here with me. I'm so happy you're still here. And I'm so sorry. I'm sorry I couldn't explain, and I'm sorry I couldn't bring you with me, and I'm sorry I had to leave you alone."

I was met with more silence for a long moment before Jonah finally responded to me. "Am I too much for you?"

The question felt like a physical blow. "No," I answered without hesitation. "You aren't too much. You're *never* too much for me."

"I'm frustrating. I'm unreasonable. I'm clingy, and jealous. I'm... I'm crazy or something."

"No," I said again, my voice firm despite the pain I felt knowing he could ever think those things about himself. "You aren't any of those things, not to me. Not ever. I love you, my rabbit, exactly how you are. I left because I had to, not because of anything you did."

"You say you had to, like you didn't have a choice. But you did have a choice. And you chose to leave me."

Guilt, heavy and sharp, expanded in my chest. I had responsibilities with the Strays, people who relied on me, but Jonah was right. No one had *forced* me to go.

"You're right. But I didn't want to."

"But you still did it."

"Yeah. Yeah, I still did. And all I can say is that I'm sorry. That I'll work on being better."

Jonah thought over that for a long moment before he shifted out of my arms, or at least he tried to before I tightened my hold on him to keep him against me, scared that if I let him go he'd slip away from me and go someplace I couldn't reach him.

He sighed, giving up and letting me keep him. "You lied to me."

"When?"

"You said you wouldn't be long, that you'd be back before I woke up."

"Did you sleep?"

He grumbled, "That's not the point."

I kissed the warm skin along the curve of his neck. "I'm sorry. It took longer than I thought."

"Will you at least tell me what you were doing?"

I inhaled him deeply, his scent a comfort unlike any other I'd ever known. "There was... a body."

Silence for a moment, and then, "Who?"

"No one you know, Rabbit. I promise."

Instead of pulling away from me like I feared he would, Jonah pushed into me. Closer. "And this... Snake... he killed them?"

"He did. It was an accident, and he didn't know what to—"

"Have you fucked him?"

I kissed the side of his face. "No."

"Promise?"

"I promise."

"What about... Cupid?"

I swallowed heavily, and my silence answered the question for him.

"When?"

"Once. A long time ago."

"Which other Strays have you slept with?"

"Can we not do this?"

"So there's more, then." Jonah tried to pull away from me again. I tightened my hold on him in a panic.

"Just Archer. But it's over. It was never anything serious. None of them were."

"But they still saw you like I have."

"No. They haven't. No one has ever seen me like you've seen me," I told him, my hold on him turning bruising. "No one. Only you. The rest of it was just sex, just fucking without feeling. I didn't care about them, and they didn't care about me, not really. Only you've seen me. Really, truly *seen* me. All of me. Only you."

He stopped trying to pull out of my hold as he contemplated that. I expected him to drag it out further, to ask me for more of the details. Instead he said, "I feel like I can't see you anymore." And my chest ached. "This morning... it felt like you were hiding from me. Like... wearing a mask. I hate it."

I inhaled deeply. "I'm sorry." I'd apologize for everything, as much as he needed to hear it, because I truly was sorry for any action that had hurt him. None of them had been intentional. In fact, everything I'd done, I'd done intending to protect him. But I wasn't doing a good enough job of it, and still I'd hurt him, and I'd never stop being sorry for that. "I wasn't trying to hide from you. I just wanted to protect you."

"From what?"

"From me. From the bad things connected to me. I only want to be good for you."

"Don't you get it yet?" Jonah shifted, and I held him still as he grunted and smacked at my arms until I loosened my hold enough for him to turn around, and his eyes met mine. He took my face in his hands. The spark was back in his eyes, his brow furrowed with determination. "I want all of you. Every single piece of you, as you are. I don't want you because you're good or because you protect me. I want you because I fucking love *you*, you dumbass."

"Baby—"

"I'm not finished. I know I'm a lot of work, Dex. I know I'm needy and demanding. Fuck, I know I'm entirely fucking ridiculous—"

"I told you you're not—"

"But you still accept me as I am. Why won't you give me the chance to do the same? I know I'm a fucking mess. I really do know. But that doesn't mean you have to hold it together for the both of us."

"I just—"

"So yeah, I'm pissed that you left me alone, but what I'm most pissed about is that you feel you can't lean on me and trust me to hold you as well when things get tough. I'm not just some kid for you to babysit. We're in this together, you and me. Aren't we?"

His eyes searched mine, open and vulnerable. I didn't deserve him. I never would. But he was mine, and I was keeping him. I'd just have to try every day to be worthy of him. "Yeah. We're in this together."

"No more hiding," he told me.

"No more hiding," I agreed. And added, "No more running."

"No more running." He nodded in approval, sealing the agreement with a kiss.

"I love you," I said as our lips parted again.

"I love you too." His fingers traced my jawline from beneath my ear to my chin. "And I wasn't going to run."

"You almost did. You made it to your car before changing your mind."

Jonah scowled. "You got cameras here or something, Devil?"

No more hiding. "No. I um... I asked Raven to keep an eye on you."

The scowl deepened, but he fought a smile pulling at his lips. "Well, she did a terrible job."

I shrugged one shoulder. "I told her to keep her distance and follow you if you left."

"Would you hunt me down and bring me back if I did?"

"Of course I would."

He didn't fight his smile this time. The fact he even doubted that offended me. Jonah was mine. There was nowhere in this life or the next that I wouldn't follow him.

42

Dex – Past

TWO BIRDS, ONE DILDO.

Fingertips gripped my jaw, holding me in place as Jonah took what he wanted, his softness turning to desperation. There was more we needed to talk about, but it felt like we'd made progress, and I needed him too.

It must have been late afternoon from the light streaming in through the window. The sun hit him just right, and I swear his eyes looked golden. Sharp and bold. Rich and deep. And I didn't drink, but I was an alcoholic for the whiskey of his eyes.

He was so beautiful.

Jonah rolled his hips into mine, his scowl deepening. "Stop just looking at me and do something about this," he said, pushing his hard cock into mine, as if I hadn't noticed it yet.

"So demanding," I chuckled.

"You like me demanding."

"Mmn, close. I like you needy." Jonah looked ready to protest, so I continued further. "And I like you desperate and whimpering."

He exhaled a shaky breath, pupils dilating. Black swallowing gold. "Then make me desperate."

It was a challenge, and one I couldn't refuse. I darted forward, catching his bottom lip between my teeth, biting him roughly before I sucked it into my mouth. Jonah groaned, his nails sinking into my skin above the waistband of my boxers. Obviously we had to lose those, but a wicked idea resurfaced in my mind first.

"Do you remember what I told you on the roof of the college?"

Jonah groaned, frustrated that I was talking again instead of acting, but I wouldn't let him have his way just yet.

"What part?" he sighed in annoyance.

"The part where I told you I'd punish anyone who hurts you." His eyes widened slightly. "Including yourself."

Jonah swallowed and then nodded.

We would need to talk more about what he'd done to himself, why he'd done it, and make a plan for what he should do the next time he felt like harming himself. And we would. After I'd punished him.

"Get on your hands and knees."

"Make me."

It was a game. One we both knew he wanted to lose, but he had to play it out first. He wanted to give up control, but only after I fought him for it. I had to earn it. I intended to do just that.

I knew what he expected me to do. He was waiting for me to grab him, to manhandle him into position, and fuck, I wanted to. But this was supposed to be a punishment. So Jonah didn't get what he wanted, at least not yet.

Rather than grabbing him roughly, my hands withdrew from him entirely, and I shifted away, rolling onto my back and trailing my fingers down my body, down to the only fabric that still covered me... beneath it. My fingers wrapped around my hard cock and I hummed.

Jonah reached for me, but I smacked his hand away with the one not currently wrapped around myself. "No. You don't get to touch me until you do as you're told."

He scowled, eyes sharp with lust and rage. I ignored it, stroking myself slowly, my thumb pressing into the metal of my piercing at the tip, making me groan again. Jonah's eyes tracked the movement, but he couldn't see exactly what I was doing, the fabric concealing all but the outline of my fist.

"Show me," he breathed out.

"I'm not doing anything you say until you're on your hands and knees, brat."

He grunted in frustration, having a rapid but large internal war within his own mind. He wanted to touch me, to see me, but he didn't want to do as I'd said. He was looking for a loophole.

"Fine, then I'll just touch myself too," he declared smugly, as if I would allow that to happen. As soon as he rolled onto his back and reached for the fabric covering his own hard cock, I was on him. He smiled, thinking he'd won, but I wasn't done.

My hands gripped Jonah's hips roughly, and I flipped him onto his front. Immediately he was squirming, his hips rocking back to find me, but that wasn't what was happening.

"Don't fucking move," I snarled into his ear, and he shivered as I got off the bed. I yanked the bottom drawer of my dresser open, snatching up a thick black leather belt, and spotting something else I'd hidden away there earlier. I grabbed that too, bringing both over to the bed.

"What are you—" Jonah started, but I didn't let him finish before I grabbed each of his wrists, pulling them behind him and crossing them behind his back. Then I reached for the belt, wrapping it around and around where his forearms crossed over each other. With the ends, I placed them in his palms.

"If you let go of either side, even for a moment, I'm not fucking you."

Jonah's hands closed into fists, quickly holding onto the belt and securing it in place.

Then I reached for the other thing I'd decided it was finally time to use—the purple dildo Jonah had traitorously bought from Maxxxine's.

"I thought—"

"Quiet, or I'll gag you."

It was a lie, because I'd be gagging him either way. I ripped open the packaging, tossing cardboard and plastic behind me carelessly. Then I slammed the silicone dick onto the headboard, its suction base sealing and remaining in place.

I wouldn't fuck Jonah with it. Nothing was ever going inside his hole but me. That was *mine*. His mouth, however? I couldn't give him that, or so I'd thought, because maybe it didn't have to be me. Maybe I could use this tool instead, like an extension of myself. He'd get to feel what it was like to have his throat fucked, and I'd be able to gag him like I'd threatened to. Two birds, one dildo.

Before settling on the bed over him, I took the lube from the nightstand and dropped it next to Jonah. Then I stripped out of my boxers, my hard cock springing free, already desperate for him. Jonah could keep his on for now, I had other plans for him.

I lowered myself over him, kissing the back of his shoulders, his neck, until I reached his ear, my tongue tracing the curve, causing him to shudder.

"I'm going to punish you now, Rabbit. But if you're actually uncomfortable, you need to let me know," I told him. Before we went any further, I needed him to understand this. "If you can't say the safeword, then you let go of the belt. I'll be watching your hands closely. So if you want to stop, just let go, and I'll stop. I won't be disappointed, and you won't be in trouble. Understand?"

Jonah nodded frantically, and when I was silent, he knew what I was waiting for. "If I want you to stop, I'll let go of the belt."

"Good boy."

I pushed up to my knees, my hands on his hips guiding him to do the same. Without the use of his arms, it meant his face remained pressed into the bedding. I smoothed my hands over the firm globes of his ass, over the fabric, my thumbs trailing his crease. Slowly. Firmly.

He was still at first, but the more I took my time just massaging him, the more impatient he got, until he was pushing back against me.

Jonah cried out, his voice muffled by the sheets, the spank muffled by his underwear.

That wouldn't do.

Thumbs slipped beneath cotton and I pulled the fabric up, exposing his pale cheeks and the permanent letters of my name. I'd never tire of seeing it there.

I spanked him again. Once. Twice. The *thwack* of my palm on his skin so much sharper this time. His voice was louder too. I alternated sides until my palm was stinging and his ass was pink and his breathing shuddered and he was soft and pliant for me.

My hands glided over the abused skin, and Jonah shivered and twitched.

"Are you attached to this underwear for any reason?"

"What do you mean?" he asked, already sounding breathy and hoarse, his voice slow, like it took a lot of effort for him to string the words together.

"I mean, do you care about them?"

"I... no? Ah!"

Fingers through fabric, I tore a hole down the center, enough to expose him to me without needing to remove them.

"Fuck," he whimpered, hips twitching as his cock sought friction and was denied any.

Then I was reaching for the lube, slicking up my fingers and circling his rim through the threads. "Open for me," I demanded, and he did, hissing through his teeth as I pressed one inside down to the knuckle. Jonah adapted quickly, and one finger soon became two, and then three. This part of him remembered my touch and yielded to it easily.

When he was sufficiently stretched, I pulled out of him and grabbed at his bound wrists, yanking him up from the sheets and pushing him forward until the dildo on the headboard was in front of his face. "Suck."

Jonah made a whining sound, but he did as I told him. Lips parted hesitantly as he took the tip of the silicone dick into his mouth. I gave him a moment to get used to it, and then I was pushing him forward, until the dildo hit the back of his throat and his whole body convulsed as he gagged. I pulled him back. Jonah coughed and sputtered, but he didn't let go of the belt, and when I pushed him forward again, he didn't fight me, opening his lips more eagerly this time.

"That's it. Suck that cock. Pretend it's mine."

Jonah muffled a groan, sucking more eagerly.

"It's not enough for you, is it? You want mine as well, don't you?"

I pulled him back, the silicone slipping from his lips as he strained to reach it again. But I'd asked him a question, and I expected an answer.

Switching to holding both his arms with one hand, I used the other to plunge three fingers inside him, curling them until I found the spot he was most sensitive and he moaned like a filthy whore. *My* filthy whore.

"This mouth is cock hungry too. Tell me. Beg for my dick, baby."

"Yes," he cried out. "P-please, I want your cock too. Please, please, please! Fuck me with your cock too! I need it!"

Fuuuuck. His needy voice sparked something primal inside me. Something more beast than man. I wanted to drag this out longer, but I was powerless to resist that siren song.

Letting him down onto the mattress again, I reached for the lube and slicked myself up further, keeping his ass up and presented to me as I notched my cock against his slick hole. Jonah was already trying to push against me, desperate for me to get inside him, the piercing and tip popping inside, and then we both groaned loudly as I slid home.

"Fuuuck, Rabbit. You feel so good. So perfect for me."

I gripped his hips, giving him a few thrusts, hard and fast. And then I was grabbing his wrists again, pulling him back up and into position, the dildo at his lips cutting off a moan as he took it in. With a cock in both ends, my thrusts pushed his body forward and my hands yanked him back, the motion fucking the dildo in and out of his mouth.

I couldn't fuck him as hard as I wanted to—I had to watch his hands, had to hold him steady so I didn't hurt him with the toy in his throat, had to pull him back enough to breathe. But Jonah trusted me completely. His body was tight and warm, clenching and twitching around me in pleasure, but he was also relaxed, open, unguarded.

I continued, holding myself back so I could hold him safely. We found a rhythm, a balance, and while it didn't yet satisfy the primal beast inside me, it was enough to send Jonah over the edge. His body tightened and shook as he came, his cry choked off by the toy until I pulled him off it and let him fall onto the mattress again.

Now it was my turn. His ass was still presented so beautifully, still swallowing my cock like that was its only purpose. I pulled out to tear his ruined underwear off the rest of the way, the fabric torn and soaked with his cum. I didn't give him a moment to recover before I balled them up and shoved them into his mouth. His eyes widened as the taste of cotton and his own cum hit his tongue.

His face was already a mess of tears and spit, and with the ruined underwear serving as his new gag, he looked thoroughly ruined. I turned him onto his side, so I wouldn't have to worry about him not being able to breathe and I could still see his hands holding the belt, then I took what I wanted.

Jonah's leg rose up in my hold as I plunged back inside him, his sobs muffled but still loud. This time I held nothing back, letting the beast inside me take control and ravage him. My cock pistoned hard and fast into his oversensitive body. Fresh tears streamed down his cheeks. The force of my thrusts jolted his body up the mattress only for me to yank him back to me again. Still he didn't let go of the belt.

Harder. Faster. More.

I gave him everything, until the heated bliss that had been building, building, building inside me reached a breaking point, and I slammed into his depths a final time, my cock kicking as I unloaded. Cum marking him as mine. Satisfying the beast. Even more so as Jonah's cock spurted again in a second orgasm.

I reached up to pull the wet fabric out of his mouth, and we both fought to catch our breath again.

"Are you okay?" I panted softly, my body feeling so heavy after my release.

"I'm perfect." His voice was quiet and raspy, but his smile was genuine and easy.

"Yeah... you are."

I pulled out of him slowly, and Jonah laughed softly as I rolled him over to watch my cum leak out of him, the sight of it next to my name something I always took the opportunity to enjoy.

"You gonna untie me now?" he groaned softly. I laughed as I reached up to gently pry his fingers out of the fists they formed, so that when he finally let go of the belt, it was because I'd made him do it and not because he'd let it go. Even completely fucked out my rabbit was still so stubborn.

I smoothed my thumb over the gauze bandages on his injured fingers. "Are you hurt?"

Jonah rolled onto his back. "I promise I'm fine. You can carry me to the shower, though."

"Anything for you, baby."

———◆◆◆———

When we were cleaned up and I'd changed the sheets again, we found ourselves right back where we had started, naked and tangled in each other's arms in bed.

Showering had lost us some of the calm we'd felt before, the need to protect Jonah's bandages and injuries from getting wet a reminder of what he'd done, and I knew he regretted it. I never wanted him to be hurt, but I didn't hold it against him. If the urge to inflict pain on himself was something he had to deal with, then it was something we would deal with together.

"We need to talk about it, baby," I told him, nuzzling into the warmth of his neck as he stiffened.

"I know, I just... I'm sorry."

"I know you are, Rabbit. I'm not mad at you. I just want to know how to help you."

"I don't know right now."

I nodded, kissing the soft skin where my lips rested against him. "Okay. That's okay. We'll work it out together." I meant it, but there was more. More I could say. More parts of myself I could show him. Jonah wanted all of me. He'd said so. He didn't just want me when I was strong, when I was good. "I understand it. Sometimes, when my mind is too loud, when I feel restless, I want pain too, just... differently."

Jonah was quiet, waiting to see if I had more to say. When I didn't, he spoke again. "That's why you fight?"

"Sometimes."

"Does it feel better afterward?"

My fingers traced slow patterns over his stomach. "Not really. It feels like it will before I do it, but after it just feels…" I searched for the word, but Jonah found it for me.

"Numb?"

"Yeah."

He nodded, shifting around in my arms so that he could press his lips softly against mine. "Will you tell me when you feel like that?"

"I will, Rabbit. I promise." I chased his lips again. "And you'll tell me when you feel like hurting yourself too?" I asked when we parted, never moving more than an inch away from each other. I wanted to breathe in his exhales, to share even oxygen.

"I will. I promise," he whispered, and I believed him.

Then he was chasing my lips again. Kiss after kiss. But it wasn't any deeper than that, both of us far too exhausted for another round. It was kissing so we had another place to touch, intimate and lazy, with no goal other than because we could. Because not doing it just wasn't an option.

I wanted to just exist here, with him in my arms and with me in his. I wanted the world to fuck off and leave us alone. I knew it then, that despite everything happening with the Strays, despite the conversations I'd had with Henrik, and the conflict Jonah was now directly involved in, I only wanted this. Everything else was a distraction. I still cared for the Strays, and they needed me, but what I needed was here. It was him. Only him.

"Jonah—"

Bang bang bang bang bang

The front door rattled as it was beaten with heavy hands. Jonah's pupils constricted as I looked into them. His face paled as he scrambled to sit up and I did the same.

"Shhh, it's okay." I spoke softly, though even I wasn't sure who the fuck could be knocking on my front door so urgently. The worst option immediately came to mind, only she wouldn't have knocked. Unless she lost her keys? She had been gone for a while. My gut twisted. Panic that was reserved just for her rose up from the depths of me. "Get dressed, baby. Quietly."

Bang bang bang bang

Jonah did as I asked, both of us creeping around my bedroom like we were the intruders in our home. Because Jonah had made this place feel like home again rather than just the house I lived in. If she was back, though, everything was about to change.

BANG BANG BANG

"Stay here, baby. I'll go answer it."

"Who is it?" I could see the storm of panic in him, rising to the surface again stronger than when I'd told him I was leaving this morning, because this time he didn't have his rage to shield himself behind. "What if... what if they know... what if they know what I did? What if they're here to take me?"

"No one is going to take you," I promised. "Just stay here, and I'll handle it."

BANG! BANG! BANG!

The sound of a fist against wood reverberated as I crept down the stairs, approaching the door with my heart in my throat. Because what I feared being on the other side wasn't the police. What I feared was my mother.

With a shaking hand on the doorknob, I disengaged the lock, seeking any strength I could muster. It was different now. I could face her. Because I had my rabbit to protect.

I opened the door.

Pastel pink hair. Golden skin dusted with freckles. Bright green eyes. My heart almost soared with relief, because it wasn't her. She wasn't here. She wouldn't hurt me.

But this was a new problem.

"Oh shweet. You're not dead. You're not answering your phone," Matteo's soft voice said, a wide grin spreading over his features, displaying perfect white teeth with a small gap between the front two.

"I'm busy. You shouldn't be here."

"Mmhmm, but like I said, you weren't answering your phone. People were worried. So it was either Rae or me coming to check you hadn't been arrested, because apparently no one else knows where you live? Anyway—"

Matteo tried to push past me into the house, but I blocked him, because there was a lot to unpack there. Of course Raven sent Matteo, knowing I had Jonah here. I'd have to deal with her about that. It wasn't what caught my attention, though. "Why would I have been arrested?"

He rolled his eyes. "You *really* picked a bad time to turn your phone off, Dexy."

"What are you talking about?"

"Well, I'll tell you inside."

"No, you'll tell me right here."

Matteo rolled his eyes again. "Deltran Police are swarming Archer's apartment."

An anvil dropped in my gut. "Why?"

"Because he murdered three people, duh. I thought you were like, the one who knew everything."

"Who?" I snapped, even though I already knew what names he was about to say.

"Hmmm, Mason Bates, Mikhail Petrov, and Sergei Kozlov."

"Who's that?" Jonah asked from behind me. Christ.

"Hi!" Matteo waved as he pushed past me and came inside. "You're Dexy's boyfriend, right? I've heard about you!" Matteo held his left hand out to Jonah for a handshake. His left, because I noticed now that his right was in a cast.

"Who the fuck are you?" Jonah scowled, his hand reaching for me instead of Matteo's as he grabbed the back of my shirt.

"I'm Matteo, but you can call me Matty." He grinned, and I wasn't sure if he hadn't noticed Jonah's hostility or he just didn't care. "Oh! Or Cupid."

Well, fuck.

43

Jonah - Present

THE ECHO OF HIM.

⸻ ✦ ⸻

I woke with a gasp. I could have sworn I heard something—a banging in the darkness. I sat up in bed, my pulse thundering. Except it wasn't dark. At least, it wasn't as dark as it should have been. Through the gap in the curtains, a flickering red and blue light poured into the motel room. *Red and blue.*

The police.

They'd found me.

They had fucking found me.

All this time on the run and it was for nothing. They were here. It was over.

"Harper!" I whispered, turning to his bed as flashing red and blue illuminated his unmoving silhouette. "Harper!" I dared to call a little louder.

Bang bang bang bang bang

The air in my lungs formed a ball, expanding, too big to fit inside me. Bigger. Bigger. Bigger. My rib cage constricted. Crushing inwards. The core of me imploded and exploded simultaneously. "H-Harper," I gasped, my trembling hands ripping back the blankets. My knees betrayed me as I tumbled to the floor.

"Hmmm?" Half-mumbled acknowledgment.

"Harper," I choked out, more sobbed than spoken.

Bang bang bang bang

"What?" he mumbled, and I wondered how the fuck anyone could sleep through that noise. The sound of the knocking echoed so loud the walls might as well have been shaking.

"P-police."

"What?"

"Police," I repeated, the word spoken like a curse.

He rolled over to face me, pale eyes opening, looking to me first then the lights pouring in through the windows. Red and blue lit up the sharp angles of his features, casting looming shadows in the room beyond him. Shadows that twisted and taunted, beckoning me to a darkness out of my reach.

"What the—"

Bang bang bang bang

His question was cut off by an avalanche of sound, my heart beating back just as loud in response, the walls of my chest threatening to crack and crumble from the force of it. That ball inside me expanded further until it cut off my airways completely, and I couldn't breathe. They'd found me. They knew what I'd done. It was over.

Pale brows furrowed in concern. His blankets were pulled back, and bare feet touched the carpet as he stood. No! He couldn't go out there. He couldn't let them in.

I grabbed at him as he attempted to pass me.

"No."

Bang bang bang bang

Harper crouched down until his eye level matched mine. I sought the mirror of my panic in his eyes and was left wanting. His were calm. Pale and solid like steel, like an anchor. "Listen to me." He spoke, and his voice was firm. Solid. Reliable.

"You're going to let me go, and I'm going to go look at what's going on, and nothing bad is going to happen."

"You don't—"

"*Nothing* bad is going to happen."

He didn't know that. He couldn't. But he spoke like he did. Like there was not a doubt in his mind. So certain. I wanted to believe him.

My hand slipped away, releasing the death grip I had on his shirt, and he stood again. Walking to the entrance. To my damnation.

The lights grew brighter as he parted the curtains. A flood of red and blue. Colors that seared my retinas. A torch to illuminate the ghosts in the haunted house of my soul. Then the lights dimmed as the curtain shifted back into place.

My chest was too tight. My mouth opened as I inhaled, but no oxygen would come to me, only coldness, only shadows. They filled me with nothing. So much nothing.

Then he was back. Harper at my side, each of his hands reaching for mine, his thumbs smoothing over my knuckles. "Jack."

My eyes burned, my vision blurred.

"Jack."

That wasn't me. I wasn't Jack. I wasn't who he thought I was, and he was about to find out. I shook my head.

"Look at me."

I couldn't. I could see only red and blue, only the shadows between flashes.

"What color are my eyes?"

The question was unexpected, hooking my attention even as I fought it.

"W-what?"

"My eyes. What color are they?"

"B-blue."

"Are you sure?"

I spared him a glance, but it was hard to tell with the brightness of the lights, his eyes seeming to absorb the color and direct it back at me.

"Blue?" I said again, uncertain. "G-gray?"

"Look at them." He moved closer until his knees brushed mine. "You decide and tell me."

I looked closer, trying to figure out the correct color beyond the flickering lights.

A door opened and slammed closed. There were voices outside the door.

"Hey. Don't worry about that. They aren't here for us. What color are my eyes?"

"They're going to—"

"No. Don't worry about that. Just look at me. Focus on me. Answer the question. Blue or gray?"

I looked between his eyes, one framed by a fading bruise. The lights flickered red and blue. His eyes were red then blue. Then white. The flashes of color disappeared as suddenly as they'd flooded through the window and swallowed me whole. Not quite. A faint reflection of pink from the neon sign across the road. A hint of warm white from the streetlamp. His eyes were blue.

"Blue," I answered, more confidently this time.

"Good." His thumbs traced my knuckles again. "What color is my shirt?"

My eyes flicked to the oversized tee covering his slender frame, the one we'd picked up at a thrift store that he'd said smelled like moths. "Orange."

"What else is orange?"

Another unexpected question, my mind grasped for answers. Flashes of neon orange pulling from my memories. Becca. "M-my friend. She has orange hair."

"What kind of orange?"

"Neon."

"What can you smell?"

Mental whiplash, but I followed his lead, inhaling through my nose, scenting the air. This motel smelled better than the usual ones, but there was still that musty smell that inhabited every cheap motel. "Dust."

"Explain it to me."

"What?"

"Explain it to me. What does dust smell like?"

"Umm..." I'd never had to describe the smell of dust before, my mind trying to think of the best words. "Stale? Umm... Old. Earthy? I don't know."

"What can you hear?"

Beyond his voice there was silence, and it felt loud and daunting.

"N-nothing."

"No. There are sounds. What are they?"

I grunted in frustration, but I tried. I listened, tuning into my surroundings. Distant voices. Distant traffic. The low hum of electricity from harsh lighting. And no more banging. No more red and blue. No more police. I inhaled deeply. The ball of panic had receded inside me before I was even aware of it, and I was breathing.

I held Harper's hands tighter, and they no longer trembled. Feeling safe enough, I turned toward the door. Still dark. Still closed. Still separating us from the rest of the world. "The police—"

"They're gone," he told me. "They weren't here for us. They were next door."

I breathed deeper. They weren't here for me. "Why didn't you tell me that before?"

"Would you have believed me?"

I swallowed, because we both knew the answer was no. Panic was louder than reason, fear louder than hope. But I could think properly now. Harper had pulled me back from the edge before I'd even realized that was what he was doing.

I searched his eyes, and still found them firm, not in a way that was cruel but in a way that was certain. Reliable. Strong. There was more to him than I'd originally seen, a strength I hadn't noticed and relied on more than I wanted to admit.

I pulled my hands back slowly. "I'm okay now," I told him, waiting for the questions, the demand for an explanation, for him to ask what I'd done.

He didn't.

He just looked at me like he saw far too much before he nodded, standing again and going to the kitchen area, and returning with a glass of water for me. I didn't want it, but I took it anyway, a stray droplet running down the side to wet my fingers.

Harper crouched in front of me again, his eyes a weight that oddly felt welcome. I didn't like being seen like that, being perceived as vulnerable. But he wasn't looking at me with pity. He didn't see me as weak. Instead, it felt like he was watching over me.

I thought about the conversation we had last night. "*Maybe I'll surprise you*," he'd said. Maybe he would. Maybe he *could* understand. I'd been keeping so much from Harper. Even last night I'd cut the conversation when it felt too real, told him I needed to smoke and lingered around the area until I'd thought he must have been asleep before coming back inside. At least that way I didn't have to face the guilt that was slowly building over all the things I wasn't telling him.

It was more than that. Even the things I had told him hadn't been honest. They couldn't be. *I* couldn't be. Not with him and not with myself.

"My love made him worse."

It had to be the truth.

Despite not wanting the water, I finished the cup, setting it on the bedside table before finding my feet again, thankful that my knees didn't betray me this time. Harper took my lead, standing as well, but as I made my way over to the two-seater table and the chair that held my leather jacket over its back, he slipped back into bed.

"You want to talk about it more?" he asked, smoothing out the blankets.

Yes. But I can't. "Maybe later? Get some more sleep."

He nodded, pulling the blankets higher. "Wake me if you need me, Jack. We're in this together now."

Would he still think that way if he knew the whole truth?

I slipped my arms into the sleeves, pulled on my boots, then parted the curtains to look over the parking lot. No police. They hadn't been here for us—for me. I inhaled deeply, steadying myself before I reached for the door handle. The moment felt bigger than it was, like I was opening a seal that kept us safely inside. But I needed to think, and I needed to do it alone.

Cool night air rushed to greet me.

The wind was eager to carry away my panic, my fear, but I held onto it. Kept it inside me because I needed it. It kept me safe.

Every sound, every movement, heightened my senses. The adrenaline that was crashing built again, fighting the exhaustion that threatened to replace it.

When I was a suitable distance away, I pulled my pack of cigarettes from my pocket. The wind turned to a blade of ice through my inhale as I went for the lighter and found it absent. It wasn't there—where I always kept it.

My heart clenched, twisted, and warped in my chest in a panic unlike anything I'd felt tonight. More pointed. More destructive. I frantically searched the other pockets, and warm relief enveloped me as I found its familiar shape tucked in beside my switchblade. I pulled it free, my thumb tracing the floral engravings.

Everything else I'd left behind or switched out over the year I'd been running. But there was no replacement for this. This was a part of him I'd never let go. It was what kept me grounded. Even though it had been there through the worst moments, it was a reminder of what was good. Of the purpose of it all. The reason. Like childish dinosaur stickers that had witnessed too much but still served as his light. I'd destroyed those, taken them from him. I'd safeguard this other piece of his father in penance. This other piece of Dex.

When I was lost, it was his voice that brought me back. I couldn't hear it anymore, but I could feel it sometimes. When my touch smoothed over the engravings that I knew he'd also touched so many times, I could trick myself into feeling the echo of him. And maybe I didn't deserve that comfort anymore, but without it I was unmoored. Without it he was gone.

44

JONAH – PRESENT

A WHOLE FUCKING CAKE.

———— ✦ ————

"We're out of cash," Harper told me, wallet open and tipped upside down as if he were trying to shake loose money hidden in its seams.

I hadn't found a job since Hollow Creek. Our hotel room was paid for two more nights, but that was it. We didn't have money for food or anything else. Even if I found a job today, I doubted they'd pay me upfront.

"Shit." An understatement, but all I had to offer.

"We're out of cash," Harper repeated, his face even paler than usual. "Jack. We're out of cash."

"I know. I'm thinking."

"I've never been out of cash. What do people do when they're out of cash? How do they get more?" His tone was tinged with panic.

"I started this without any cash, Harp. We'll find a way. There's always a way."

"How?"

"We'll find a job. We'll find *something*."

"I've never had a job. How am I supposed to get one?" More panic. "Maybe if I just use my card, and then—"

"No. That can be tracked, Harper."

"But how are we supposed to eat?"

"We steal."

Bright blue eyes blinked at me. "What? I've... I've never stolen anything... have you?"

I stared at him for a long moment, wondering just what kind of life he'd lived before now that theft hadn't even crossed his mind. Of course I'd stolen things before. When I'd first gone on the run with nothing but my car and the clothes on my back, I'd had to steal everything. I'd eventually found work and had built a tiny amount of emergency cash. Cash that had been left behind between the pages of a Bible back in Hollow Creek for someone to stumble onto and call it a fucking blessing.

"I'll do it. You can wait here."

"No." Harper stood to his feet, determination replacing the panic. "I want to help. Let me help."

This was probably a bad idea.

⎯⎯⎯◆⎯⎯⎯

"Confidence is key. Don't act shifty or they'll pay more attention to you. Act normal. Acknowledge the people around you. If you act like you're supposed to be doing what you're doing, people don't even question it," I told Harper at the front of the grocery store.

He was buzzing with nervous energy, but also seemed weirdly excited by the prospect of committing a crime.

"Okay. Cool. I'll follow your lead."

"No. Just pretend you don't know me. Then we have double the chances. Just... don't make it obvious. And if anything goes wrong... run."

Harper nodded quickly.

Well, here goes nothing.

We walked into the store, Harper already looking around way too obviously. I sighed and pushed forward, headed to the first aisle we needed and grabbed a few protein bars, slipping them into my jacket pocket and keeping my head held high as I looked at something else. When I pulled my hands out of my pockets again, they were empty.

I grabbed a box of cereal to stare at the words on the back before putting it back where I'd found it and continuing onward.

When I ran out of pockets to fill, I carried a couple of essentials in my hands, just like anyone else, except when I was done, I walked briskly toward the entrance rather than the registers.

"Hey!" a voice called behind me, and I was about to run as fast as my fucking limp would carry me before another voice halted my escape.

"Let go of me!"

Fuck. I turned to see Harper, arms *full* of items, wrist captured by a security guard.

There was only a moment to consider how to play this. The door was only a few long strides away, close enough that the breeze beckoned me, offering me freedom each time it opened. I had what I came for. I could walk out right now, and no one would even notice me. The security guard was reaching for his radio, his focus on Harper alone. What would happen to him if they called the police?

Fear told me to leave him behind.

I moved, my legs acting before my mind could think it through fully. My body slammed into a much bulkier body, knocking the security guard to the ground. "Run!"

Plastic packages slipped from Harper's hoard, but we were moving, leaving them abandoned as we bolted out the entrance. Curses were being shouted behind us.

We weaved around buildings and alleys, taking an unpredictable path until we were far from the store and certain nobody was following us. My leg ached and had slowed me down, but Harper had kept pace with me this time. He hadn't left me behind either, and as we both panted against a brick wall, I was suddenly so fucking grateful for that. I hadn't had to watch the distance between us growing like I knew it could have, like it had before when he was running from Benny. Harper was faster than me, but he'd stayed by my side anyway.

He still had his arms full of items—snacks, bright-colored packages, and things that weren't at all essential. I could have smacked him, but I found myself laughing.

Real genuine laughter pulled from the depths of me, and a moment later he followed, laughing just as loud. We would have looked foolish to anyone who peered down the alley and spotted us, but it didn't fucking matter. I couldn't remember the last time I'd laughed like this, and fuck, it felt so good.

"Is—" I could hardly breathe. "Is that a whole fucking cake?"

Harper clutched the box closer, the package warped from holding onto it so tightly, its contents undoubtedly shaken into a complete mess. "I wanted cake."

"Maybe I should have clarified. People usually just go for the essentials when they can't afford them."

"Where's the fun in that?" he laughed, but then his smile turned. The edges of his lips dropped, the creases in the corners of his eyes smoothed out. "I thought I was fucked there for a moment. You saved me... again."

"Yeah... well, we're in this together, right?"

I expected the words to comfort him, but they seemed to have the opposite effect. His aura turned somber. "Why, though?"

"What do you mean?"

"I mean, you helped me now, but also back in Hollow Creek... when Benny... You tried to follow us then too... tried to help. And then you brought me with you."

"No offense, Harp, but you wouldn't make it out here on your own."

"Right," he answered, sounding distant.

I'd been aiming for teasing, but it seemed like I'd struck a nerve. "Hey, I'm sorry. I'm just messing around. You just... you needed someone. So did I. And now we have each other, right?"

"Right." He held his items closer to his chest, packages crinkling as he squished them.

"Let's go back to the motel... have some of that cake. Okay?"

He nodded, and we started on our way back, keeping a lookout for police or security or anyone who might be after us.

Harper was quiet the whole way back, deep in thought even as we closed the motel room door and sealed ourselves away from the rest of the world. I started unloading the items from my pockets onto the table, and he did the same, dumping his crumpled boxes and packets of snacks in a heap.

Something was still bothering him. I understood it—the weight of being cared for, of being helped, how uncomfortable it could feel. I'd spent so long not caring about anyone but myself, but I cared about him, and it didn't feel like a burden. It felt like purpose. Like hope. The weight of running lessened because we shared it.

I was going to tell him as much, but he spoke first.

"I appreciate everything you've done for me, Jonah. I really mean that."

It took a second.

His words felt like comfort until they didn't. Until I realized he'd said my name. My real name. Not Jack. He'd said Jonah.

Silence rang in my ears as I looked at him, his eyes cast downward, brow furrowed.

He knew my name.

I'd wanted to tell him so badly. I'd ached for it. Ached to connect with him in a way that was real and true and honest. Ached to hear *someone* say my name. And finally, someone had. But I hadn't told it to him. Instead of relief, instead of belonging, I felt the icy claws of dread unleashing in my gut, clawing their way up from the depths of me.

"What... what name did you say?"

I'd misheard him. I must have. I needed to have misheard him.

Harper was quiet, his expression doing something complicated before he smiled sweetly again, a mask sliding into place. "I said Jack."

"No." I stood up so fast the chair I'd been sitting in tumbled over onto the floor. "No, you didn't."

"What else would I have said?" He still smiled, and it looked like it always did when he smiled, but it felt wrong. It felt like a lie.

"Who are you?" My hand dipped into my pocket, trembling fingers seeking the switchblade. Pale eyes tracked the movement.

"Let's not do anything hasty."

"Who the fuck are you?" I shouted, pulling it free but not clicking it open. I was scared, but I didn't want to hurt him. But what else was I supposed to do when it felt like the walls were closing in and crushing me?

Harper's eyes were fixed on my hand. "I told you who I am."

I shook my head, taking a step back, a step closer to the door. "No. You're lying."

I could see the exact moment when he decided to drop the pretenses. His whole face shifted. His eyes were cold, and the way he stared had me wanting to take another step back. I was bigger than him, by a decent amount, but there was something about him that reeked of predator.

"Fine." Even his voice seemed colder.

"Who are you?" I asked again.

"I told you who I am. That part wasn't a lie."

"So what parts were?"

"Oh, you know... just... everything else."

I couldn't swallow past the lump in my throat. It felt like the ground was opening up beneath me, and I didn't know which way was up anymore. What was real?

"Are you really running from Benny?"

Harper laughed, and it was nothing like the sound I'd heard in the alley. Which one was real?

"My man would cut off his own hands before he ever harmed me with them. No, this—" He gestured at the fading bruise. "This was all *your* man."

Bile rose up my throat. Dex. He'd found me. The what-ifs, the fears, the doubts, the questions that ran through my head over and over at any moment in time. Is he alive? I finally had an answer. He was alive, and he was closing in. Through Harper he had me in his grasp.

"You're a Stray." My voice sounded distant.

His smile widened. "Now you've got it. They call me—"

"Little Snake Prince."

Harper winked.

And I ran.

45

JONAH - PAST

THE TWINS.

Pink. Everything that could be pink on "Cupid" was. Their hair was pastel pink, falling in perfect natural curves to frame their heart-shaped face, and their shirt was a light pink with a darker pink chunky-knit cardigan over the top. Knee-high socks traveled down hairless legs, and were tucked into pink shoes with a couple of inches of platform on the bottom that still didn't bring them up to my height.

I would have told Dex to get them the fuck out of here immediately, but my eyes caught on something I needed to clarify first. Along with the dusting of glitter over their eyelids, there was the pink tartan skirt. I was sure Dex had referred to them as "him," and that he wouldn't intentionally misgender someone. But if I wanted to insult this person, I needed to make sure I referred to them correctly.

"What are your pronouns?" I asked, and the smile that spread across full, glossy lips just made me hate them more.

"Oh! He/him is fine. I just like wearing sk—"

"Get him the fuck out of here," I said to Dex, not waiting for Matteo to finish speaking.

Dex was tense. He should be. It was one thing knowing he'd fucked this guy before, it was entirely another to know he just came around whenever the fuck he felt like it. Before I'd seen him, I could have at least convinced myself it was just a convenient hookup of the past. But the fact was that Matteo was fucking beautiful... I tried and failed to find any part of his appearance I could rip into.

"*I've never had someone in my bed in the* daylight *before*," Dex had told me once. That meant he'd had guys in his bed at night. If Matteo knew where Dex lived, did that mean he was one of them? Had they fucked in the same bed Dex fucked me in?

"Rabbit," Dex sighed, but I cut him off too before he could try to talk me down.

"I said get him the fuck out, Dex. Now."

"Oh. You guys in the middle of something?" Matteo asked, blinking innocently. My lip pulled up in a snarl.

"Matteo is here because apparently the police have arrested Archer."

The mention of police gave me pause. The fire building inside me simmered down enough to at least seek more details before demanding again that Dex throw Matteo out. "Why?" I asked, snapping attention back to the pink-haired bitch invading our space.

"Well, actually, they didn't arrest him," Matteo added.

"What? You just said they're swarming his apartment."

"Yeah, but he wasn't there."

"Then where is he?" Dex asked, and at least he sounded pissed.

Matteo didn't seem to care as he shrugged. "Dunno. Was hoping you did."

"No, I don't know. I saw him last at the Strays house."

"He's not there. But Raven says it's just a matter of time before the cops end up there, so not to go there."

"What's he being arrested for?" I asked. I was sure the list of shady activities Archer was involved in was long and vast, but there was something uncomfortable building in my gut.

"Murder of three Drakes," Matteo answered casually.

My mouth and throat dried up. "How do they know it was him?"

"His knife was found at the scene of the murder."

His knife... Archer's knife was found at the scene. My mind brought back that fucking switchblade with the pale wood handle, the one that had felt so heavy in my hands. The one with a history I didn't dare ask about. My own secrets now mixed with it. Henrik had insisted I use it, had handed it to me then taken it and used it himself. The whole fucking time he'd only used that knife.

"And his blood."

"His blood?" I asked, my voice softer than I wanted it to be.

"Yeah, it was like everywhere, apparently. They narrowed it down to the twins, but Henny was with his dad, so that just leaves Archy."

The scene replayed in my mind.

"Your blood is fucking everywhere!"

"Allegedly."

"What does that mean?"

"It means don't worry about me."

"You... you just killed three people..."

"Allegedly."

Allegedly. Henrik had planned this all along. Now Archer was a wanted person in the murders his twin brother had committed—the ones I'd witnessed. My mind was spinning. Did that mean the police wouldn't come for me? Were they just satisfied that Archer was the one who'd done it? What if he could prove he hadn't? What if they turned to Henrik instead? Would he then turn on me as well? Put the blame on me instead?

Warm hands grasped my shoulders, thumbs smoothing the tension from my neck. "And Archer hasn't spoken to anyone?" Dex asked.

Matteo shook his head. "Nah, no one can reach him. That's why they sent me to check with you."

"My phone's been switched off. Can you get it for me, baby?" Dex asked, placing a soft kiss on the side of my head. I nodded, accepting the request for what it was, a moment to step away and process.

The world was spinning as I went up the stairs to shut myself in the bedroom. Was this a good thing? Or was this a problem? I couldn't determine whether this put me further in danger or out of it, torn between panic and relief, somehow feeling both and neither.

Dex's phone was in the pocket of his clothes. Still switched off. I clenched it in my fist as I took a seat on the edge of the bed.

I must have taken too long. I could have been there seconds or minutes—longer, I wasn't sure—but Dex knocked softly on the door before entering. He kneeled in front of me with his warm hands covering mine.

"Everything's going to be okay," he told me, and I wanted to believe him, but doubt circled inside me like a predator going in for the kill.

"How do you know?"

"Because Henrik is a fucking asshole, but he's competent. I don't know why he did what he did, but I know if he wants to frame Archer for this, then that's exactly what's going to happen. His family's very powerful, Rabbit, and if his dad is his alibi, then we have to assume they're also trying to put this on Archer. No one will know you're involved. And you didn't do anything wrong."

"I didn't do anything wrong." I nodded, repeating his words, holding onto them like a lifeline.

"That's right. You were just protecting yourself. Protecting me. You did nothing wrong."

I did nothing wrong. I repeated the words like a mantra. Dex was so certain as he spoke them. My eyes searched his for doubt and found none. He truly believed it. So I could as well.

"Matteo..."

"He's gone, baby. I sent him away. It's just you and me."

I nodded again, tilting forward until I slipped from the bed to kneel on the floor in front of him, my arms wrapped around his neck and his around my waist.

"I've got you. Nothing bad's going to happen to you, I promise."

I believed him.

———◆◇◆———

With Archer missing, there was chaos among the Strays, all of whom had unfortunately ended up in Dex's kitchen. No one had heard from their gang leader. Dex had dozens of missed calls when he switched his phone back on, but none of them were from Archer. Apparently, Henrik had also been impossible to get a hold of.

There were two missing twins, and a whole fucking lot of chaos.

I'd wanted to be in the room as they discussed everything, but the group—particularly Reaper—hadn't at all been pleased by my presence there. Dex promised me he'd update me on everything when he'd pulled me aside and asked me to wait in his bedroom for him.

So here I was, trying not to throw things at the wall while I waited around like a pet. Anxiety swirled around inside me. Fear that one of them could verify Archer's whereabouts that day and they'd know he hadn't done it. And maybe that should have been the biggest fear I had, but it wasn't.

If Archer was out of the picture, the Strays would need a new leader, and the fact that they were all in Dex's kitchen right now, and that they'd been calling him for everything leading up to this, it was pretty fucking obvious who that would be.

I didn't want to share him—not with the Strays or anyone else. I wanted him to be mine and mine alone. I wanted to be his priority, and as long as the Strays existed, I wouldn't be. He'd chosen them over me before, and if he officially became their leader, it would only happen more. I hated it, hated them for needing him. Why couldn't it be someone else? Why did he have to always take care of them and let them rely on him?

By the time I heard the front door opening and closing, various bikes roaring to life and speeding away, it was well into the night, and I was fucking pissed.

The stairs creaked under footsteps, and Dex opened the door quietly, his eyes finding mine. "I thought you might be asleep."

I glared at him. "Really?"

"No." He smiled softly. "But you should be. It's late."

"What happened down there?"

Dex sighed. "No one's heard from Archer or knows where he might be."

"We already knew that."

"No one's been able to get in contact with Henrik either."

I stared at him, waiting for him to continue and prompting him when he didn't. "What's happening, Dex? Who's taking Archer's place?"

His jaw clenched, and my fears were confirmed. "Me. Just for now. Just until we figure out something more permanent."

I laughed, but there was no humor in it. "As if. Something more permanent, come on, Dex. You don't really expect me to believe that, do you? You're it. They all need you, and you let them. This is just it now, isn't it?"

"Just for now, Rabbit." He crossed the room, hands finding mine. I pulled away from him, but he grabbed me again, pulled me into him, his arms trapping me in. "Just for now, I promise. Just give me a little time to sort this out, and I'll set Raven up to take over. Then I'll be done with it all."

I pulled back to look into his eyes, to search for the truth in his words. "You... you're going to step away from it? From them?"

Dex nodded. "I had nothing but them for a very long time, baby. They were the closest thing to a family I'd ever known.

But they aren't anymore. Because now I have you. And you're the only home I'll ever need."

His words broke through the shield of rage I was holding between us and punctured the heart of my fear. "You... you really mean that? You'd give it all up for me?"

"Of course I would, Rabbit. And I will. Just give me a little bit of time. Can you do that?"

He wasn't choosing them. He was choosing me. My arms wrapped around him as I pulled him closer, burying my face in the curve of his neck. "You're my home too," I whispered into his skin.

Just a little more time and he'd be mine completely, and I'd be his, and we wouldn't have to worry about anything but each other.

I sought his lips and found them eager. Promises passed between us in the form of kisses before we were on his bed, pulling at each other's clothes, tasting each other's skin. Until he was inside me and we were as close as we could be. Until he was home within my body and I wished I could keep him there always.

46

DEX - PAST

THE DEVIL'S HOME.

Jonah stirred but didn't wake as my phone vibrated on the nightstand. I pulled away from him gently, already missing the heat and warmth of his body as I grabbed the device and shuffled out of bed. I'd meant what I told him—he was all that mattered. As soon as I knew the Strays would be okay without me, I was out.

Raven was my choice to replace Archer, but I knew not everyone would feel the same, and I had concerns about what the others would think when I tried to leave. My biggest concern being Reaper. I was one thing—he had little ground to stand on by challenging me—but Raven was another.

Closing the door quietly behind me, I glanced at the screen before answering.

"Snake," I answered, murmuring as I made my way downstairs.

"I got what you wanted," Harper responded, as blunt and cold as usual, his emotions shielded again, unlike the last call I'd received from him. He hadn't made it to the group meeting, neither had Bull.

"Good. I'll come get it later today."

"Fine. We're even now."

I laughed. "Not even close."

"This is an expensive piece of tech, Coyote. Do you have any idea how hard it was for me to—"

"You still owe me," I interrupted. Expensive tech for someone like me probably, but it was nothing to a billionaire. I liked Harper, but I wasn't letting him get out of debt to me that easily. He was a powerful person to have a favor owed from, and I intended to use it wisely.

There was silence for a long moment before he conceded with a sigh. "I can pay you."

"This isn't blackmail, Snake. I helped you, and someday you'll help me. I don't want your money."

"I don't like owing people."

"Well, you should have thought of that before you asked me for help."

Silence, and then another long sigh. "Whatever. Don't take too long, I am very busy, you know."

"I'm sure you are."

"Hmm."

The line went dead as he hung up on me. I rolled my eyes, returning to the bedroom to put on pants before heading to the kitchen to make Jonah breakfast.

Soon I'd be out. I'd take my Rabbit, and we'd get the fuck out of this place. We'd go somewhere no one knew us and exist only for each other.

The thought put an extra bounce in my step as I busied myself around the kitchen, feeling none of the unease that usually came with being in this room. Jonah had filled it and all the others with a new sense of home. Since the first night he'd stayed here with me, he hadn't left. There hadn't been a night we'd slept apart, and I wanted to make sure there never would be.

Bang bang bang bang

The echo of fists on the front door had my good mood evaporating, as I looked to the ceiling and prayed to a god that had never heard me before for patience. I'd expected that now most of the Strays knew where I lived they might drop in unannounced, especially with the agreement that we'd be staying away from the Strays' house. I just didn't expect it would happen so quickly.

I left the bacon cooking as I made my way to the door, expecting Matteo again, or Raven. So when I unlocked it and pulled it open, I was entirely unprepared for the way my heart plummeted like an anvil to my gut—lower, like the weight of it could send me crashing through the floor and down into hell itself.

I wished it had. I wished for anything else other than to have opened the door to the person standing in front of me.

"You just gonna stand there and look at me like you're stupid? Move!"

A pointed fingernail stabbed at my shoulder, but I didn't budge even though it stung. Because hell was real, and it was here, but I wasn't its devil, my mother was. And the devil was home.

"Move, Dexter. This bag is fucking heavy."

Jonah. All I could think about was Jonah. I stood my ground despite the years of instinct that told me to back down, to keep her happy or suffer the consequences. My bones seemed to shrink in her presence, her shadow distorting and looming until she felt so much bigger than I was, so much stronger.

"Move out of my way!"

"No," I told her, my voice barely above a whisper. All other words evaded me.

I couldn't protect myself from her—not now and not ever—but I could protect my rabbit. I could keep her out for his sake. I wouldn't let her get to him.

As if my thoughts summoned him, I heard the creak of my bedroom door. Eyes as pale and pointed as blades flickered from me to beyond me, to the house that Jonah had transformed from a cage to a home again. "Go away," I told her.

Her gaze cut into me again, the monster beneath her skin twisted in fury. She looked older, more withered than the last time I'd seen her, but that beast still lurked there, just as bloodthirsty. I'd be its willing target if it protected my rabbit.

"This is my fucking house!" she roared, each word doubling in volume.

A heavy bag thudded to the floor, and then she attacked, sinking her claws into my arms as she tried to pull me aside, but I still didn't budge—still didn't let her past me—so she went for my face. She always liked going for my face. It was how I'd lost the eyebrow piercing Jonah had asked about. Ripped from my skin for reasons I couldn't even remember.

I grabbed for her wrists to stop her, but lingering fear made me slower than I needed to be, her nails sinking into skin as she swiped, a sharp sting from my eyebrow to my cheek. Still, I wouldn't move out of her way.

"Dex?" Jonah's heavy footfalls pounded down the stairs behind me.

"Go back upstairs, Rabbit," I told him without turning to face him.

"Let go of me!" my mother shrieked, as if she hadn't been the one to attack first. No, she was the victim. Always the victim.

Holding on to her meant I couldn't hold the door closed, and she kicked at it, the force slamming it open only for it to ricochet off the wall with a bang and slam back into my side. I grunted, but I didn't let it sway me. Not with Jonah at my back.

"Go back upstairs, Jonah!" I raised my voice, but he didn't listen, of course he didn't.

His toned body slipped between me and the door frame, and then she was ripped away from me, her wrists leaving my hold as Jonah threw her backward, off the porch and into a pile of junk she kept on the front lawn.

Jonah stood tall between us. My rabbit protecting me when I should have been protecting him. "Who the fuck is this bitch?" he snarled.

"My mom," I admitted, and he turned to face me, honey eyes wide with shock before he saw what she'd done, the red of my blood as it dripped from the fresh cut on my face igniting something red in him. Something big and destructive. Fire ten times larger than any I'd seen burn inside him before.

"Jonah!" I grabbed at his arm as he tried to march forward, tried to follow the woman he'd thrown off the porch before he'd even fully grasped the situation. I didn't know what he'd do to her, and I didn't care about her, but I wouldn't let him taint his perfect hands on my behalf.

Then she started screaming. "How fucking dare you! You fucking bitch! Who the fuck do you think you are throwing me out of my own fucking home? I'll call the fucking cops!"

Jonah tensed in my hold, and I used his pause to pull him to my side, desperate to get him behind me. He wouldn't let me, fighting to do the same thing to me, both of us trying to put ourselves between her and each other.

"Get out!" she screeched. "I'll call the cops for real. I'll tell them you're assaulting me in my own fucking home! I'll tell them what you did to Pierce, Dexter."

Ice in my veins, and I was suddenly sixteen again, staring at a mangled corpse in the kitchen. "Y-you did that."

"You think they'll believe you over me? You're the one who knows where he is, not me. You're the one mixed up in all sorts of shit." She waved her hands, gesturing vaguely at everything, because she didn't know the first thing about me or what I was mixed up in. But if she called the police, it wouldn't take them long to find out. If she told them I was the one to kill Pierce, especially with the recent murders already connected to the gang, they wouldn't believe me over her. I'd be charged over the murder of my abuser without any of the satisfaction that would have come with actually committing the crime.

"You disgusting fucking maggot of a fucking—" Jonah tried to go for her again but I pulled him back, because I didn't doubt she'd follow through with her threats.

"Let's just go, Rabbit."

He halted, turning to look at me. "What do you mean? Go where?"

"Somewhere. Anywhere. Away from here."

"This is your home."

"No, you're my home. Let's go." I turned to my mother, to the person who should have been a safe space for me but never had been. "We'll go."

"Damn right you'll fucking go," she sneered, happy in her victory. "'Cause you're a fucking coward, aren't you? Just like your dad was a fucking coward."

Her words cut deeper than her nails ever had, than anything else she'd ever thrown at me, and Jonah fought to get free from my grasp to go for her again.

"Just... I'll get my stuff."

"You've got five fucking minutes before I'm calling the cops." She held her phone up in her hand, waving it at us to emphasize her point.

I pulled Jonah along with me back into the house, because I wasn't ever leaving him alone with her. He fought me each step of the way. I had to put my hands on his shoulders, physically turn him around, and march him forward in front of me. She followed right behind us, not letting the front door close with her outside again.

"Dex—" Jonah tried to talk to me once I'd pushed him into the bedroom, but I cut him off.

"Not now, baby, please," I pleaded with him. "Let's just get our stuff and go. Nothing else matters if we have each other. Please."

His brow furrowed as if he were in pain, but he nodded, grabbing his things and shoving them in a bag beside mine.

We had what we needed and then we were making our way down the stairs, my mind already racing about what this meant, about where we would go.

She was still standing by the door. Apparently we were taking too long, and it had just riled her up more. Because throwing me out wasn't enough anymore, she had found her weapon in threatening to get the police involved, but why not twist the knife further?

"Should have kicked you out years ago." Verbal vitriol. "You're what made him do it, you know. He killed himself cause he didn't want to put up with you anymore."

I only just managed to catch Jonah as he launched himself at her again, my vision blurring with tears that I didn't want to give her the satisfaction of seeing.

"You or your bitch girlfriend ever come back here and there'll be more fucking bodies to hide. You hear me, Dexter? Don't you ever fucking come back."

I expected the threat to spur Jonah on further, instead he stilled. With my arm around his waist, I couldn't see the expression he was giving her, but I saw something in her eyes I hadn't seen in a long fucking time. Fear. Just for a moment, then she was holding up her phone again. "Get out. I'm calling the fucking cops. Out fucking now!"

Jonah's hand grabbed my wrist, and he pulled it off him, standing tall and giving her another long glare before he turned and walked out the door ahead of me.

47

Dex - Past

WHAT COMFORT FEELS LIKE.

Pale blue eyes looked us over, and without asking a single question, Roy stepped to the side, holding the door open.

Jonah had followed me in his car, the one bag containing everything we now owned thrown in his back seat as I started up my bike and led him here, to the only place I could think of going.

My head wasn't right, never was around that woman. I couldn't think clearly. She'd been bad before, said mean things, and she'd hurt me—fuck, she'd even threatened to kill me before—but she'd never thrown me out. I'd never challenged her before, though. Never wanted to risk what would happen if I did. Because maybe they weren't just idle threats.

Roy closed the door behind us.

"Staying a while, then?" he asked, eyes on the bag in Jonah's hand before they flicked to mine.

Just having him look at me made the heat I'd fought back on the ride here resurface. I shut my eyes tight so they wouldn't spill my secrets and I nodded. When I opened them again he nodded as well.

"Right. This way."

With no further preamble, Roy led the way down the hall of his home. It was aged but well maintained. Light gray carpet streaked with uniform lines from a recent vacuum, and wood-paneled walls absorbed the late morning sun. The air smelled of warm pine and something sweeter... something comforting.

The room he led us to had a completely different vibe—a bed much bigger than mine, covered in floral bedding and decorative pillows, the furniture all white unlike the dark-wood theme throughout the rest of the house. It wasn't overly spacious, but it was tidy, with a vanity to one side and a tall white wardrobe on the other. A large window filled the space with scattered sunlight shining through its lace curtain.

I turned to Roy, raising a tired brow.

He shrugged a shoulder. "Was the wife's room." He cleared his throat. "Right, then. I'll be... around. If you need me."

With that, he shuffled off toward the kitchen, and I knew I owed him more of an explanation. I'd make sure I gave it to him, but I didn't have the energy for it right now. Jonah closed the door and locked it behind us before taking a seat on the edge of the bed.

He'd been so very quiet. I knew there was a fire burning inside him, desperate to be unleashed upon the woman who had just shaken our world, but he kept it in. His eyes searched mine, seeking another way forward.

I didn't have answers for him. There weren't any words. I didn't know how to comfort him or how to ask for comfort. Because I'd dealt with this on my own my entire life, all I wanted to do was shrink into the shadows and hide until things felt quiet and calm again.

They should have been calm. I was out of her reach, and these walls had never seen me hurt. Still, her claws sunk into me from the inside, from the memories and the scared little child I kept locked away in my core. He was safer there, locked away always, but he was scared, and he was alone.

Jonah kicked his shoes off, shuffling on the bed until his back rested on the pillows before he held his arms out to me. My inner child reached for him, longing for a comfort forever denied to him, hands that would hold and soothe rather than destroy. I went to him, lay over him, my face buried in the fabric at his chest, my legs slotted between his like a perfect puzzle piece. His arms wrapped around me, and mine around him, and I cried. I wept like that small child inside me wanted to weep all those years, because there was finally someone who would listen.

Jonah held me as if he could reach through time and cradle all the past versions of me that needed this, that needed *him*.

So this is what comfort feels like. This was what it felt like to be held by hands that would never harm me, to be touched by a soul that wouldn't leave me. Jonah was nothing like my mother, and he was nothing like my father because he wouldn't leave.

I cried until my eyes felt heavy, until all the fear drained from my soul and soaked into his clothing, the hurt smoothed away by his hands as he ran them gently over my back. Soft fingers dipped under fabric to trace invisible patterns directly over my skin.

I wasn't certain when I fell asleep, or how long I was out for before a gentle knock on the door pulled me back. Jonah was still here, his fingers combing slowly through my hair. I pulled back to look at him. His expression was soft, open, safe. He sat up just enough to place a lingering kiss on my lips.

"Want me to tell him to go away?" he whispered.

I huffed in amusement. "No, baby. I'm okay now."

Except when I opened the bedroom door, Roy wasn't there. The hallway was empty, but I looked down and saw a tray resting by the doorway with a plate of sandwiches and a carafe of water with two stacked glasses. The gesture threatened to bring heat to my eyes again, but I'd done enough crying for one day. I shook them off, picked up the offering, and brought it inside to share with Jonah.

⎯⎯⎯◀◯▶⎯⎯⎯

As much as I wanted to stay locked away in this room with Jonah for the rest of my life, the world wouldn't stop and wait for me to be ready to go on. There were things that needed doing, most unfortunately by me.

It was already dark, and I'd ignored a few phone calls. I had no doubts about who they were from. I'd kept Harper waiting, and he was no doubt pissed off about that.

"I have to go out for a bit," I told Jonah, even though I knew I didn't have the energy for the battle that leaving would probably trigger.

"Where are you going?" he asked, surprising me slightly.

"Have to see one of the Strays."

"Will you be safe?"

"Yeah, baby, I promise. Just picking something up."

Jonah frowned. "How long will you be gone?"

"A while. But I'll have my phone on me if you need me for anything."

I waited for the arguments, but none came. He simply nodded. "Okay. I'm going to visit Bee for a bit, then."

"Okay, baby." I kissed him softly, and then again. "You call me if you need anything, okay?"

"I will."

I left the room and caught the scent of roast meat and herbs. Roy was busy in the kitchen, chopping up vegetables. A tendril of guilt coiled in my gut. "I'm um... I need to head out for a bit."

Roy turned to face me, and looked me over, no doubt trying to figure me out and the situation I was in without directly asking about it. He nodded, eyes straying to the food he'd been cooking before finding mine again. "You don't need my permission for that, son."

"I know... just... I want to explain, but... later?"

He nodded again, turning back to his cooking. "Anytime, kid. I'm here."

"Were you... cooking for us?"

"No," he answered quickly. "I'm just cooking. But there's enough, and you boys need to eat, so..."

"I'll eat when I get back. It smells really good."

"Right. Good."

A smile pulled at my lips. "Thanks, old man."

"Get outta here, brat."

I laughed, feeling a bit lighter as I left the warmth of his home.

I needed the ride more than I'd thought—the open road, the wind whipping past as Delilah and I weaved through traffic and headed for the city.

The building Harper lived in was massive, all cold glass and steel, and I was met with scrutinizing eyes as I entered the lobby. The man behind the reception desk was wearing a suit that cost more than everything I now owned. His eyes were sharp and probing, lingering on the tattoo on my neck. "Mr. Weller, I presume."

Something about him made me want to poke at him, to break through his composed exterior by causing a scene of some sort. He was clearly already judging me, and had I not been so eager to get back to my rabbit as quickly as possible, I might have dragged this out just to cause a little drama.

"Mr. Lorens has been expecting you."

"I'm sure he has."

"Hmm." He pursed his lips, offering another judgmental once-over before he directed me to the elevators.

Harper's penthouse was much larger than any apartment ever needed to be. The air was warm, but the aesthetic was cold. Dark gleaming floors and dark marble walls. Even the black leather sofa looked hard and uncomfortable, and I wondered why someone with so much money would actively choose to live in a place with so little comfort.

Floor-to-ceiling windows took up one wall, offering a view of the city, but what really caught my attention were the glass panels that separated a wall length enclosure from the living room. It's inhabitant, a huge, bright yellow python, curled around itself, bronze eyes staring back at me. The thing must have been fourteen feet long.

"You're late." Harper spoke, snapping my attention away from the snake. His arms were crossed, his clothing as dark as the rest of his apartment, and another much smaller snake coiled up his arm and around the back of his neck, this one as white as snow.

"I'm very busy, you know." I offered his words back to him, enjoying the annoyed twitch of a well-manicured eyebrow.

"Are you forgetting this was a favor you specifically asked me for, Coyote?"

"Devil."

"What?"

"It's Devil now."

"Of course it is." Harper rolled his eyes. He stepped up to me, his presence feeling so much larger than the small body he existed within. "Here."

He pulled a card from his pocket and slapped it—along with what I'd come here for—into my palm. Just holding it again brought me much-needed comfort. "How does it work?"

"Everything you need to do is on the card. Just download the app and follow the prompts."

"I don't have a smartphone."

He huffed. "Of course you don't. You know we're in the twenty-first century, right? You're asking me for stolen, experimental, top-of-the-line tracking technology when you don't even have a smartphone?"

"I'll get one. Just tell me how it works."

Harper sighed, muttering something under his breath that sounded like "Neanderthal" before he continued. "It's a low-energy GPS module—no lights, no vibrations, no sounds. Complete stealth technology. Pings its location every twelve hours, hence the need for the app, unless you're expecting me to mark an X on a map every morning and send it to you by carrier pigeon."

"Anyone ever tell you that you're a little dramatic?"

If looks could kill, I'd be a dead man, but Harper continued. "Even if the fluid is refilled, the modifications should be completely unnoticeable unless you're measuring the internal chamber down to the millimeter."

"The battery?"

"Like I said, it's a prototype. I wouldn't expect it to last more than a year max."

I traced my thumb over the engravings as familiar to me as my own skin.

"You're welcome." He waved his hand at me dismissively. "Now go away."

48
JONAH - PAST

FIRE.

—— ✦ ——

I lied. Dex told me he was leaving, and I lied to him. I didn't want him to go, didn't want him away from me, but there was something I had to do, and he couldn't be with me. He couldn't know.

I waited five minutes, pacing the bedroom after he'd left, before I couldn't stop myself anymore. The scent of warm food tried to lure me toward the kitchen but was unsuccessful. Alarms pinged in my brain, sirens and logic blaring at me to stop, go to Becca's like I'd told him I was going to. *This isn't the answer.* My demons were louder.

Cold air hit my face as I stepped outside, but I couldn't feel it. Then I was in the car. I drove in silence. This was the first true trip I'd taken on my own with this gift—the car he gave me. He gave me so much. What did he get in return? Who gave things to him? Who had ever held him like I held him as he cried? Who had ever made him feel safe before me? His father, maybe, but he was gone, and what was he left with? That disgusting, vile woman.

No.

The car stopped, and I was just a street away. I went the rest of the way on foot, and not even the ache in my leg would slow me down.

Then I was standing in the dark, watching the house that we'd made a home only to have it ripped away from him by that *thing*. It lurked in there now, its presence contaminating everything good.

Dex was scared of her. I wasn't. He couldn't face her, and I didn't blame him. Because I *saw* him. I saw *all* of him now.

The rest of the world saw him as big and scary because he wanted them to. He'd worked hard on it, because the house he came from made him feel small and afraid. Even now. In that house, and in the presence of that *thing*, he was still a lost, scared child, unable to grow up. She kept him small—those walls kept him small. I hated it all.

So I'd set him free.

I would protect him. That monster would never hurt him again.

I'd known I was going to do this from the moment that threat spilled from her lips. The decision shaped my rage into something solid and certain in my gut, as tangible as any weapon.

There were demons beneath my skin, and they lived to serve my devil. There was nothing I wasn't capable of doing for him. All I had to do was surrender.

Light flickered from the TV in the living room. I could see her through the window—stringy blonde hair tied in a messy bun, a stained pink robe barely wrapped around her, a bottle in one hand and a cigarette in the other.

I watched. I waited.

Then she was still.

I wondered if she even knew where he kept the spare key. I knew. Found it waiting for me like a willing accomplice. The door unlocked, and I was greeted by silence and darkness. The dim light from the TV spilled into the hallway like a beacon. A siren call to my demons.

She was asleep, mouth half open, sprawled gracelessly over the sofa, the bottle still in her hand. How often had she slept here drunk while her child was terrified in his room? Was this where she was while he was being harmed by another monster?

Even the air surrounding her was tainted. When we'd left this morning, this house had smelled like warmth with the breakfast Dex was cooking. Now it smelled cold—of beer, cigarettes, cheap perfume, and decay.

I'm not sure how long I just stood there watching her. Long enough that the disgust I felt in her presence and the rage that bubbled and brewed inside me drowned out any doubt.

I wanted to do it myself. Wanted to wring my hands around her neck. Wanted to inflict on her every bit of pain that she'd ever dealt to Dex. But even in all my rage, I wasn't *that* reckless.

This would have to do.

I pocketed her phone from beside the half pack of cigarettes and lighter on the dinged-up coffee table.

The flame was so small and unassuming as I lit one, taking a drag to get it started. White turned to black as the paper burned.

I dropped it. At first, nothing happened. The glowing ember shrank and dimmed. Then it caught. Synthetic carpet bubbled. It grew.

Like a ripple on the surface of a pond, a wave of fire.

The smoke didn't even rouse her from her drunken stupor.

I tried to leave, making it as far as the doorway before halting.

Not yet.

It wasn't enough to leave her to burn. She had to know why.

I waited. Until the flames were blazing, swallowing the couch, and then finally she woke, startled at first before her drunken mind could piece together the situation. Then she was screaming, stumbling away from the sofa, flames licking at her haggard skin. She shuffled to her feet, attempting to run.

Her eyes met mine.

Confusion. Recognition. Understanding. Rage.

"You fucking—"

"It should have been you." Words spoken from somewhere deep inside, a direct tether from the darkest corners of my soul to my lips. "You who died. Everyone would have been better off if it had been you."

She shrieked as she charged at me. I closed the door.

I heard the rattle of the handle. The door didn't budge, betraying her as it had betrayed me. Sealing her in with the growing flames. Her words of rage morphed—desperation, pleading, and screaming. Then silence.

Smoke filled my vision as it bled out from under the door. A tendril danced in front of my face before billowing toward the exit.

I left her phone on the table in the hallway, and when I left the house for the last time, I locked the door with my secrets inside to burn along with her body.

By the time I made it back to the car, the flames had taken the whole house, the glow and stench of fire lighting up the night sky and half of Meadow Park.

Then I heard the sirens. Time to go.

I expected to feel something, some noticeable difference from taking a life, perhaps some sort of invisible weight I'd have to carry with me always. I didn't. I was calm.

My rage was usually so loud, so destructive, explosive and uncontrollable. This had been different. This time it had a purpose. A destination. A shape I could understand. A form I could use. And now it was done, and I could let it go, finding comfort in the knowledge that it had protected him. That she could never hurt him again.

Roy's home was dark when I returned, Dex's bike still missing from the driveway.

I expected the old mechanic had gone to bed already, leaving the front door unlocked for us to return. I was proven wrong when I bumped into Roy leaving the bathroom on my way back to the guest room. He looked me over slowly.

Then he leaned in, and I held my breath.

"Smell of smoke tends to linger in clothes and hair." He spoke low, and fear sparked in my gut. "Use the green soap."

Then he brushed past me, walked down the hall, and closed himself in his room.

I rushed to take his advice, whatever adrenaline still fueled me washing away under the scalding stream. That calmness was fading, the beast that lent me its strength receding because it was no longer needed. I wanted to crash, to sink to my knees and wait for the water to wash away my sins. But if I was still here when Dex came home, then he'd know. He'd see it on me.

I wanted to be a safe place for him always, so he could never know what my hands were capable of. He could never know that I'd killed the monster that called itself his mother.

49

Dex - Past

REAPER.

───────── ✦ ─────────

Jonah's car was already in the driveway when I pulled in and killed Delilah's engine. I hoped he had actually taken the chance to see Becca and hadn't lied to me just so I wouldn't feel guilty about leaving him. He hadn't tried to call or text me while I'd been gone, and I was almost disappointed by that. I liked when he was needy. It made me feel wanted.

Inside, it was quiet and dark. I went straight for the guest room, *our room* for the foreseeable future, and found the lights already off. The low light through the window from a distant streetlamp outlined the shape of Jonah beneath the covers on the bed. My home.

I stripped off quietly, unsure if he was already sleeping and secretly hoping he wasn't as I slid in beside him. This bed was softer than mine, and far more spacious, but I still slotted my body along his like we were magnets.

Jonah was tense, his breathing a little fast. A few lingering kisses over the curve of his neck and he melted back into me. His hair was damp, and he smelled like apples. I much preferred when he smelled like me.

"Did you keep your bandages dry when you showered?" I whispered, knowing he was awake, even if he seemed intent on pretending otherwise.

He nodded, pushing back against me.

"Are you okay, baby?"

There was a long pause before he answered me. "Yes."

"It's okay if you're not. We don't have to talk about it if you don't want to. Just... be honest with me?"

Another pause. "I'm okay. We're okay. We're... safe."

He spoke quietly, his words not exactly a question but still sounding on the edge of one.

"We're safe," I promised him.

"I love you," he answered. "So much."

"I love you too, baby. More than anything."

"No matter what?"

"No matter what."

Jonah relaxed into me further, and I kissed along the skin at his neck and shoulders. My fingertips traced patterns over the bare skin of his sides and his stomach until his breathing deepened and he fell asleep. I followed him shortly after.

—◆—

It was early when I stirred awake again at the movement beside me. Jonah wriggled out of my arms and out of bed.

"Okay?" I grumbled, my voice sleep-deepened.

"Yeah. I just... I want to go for a run."

My brows pulled together, and I attempted to chase the remnants of sleep away as I rubbed my eyes. Jonah rarely woke up before me, and he certainly didn't go for runs.

"What's wrong?"

"Nothing," he answered too quickly. "I just want some fresh air."

"Baby—"

"I'm fine, Dex. I just want to go for a run."

"But... your leg."

"You think I don't know about my leg? Trust me, I fucking know, but I'm going to try. Okay?" Jonah huffed.

I had no idea what was going on with him, but I didn't like it.

"I'll come with you."

"No. I want to go alone."

Something twisted in me, some dark urge, similar to panic but not quite. I didn't want him to do anything alone. Didn't want him to push me away like he seemed intent on doing. I preferred when he was unreasonable and wouldn't even let me go to work without him coming with me. Because that was honest.

"Talk to me." My voice sounded more pleading than I intended, but it reached him, and conflict clouded his features.

"I will. Just let me go clear my head, and we can talk when I get back."

I fought the urge to grab at him, to hold him to me until whatever this distance was faded away. "I have something I want to give you," I said instead.

His eyes flicked to the door, as if he was desperate to escape. I didn't give him a moment to try, pulling back the covers and heading for my jacket.

I found what Harper had given me in the pocket, and clutched it tightly in my fist as I brought it over to Jonah, offering him my most precious possession.

"Your father's lighter?"

"I want you to have it."

His eyes were wide when they snapped to mine. "Why?"

"I lost it once, Rabbit, and you brought it back to me. It's safer with you."

Tears beaded and fell faster than I could process, and then his arms were around me. Like a vise. Emotional. Desperate. Not leaving even an inch of space between us. I held him back the same way. My hands smoothed over his back until he loosened his hold on me long moments later.

"Sorry," he sniffed, as he wiped the dampness over his cheeks away with the back of his hand.

"Hey." I captured his face in my hands. "Don't say sorry. I always want to know what you're feeling. Don't hide from me."

Jonah nodded, and my lips pressed against his. His pressed back a moment later.

"You want to talk about what's going on?" I asked him when we parted again.

He nodded. "When I get back?"

"Okay, baby."

I hadn't told Jonah about the tracker in the lighter, maybe I would when he got back and we talked out whatever was going on with him. I hadn't intended for it to track him. After Mason had stolen it I just needed to make sure I'd never lose it again. Still, Jonah had been a little unpredictable lately, so having it on him gave me extra peace of mind when things were so unstable in our world.

We both dressed for the day, and Jonah set off on his run. I only hoped it would help him the way he seemed to believe it would, and not make him feel worse about his injury and limitations.

Roy was in the kitchen, scowling at the contents of the fridge like they'd betrayed him.

"Alright, old man?"

He grunted in response, closing the door again. "Ain't got enough to make breakfast."

"So we'll just eat leftovers."

"That ain't breakfast. And don't think I didn't notice neither of you ate dinner."

I shrugged one shoulder. "We'll eat it when Jonah gets back."

Roy looked me over, hands moving like they were looking for something productive to do until they rested on his hips. A beat of silence, and then, "I'll just go pick something up."

"It's fine, Roy," I huffed.

"I'll not be long." He was already grabbing his keys off the counter.

I knew what he was doing—trying to be useful and helpful when he had no idea what we were going through, or what to do about it. Who was I to tell him how to care?

"I'll be here."

Roy nodded, and then he was off too.

With nothing to do but wait, I pulled my phone from my pocket to call Raven and check in on anything new she might have heard. Only, when I glanced at the pixelated screen, I saw I'd already missed several calls from just about the last person I would have expected. Reaper.

Knowing that bastard wouldn't have reached out to me unless it was absolutely necessary, I called him back first.

"What?" came his abrupt voice as soon as he picked up.

"You're the one who called me, like five times. You tell me what."

"You're alive, then."

"Why wouldn't I be?"

"Thought maybe you weren't. Fire and everything."

Fire? This wasn't a conversation to have over the phone. Not when the police were already scanning through Archer's connections and the Strays.

I couldn't leave here to discuss it with him, though, not when Jonah might return at any moment and need me to be here for him.

With a sigh, I gave Reaper my current address. Later, I'd apologize to Roy for not asking him first. I'd tell him every-thing, and if he decided it was too much and kicked us out again, then I'd deal with that.

Reaper arrived much faster than I expected, and not alone. Toby was with him, shifting from foot to foot behind him, his eyes locked on the house next door. The two Strays I trusted and liked least.

Better get this over with. I turned and stalked toward the kitchen, and they followed.

"What's this about a fire?" I asked as I fiddled with Roy's coffee machine.

There was a sharp sensation in my lower back, pressure applied and then released. It sparked like electricity, a thousand tiny pinpoints that all caught flame until it was searing. When I reached for the area, my fingers came away wet.

"This isn't what we fucking talked about, Reaper." Toby's panicked voice came from further in the room.

"I'm done talking."

I stumbled as I turned to face them, my eyes dipping to the knife in his hand, red with blood. My blood.

He'd stabbed me.

Adrenaline unlike any I'd ever known released in my system like a bomb. My eyes darted to the dish rack. Reaper tracked it, and launched at me as I went for the chef's knife.

Another surge of heat in my side, but then I had it. My blade swiped through the air, catching fabric as he barely dodged it. I knew I was fighting at a disadvantage. If I had any hope of coming out of this alive, I needed to overpower him, and I needed to do it quickly, before the blood loss and the pain slowed me down.

The searing pain in my back and side grew, molten heat spreading as I dove for him. More heat to my shoulder, but I got him this time, my steel coming away as wet as his.

"Fucking do something, Jackal, you worthless piece of—"

I threw myself at him, the weight of my body sending us both to the ground, my knife in his bicep, his knife embedded in my thigh. That one hurt more. Still the fucker wouldn't let it go. He wrenched it free, plunged it into the same spot, and I roared in agony.

Instinct propelled me back before he could do it again, but the shift gave him the upper hand and he swung his leg up. His knee collided with my burning, bleeding side.

I fought just to take air into my lungs as he knocked me sideways and followed closely, straddling me. There was a wet crunch as his knife carved through my flesh to grate against the bone in my forearm, and my hand spasmed. My blade clattered to the ground. Reaper grabbed it—tossed it behind him.

"You think you're so fucking good, Coyote." He panted above me, more light in his eyes now than I'd ever seen in them before. "Fucking slept your way to being Archer's right-hand man. Jumping in to take his place the same day he goes missing. You think we'll all follow you blindly? No, we don't need you. I'll lead the Strays, and I'll make them stronger than you ever could."

I should have listened to Jonah. Should have abandoned the Strays and left them to figure it all out on their own. Then I could've been with him. Only him. He was all that mattered, and now I was going to die because I'd hesitated.

"I don't want the fucking Strays." My eyes remained focused on the knife in his hand. My only hope now was to talk him out of the killing blow. "I never did. I was going to leave."

"Lies from a coward," Reaper sneered.

"Reaper." Toby's voice came from somewhere beyond my line of sight. Small and panicked.

"You're done, Dex. Enjoy hell." His blade rose, ready to plunge.

"Reaper!" Toby shrieked.

Then Reaper's eyes went wide as his breath was knocked out of him. His body jolted once. Twice. Three times. Blood trickled from the corners of his mouth and he fell forward, landing over me.

Only for a moment. The weight disappeared just as fast. His body was yanked to the side, and my rabbit was on him. With the chef's knife in his hand, he plunged it into Reaper over and over.

50

JONAH - PAST

LET ME GO.

─────────⭐─────────

There was no escaping what I'd done. Even if I had been able to run without my leg threatening to give way, no amount of fresh air and exercise would change the fact that I'd killed someone. Not just someone. I'd killed Dex's *mom*.

It was the right thing to do. I had to. I was protecting us. She'd deserved it. All things I told myself over and over. I'd believed those whispers from the demons under my skin last night when I'd done it. It was harder to believe them in the daylight.

New fears. New panic. What if Dex found out? What if he hated me for it?

My mind raced at a speed my feet couldn't keep up with. The stabbing ache in my leg was amplified by the ache in my head. It was too late now. My decision burned into my soul like the fire that had erased hers.

I pushed onward, until the itching from my self-inflicted wounds proved to be the final straw, and I screamed my frustration, my rage, and my anger to the world, not caring who the fuck heard me or what the fuck they thought.

Lost. Adrift. Unmoored. A storm of emotions that I couldn't face, not alone. I needed him. And maybe I didn't deserve to be comforted after what I'd done, but I needed him anyway. Needed the only person my demons would listen to. Only he could calm them again.

It was time to go back.

I turned around, heading to my home, to my devil.

There were two extra motorcycles in the driveway when I returned. New emotions joined the storm. Because of course they needed him again.

I didn't want anyone but him to see me, so I entered quietly, intent on sneaking off to the bedroom to wait for him to be done.

Then I heard him scream. An awful sound I'd never heard before, but I knew in my bones it was him. My demons rose to the surface, and I let them lead me.

Toby was the first thing I saw. Then the blood. Dex on the ground. Reaper over him. A bloodied knife near my feet.

Red.

Toby noticed me. "Reaper."

The knife was in my hand before I could process the situation. Thoughts evaded me. There was only red. *Red. Red. Red.*

"Reaper!"

The knife plunged into Reaper's back. Again. Again. *Red. Red. Red.*

He fell. I ripped him away from my devil. Again. He wasn't moving anymore. I didn't stop. Over and over. Until I couldn't see. Red in my eyes. I wiped it away. Rage still bubbled away like acid at my core. Not enough. He still wasn't safe.

I turned to Toby. Tears streamed down his pale cheeks. "I'm sorry," he whispered. "Reaper said we were going to talk. We were just supposed to talk. He said to back him up if things got violent, but I didn't think—I didn't know—I'm sor—"

Red.

"Rabbit." A voice that almost reached me. Not quite.

A sob. A choked cry. More red. New blood on the blade.

"Rabbit. Stop!"

The wet squelch of the knife as it impaled an unmoving body again and again. So much red.

"Jonah!" A hand on my shoulder, pulling me back. Eyes the color of an overcast sky through the clouds. Soft.

"D-Dex?"

"I've got you. It's okay. You can stop now. We're okay."

My fingers trembled around the handle of the knife, then released it.

The demons shrank back inside me, and I looked down at the body... No. Bodies. Two. I'd killed two more people. Ice in my core. Fuck.

Too much. Everything was too fucking much.

"I can't do this." My thoughts poured out of me without filter. "I can't fucking do this."

"W-what does that mean?"

"I can't do this!" I raised my voice. "I'm not this person. I can't do it anymore."

Dex's hand tightened around my arm. "We'll figure this out."

"No." I tried to shake him off, but he wouldn't let me. He groaned as he used his other hand to grab me as well, the grip weaker in that one as blood streamed onto the floor. "I can't do this! I can't! It's too fucking much! Let me go!"

"No! I won't ever let you go!"

I couldn't breathe. Couldn't think. "I can't do this, Dex! I've killed three fucking people in two days. I don't know who the fuck I am anymore!"

"Th-three? Who else did you kill, baby?"

Fuck.

"Let go of me!" I tried again to pull away, needing to escape, needing to run.

"No!" He tried to tighten his hold on me. "I'll die before I let you go!"

I needed air. I couldn't get any. Not here, not where there was so much red. I tried again to pull away from him, but he wouldn't let me. His hold on me was bruising.

"I said let go!" I shoved him this time. Hard enough that he was forced backward. A step on a tile covered in red. His bloodied leg failed to support him, his foot unable to find traction. He slipped.

The sound of his head hitting the counter made me want to hurl.

"I'm sorry!" I sobbed as I kneeled at his side. But he wasn't moving anymore.

Fuck. Fuck fuck fuck fuck.

FUCK!

"Dex?"

More red pooled around his head like a halo of death.

I wasn't sure if it was blood or tears that obscured my vision, but his face blurred. So still. The silence like a blade to my heart.

I tried to scream, but even my voice had died, a void of regret and grief tearing open at the core of me. My fingers shook as

I checked for a pulse, the void tearing me up further when I couldn't find one.

'I'm sorry,' I wanted to scream over and over, but my voice remained out of reach. My soul reached for his and couldn't find it. My love. My purpose. My home. In losing him, I lost them all.

A sound from the doorway. I turned from the horror I had created to see it reflected back at me in wide eyes. Roy.

Too much. It was all too fucking much.

Run.

I stumbled to my feet. My legs threatened to give out with every step. Roy remained frozen in place, his eyes on the carnage as I pushed passed him. Bloodied handprints smeared over the walls as I made it to the door.

Run.

A cold breeze chilled the red on my face, on my clothing.

Run.

Keys shook in my hand as I unlocked the car.

Run.

I slid into the driver's seat and started the ignition.

Run.

The car jerked backward onto the road.

Run.

My foot hit the gas. Tires rolled forward. I didn't know where I was going. All I knew was the voice in my head and the one word it repeated over and over.

RUN.

51

Jonah – Present

Found.

✦

He's alive.

A year of not knowing. A year of forcing that day out of my head. A whole fucking year of being without him.

Then he'd sent Harper. I didn't understand it. Why hadn't he come himself? Was he unable to? Was he still hurt? Where was he now, and how had they found me? With one big answer, I'd found only more questions.

It had been two days since I'd ditched Harper, once again on the run with no cash or a single possession. All of it left behind except my switchblade and the lighter in my pocket.

The sting of betrayal followed me. I'd trusted Harper. Trusted the *snake*. I thought I'd made a friend. Yet more than the betrayal, there was a twisted sense of relief, because Harper might not have actually given a shit about me, but he was there, which meant that Dex still did. For some unknown reason, Dex had sent him to me. It had to mean he still wanted me.

But he wasn't the only thing hunting me down.

There was something bigger. Something worse.

The truth.

The knowledge that he was alive, that I hadn't killed him, was a battering ram to the shield I'd built around my mind. I told myself I was running from him. That I was afraid of him. That I needed to escape him. *My love made him worse.*

Lies. All of it.

The shield fractured and crumbled, and the ugly truth couldn't hide in the darkness and the shadows any longer. It was never him I was running from. It was myself—what I'd done. I'd run from the possibility that I'd killed him. Because if I ran, I didn't have to face it, I didn't have to confirm it. I could live knowing there was a chance.

Of course, there was still the possibility that he hated me now. Why wouldn't he, when I'd left him bleeding out on the ground? I hadn't been there when he woke up. I hadn't been there to help him recover.

He'd know about the fire by now too. He'd know I'd killed his mother.

"I'll die before I let you go."

He would still come for me. I just didn't know if what found me would be the home that I'd left.

Run. The word still echoed.

Stay. A new voice joined it. *Let him find you.*

The memories circled. The real ghost that had been haunting me all this time.

"It's time to stop running... It's time to stop now. I know you're tired of it. It's okay to stop."

"I don't know how."

I still didn't know. But I was more tired of running now than I'd ever been.

Another day. At least tonight I wouldn't have to sleep in my car. I'd stolen the tip jar from a bar, the cash just enough to pay for a room so I could shower for the first time in days rather than just wash up in a gas station bathroom sink.

I was so fucking tired. Driving with no destination. No plan. No rules. None of it mattered anymore.

I barely registered the heat of the water over my skin. The only clothing I owned was in the shower with me so I could wash them using the motel's complimentary "lemongrass-scented" body wash.

After I'd hung them in front of the heater to dry, I collapsed onto the bed. I hated the way the sheets felt against my skin, hated the old musty smell that all motels seemed to magically possess. Mostly, I hated falling asleep without his arms around me, or his body slotted perfectly against mine.

Did he miss that too?

The thought prevented my exhaustion from taking hold. It was more pressing than sleep. In the year I'd been gone, had he found someone else to warm his bed?

I was the one who had left him. Yet the thought of him moving on with anyone else sent a wave of nausea through my empty stomach. If he was hunting me down, that had to mean he hadn't moved on from me. It had to.

The tingle of tears forming in the corners of my eyes gave me something to focus on besides the popcorn ceiling of the room, until they left me, dispersed into my hairline.

I didn't sleep. The darkness of the room eased as the sun rose and light filtered through the half-closed curtains. Outside, other guests were waking up, getting the fuck out of this piece of shit motel. They all had somewhere to go. A destination. A purpose.

I listened to the footsteps outside my window. The steady clink of something metal against the concrete. It slowed outside my door before continuing on.

How much longer could I keep doing this?

I was tired in ways sleep wouldn't fix.

My phone buzzed on the nightstand with my alarm. With a groan, I sat up and let the covers fall away.

Another day.

My clothes were *mostly* dry. The slight dampness made my skin itchy as I dressed. It didn't matter. It was time to go.

I had nothing else to pack. I'd run out of cigarettes and hadn't had money to buy more. Still, I pulled the lighter from my pocket, my thumb tracing over the patterns. He'd probably want this back. Probably regretted ever giving it to me in the first place.

Well, he'd have to catch me first.

I put it safely back where it belonged, in its pocket, and made for the door, uncertain where I'd end up tonight, or even what direction I was going to drive in.

Lost in my thoughts, I almost tripped over the bag in front of my room.

Rage sparked in my core that someone would just leave their shit in my way. But then I looked at the bag properly, and rage turned to ice. Because I'd seen it before. It was *my* bag. The one I'd left behind in Hollow Creek.

"*Run, Jonah, run,*" said the logical thoughts.

"*Find him. He was here. Find him,*" said the demons.

My hands gripped the railing, my upper body hanging over the edge as I searched for any sign of him. My eyes flicked over all sources of movement with desperation. A couple in the parking lot, a man walking his dog across the street. No Dex.

I returned to the bag like it was a bomb I didn't know how to defuse and wasn't sure I should even try. But what if there was something in there? Some message? *Something.*

In the next moment I was back in the room, the zipper of the bag busted open and the contents spilled over the bed. My clothing, and a familiar old Bible with the little savings I'd collected still tucked safely in its cover.

My eyes burned. What was this?

A threat? A peace offering? If he was here, why didn't he just catch me and be done with it?

I shoved everything back into the bag, taking it with me back to my car. Maybe he'd snuck a tracker into the seams of something. I thought about it and decided I didn't care. He clearly had ways to find me already anyway.

Then I was on the road again. My car sped down the highway as if I had someplace I needed to get to. Further. Faster. As if I could drive fast enough to escape my own thoughts.

The engine hiccuped. My eyes flicked to the fuel gauge to see the needle hovered well below empty. *Shit.* No, no, no. I just needed to get to the next town. I had money for gas now. I could fill up and keep going. Somewhere. It hiccuped again. Then it groaned. Sputtered. And it was out.

I coasted to the side of the road. Tears of frustration welled and fell, and my head slammed against the steering wheel. The sound of my scream was drowned out by the blare of the horn.

Again, I smacked myself against it as if getting angry enough would motivate the fucking car to just *move* again.

Then I was out. The door slammed as I inhaled a lungful of air just to scream it back out at the dense forest the highway cut through. "FUCK!"

My knees hit the gravel, and I crumbled in on myself. The weight of this, the final hurdle, broke me. I was done. I couldn't go on anymore.

Let the forest claim me if Dex didn't find me first.

Nothing happened for a long time—it was just me and the forest, the birds and the wind—until another vehicle approached. Its heavy tires slowed and pulled to a stop a short distance in front of my car.

I really didn't have it in me to deal with a stranger, even if it was one who had stopped to help me. I was going to tell them to fuck off, snap at them like a starving feral dog snaps at someone trying to feed it.

Footsteps crunched on gravel, the rhythmic clink of metal.

Familiar boots stopped in front of me, out of place with the cane beside them. I followed long legs up, and then I was looking into the icy eyes of my dreams and nightmares.

The first thing I thought was that the short hair suited him. The first thing I felt was overwhelming relief.

Dex.

It was over now. Whatever he wanted to do with me, I was ready.

52

Dex – Present

SAFE AND LOVED.

———— ✦ ————

I didn't know the man at my feet. He'd lost weight, his cheeks were hollow, his skin pale. His hair was dull and greasy. He was smiling up at me, but beyond the smile, beyond the tears that filled his eyes, my honey-eyed inferno was missing. There was no life in him. No spark. This wasn't my rabbit.

A year had taken a lot from both of us. It had started with what had almost been the end of my life, and it ended now, with the shell of his. Because I might have been the one who nearly died, but Jonah was the ghost.

"I missed you," he said, dull eyes glassy and blurred with fresh tears.

Pain laced with rage coursed through me. I reached for him, my fingers threading through his hair, tightening, pulling his head back so he couldn't look away from me if he tried. Because how dare he? How dare he say that to me when he was the one who left?

Despite the burn he must have felt in his scalp, Jonah didn't react. He still smiled and didn't try to pull away.

"I thought I killed you." He sniffed, but it did little to help with his current state, tears and snot weeping like open wounds. "I didn't know what to do. I thought I could outrun it. But I couldn't. Wherever I went, you followed me." His smile faded. "You are here, aren't you?"

The days, the weeks, the months I'd spent without him had built something huge and ugly inside of me. But now that he was here, now that I was looking at him again, touching him again, all I wanted was to hold him for the rest of our lives.

My grip in his hair loosened, my hand smoothing over the strands. My fingertips trailed over his cheek. He turned into my palm, soaking up the warmth from it like he was starved of it.

"I'm here," I told him.

"You're real?" he asked, as if he still didn't believe me.

"I'm real."

Before I'd sent Harper to Jonah, there had been so many emotions at war within me. Betrayal because he had left me. Rage because he promised he never would. Grief because I had lost him. Mostly, though, there was a deep ache in my chest. A void deeper than anyone else had ever left behind. I longed for him with every breath.

Harper had updated me on the state Jonah was in when he left him. Jonah was alive, but he wasn't *living*. He existed in a constant state of survival, stuck between the life he'd destroyed and the way forward. Unable to find it for himself.

Seeing it for myself was different. I wanted to hold onto the rage, to the hurt, but how could I? He had hurt himself far more than he'd ever hurt me.

He had run because it was his instinct to run, and I'd chased him for the same reason. But it was more than instinct. It was purpose. Through it all, we were still each other's purpose.

I could have caught him months ago, but he hadn't been ready. *I* hadn't been ready. His words that day hurt me more than any stab wound. I couldn't show up, have him see I was alive, then turn and run from me again anyway. I'd survived it once. I couldn't do it again. I needed him to give up, and he needed me there to pick him up when he did.

It's why when I'd seen him slowing down I'd sent Harper to him. Because I needed to see him without giving him the chance to reject me. I'd sent Harper to change out the tracker so I wouldn't lose him if Jonah wanted to keep going, but I'd also asked him to test Jonah. To befriend him. To see if he was still loyal to me. To get a glimpse into the man I'd get back no matter what. But also so that I'd know how long to wait. So I'd know when it was safe for me to give my heart to him again.

Harper didn't have the chance to report back until after Jonah had discovered who he really was. As soon as he'd told me everything, I was there.

Now that I had him, I had to *find* him again. I had to bring him back to himself. He was in pieces at my feet, and he needed me to put them back together. I would. I always would.

He sobbed. Arms wrapped around my legs. Tears soaked into my jeans.

There was so much we needed to talk about, but it wasn't the time for that. Now it was time to pick up his pieces and carry them home. "I'm here, baby."

He sobbed harder. Loud, guttural sobs from some place deep inside him. I attempted to take a step back, but he only clung to me tighter.

"I'm not going anywhere," I assured him, but he still didn't want to let go.

Letting my cane drop to the ground, I pulled at his arms until I eased his hold enough to sit down. Without prompting, he was on me again, crawling into my lap. His arms wrapped around me, his wet face buried into my neck.

My hand smoothed over his back, and through the fabric I could feel the ridges of his spine. Heat rose inside me. His tears beckoned my own. Jonah's pain called out to me, and mine to him. Both demanded to be seen, to be soothed, to be released. It wasn't needed anymore. Because we finally had each other again.

"I'm sorry," he cried into my skin. "I'm so sorry."

I knew he was. Knew he had been all this time, but he was scared, and he hadn't known what else to do. My tears fell... for him, for myself, for the time we'd lost together and the mistakes we'd both made.

"Sorry," he repeated over and over, his voice hitching with his sobs. I held him tighter.

We cried until the pain eased. Until it was freed. Leaving us empty and ready to fill its place with comfort. Only comfort from now on.

"Will you come with me?" I whispered, long after we'd fallen silent.

Jonah nodded, finally ready to allow a sliver of space between us again. He stood and reached for my cane before I had the chance to. New tears welled in his eyes as he stared at it.

"Hey." I smoothed them away with my thumb. "I'm okay."

A wet sniff as he nodded.

In silence, we collected his things from his car and took them to my truck. In silence, we drove to the closest town, and I paid for a room. In silence, we entered it, shed our clothing, and showered together.

Jonah cried again as I washed him, my fingertips learning the ways his body had changed. Then he washed me and cried even harder, his fingers lingering over the jagged scar on my forearm, on my thigh, at my side, on my back. They trailed higher, so gentle as they parted the short curls of my hair, seeking the scar he feared the most. The one that hurt him far more than me. I let him take his time to meet it properly so he could let go of the fear.

"I'm so sorry," he sobbed.

"I know, Rabbit." The truth.

"It was an accident."

"I know."

I turned slowly to face him, and his body stiffened as our eyes met again. He still wasn't in them, his fire extinguished. I needed to bring it back.

After shutting off the water, I reached for a towel, drying him and then myself before taking his hand and leading him back to the bed. Short distances without the cane were manageable, if uncomfortable, but with Jonah's hand in mine it was the best I had felt all year.

We slipped under the covers, his body against mine for the first time in so long. Another wound healed.

"Where have you been?" he asked me, voice tired.

My fingers tucked a long strand of damp hair behind his ear. It wasn't an easy story for me to tell, and it wouldn't be easy for him to hear. But there had been enough secrets between us. Enough distance. Jonah deserved answers.

"After you left." My throat caught on the word, and I cleared it, composing myself before I continued. "And Roy found me, he called Bryce. Bryce called Bull, and Bull did the rest. He was a doctor once, and he saved me. I was asleep for a long time, Rabbit. And then I wasn't. When I woke up, I couldn't move much. Talking was difficult for a while, and I had to learn how to walk again."

Tears flowed freely, a damp circle forming under his face on the pillow.

"I fought a lot with Bull. I was determined to get to you, and he wouldn't let me leave before I was healed. But I knew where you were, and I watched you as you went. I was always coming for you. It just took longer than I expected. And when I was ready, you were still running from me. I thought maybe you needed to. So I stayed close by, and I waited for you to stop."

This time I didn't fight the heat as it pulled from inside me again. There was a wound that still needed to be soothed. "No. *I* wasn't ready to see you. I couldn't watch you run away from me again. You have stopped now, haven't you, Rabbit?"

Jonah sobbed, arms around me, then legs. "I've stopped. I'll never leave you again. I didn't mean it when I said that. I never wanted to leave you. I was just so scared. I did so many bad things, and I didn't know how to deal with it. It was all too much too fast."

"You're not bad, baby. You know that, right? No matter what you did, you could never be bad. You protected me. You did the best you could."

He trembled in my arms, his face wet on my skin again. "W-what happened... to the bodies?"

I held him tighter. "Bull dealt with it all. They're gone. No one will find them. No one will come for you. You're safe. We're safe."

"And... the fire?" He whispered the last word, as if he wasn't sure if he should bring it up. As if I still didn't know.

"Police deemed it an accident."

"That's... not what I meant."

"Look at me." I forced him back, just enough to look into his eyes again. "You killed a murderer. An abuser. A monster. One that kicked us out of our home. One that—" My voice caught but I pushed through. "One that hurt me so many times. I love you for what you did for me."

I meant every word. Jonah had killed for me. Had protected me far more than anyone else ever had. I'd kill for him too if anyone ever threatened him. It didn't matter if they were supposed to be family. Nothing mattered except him. I'd burn the world down to keep him safe, just as he would do the same for me.

"Say it again," he whispered.

"I love you."

"Again."

"I fucking love you. I love you more than I thought it was possible to love someone. I love you in ways I can't ever put into words. I love your fire. I love your temper. I love when you're needy and clingy and entirely unreasonable. I love your body, and I love your mind. I love every moment when you're with me. You're fucking mine, Jonah Hargreaves. And I love you."

His pupils dilated, and I saw it, his spark. It was small, but it was there.

"Show me. Let me feel it. Love me, Devil. Show me I'm yours. Love me and let me feel it. Let me taste the love on your lips, let me drink it from your skin and feel the heat of it burning inside me. Burn me with it."

53

DEX - PRESENT

MINE.

His mouth was mine. I claimed it, my tongue demanding every inch. Jonah tried to meet me, match me, but that wasn't what was happening here. This was me claiming him as mine and making his body and mind understand that. The kiss was messy. Brutal. His tongue slipped into my mouth, and I bit it. Sucked it. Tasting red. He groaned.

I released it to give his bottom lip the same treatment, sucking it between my teeth before I bit him. Tugged until he whimpered. Again, until it was red and plump.

His face was mine. I licked a stripe over his cheek and along his jawline, teeth nipping at the skin until he angled his head back to give me his neck.

That was mine too. My teeth sank into his flesh, and he cried out, his body jolting beneath mine, but I was only just getting started. I sucked until red bloomed to the surface. A beautiful bruise marking him as mine. Again, until his neck was covered. Until there was no way he'd be able to hide these marks with any clothing.

Lower. His chest was mine. I nipped at his collarbones. Marks from sucking and biting surrounded his nipples before I targeted them. Because they were also mine to claim.

Jonah was writhing beneath me, his voice loud and beautiful. Unrestrained. His hands on my shoulders, nails digging into my skin, spurring me on. When I'd finished with his nipples, they were red and swollen and perfect, sensitive to the point of pain, and Jonah loved it. That tiny spark in his eyes grew brighter.

"More," he breathed.

I continued, marking my way down his body, so much thinner than it had been the last time I'd held him. He was still so beautiful.

My teeth sank into his thigh until he yelped. Mine. Again, until he was in tears. His hands still clawed into my back, keeping me close.

"More," he cried.

I switched to the other thigh and marked that as mine too. His cock twitched impatiently, demanding my attention.

Mine.

I swallowed him down to the base in one movement. Until he was in my throat, and a sharp moan ripped from his chest. His hand moved to tangle in my hair, just long enough for him to grip onto. I sucked hard up to the tip only to drop and take him into my throat again. Then I pulled off, because he wasn't allowed to come yet. Not until I'd marked all of him. Jonah whimpered. More tears decorated his beautiful face.

I lowered to suck at his balls. Then I made my way down his legs. Kissing. Biting. All mine.

I gripped his ankles. Tugged him roughly. Flipped him onto his stomach. He gasped, hands scrambling to steady himself on the sheets.

There it was. My name. My permanent mark on him.

Beautiful.

Mine.

With my hold on his ankles, I dragged him closer to me. Then my teeth were sinking into pale skin again. The backs of his thighs this time. Then his ass, my tongue tracing the letters of my name. "This is my ass," I told him. "Say it."

"It's yours."

A crisp *thwack* as my palm came down on the pale skin of his other cheek.

"Say it louder."

"It's yours!"

Thwack.

Jonah sobbed, flinching away from me on instinct before he pushed back for more. His ass was still perfect, toned and round. The skin I'd spanked flushed pink in the outline of my handprint.

Thwack. Thwack. Thwack.

More cries muffled by the sheet beneath his face. And that wouldn't do. Because those were mine too. He wasn't allowed to keep them from me. I gripped his hips. Yanked him up to his knees.

Thwack. Thwack. Thwack.

This time, the raw sound of his voice on every strike was exposed. Clear. Unrestrained. Beautiful.

The pink darkened, the color beckoning me until my teeth were embedded in the oversensitive flesh and he cried again.

"Ah—yes! It's yours. I'm yours. More! I need you to fuck me! Please!"

"Soon. I need to mark you on the outside, Rabbit, before I mark up your insides."

He whimpered. "Hurry. Please. I need you. Ah!"

Thwack.

My hands smoothed over reddened flesh. Parted the perky globes. Exposed his hole to me. Fuck, I'd missed the sight of it. "Has anyone else touched what's mine?"

"No one."

"Have you?"

Silence.

Thwack.

"Have you touched it?"

"Yes." His voice hiccuped. "Just my fingers."

The next spank I gave him was the hardest one yet, the crisp sound of it almost echoing in the small room. The ragged groan from Jonah's throat rivaled it in volume.

I hoped these walls were thick, otherwise we were about to get some noise complaints. Jonah had touched what was mine and only mine, and I intended to punish him severely for that.

My cock was hard and ready, desperate to feel the tight heat of my rabbit again. Soon. I wrapped my hand around it, intending to deal with it as quickly as possible so we could move on. I stroked with purpose, knowing it wouldn't take me long, because my rabbit was finally here in front of me, so perfectly marked up and presented.

"Please," Jonah sobbed, trying to turn and look at me. I stopped just long enough to spank him again before forcing him back into place and continuing. "P-please, please, please. I n-need you to fuck me." His voice was frantic, bordering on hysterical. "I'm sorry," he hiccuped. "I'm so sorry. I'll never do it again, p-please fuck me. I need it. Please. I n-need you."

"I'm going to fuck you, Rabbit," I assured him through gritted teeth.

"Then why are you—" He cried, a broken, ragged sound as my cock fired. Cum sprayed over his spank-reddened skin. "No! I w-wanted it." He sniffed, struggling to breathe. "W-wanted it inside."

"That was your punishment," I panted. "For touching my hole."

His response came in the form of another broken sound, as if I'd wounded him by coming on his ass instead of inside it.

Two birds, one orgasm. Jonah had been punished, and now we had lube.

While his body trembled, I ran my fingers through the mess, collecting as much as possible before smearing it over his hole. He stiffened at the contact. Cries sniffled out as he realized this wasn't over. My finger probed at the tight entrance, and he arched his back, presenting himself to me eagerly again, quickly on board with this new idea.

It slipped inside, and he rocked back to meet it, not caring about the way it must have burned. Instead, he seemed to crave it. I pushed it in completely, coating his insides with my cum before I pulled out to collect more of it, this time pressing two fingers inside.

Jonah hissed at the sensation, but his hips still pushed back against my hand, chasing more. I fucked him with my fingers, pulling them free only to collect more cum and stuff it inside him. His hole was so tight, but he was so eager, forcing his body to adapt to me quickly. "More!" he demanded.

This time when I collected more of my cum, I plunged three fingers inside him. He yelped. The sound of his fucked-out voice, the sight of his tight hole around my cum-coated fingers—it was enough for my cock to perk right up again, already aching to be involved.

"Fuck. F-fuck. Fuck me. Now."

I pulled out, collecting what was left and smearing it over my dick. Then my piercing notched against his opening, and Jonah was already trying to push against it to fuck himself with it. His body wasn't as eager as his mind, but what he lacked in prep he made up for in determination. All I had to do was hold my cock in place for him, and Jonah did the rest, pushing back until the resistance gave way and the head of my cock popped inside him.

He whined, trembled, and I held perfectly still even though the exquisite heat beckoned me to slam home.

"Fuck me!" he screamed at me. And any hope I had of holding back shattered.

In one quick thrust, I was fully inside him, his body tighter than I'd ever felt it. Jonah cried loudly, and his body spasmed as he came. Just having me inside him was enough to send him over the edge. "Fuck, Rabbit," I groaned as he tightened even further.

All he could do was grunt and take it as my fingers dug into his hips, and then I was *fucking* him. Sinking as deep inside him as it was possible to reach before pulling out to do it again.

There was an entire year of pent-up desire and frustration. Of longing to be inside him. Of dreaming about exactly this. I unleashed it all on him now. My fingers bruised his hips as my cock pistoned into him, intent on bruising his insides.

The force of my thrusts rocked his body up the bed until my hands yanked him back, the bed shaking until the headboard thumped against the wall.

My grunts, his cries, the slick slap of skin on skin, and the rhythm of wood against wall made for a brutal melody. A short song.

We were burning too hot to last, but it didn't matter. He was mine now. And we weren't leaving this fucking bed until I'd fucked him stupid. Until he couldn't walk, let alone run away from me again.

Pressure built and built. The song reached a crescendo. I roared as my cock kicked inside him, marking his insides up the way I'd promised him I would. Jonah screamed as he came again.

Then his body went limp and heavy in my hold. I'd fucked him unconscious. I kissed over sweat-soaked skin, repositioning us carefully on the bed so I wouldn't slip out of him, and followed him into the darkness. My arm a cage around his center, keeping him to me. Right where he belonged.

54

Jonah - Present

NO MORE SECRETS.

———— ✦ ————

Soft lips and sharp teeth caressed my shoulder. For the first time in a long time, waking up was a slow thing. Because I was warm, I was comfortable, I was exactly where I wanted to be. I was in the arms of my devil.

"Are you marking me more?" I didn't even try to hide the amusement in my voice.

His warm tongue licked over my skin. "I missed a spot."

My lips pulled into a lazy grin. "I'm just going to be one giant bruise from now on, aren't I?"

"Is that a complaint?"

"Nope."

Teeth clamped down again, harder this time. I squirmed, rocked my hips against him, and gasped at the throb where we were connected. His cock was still hard and buried deep inside me.

"Are you sore?" he whispered. His tongue traced the shell of my ear and made me shiver.

"Yeah," I breathed.

"Want me to pull out?"

"No!" I answered quickly. My hand snapped to his hip to keep him in place. "I like it."

The ache was pleasant. The pain was an anchor. It was real. To prove I was being honest, I rocked my hips again, feeling his length glide out then back in. The piercing at his tip rubbed at my insides. The slight burn at my hole made me groan and clamp tighter around him.

"Fuck," Dex groaned. "Fuck, I've missed you. Missed this."

"Mmnn." I moaned my agreement.

"I'm gonna fuck you again."

"Please."

Strong fingers gripped my hip, and then he was thrusting again. Short, sharp strokes that lit me up from the inside. My hand was still on him. My nails dug in deeper, encouraging him to go faster. Harder.

Teeth found my shoulder again, and I cried out at the sting. *Yes.*

"Hurt me," I begged him. "Bruise me. Make me feel you everywhere. Make it last. Fuck! Yes!"

Dex pulled out, and I was about to go absolutely feral before he pushed me onto my stomach, his legs straddling my thighs before he pushed back in again. Any complaints I had choked out into moans.

Warm hands braced on my shoulders, pushing me into the mattress. Then he fucked me harder. His thick length was slick with his cum. I wanted more. I wanted to be full of it. Stuffed until no more would fit inside me. Until he had no more to give me.

My dick rubbed against the sheets beneath me. Each of his thrusts forced me to grind into the fabric. The friction added to the pleasure that built rapidly in my core.

"F-fuck." I knew I wasn't going to last long. I was out of practice, but that was okay. Because we were together now, and we could fuck as much as we wanted. "G-gonna— *hnng*."

I fisted the bedding as my body spasmed around him. Cum soaked into the sheets below me, and Dex continued to fuck me through it. Even after the waves of pleasure passed and my hole felt tender and oversensitive, he kept fucking me.

"Your hole is still so fucking tight," Dex grunted through clenched teeth. "Won't be—*mnn*—won't be when I'm done with you. You'll be so fucked open. Gaping for me."

A verbal aphrodisiac. My body spasmed again in response, like it was challenging him, tightening as another smaller orgasm pulled from my depths. I whined.

"Fuck, Rabbit. So fucking good!" He slammed balls deep, filled me up completely, and then filled me more as hot cum claimed my insides again.

We both panted as he collapsed on me. Sweat stuck our heated bodies together, but I didn't care. Dex crushed me with his body weight, and I fucking loved it.

We drifted off to sleep again after that. When we woke up again, the room was dark, the day was over. I didn't care. Time had no more meaning now that we were together.

He fucked me again. Filled me up more. Marked me more.

We stopped only for him to order us food and to use the bathroom. Then he folded me in half and filled me up again until we were boneless and exhausted.

When I opened my eyes next it was morning—well, *daylight*. I didn't know what the actual time was. My body ached all over, inside and out.

I was tired in a whole new way: heavy with exhaustion, but the weight of my mind and soul had eased. The tiredness that draped over me like a giant blanket I couldn't escape from had eased.

The weight of the last year couldn't reach me when Dex's body was over me instead.

"You awake?" Dex's voice was low and hoarse. A tingle of lust sparked in my gut again, but this time it didn't feel so urgent.

"Mhmm."

"Feeling okay?"

"Perfect," I answered honestly. "I want to look at you."

He grunted as his hands pushed him up. I winced as his cock slipped out of me and he rolled to lie beside me instead.

"Don't let any spill out," Dex ordered, giving my ass a playful smack, but it lacked any real heat. Still, I did my best to clench up and keep his cum inside me. "Good boy."

"I love you," I told him, shuffling so I was half lying over him.

"I love you too, Rabbit. More than anything."

Words didn't feel like enough, and I'd never been good with them anyway. "Will you let me show you?"

"Baby, I'd let you do anything. As long as you never leave my side again."

"Deal."

I found his lips. This kiss wasn't as urgent as the ones we'd shared yesterday, but it was deeper, my tongue against his, slow and comfortable. I pulled back just so I could look at him. His beautiful face. As bright and brilliant as the sun.

My fingers combed through his short curls. "When did you cut your hair?"

"Bull had to shave it." His brow furrowed slightly, and my gut twisted as I realized why. Stitches, for the wound I'd caused. "But then I decided to keep it short," he continued, not letting us linger. "I... liked to feel it. What you left behind. Something permanent. Like a tattoo."

"That's a terrible fucking tattoo," I said, my mouth working faster than my mind.

For a second I panicked, it was a shit thing to say, but then his lips curved and he laughed. The sound was so beautiful I couldn't help but echo it. My laugh joined his.

Dex's pupils expanded. His hand moved to cup my cheek. "There you are."

Emotions clogged my throat, but I'd cried enough for the foreseeable future. I had my devil with me. Now it was time to show him how much I appreciated him.

With one more lingering kiss to his lips, I turned into his palm and placed a kiss there as well. Then I trailed my lips over the inked skin of his wrist... then to his forearm where they brushed over the soft, slightly indented skin. A tear through the ink. One of the scars that I should have been there to help him heal from.

I kissed my apology over the skin then turned his arm to kiss the other side as well.

Then I sought the others... kissing the mended skin down the side of his torso, then his thigh, my lips soothing a wound now healed. He needed the cane because of this one. Had needed to learn how to walk again. I hadn't been there, and I was so sorry.

"Turn around?" I asked, and he did without question.

Fingertips traced the smooth line on his lower back. I followed them with my lips… firm, lingering kisses.

Then it was time for the one that needed my apology the most.

It was barely hidden by his short curls. My fingers exposed it fully. His hair no longer grew from the light pink line, only a few inches long and a couple of millimeters wide. So small, for what it had almost cost us. My lips gave their apology slowly. Completely. Over and over until he shifted, rolling onto his back and hiding it from me again.

There was a smile on his lips and tears in his eyes.

"I forgive you, Rabbit."

This time when my emotions tried to overwhelm me, I let them. My tears fell onto his face as I stole his lips again. My leg lifted over his body until I straddled him.

I'd thought about this so often, connecting with him like this. I'd worried in the past that my leg wouldn't let me ride him for long, that I'd have to stop and I'd look weak. I realized now that was okay. I could be weak with him. It was safe.

My hand reached back until I found his cock, once again hard and ready for me. Dex's hands held my hips steady as I angled it toward me. Then I lowered myself, and he sank back inside. Cum squelched and leaked out of me, and I shivered at the sensation.

"I love you," I told him again once he was fully seated inside me.

"I love you too, baby."

Then I rode him. My hands on his chest, my legs already trembling from the amount of times we'd fucked over the past day.

I pushed through it. Through the burn in my thighs, the ache in my leg, until it was too much. Then without even needing to ask him, he flipped us, pushing my legs up to my chest before plunging back into me again.

My tears turned to ones of pleasure as he filled me over and over.

When his leg started to ache too, we switched again. Slow, deep thrusts as we lay on our sides.

The fast, hard fucking had been necessary, but so was this. This sex so much deeper than pleasure and release. I came first, and he followed me shortly after.

Then we just lay there, limbs entangled and bodies connected, simply breathing each other's air.

"How did you find me?" I asked long minutes after we'd both caught our breath.

He pursed his lips as if trying to decide whether he wanted to tell me. "No more secrets," he sighed.

I kissed him again. "No more secrets."

"Snake."

"Harper?"

"Yeah, Harper Lorens from Lorens Industries. They make security tech. He gave me a tracker, and I gave it to you."

My brow furrowed, my mind flicking through my meager possessions to determine what he could possibly have been tracking. I'd traded phones, cars, and clothing. What had I had with me this entire time? Then I found it. "The lighter."

Dex nodded.

This whole fucking time he'd known exactly where I was. I was running, but I'd never been lost. He'd been with me from the beginning.

Maybe it should have made me angry, how pointless it all had been. All my rules. All my paranoia, and I hadn't gotten rid of the one thing he'd actually been able to track me with.

I laughed. Deep, genuine laughter from somewhere inside me I'd thought was lost. Dex smiled, his own laughter joining mine.

"Of course it was the fucking lighter." I gripped his cheeks so tight that his lips puckered before placing another firm kiss on them. "I'm still not giving it back."

It was mine. And so was he.

EPILOGUE

One Month Later.

---⭐---

JONAH

It took us a month to get back to Port Skelton.

We weren't in any rush. Port Skelton was where we had come from, but our home was with each other.

We found work on the road. Used fake names at shitty bars, not because we had to, but because it was fun. No one knew us and that was the way we liked it. We worked just enough to pay for a room and food, and whatever time wasn't spent working or traveling was spent with our limbs tangled up together.

Dex updated me on the Strays. Raven was in charge now, and after Reaper and Toby had gone "missing" there was very little conflict between everyone else. Henrik and Archer were still yet to be found. Bryce had left too. The Strays also had some new members. But after Dex told me he'd left them, I had little interest in the rest. He was all mine now, and that's all that mattered.

Roy had moved away after selling the auto shop. We planned to visit him eventually, though that was more for Dex's sake than mine. I'd be happy if the only face I ever saw again was his—well, and Becca's. If she didn't murder me the moment I was within reach.

Every time I'd thought about contacting Becca, my stomach would twist with nerves until I felt physically nauseous. It wasn't the kind of conversation to be had over the phone. Dex had asked me over and over when I wanted to see her, but I hadn't been able to give him an answer apart from "*soon*."

We pulled to a stop in front of an unfamiliar apartment building.

"What are we doing here?" I asked Dex.

He pulled our laced fingers to his face to kiss along my knuckles.

"Need to do something. Come on."

Then he got out of the truck before I had a chance to protest.

With a groan, I unbuckled and got out as well, then followed him up the concrete steps. It was an older building, but it seemed well maintained.

"Who lives here?" I asked, my hand reaching for the back of his jacket.

He didn't answer, just knocked on the apartment's red door.

A few moments later, it opened to reveal Raven.

She smiled and held her fist out for Dex to bump, shaking it at him when he didn't. Then she turned to me. "Well, look who it is." Before I had the chance to respond, she turned back into the apartment. "It's for you, babe!"

My stomach twisted, because I had a feeling I knew who she was talking to, and I still didn't feel ready.

Her hair was purple now, and much longer. Familiar amber eyes looked annoyed until they caught on me and widened. Becca.

She walked toward me with purpose, and I stood frozen like a deer in headlights.

Thwack.

Pain seared over the side of my cheek as she slapped me, but before I could even process that, she yanked me into the tightest embrace I'd ever felt.

She was so warm.

She hugged me like she'd missed me.

"You fucking dick!" Her voice caught with emotion. "I thought you were fucking dead! I cried for you, you bastard!"

Once her embrace had felt like it was putting the broken, jagged things inside me back together, but this time I knew I'd be okay when she let me go. Those pieces would stay together, because it wasn't the end, and there would be more hugs just like this one. "Welcome home."

My eyes burned, and I let them. I didn't fight the tears, and neither did she, and we just stood in the doorway hugging and crying until Raven cleared her throat behind us. "Maybe... come inside?"

Bee didn't give me a choice in the matter; her hand found my wrist and dragged me in after her. I heard Dex chuckle as he followed us.

Then we were sitting on the sofa, both her hands held mine.

"What happened, JJ? I tried to contact you, and I couldn't. My calls and texts weren't going through. I made Rae take me to Dex's place to find you." My throat tightened in discomfort, but she continued. "And it was fucking burned to the ground, so I went to your dad's, and he hadn't heard from you either. He was fucking useless by the way. I hate the bastard, just so you know."

I couldn't help the huff of breath as too many emotions tried to escape me at once. "I... I can't tell you everyth—"

"Don't give me that shit! You can tell me. You can tell me anything. Whatever happened, I'm on your side. I'm always on your side, and I have your back."

I looked to Dex, who smiled softly and gave me a nod.

So I did. I told her everything. I told her what I'd done and why I ran. I cried more, and so did she. Then she pulled me into another crushing hug.

"You stupid prick!" she sobbed. "I told you I'd help you hide a body, you dumb fuck. I meant that. If you'd just fucking called me—"

"I'm sorry." I truly was.

I'd done a lot of bad things that I couldn't change, but I'd also done a lot of things *wrong*. And those I could make up for, starting from now. With the people who loved me unconditionally.

DEX

We spent the night on Becca and Raven's pull-out sofa. I didn't have a place here anymore, but that didn't bother me, because I had my rabbit, and wherever we slept together was home.

After breakfast, I had to pry him back out of Becca's hands. There were other things left to do. Jonah gave her his new number, and Becca threatened me with death—"*a permanent one this time*"—if I ever made him run again.

Our first stop was the Port Skelton cemetery, where Jonah took me to meet Adaline. He told her that she would have liked me and that he was okay now, that he'd found a new family who loved him unconditionally.

Then we went to my storage unit to swap the truck for Delilah. Driving was more comfortable for my leg than riding, and I couldn't bring my cane with me when we took the bike, but where we were going next, I wanted her to take us.

With the new modifications, Jonah was more comfortable and secure as my passenger, but he still clung to me tightly as we cut through the wind, heading to a place I had wanted to take him for so long.

We left Delilah to watch over us. Then my hand was in his as we trekked through the brush to get to the cliff.

The roar of the ocean was familiar. This place had always been more of a haven to me than the house I'd grown up in. It was where I went to be close to my dad, and now it was where I'd brought Jonah so they could finally meet each other.

We sat on the stone, beside where I'd carved his name.

DECLAN IAN WELLER

The letters bold and distinct from how many times I'd run my blade over them.

Jonah's fingers laced through mine as we stared out at the sea. I cleared my throat.

"So, I told you about this guy." I pulled Jonah's hand so I could kiss the back of it. "I'm in love with him. And he's in love with me."

Jonah's head rested on my shoulder.

"I feel things I've never felt before with him. He's everything to me, Dad. You'd really like him."

My chest felt tight and heavy. I wished more than anything they could have met each other. That Dad could have smiled and pulled Jonah into a hug he'd have been extremely awkward about. That he could have slapped him on the back and welcomed him into the family like I *knew* he would have.

"I'm really happy now," I continued. "*He* makes me happy. And I'll never let go of you, Dad. But I won't be able to visit you as much. There's a whole world out there that we want to see. But I know that you're with me, and I'll carry you always."

The ocean roared louder. As if he were in the waves. As if he were cheering for us, telling me it was okay to move on.

"I wish I could have met you." Jonah spoke up after I'd fallen silent for a while. "But I promise that I'll keep him safe from now on. You'd be really proud of him. He's such a good man."

Good. There were already tears in my eyes, but that word pulled something deep and raw from my chest. Because Jonah meant it. He saw me as *good*.

It didn't matter if the world didn't agree with him. Jonah was my world, and he thought I was good. It was all I had ever needed—to be good for *him*.

We sat there telling Dad about our plans until it was too cold. Until I felt ready to leave again, not knowing when we'd be back.

Then we took Delilah back and strapped her to the truck, to take her with us.

Our plan was to keep going. To live on the road until we found some place that felt enough like home to stick around. If that took months, or years, or never happened, I didn't really care.

Jonah and I had had a rough start to life and to love, but we'd found our way through. We were together now and always would be. This was just the beginning, and our story was far from over.

THE END... FOR NOW.

Thanks for Reading!

Thank you so much for reading my debut novel.

You may have some questions. What's the situation with Benny and Harper? How is Harper a Stray when he's a billionaire? What happened with the twins? Who is Bull? Why did Bryce leave the Strays? Where did Roy move to? I promise you, all of these and more will be answered in the books to come.

For preorders, and to access my reader groups, website and newsletter, please visit my Linktree by scanning the below QR Code.

Acknowledgements

This book wouldn't be what it is without my amazing friends, support system, and alpha readers. Lys, Tee, Lux and Sam, your comments and support have meant the world to me and I am truly grateful from the bottom of my heart for everything you do and are.

I also thank my wonderful beta team, sensitivity readers, and my cat, Oni, for his hairy cuddles when I was at my lowest points.

Until next time,

Ronan

ABOUT THE AUTHOR

Ronan Marlow loves to read and write queer romance. He loves creating deep, complicated, and broken characters that find love and healing. While his books may contain dark themes, you're always guaranteed a happily ever after. Ronan lives in Victoria, Australia, with his cat Oni, and is probably reading, writing, drawing, or drinking a ridiculous amount of coffee.

Sign up to the newsletter to receive updates, teasers, exclusive art and more; ronanmarlow.com